The shining splendor of our Zebra Lovegram logo on the cover of this book reflects the glittering excellence of the story inside. Look for the Zebra Lovegram whenever you buy a historical romance. It's a trademark that guarantees the very best in quality and reading entertainment.

ALYSSA TREMBLED AS JASON'S FINGERS TOUCHED HER . . .

She stared into the blue depths of his eyes and found herself thinking of the ocean, found herself wondering if she might not be swept up to drown in his eyes as she had feared drowning beneath the waves.

His lips touched hers. She felt light-headed, realizing she'd never experienced anything like this before, never thought it possible that deep within her she could feel herself melting, moving, flowing. His arms tightened around her and drew her close. Her body bent to him, warm and pliant under his hands, and she found herself floating under his touch. She hardly realized it when he lifted her in his arms and then lay her on the soft sand, hardly knew when he pushed the shirt back from her shoulders. All she could think of was the feeling of his lips, the heat of his hands gently stroking her body. She dropped her head back, letting herself become lost in the sweet mystery he released inside her . . .

SURRENDER TO THE PASSION

LOVE'S SWEET BOUNTY (3313, $4.50)
by Colleen Faulkner

Jessica Landon swore revenge of the masked bandits who robbed the train and stole all the money she had in the world. She set out after the thieves without consulting the handsome railroad detective, Adam Stern. When he finally caught up with her, she admitted she needed his assistance. She never imagined that she would also begin to need his scorching kisses and tender caresses.

WILD WESTERN BRIDE (3140, $4.50)
by Rosalyn Alsobrook

Anna Thomas loved riding the Orphan Train and finding loving homes for her young charges. But when a judge tried to separate two brothers, the dedicated beauty went beyond the call of duty. She proposed to the handsome, blue-eyed Mark Gates, planning to adopt the boys herself! Of course the marriage would be in name only, but yet as time went on, Anna found herself dreaming of being a loving wife in every sense of the word . . .

QUICKSILVER PASSION (3117, $4.50)
by Georgina Gentry

Beautiful Silver Jones had been called every name in the book, and now that she owned her own tavern in Buckskin Joe, Colorado, the independent didn't care what the townsfolk thought of her. She never let a man touch her and she earned her money fair and square. Then one night handsome Cherokee Evans swaggered up to her bar and destroyed the peace she'd made with herself. For the irresistible miner made her yearn for the melting kisses and satin caresses she had sworn she could live without!

MISSISSIPPI MISTRESS (3118, $4.50)
by Gina Robins

Cori Pierce was outraged at her father's murder and the loss of her inheritance. She swore revenge and vowed to get her independence back, even if it meant singing as an entertainer on a Mississippi steamboat. But she hadn't reckoned on the swarthy giant in tight buckskins who turned out to be her boss. Jacob Wolf was, after all, the giant of the man Cori vowed to destroy. Though she swore not to forget her mission for even a moment, she was powerfully tempted to submit to Jake's fiery caresses and have one night of passion in his irresistible embrace.

Available wherever paperbacks are sold, or order direct from the Publisher. Send cover price plus 50¢ per copy for mailing and handling to: Zebra Books, Dept.3629, 475 Park Avenue South, New York, NY 10016. Residents of New York and Tennessee must include sales tax. DO NOT SEND CASH. For a free Zebra/Pinnacle Catalog with more than 1,500 books listed, please write to the above address.

SUSAN SACKETT

SEASWEPT

ZEBRA BOOKS
KENSINGTON PUBLISHING CORP.

ZEBRA BOOKS

are published by

Kensington Publishing Corp.
475 Park Avenue South
New York, NY 10016

First printing: January, 1992

Printed in the United States of America

Chapter One

Alyssa Whitlock searched her memory for some sin she might have inadvertently committed in the immediate past. Her conscience might be clear, she realized, yet still that would not mean she had not in some way transgressed in her uncle's eyes. And in her uncle's house, she was only too aware, her uncle's eyes were more important to her immediate existence than even the eyes of God.

She closed her eyes and whispered an earnest prayer.

"Please, Lord, please don't let him be angry with me."

Chances were, she realized, that he was angry, and that the prayer would do her little good. She told herself the wisest course was simply to steel herself to face whatever penance he would impose upon her. That way, she would be prepared for the worst.

She knocked tentatively on the door. There was an extended moment of silence as she waited for some response. Finally, she heard her uncle's abrupt "Come!" It was only then that she put her hand to the knob and pushed the door open.

"You wanted to see me, Uncle Silas?"

He didn't bother to look up at her from the letter he was reading, just lifted a hand to wave her into the room from where she was standing by the door. Alyssa soundlessly closed the door behind her and advanced to the desk, stopping at the straight-backed chair that stood facing it and seating herself, all the time taking great care to make no noise that might distract him from his work. It would be sheer stupidity, she warned herself, to add another sin to whatever others she had already unknowingly committed.

She swallowed nervously, wondering why a summons to her uncle's study need always be so frightening to her. After all, she told herself, he was her guardian, not God. But logic failed her in her uncle's presence. It was hard to consider eternity when faced with the immediacy of Silas's determination to see that the unrighteous were condemned to their fair share of hellfire and damnation in the present. For some reason her uncle seemed not to trust to the hereafter for the fair payment of a sinner's wrongs, but had determined that a strong hand here on earth was the only way to redeem a lost soul. And since coming to live in his house, Alyssa had grown to realize that her uncle was convinced she was a sinner in grave need of saving, a task to which he'd diligently applied himself.

She found herself squeezing her hands together as she waited for him to get on with the purpose of his summons. She wondered if he always let her sit and wait like this because he knew it made her nervous, wondered if he enjoyed the discomfort she could never quite manage to hide.

She considered what she saw of him as he leaned over his desk, the austere black jacket of his suit that could not disguise his tall, bony frame, the white collar at his throat seeming to Alyssa at that moment like a bandage for some unspeakable wound, the thin, dull brown hair framing a face whose principle feature was a sharp, overlong nose. Why, she wondered, was there absolutely nothing about him that was pleasant, nothing about him that she might find likable? At first she had wanted to care for him, and had made the effort, for he was her mother's brother, and all the family she had left.

Silas finally looked up. It took only a glance at his face for Alyssa to realize that her prayers had been for naught. From his expression she realized she had sinned, and, in her uncle's estimation, at least, sinned grievously.

He offered Alyssa no greeting, but let his eyes narrow as he considered her.

"Mrs. Trumbull tells me you entertained a young man alone in my house," he intoned in a voice that somehow conveyed injury, regret, and threat, all at the same time.

He was not asking her for an explanation, Alyssa realized, but telling her that between himself and Mrs. Trumbull, the housekeeper, they had already tried and convicted her. Alyssa saw her hands flutter in her lap and wished she could keep them quiet, wished her nervousness did not make her behave as though she were guilty.

"It-it was one of your students, Uncle Silas—Mr. Peabody. But I didn't entertain him, or even invite him here," she blurted out, wanting to explain, to make him realize she'd done nothing wrong. In their haste to be said, the words seemed to tumble into one another on her tongue. "He came to see you, and as you weren't here, I offered him a cup of tea. That's all. When Mrs. Trumbull returned from the market, he decided he couldn't wait any longer and left."

There, she thought. Surely he couldn't condemn her for anything so innocent as offering one of his seminary students a cup of tea.

But it seemed he could.

"He was alone with you in my house, was he not?" he asked her. "Need I belabor the fact that it was inappropriate for you to be alone with him and completely improper for you to ask him in, under the circumstances?"

"But he came to see you," Alyssa protested, even

though she knew the effort was useless. He'd already condemned her, and she could only wonder what penance he would exact for the sin.

Silas wasn't moved in the least. "All my students are aware I work in my office at the seminary on Saturday afternoons. Mr. Peabody is, I am sure, no exception. Therefore, he came here to see you." He cleared his throat, the sound deep and unpleasantly liquid. "It would seem, Alyssa, that despite the efforts both Mrs. Trumbull and I take with you, you remain perniciously willful in refusing to conform to the most basic precepts of decorum."

Alyssa looked down at her lap. She wiped her sweating palms against the fabric of her skirt. She hated being lectured to this way, hated when he used phrases like "perniciously willful." She wasn't even sure she knew what it meant, and with a stab of perversity, wondered if perhaps he didn't, either. She felt an unexpected wash of useless anger and asked herself, as she had innumerable times in the previous three years, why her mother had died and left her to live with this mean-natured prune of a man.

She forced herself to swallow the anger before she looked up at him. It would do her no good, she knew. If she gave in to it, things would only be worse for her.

"I've tried to do what you would want me to do, Uncle Silas," she murmured, even as the thought occurred to her that she had absolutely no idea what he wanted from her except to make her life as drab and unpleasant as he had made his own.

He pursed his lips. "I don't suppose it's your fault," he told her in his superior, lecturing nasal voice. "After all, it's in your blood. If my sister hadn't seen fit to marry that godless sailor . . ."

This was too much. Let him think what he wanted about her, Alyssa told herself, but she would not sit there and calmly listen while he said anything against her father. She jumped to her feet.

"Stop it!" she cried out. "I won't have you talk about my father that way. He was kind and brave and good, and if he hadn't died . . ."

"But he did die," Silas shot back, silencing her with the finality of those words.

She stared at him and forced back the threat of tears that nearly choked her. That pain never seemed to age or lessen. It was always new to her, and the realization that her father and mother were dead, that they had left her with nothing but her relationship to this mean-spirited man, always seemed to bring her a fresh shock of hurt. She stared at her uncle and saw the condemnation staring out at her from his dark, round eyes.

"Sit down, Alyssa," he ordered.

Defeated, she reseated herself.

"Surely you see, Alyssa," Silas returned to his lecturing tone, "how you condemn yourself with these outbursts. The good Lord knows I've tried with you, but I have come to the realization that I am unable to provide you with the sort of guidance you need. Perhaps it is because I am unmarried and unused to dealing with young women. Whatever the reason, it is apparent that you need a different sort of hand to guide you than that which, out of compassion for my dead sister, I have offered you."

Alyssa felt her heart begin to throb in her chest. She wondered if she had misunderstood, as she couldn't believe what it seemed to her he was saying. He was sending her away, she told herself. He was saying he was sending her away.

All she could feel at the prospect was a wave of pure, unadulterated joy. It didn't matter where he sent her, she told herself. Whatever it was, it would have to be better than the pinched life she led under his roof.

Silas tapped the piece of notepaper on his desk.

"This is a letter from one of my former students, a fine young man named Owen Remsen," he told her.

She said nothing, as she had absolutely no idea what

a letter from one of his seminarians could possibly have to do with her.

"He is part of a mission on Banaba, in the Gilbert Islands."

Alyssa shook her head as though trying to clear away a cloud of cobwebs.

"Banaba?" she asked.

"The South Pacific, Alyssa. A part of the world which is much in need of the civilized word of our Lord."

The explanation had little effect on her confusion, and she simply stared at him. He looked down, lifted the letter from his desk, and scanned it.

Owen Remsen opened his letter by telling Silas he was writing to him for advice, telling him that his old teacher was the one person to whom he could go for counsel about so delicate a matter. When he'd first read the letter, Silas had found himself pleased that one of his favorite students still found his advice worth seeking. But as he'd read it through, he'd found himself less and less pleased with Owen Remsen's problem.

Owen asked Silas how he was to deal with the natural urges with which a young man found himself constantly assailed, living, as he did, in a godless and shameless place. He described the native women in florid detail, detail which made Silas wonder if he had somehow missed some prurient flaw in Owen while the young man had been his student. But he reserved his condemnation when Owen assured him that he had so far kept himself aloof from the temptation that surrounded him. The strain grew greater as time passed, Owen wrote, and he feared he might waver, might endanger his soul by his own weak nature. The confession left Silas fearful for his former student, yet touched that Owen was willing to bare such private matters to him.

The letter had been locked away for two days in the drawer of Silas's desk as he pondered Owen's dilemma.

He'd been tempted to write back, preaching abstinence, reminding Owen of the danger to his immortal soul were he to give in to these eternal temptations. But that morning he'd realized that Owen's trials had perhaps been given him by God. Silas saw in his former student's distress a unique opportunity to relieve himself of the unpleasant situation in which he found himself with his sister's daughter without in any way staining his conscience. The answer to helping Owen with his problems lay, Silas told himself, in the simple expedient of equipping him with a wife.

"Mr. Remsen writes to me about the difficulties he has encountered living in such a remote place," Silas told Alyssa, "of his need for a helpmate. It is an excellent opportunity for a young woman to find a meaningful, useful, moral life."

Alyssa shook her head slowly. Surely she had misunderstood. Even so great a sin as allowing herself to be alone with one of his students for an hour and sharing some tea could not possibly warrant banishment to some island in the South Seas as the wife of a missionary.

"Helpmate, Uncle?" she gasped. "Am I to understand you intend to send me to the other side of the world to marry some stranger?"

He returned the letter to his desk, placing it carefully in the center of the blotter before returning his gaze to meet hers.

"He is not a stranger, Alyssa. He was one of my finest students, a decent, moral young man."

Decent and moral . . . they were words that seemed to have a vastly different meaning to Alyssa than they did to her uncle. To him they were attributes, but to her all he was saying was that this Owen Remsen was dull and humorless, and doubtless as sour as Silas himself.

"Do you intend to send me off to marry him, Uncle?" she repeated.

Silas's eyes narrowed meaningfully as he stared at

her. "You could do a great deal worse, Alyssa," he told her sharply.

She knew what he was saying: that like her mother, she *would* most probably do a great deal worse, and he intended to see that it did not happen.

This is all absurd, she told herself. He couldn't simply send her off like a piece of unwanted baggage. She was, after all, a human being.

But the more she considered her options, the more she realized that he could do precisely what he wanted and if sending her to some island on the other side of the world to marry this Owen Remsen was what he intended, there was little she could do to keep from complying. She was dependent upon him for the room in which she slept, for the clothes she wore, and for the food she ate. He could not force her to marry, certainly, but he could turn her away and leave her with no means to provide for herself.

She considered the alternatives open to her, the possibilities for a woman, alone and with no means of support, in a city like Plymouth. There were, of course, means by which a woman could earn money. She was not so great an innocent as to be ignorant of them. But the thought was physically repugnant to her. Better, she told herself, to sell herself to one man in marriage than to a different one on the street each night, as some women did.

And then she considered the seminary students with whom she had come into brief contact over the previous three years. Mostly they were earnest, intense young men like the young Mr. Peabody, whose presence the previous afternoon had precipitated her predicament. If they were not the romantic sort of hero of whom she secretly dreamed at night, they seemed at least pleasant and reasonably kind. Perhaps marriage to one of them would not be so horrible a thing after all.

Of one thing she was absolutely certain: becoming

Owen Remsen's wife could be no more odious than living with her Uncle Silas.

She looked up to find her uncle's expression had become fixed and determined. He's already decided, she thought, and he knows I haven't much choice but to agree.

"I'll give what you have said some thought, Uncle Silas," she said.

"Think all you like, Alyssa," he told her. "But do it quickly. I have made arrangements for you to sail for Papeete next week. Our mission there will see to your passage to Banaba." He made a sharp movement with his hand, dismissing her. "Now see if you can help Mrs. Trumbull with the preparations for dinner."

Alyssa took one last, long look at the rooftops and church spires of Plymouth. Everything was sharply brilliant in the crisp October sunshine. The autumn-tinted leaves provided a riotously lush, colorful backdrop to what might otherwise seem a sharp and austere view. She had lived in this place all her life. For the first time she found herself realizing how bleakly ordered, angular, and severe a place it was. It amused her to think that while man tried to make his surroundings neat and orderly, nature persisted in interjecting her own chaotic disorder, dispensing beauty without prejudice to those who seemed determined to ban it.

She let her gaze drift along the coast to the far edge of town, searching among the rooftops for one that was uniquely familiar to her, the one where she and her mother had spent innumerable hours along the widow's walk, searching for a sign of her father's ship and sharing the sort of conversation that could not be exchanged in the company of others.

All that seemed impossibly long ago. Another family lived in that house now, she knew, and another child slept in what had once been her bed. She really wasn't leaving much behind, she told herself. She'd lost it all when first her father, and then her mother, had died.

"Departures are always sad."

Alyssa turned to find Emily Carver, the wife of the Reverend John Carver, one of her uncle's former students, at her side by the rail. The Carvers, like Alyssa, had taken passage on the clipper for Papeete, where they would continue on to their posting in Samoa. Although Emily was roughly Alyssa's own age, she was already as prim-lipped and superior as an elderly matron.

Alyssa had a distinct feeling that Silas had enlisted her as a guardian until she could pass Alyssa on to the Reverend and Mrs. Styles in Papeete, there to be forwarded on to Banaba. In any case, it hadn't taken Alyssa long to realize that Emily seemed determined to provide a motherly, or at least sisterly, presence that was entirely unwanted at that moment.

Alyssa looked back to the rapidly shrinking outline of the coast. "I've always loved autumn," she replied. "I shall regret not seeing it again."

"Oh, I don't think we should decide that anything is ever lost to us," Emily pronounced. "After all, we are sent on God's mission, and he cannot but see that we never lose those things we really care for."

Alyssa scowled slightly. She was, she realized, going to find Emily's tight-lipped sanctity almost as grating as her uncle's superior lecturing.

But as Plymouth dwindled into a tiny toy village in the distance, she smiled. She inhaled thick, clean breaths of the brisk sea air and found herself decidedly cheerful.

"Well I, for one, have decided this is one great adventure, and I don't intend to spend a moment of it mourning what I've lost." She turned back to Emily and grinned a slightly devilish grin. "I've been reading a bit about the South Seas," she went on, "and it all seems like a fairy tale: half-dressed natives, and lush, flowering jungles, and even cannibals."

Once again Alyssa offered Emily the slightly wicked grin. The grin only widened when she saw the look of shock and sheer revulsion that widened Emily's eyes behind the glass of her spectacles and drained the little color that decorated her too pale cheeks.

"Oh, no, I don't think we'll see cannibals or anything of the sort," Emily responded. She shook her head and pursed her lips. "John assured me we were going to a godly, well-established mission."

Alyssa turned away, hiding her smile by pretending to concentrate on her last glimpse of Plymouth.

"Oh, I'm sure where you are going is quite civilized," she agreed. Her smile faded and she found herself suddenly very sober. Her eyes narrowed in concentration. "But as for me," she continued, "I hope I find anything but civilization out there. I'm sick to death of civilization. I want to have an adventure before I'm too old to enjoy it."

Emily's expression turned to one of outright disapproval. Alyssa could almost hear her think that it would not be easy to maintain a watchful eye on a person who seemed determined to dwell on matters a reasonable woman would not wish to consider. She found herself hoping that Emily would grow tired of the task and quickly abandon it.

A silence fell over them and Alyssa quickly decided that she rather preferred it to Emily's conversation. It dragged on and seemed to make Emily a bit uncomfortable, for she cleared her throat noisily and began to consider her hands, at that moment, white-knuckled as they grasped the rail. Alyssa realized she had no pity at that moment and did nothing to relieve either the silence nor Emily's discomfort.

"I think I'll go to my cabin," Emily said finally. "I have so many letters to write." She pressed what Alyssa assumed was her most sincere smile onto her lips. "Perhaps you might like to stop by later on. John and I always read aloud a passage of inspiration before dinner."

"That does sound intriguing," Alyssa replied. She returned Emily's smile. "But please don't put yourselves out by waiting for me. I sometimes lose track of the time, I'm afraid." She darted a quick glance to the helm, where the ship's captain and first mate directed the navigation. "And this is my first sea voyage. There's so much to watch. Captain Howard even promised me he would show me how nautical maps are used to find our position. Don't you think it's all fascinating?"

Emily nodded, but her expression clearly said that she couldn't think of any pastime less useful to a woman who might be otherwise occupied in the far more important task of listening to an enriching and highly moral tract.

"Until later, then," she said, before she turned away and started unsteadily across the deck.

Alyssa watched Emily disappear with absolutely no regret. She ought to feel guilty, she told herself, for having behaved that way, for purposely shocking her. But she didn't. She felt happy and free for the first time in what seemed like years. She looked away and smiled as she found herself thinking that when she married, she certainly hoped she and her husband could find some way to amuse themselves that was more interesting than reading an inspirational passage or two.

Her last thought startled her. It was one, she was certain, of which neither her uncle nor Emily Carver would approve.

For a moment she pondered what had gotten into her. All the passivity she'd cultivated in her uncle's house, all the desire to please at any cost, had suddenly left her. And then she realized that what she had told Emily out of a desire to shock had been absolutely true, no matter that her uncle had banished her to Banaba to become a meek and subservient missionary's wife. She was embarking on an adventure, and she intended to take advantage of the opportunity and relish every moment of it.

And she would not marry Owen Remsen simply because it was what she was expected to do. After all, she could not be forced to take some stranger as her husband. She'd wait until she met him before making her decisions. If he was pleasant and earnest and sweetly shy, like the poor, unmissed Mr. Peabody, whose presence in her uncle's house had precipitated this voyage, she would consider the match. But if Owen Remsen did not please her, she would simply refuse, and that would be that.

She'd find some way to survive. She wasn't, after all, helpless. And all that was still months in the future. For now she had the prospect of a sea voyage and an adventure to consider. And she determined to think of nothing else.

Alyssa had watched the calm waters of Cape Cod Bay turn into the angry gray of the Atlantic. She found herself intrigued by the way the gulls that had followed after them had turned away to return to shore, by the way clouds began to scuttle across what had been a perfectly clear sky and then disappear as the last of the sun settled beyond the horizon. Commonplace things suddenly seemed wonderful to her, and she realized it was because she stared at them with the eyes of one who was now free to find in them whatever she wanted to find, not what she was expected to.

Dinner, in the officer's dining room and in the company of the gray-haired and formal Captain Howard, his officers, and the Carvers, was a dry but not unpleasant affair. Afterward Alyssa had gone to her cabin, relishing the thought of her first night in three years not spent under her uncle's roof.

She was soon to learn that expectations are seldom completely met by reality.

She woke not long after she had dozed off to find her stomach lurching in sympathy with the clipper's movement, the rise and fall inside her soon making her feel more sick and uncomfortable than she ever remembered feeling. She dragged herself out of the narrow bed and across her cabin to find the washbasin just in time before her stomach decided to empty itself. She clung to the side of the wash table, heaving miserably, too weak and ill to think of anything but that this was a decidedly ignominious way to begin her adventure.

When her stomach had finally nothing left to expel and she crept back to her bed, still she found she could think of little else. Adventures were to be met with bravado and excitement, she told herself firmly, not by miserably cowering with the blankets up to one's chin, one's stomach lurching all the while.

Nonetheless, she told herself as she lay back and allowed herself to groan slightly with her misery, even this was better than growing old in her Uncle Silas's house, afraid to talk or act in some way that would be criticized. Even if she were to die at sea sometime during this voyage, she would at least die free. Better that, she told herself with firm resolve, than an endless number of years meekly trying to please a man who had shown her it was impossible for her to do anything right.

Her stomach shifted angrily, and she realized it had not emptied itself completely, after all. She scrambled across the cabin to the wash stand once again, and leaned over it, paying homage to the god of adventure.

Chapter Two

Alyssa stared at the flurry of activity on the deck of the *South Seas Empress.* Had she been in a more light-hearted mood, she would have been amused by the conceit of giving a copra trader's barque any claim to a title of nobility. The small, square-rigged ship had a slightly scruffy and well-used air about her, hardly the aristocratic demeanor that might be expected of an empress. At that moment, however, Alyssa had far darker matters to occupy her, and no thought to be amused.

The first and most pressing was the realization that she would actually have to board the boat and stay on it for the next three to five days. Her stomach had begun to rebel from the moment she'd set foot on the wharf, and the closer she drew to the barque, the harder she found it to force herself to take another step toward it.

She knew that the unpleasant feeling had no physical cause. After all, she'd accompanied the Carvers to the ship that was to take them on to Samoa, and felt nothing beyond the pleasant anticipation of the peaceful quiet that would reign once they were gone. Whatever caused the lurching in her stomach had nothing to do with the mere sight of the barque and she firmly told herself that she would not countenance it. Unfortunately, her decision had little effect on her stomach.

It had been torture for her during the passage from Plymouth to Papeete, enduring the bouts of sea sickness that attacked her each time there was a span of rough water, and they seemed to have been the rule, not the exception, over the nearly three-month voyage. After that first night, there had been countless others when she had been certain she would never live to set foot on dry land again. Now that she had, she had no desire to embark on yet another journey on the ocean. Her stomach obviously felt the same way.

Added to the physical unpleasantness was the trepidation she felt at the prospect of actually meeting Owen Remsen in only a few more days. She'd managed to forget during most of the voyage from Plymouth that she was being sent to marry this stranger. As long as the prospect was still distant, both in time and place, she could force it from her mind. Just as it had been easy to tell herself she could simply refuse if she so decided, it had been no great matter to convince herself that if she didn't think about him, he didn't exist.

Now, as she was about to begin the last leg of the long journey, she found herself wondering at her naiveté. Perhaps she had been rash in her expectation that she could find a life of her own if she decided that marriage to Owen Remsen was not what she wanted. This place was all so strange, so foreign to her. Perhaps it might have been better had she refused her uncle's offer and stayed in Plymouth. Even if Silas had turned her out of his house, even if she had been forced to do whatever necessity dictated she do to survive, at least there she would have known her surroundings.

She looked around her, at the jungle that seemed to reach out into the village, as if it intended to swallow everything man's puny efforts had managed to erect there. As many times as she told herself that nature was no different here than it had been in Massachusetts, still she could not convince herself that this part of the world was not something alien to her, that the people were not different.

Despite the fact that she'd been reasonably warmly

welcomed to Papeete by Reverend Styles and his wife, the missionaries on the island, she could not shake the feeling of being more than a little foreign here, of being entirely out of her element. The weather was hot and muggy and everywhere she looked the jungle seemed reaching out for her, something alive and predatory.

And she seemed to always feel uncomfortable. The little clothing she had, the heavy, dark, primly decorous dresses with which her uncle had deemed it appropriate to provide her, stuck to her skin and set thin rivulets of perspiration running down her back. It had become a chore simply to move about bearing the weight of the fabric.

No matter how hard she tried to find similarities to what she knew, nothing here seemed the least bit familiar about this place: not the plants, nor the birds, nor the animals seemed like anything she'd ever known before. Rather than accepting it all as an adventure to be warmly embraced, as she had promised herself she would, she could not help but find herself longing for a crisp New England fall afternoon and a solitary walk in an orchard filled with the scent of ripening apples.

She felt herself completely ignorant in this strange environment. Everything she knew, everything that was familiar, seemed irrationally far away. And she realized that that fact frightened her despite her determination not to allow it to.

Perhaps the worst of it was that she found herself constantly staring at the native men and women. They were certainly handsome enough, with golden tan skin, thick dark hair, and round, wide eyes. But they all dressed with absolutely no attempt at the modesty which she had been raised to expect as necessary. As bravely as she had touted to Emily Carver, the prospect of finding half-naked natives, still she found the expectation a far cry from the actuality. Although she had quickly put aside her own feeling of dismay at the sight of all this semi-nudity, she could not quite stifle her curiosity. To put it simply, she had never seen quite so much bare flesh in her life as she had since her arrival on Papeete, and if she could not find it within herself to be shocked by it, she realized she was more than a little disconcerted and intrigued a good deal more.

Reverend Styles had made a point to tell her on several occasions that Papeete was quite civilized compared to what she might expect to find once she arrived at Banaba. Part of her had begun to wonder if her reaction wasn't caused by some deep-seated prudishness she didn't want to admit to herself, if she wasn't almost as sanctimonious as her Uncle Silas.

One thing she could not deny to herself, however—she was more than a bit jealous. When the heat of the afternoon seemed to drag at her, she secretly wondered what it would be like to dress as the native women did.

Standing there on the sun-bleached wharf staring at the *South Seas Empress,* Alyssa suddenly realized she was afraid. She was about to board that ship and it would take her into a world where she was virtually alone, where she would have to learn to live with these strange people, learn to reconcile the life she had known with their lives.

She sharply amended the thought: she would have to learn to live, not only with these people, but with a stranger she was supposed to call husband as well. And if she could not bring herself to do that, she would have to do something even more frightening—live without even a single person to tie her to her memories of the sort of life she'd left behind.

Emma Styles patted her hand.

"Don't look so worried, my dear," she said. "We're all a little afraid at the start. But once things get settled, you'll find your life will arrange itself to your liking."

Alyssa looked at the older woman's sympathetic expression. Emma Styles peered back at her, her pale eyes shadowed by the wide brim of the plain, dark bonnet that primly covered all but the smallest wisps of her graying hair.

Emma was, despite the four days she had spent in her house, still an enigma to Alyssa. Her expression grew pinched and sour whenever she addressed one of the native people, especially the women who worked as servants in the Styles household and who seemed incapable of doing anything to please her. Still she labored several hours each day teaching in the small mission school. She was apparently tirelessly patient with the children, finding for them what she seemed incapable of finding for their elders. And Alyssa had to admit that since her arrival Emma had been the soul of kindness to her, taking great pains to make her feel comfortable and welcome. She had been unable to think of her with the same sort of indifference with which she had thought of Emily and John Carver.

"Is it so obvious?" Alyssa asked her with an attempt at a smile, wondering how Emma seemed able to read her mood so well.

"Only to someone who has been through it herself," Emma told her. "Of course, I was already married to Richard when I came here, and had to face the prospect of living in a strange place among strange people. I do understand the hesitation you feel. Part of it is the fear of the unknown, and that soon goes away. And part of it, I suspect, is the uncertainty, something all brides feel." She smiled. "Believe me, that too is fleeting. Once you decide you love a man, the prospect of marriage is nothing to fear."

Alyssa felt a lurch of discomfort as she heard the word *marriage.* It was no longer a distant possibility, but a close eventuality, something she could no longer avoid thinking about, something she could not simply ignore.

"I've never met Owen Remsen," she murmured. There seemed no other way to explain her distress, and no other way to say it but as she had, bluntly and without preamble.

Emma seemed startled by that revelation.

"Oh," she said. She took Alyssa's hand and squeezed it.

"No wonder you look like a frightened little pigeon. Well, if it comforts you at all, I can tell you that I met him last June. He stayed with us here on Papeete just as you did, waiting for passage to Banaba. And I remember thinking him a decent, diligent young man."

Alyssa found herself wondering why Emma's description was not at all that comforting, thinking that however laudable decency and diligence might be, still she yearned for something more in the man she was to marry. But she squelched her feeling of disappointment and smiled at Emma.

"Thank you," she said. Then she shook her head. "Do I really look like a frightened pigeon?" she demanded with a small laugh.

Emma stared at her, making a point of showing she was considering what she saw.

"Well, perhaps just a little," she replied.

"I suppose it's just the feeling of walking off into the unknown," Alyssa told her.

Emma nodded. "I remember how strange it all felt, and how completely alien I thought myself. I can only tell you that despite all that, and despite the work and the discomforts that were necessary, still I wouldn't trade my life here for any other."

With those words of encouragement, Emma marched Alyssa forward to where her husband was waiting by the gangway, making last-minute arrangements with the barque's master.

Richard Styles turned his rheumy, slightly nearsighted eyes to the two women as they approached, then settled his gaze on Alyssa.

"Alyssa, my dear," he said, "may I introduce you to Captain Draper?" He turned to Draper. "Captain, your passenger, Miss Alyssa Whitlock."

Alyssa swallowed. The captain of the *South Seas Empress* was not at all what she had expected, not at all like Captain Howard, the gray-haired, remotely formal master of the clipper that had brought her from Plymouth to Papeete. Nor did he in any way resemble the cheerful and talkative captain of the ship that had left with the Carvers two days before.

Captain Jason Draper was at least twenty years Captain Howard's junior. And it was obvious from his tight-jawed, silent stare that he wasn't smilingly loquacious. He was tall, dark-haired, muscularly built and handsome. And there was nothing in the least remote about the way his steely blue eyes were looking at her at that moment.

Alyssa felt suddenly very grateful for the modest, dark dress that had seemed so oppressive in the previous few days. At that moment it was the only protection she had from those evaluating blue eyes, eyes that seemed quite capable of staring through a few folds of fabric. She certainly had never been exposed to this sort of inspection from any of her uncle's seminary students, of that she was entirely sure.

It pained her to realize it made her decidedly uncomfortable when she ought to have been able to ignore such trivialities as a stranger's stare. After all, she was more than certain that Reverend Styles would never have secured passage for her with him if Captain Draper were not totally reliable. She had no need to feel shaken simply because the man was rude.

But after a moment, she realized that it wasn't Jason Draper's lack of manners that unsettled her. It was the unpleasant feeling his inspection gave her that she had miserably failed to provide whatever it was he was looking to find. That, for some reason that quite baffled her, seemed a great and unforgivable failure to her.

Alyssa ventured a subdued, "Captain Draper?" and offered her hand.

Jason Draper made no effort to take it. He turned to Styles.

"My mate will see to the lady's baggage. If you intend to see her settled into her quarters, keep in mind that the *Empress* sails within the hour." With those words he turned and strode up the gangway, calling out orders to his crew.

Alyssa stared numbly after him. She was so bewildered by him that she hardly heard Emma Styles's pained mutter.

"The nerve of that man," Emma said angrily. "At least he could make an effort to be civil."

"Indeed," Styles agreed. He turned to Alyssa. "Captain Draper has a reputation for being honest and dependable, if not entirely mannerly," he assured her. "If it were otherwise, I should never have secured passage for you with him. And his ship is the only one stopping at Banaba for several weeks."

Alyssa nodded absently. "It doesn't matter," she told him. "I'm sure I'll be too seasick even to notice Captain Draper."

Styles smiled encouragingly.

"You should not be too pessimistic, my dear," he told her as he took her arm. "I am sure our Lord will watch over you and make your trip safe and comfortable."

Alyssa swallowed any words of confutation. It wasn't that Alyssa hadn't expected some sort of similar response from him. It was simply that she was not entirely sure she agreed with him. If the previous months had taught her anything, it was that she ought to have very little expectation of being comfortable while she was at sea.

She shook off her preoccupation with the strange Captain Draper, letting Reverend Styles take her arm. As she started up the gangway under his and Emma's guidance, a huge, barrel-chested man lumbered up to them from the far side of the deck.

He stared at Alyssa for a second. Whatever it was he saw in her, it seemed to leave him having trouble knowing what to say or where his hands ought to be. He finally settled with a slightly choked "Miss," and let his hands remove his cap and cling to it.

Alyssa had the distinct feeling he'd seen precious few American women in quite some time, at least few who were younger than the fiftyish Emma. However rude and disdainful the captain of the *South Seas Empress* might have behaved toward her, it was obvious the feeling was not shared by his mate.

"That the lady's luggage?" he asked Reverend Styles and pointed to the trunk and small heap of boxes that had been deposited on the wharf by the Styles' houseman.

Alyssa admitted ownership, and the mate bounded down the gangway, barking out orders to one of the sailors as he ran. Between the two of them they easily hoisted the whole of her belongings to their shoulders and returned to the deck.

"Follow me, miss," the mate told her.

They formed a small procession, the mate bearing her trunk and leading, then Alyssa, sandwiched between the Reverend Styles and Emma, and finally the sailor, a tall, dark-skinned. muscular Polynesian whom the mate addressed as Peli, carrying the odd boxes, bringing up the rear. The five of them managed to navigate the narrow passageway to Alyssa's small cabin without mishap. The two seamen deposited her belongings in an orderly heap that covered nearly all the available floor space of the cabin and left her, Emma, and the Reverend Styles standing awkwardly in the corner by the door.

The mate accepted Alyssa's thanks with a wide smile and a slightly awkward bow.

"If there's anything else you'll be needin', miss, just ask for me," he told her. "I'm Argus, Liam Argus."

"Thank you, Mr. Argus," Alyssa replied. She smiled first at him, then inwardly as she realized he actually blushed in response.

Argus turned, nodded to the other sailor, and the two departed to go about readying the *Empress* to leave port.

"I think it wise that I leave you ladies to settle those things that need to be settled," Reverend Styles said, and he too withdrew.

Once he was gone, Emma helped Alyssa arrange her belongings so that they cluttered the tiny cabin a bit less.

When the women were done, Alyssa found there was a small open area in the center of the room, only a few paces wide, but leaving her with enough room to get from the door to the narrow bed and tend to herself. If it was not commodious, it would suffice for the next few days.

The two returned to the deck.

"I'm afraid this is good-bye, my dear," Emma said as she embraced Alyssa and kissed her cheek.

Alyssa returned the embrace warmly, surprised to find that she sincerely regretted leaving and to realize that she would miss Emma.

The Reverend Styles offered her his hand.

"Our very best wishes to you, my dear," he said, and he pressed her hand. "You and Mr. Remsen will be in our prayers."

"And you will both be in mine," Alyssa replied, sure it was true.

And then Alyssa watched them make their way down the gangway back to the wharf, two stiff, quiet, darkly clad figures that seemed entirely out of place in the riot of color and noise. Alyssa stared at Emma's back, wondering if she would someday become the same sort of dignified, serious woman Emma was, if she would someday be a proper missionary's wife.

She stood by the rail as the *Empress* crew cast off the lines, pretending interest in the activity when she knew all she really felt was trepidation. Then she waved to Emma as the *Empress* slowly pulled away from the wharf, watching her and the Reverend Styles grow ever smaller until they were simply tiny dark smudges in the distance.

She didn't move for a good while longer, staring, trying to find Emma on the now minuscule-seeming wharf, wishing she could stay behind with her, clinging to a life that was at least a little familiar, for just a while longer.

Only a few moments in her tiny cabin were enough for Alyssa to find the heat and clutter sufficient to make the thought of remaining there unbearable. She was heartily thankful that her passage on the *South Seas Empress* would not be a long one. The unpleasant reception she had received from the barque's master made it only too clear to her that she ought not to expect her presence on deck to be especially appreciated. Between Jason Draper's antipathy and the seasickness that assailed her in the small, enclosed cabin, she was at a loss as to where she might find a little peace.

It didn't take her long to decide that a certainty of unpleasantness, the seasickness, was far more odious to her than the prospect of an uncertain one. She decided to try her luck on deck, where the fresh air would calm her stomach. She would deal with the *Empress's* captain when and if she encountered him. Perhaps, she thought, if she made an attempt at being inconspicuous, he might not even notice her there.

She camped on a tiny piece of the deck near some of the cargo bound for Banaba, settling herself on a huge coil of rope. She was, she told herself, completely out of the way of the crew, and couldn't possibly get into any trouble if she remained there.

She inhaled a half dozen deep drafts of fresh sea air. It was like a balm, curing the queasiness that remained after her short visit to her cabin. Then she turned and stared out at a seemingly endless expanse of blue water that sparkled with reflected sunlight. She couldn't help but wonder how what appeared to be so beautiful while she was on deck could make her feel so miserable when she was in the confines of the cabin.

Her thoughts were interrupted by a stirring in the air behind her, a feeling that she was not alone. She turned and looked up. With an unpleasant feeling she couldn't quite understand, she found Jason Draper was standing beside her, staring down at her with an icy glare she did not consider one of welcome.

"I don't suppose, Miss Whitlock, you are here to any purpose?" he asked.

She had no thought that he was even remotely pleased to see her. His tone told her that only too clearly, even if his stare had left any question in her mind on the subject. She found herself looking around, wanting a place to which she might flee and not finding one. His stare made her feel guilty, although she couldn't think why, as she was sure she'd done nothing even remotely objectionable since boarding the *Empress*. For the life of her she could not imagine how she had offended him, even though it was more than plain that she somehow had.

"I'm sorry," she murmured. "I didn't think I'd be in the way here."

"Then you were wrong," he told her. He pointed to a heap of coiled line on which she had perched and turned to call out to his mate. "Have one of the men use that to tie down those barrel staves, Liam," he said. "I have a feeling we may be in for a blow tonight, and I don't want anything free to move on deck."

Liam Argus looked up to evaluate a clear, nearly cloudless sky. He shrugged, his movement saying quite clearly he thought there was little possibility of a storm brewing. Alyssa followed suit, looking up and deciding that Jason Draper's prediction had little to do with the weather and a great deal more to do with ridding his deck of her presence.

Argus made no attempt to question his captain's order. Instead, he approached Alyssa, smiled at her, and offered her his hand.

"Excuse me, miss."

She accepted it, quickly scrambling to her feet. She felt Jason Draper's eyes on her as she stepped aside, and knew he was thinking the worst of her.

Argus set to work, easily lifting the heavy coil of rope with a single, hugely muscled arm. Alyssa watched him and the man Peli work for a moment, intrigued by the seemingly effortless way they handled the huge coil of rope, neatly encasing the pile in a tight mesh. Then she turned her attention back to Jason Draper.

She stared up at him, waiting until he glanced her way. "Perhaps if you told me what part of the deck I should avoid so as to give your men the least bother, Captain?" she asked.

She hoped she sounded pleasant. She didn't care that she thought his manners intolerable and under other circumstances might have considered telling him so. At that moment, all she wanted was to convince him that she would be no bother if she remained on deck. The thought of being banished to her cabin was odious enough to outweigh the dislike of him that she had begun to harbor.

He wasn't swayed in the least.

"All of it," he replied.

Alyssa pursed her lips. She had had three years' practice in her Uncle Silas's house swallowing words that sprang to them when she was angry, but she still found the effort surprisingly taxing. The *South Seas Empress* was hardly huge. It would be, she realized, impossible for her to spend the whole of the voyage to Banaba trying to avoid Jason Draper. And it was entirely unfair of him to act as though that was what he expected her to do. After all, her fare had been paid, and he owed her some reasonable consideration.

She would not, she decided, be cowed by this man for the next five or six days. If he had a reason for treating her as he did, at least she had the right to know what it was.

She stared up at him, calming herself, telling herself that she would behave rationally even if he did not.

"I seem to have offended you, Captain," she said. "Perhaps you might enlighten me as to how?"

He eyed her, apparently surprised by her question.

"I don't recall telling you that you've offended me, Miss Whitlock," he replied.

"Not in words," she agreed. "But you have said so nonetheless. If you will tell me what it is I've done to make you angry with me, I will earnestly endeavor to make a sincere effort to remedy my actions in the future."

She expected at least a softening of his expression. After all, her little speech sounded ridiculous to her own ears. Surely he must think the same of it.

But if he felt any amusement, he hid it quite well. He turned icy blue eyes to meet hers. It seemed to Alyssa almost as though he was looking through her. As she had when he'd been introduced to her on the wharf, she felt unsettled by his stare, as though he were telling her she had in some way failed.

But despite the distance Alyssa saw in his expression, Jason Draper was far from indifferent to her. In fact, at that moment, he was staring at her wide green eyes and the soft wisps of blond hair the wind had pulled free from her hair pins and sincerely wishing he found her less attractive.

Not that the dark, prim little dress she wore exposed a great many charms, he mused. But still, he had a practiced eye, and was more than convinced that her small frame was constructed in an entirely pleasing fashion. If she were old or plain, he thought, it would be a simple matter of ignoring her. But as she was decidedly not old and anything but plain, he found himself entirely incapable of disregarding her. And that, he realized, only increased his already smoldering anger.

"As you ask, Miss Whitlock, I will accommodate you. To put it as simply and succinctly as possible, your presence here is an offense to me."

She shook her head, baffled by his words.

"I'm sorry, Captain?"

"You. All of you missionaries. You come to these islands, you preach religion as though you were the only guardians to the gates of heaven, you teach the natives to become good Christians, and more often than not that means becoming good servants for their western masters. You tell them to give up the lives they've lived for centuries, tell them they're slothful and idolatrous, tell them that work on the copra and pineapple plantations is their only path to salvation. That is what offends me about you, Miss Whitlock. All of you holier-than-holy missionaries offend me."

Alyssa was shocked by the intensity of his attack. She'd certainly harbored uncomplimentary thoughts about her Uncle Silas over the years, but they were caused by a lack of personal warmth, by the failure to create any kind of bond of fondness between them, something she felt ought to exist between members of a family.

She'd never once thought, however, to question the work done by the missionaries he instructed. After all, for years she'd heard how these men and their wives selflessly gave up everything to better the lot of those poor pagan souls to whom they ministered. It was akin to sacrilege to so much as question the basic premise that they dedicated their lives to saving others. Whatever sins she might have committed while under Silas's roof, sacrilege had not been one of them.

"But, but that's not true," she stammered, automatically defending those she had never thought might need defending. "The missionaries do a great deal of good. They teach schools, they provide medicine . . ."

He wasn't interested in her argument.

"Schools that teach only what you believe," he interrupted. "And each dose of medicine comes accompanied by a sermon."

Alyssa wanted to say something, wanted to show him how wrong he was, but found herself without any words to refute his. After all, she had never had direct contact with any but her uncle's students, and however sincere they might have seemed, she had no idea how they actually put their principles into practice.

She backed a step away from him, as though what he'd said had distanced them in a way that could not be broached.

"It would seem that the only way I can accommodate you, then, Captain Draper, is by absenting myself from your presence."

"I believe I suggested as much, Miss Whitlock," he

agreed.

Alyssa swallowed. The prospect of spending even a moment more than necessary in her cabin was physically repellent to her. But the thought of being subjected to any more of Jason Draper's animosity suddenly seemed even worse.

"Very well," she said, and turned sharply on her heel.

Jason watched her make her way along the deck to the hatchway leading to her cabin. He told himself that he was well rid of her, but still, despite his determination, he couldn't quite stifle the realization that he regretted to see her go.

Chapter Three

Alyssa managed to divert herself for a short while by rearranging her belongings, telling herself as she worked that if she were to be forced to spend any time in the tiny cabin she might as well make it as comfortable as she possibly could. But try as she would, there was nothing she could possibly do to change the fact that the air in the cabin was close and stuffy. Out of the sea wind, it immediately became unpleasantly thick and still. The tiny breath of a breeze admitted by the small porthole did almost nothing to improve the atmosphere.

It was not long before she began to feel the unpleasant heaving in her stomach that had become so familiar to her during the long trip from Plymouth.

She removed her dress and clad only in her shift lay down on the narrow bed. If she slept, she told herself firmly, she would not feel the uncomfortable lurching in her stomach. She set her mind to it. Sleep would relieve the discomfort, and she would therefore sleep.

She couldn't. Although she closed her eyes and tried diligently to empty her mind of all thought, still she could not force herself to sleep. Each time she closed her eyes, Jason Draper's image filled her mind, his deep blue eyes seeming to stare right through her, his expression disdainful as it had been when he'd told her exactly what he thought of her and everyone like her.

She told herself she ought not to care, that whatever he

might think of her, it meant nothing. But somehow she could not dismiss her thoughts of him, and the harder she tried, the more insistent they became.

And she knew why.

Jason Draper, she realized, was the image of the man who had filled her dreams since the day she'd gone to live with her Uncle Silas.

A sea captain was independent and strong, like her father, a man who did not allow convention to dictate his life to him, a man who seemed to care for nothing more strongly than what he felt to be right. From the first day she'd gone to live in Silas's house she'd begun to dream of a man like that, a man who would take her away from the petty meannesses, from the sort of pervasive, drab tyranny under which she'd been forced to live, the tyranny Silas seemed to delight in exerting under his own roof.

And although she told herself such things were of no importance to her, she couldn't completely deny to herself that it didn't hurt that Jason Draper was handsome, that his blue eyes and dark, wavy hair gave him a sort of rakish, almost dangerous air. In fact, she realized, those things only made him that much more attractive.

And here she was, on his ship, half a world away from Plymouth and her Uncle Silas. A voice inside her was shouting at her, telling her that this was her fantasy, her dream. And it was real.

She forced herself to quiet the voice, reminding herself that she was on Jason Draper's ship because she was on her way to marry another man, a man still a stranger to her. And then she told herself that Jason Draper had made it only too clear that he hated her and everything about her, and finally managed to stifle the voice completely by telling herself that fantasies don't come true, and what's more, they never, absolutely never, came accompanied by the discomforts of seasickness. If she hadn't felt so entirely miserable, it all would have made her laugh.

When she realized it had begun to grow dark and she

still had not slept, Alyssa rose and lit the small brass lantern that hung in the corner of the cabin. She thought longingly for a moment about the books that had lined the walls of her father's small study, of the hours she had spent there, reading and thinking of him while he was away. It would be good to have one of those books with her now to distract her, the poems of Walt Whitman or a book of stories by Edgar Allen Poe, stories that had made her shiver with a delicious thrill of terror. Even when word had come of her father's death, she had still felt him close when she sat in that small room and read one of his books. If books could ease that hurt, they certainly could relieve the discomfort of seasickness.

Even the distraction of memory, she discovered, was not without its price. She recalled how the house had been sold after her mother's death and how she'd felt leaving it and going to live with her uncle. As for the books, they had been banished by Silas. He told her with great emphasis that such books were ungodly and unfit for a true Christian. She didn't believe him, of course, but she couldn't keep him from disposing of the books, taking from her the last tie she had with her father.

Silas, of course, had made a great deal of replacing the banished volumes with a handful of books he considered more appropriate, such dry stuff she had not even wanted to take them with her when she left. They were packed up somewhere, in one of the boxes, to be presented, she assumed, to her future husband, Owen Remsen.

She roused herself from her thoughts, telling herself that dwelling on either the past or the future was valueless. It was the present that had to be endured, and that was all that mattered.

The arrival of dinnertime did little to improve either her mood or the unpleasant heaving in her stomach. Had her cabin not already become totally odious to her, she would have simply forgone the meal, knowing full well that feeling as she did, she would be able to eat little or nothing anyway. But it was a chance, she decided, to get out of the confines of the small room, and might even provide her the opportunity of a walk on deck afterward, something she was sure even one so ardently opposed to her very existence as Jason Draper would not deny her.

She washed in the pail of tepid water that had been left in her cabin for that purpose, pulled on her dress, and carefully, because she felt rather unsteady, did up the buttons. She had just finished brushing her hair when there was a knock on the door.

She opened it to find Liam Argus, tongue-tied and embarrassed to be alone in her company, facing her.

"Mr. Argus," she said, and smiled at him, thinking that his distress seemed greater even than that which the seasickness caused her.

His cheeks, tanned dark by endless days in the sun, improbably managed to color.

"With the captain's compliments, miss," he said. "Dinner's about to be served. I'd be pleased to accompany you to the dinin' room."

"Dining room?" Alyssa asked with a questioning smile. She thought of dining room on Captain Howard's clipper. The *South Seas Empress* hardly seemed large enough to have any such accommodations.

Argus grinned. He seemed to be reading her mind.

"Well, in all honesty, miss," he told her, "there is no mess. In fair weather we take our meals on deck."

Alyssa's mood lifted at the prospect. Out in the open, she knew, the seasickness would disappear as it had always done before. She might even feel like eating something.

"That sounds lovely," she replied.

Argus nodded. "But it seems the captain's prediction is coming true." His expression grew slightly puzzled at that, as though he were not quite sure how Jason had foreseen what seemed to him entirely unforeseeable. "It's already begun to rain a bit. We'll be dinin' in the captain's cabin tonight."

"Oh."

As quickly as it had lifted, Alyssa's mood fell. Rain did not bother her, but the prospects of what would surely accompany it, wind and rough water, decidedly did. She began to wonder if Jason Draper had somehow conjured up a storm just to make her suffer.

Feeling deflated and disappointed, Alyssa followed Argus along the narrow passageway to the stern of the ship. The cabin door was open, and Argus waved her inside. Alyssa hesitated, not at all sure she wasn't being invited into the den of some ferocious beast.

But there was no ogre to be seen inside, and no sign to indicate that one inhabited the space. Draper had not yet arrived, and there was only the cabin boy, who busied himself with setting three places at a narrow table against the wall of the room. He smiled and nodded at her when he saw her standing by the door and then returned to his task.

Alyssa walked in, curious to find that Jason Draper's quarters, although certainly not extensive, were pleasant and comfortable. For some reason she had anticipated something dark and foreboding, much like that part of himself he had seen fit to show her. In fact, it was entirely otherwise.

There was a desk, neat and carefully organized, placed against the wall beside the head of his bed. The latter was not quite as narrow as the one on which she'd tried unsuccessfully to sleep, but certainly not a great deal larger. But Alyssa's glance did not dwell on those things. Instead, it traveled to the foot of the bed. There, obviously set so that he could put his feet up on the bed if he chose, was an oversized armchair. Above it hung a shiny brass lantern, and beside it, firmly secured to the wall, was a well-stocked shelf of books.

She wandered to it, letting her eyes scan the titles, surprised at what she found. There, closest to the chair and in a place that said quite clearly it was a favorite, was Walt Whitman's *Leaves of Grass*.

Alyssa lifted the volume and found the pages well thumbed. She touched the cover fondly and closed her eyes. The words came back to her as vividly as if she had last read them only days before, not years:

I sing the body electric. . . .

She remembered how she had sounded out the words the first time she'd read that passage. She couldn't have been more than nine or ten at the time, and the words had meant nothing to her except that the sound of them as she mouthed them was pleasing. And she remembered her father's voice, a deep *basso* rumble, reading those same words to her and making them sound even more wonderfully lyrical. She closed her eyes and could almost hear his voice again, a faint echo of him that remained with her always.

"Hardly suitable literature for a missionary, Miss Whitlock. I should think you'd be burned by simply touching that particular volume."

Jason Draper's words seemed to have the effect of freezing her. Alyssa found she couldn't even muster a response. Instead, she stood there, still and dumb, as he took the volume from her hand and returned it to its place on the shelf.

It occurred to her that in a way he was right. She remembered her uncle's reaction when he'd seen the volume in the house while her parents were still alive, remembered the argument that had ensued over it, an argument that had ended with Silas refusing ever to return or even speak to her father again. When Alyssa had been orphaned, when Silas had taken her into his home, he had burned that particular volume with great and obvious relish.

"It would seem you've been shocked despite my intervention, Miss Whitlock. You've gone quite pale."

She looked up at him and realized he was amused at the thought. He was staring down at her and for the first time since she'd met him she thought she saw laughter in his expression. Her immediate reaction to it was to smile in return, for it was an unexpectedly pleasant expression, and quite handsome.

But then she realized he was laughing at her, and her own smile died stillborn. She felt like telling him that it wasn't the poetry that drained the color from her cheeks, but rather the previous hours spent in her cabin combined with the *Empress*'s lurching movement. Instead, she turned away, deciding it wasn't worth the effort, that he probably wouldn't believe her in any case.

"Will you do the honors, Liam?" Draper asked as he turned to wash his hands.

Not at all displeased with the suggestion, Argus raced forward and pulled back one of the three chairs by the table for Alyssa.

"Miss?"

Alyssa crossed the cabin and sat.

"Thank you, Mr. Argus."

Argus settled himself at the place next to her, and Jason finished washing his hands and took the seat at the opposite end of the table. There was the mealtime bustle as the cabin boy and the cook distributed the plates of food and filled the glasses from the decanter they'd left on the table by Jason's place. The service completed, they exited, leaving Jason, Argus, and Alyssa alone in the cabin.

Jason cleared his throat, and Alyssa wondered if he intended to put himself out and talk to her, or if he would simply ignore her throughout the meal. By now she'd come to consider that being ignored by him might be preferable to his taunting attention, and was therefore not the least surprised when he leveled a stare at her and spoke. She was starting to think he planned to make her uncomfortable in any way he possibly could for no other reason than that it seemed to amuse him. And as his conversation could only prove unpleasant to her, he would therefore, certainly, not remain silent.

"I believe the Reverend Styles mentioned you were going to Banaba to marry one of the missionaries there," Jason said as he attacked the healthy plateful of stew in front of him. He raised an arched brow. "It seems to me you must be very much in love with a man to travel halfway around the world to wed him."

Alyssa bit her tongue. This was not the sort of conversation she wanted to get into with Jason Draper.

She lifted her fork and poked at her stew. The meat, she realized, was fresh, as were the vegetables. And there was a bowl of fresh fruit in the center of the table. All this, she knew, was a great luxury at sea. The *Empress*'s cook had no doubt taken on fresh victuals in Papeete. The food on Jason Draper's table was a far cry from the roasts of salted meat and boiled root vegetables that had been the diet of Captain Howard and his crew.

Despite all that, Alyssa found she could not muster much of an appetite. She wished it were otherwise. Even though her stomach was lurching with the movement of the ship, she knew she should put something into it or she would only feel sicker.

"Missionaries?" she asked disinterestedly, pointedly ignoring his last statement. "I was under the impression there was only one missionary on Banaba."

Argus nodded and swallowed.

"There usually is," he said. "But when a new one comes as your young man did to Banaba, the old one stays on for a while before he retires, to get the new fellow settled in." He reached for a piece of baked breadfruit. "I've never met your gentleman, but old Reverend Merricomb is a nice enough fellow."

"Do you know him well?" she asked.

Argus shrugged. "Passing well. We put into Banaba four or five times a year, but usually on the opposite side of the island. There's a copra plantation there. That's the *Empress*'s usual cargo. But sometimes there's a box or two for old Merricomb that we bring from Papeete, and we put in for a few hours on the eastern end of the island first. Merricomb likes his occasional bit of company, a little word of the outside world."

But Jason was obviously not quite as interested in imparting information as he seemed to be in gathering it. Or perhaps he only sensed that Alyssa seemed disinclined to talk and therefore determined to force her to do so.

"For someone about to marry into the family, Miss Whitlock," he said, "you seem remarkably uninformed."

He had been eating his dinner with relish, but he stopped, putting his knife and fork down on his plate, to stare at her, to consider her reaction to his words.

Alyssa swallowed. There was no question in her mind now but that he was enjoying making her feel uncomfortable. What she couldn't understand was how he seemed to know just what to say to her that would be the most unsettling thing possible. She had an unpleasant feeling that he might be able to read her mind.

She looked down at her plate, forked a piece of meat and put it into her mouth. She braced herself for the rebellion in her stomach as she chewed and swallowed, then breathed a small sigh of relief as it accepted the offering without too much contention.

"It was all rather rushed and unexpected," she replied finally, aware that she was being purposely evasive. She darted a glance up at him. Why, she wondered, should it matter to her what Jason Draper thought?

His eyes narrowed, and for the second time that day she felt as though he were inspecting her, looking for something beneath the surface that she was not quite sure she had for him to find.

"I never thought missionaries married in a rush, Miss Whitlock," he said. "I thought that was for impulsive, weak-natured men like us poor sailors, not for the strong-willed and moral."

She looked down at her plate again. He was making her feel like a fool, and she was sure he knew it, sure he was pleased by it. She forked some more stew, but dropped her fork with the food untouched, suddenly aware she was unable to swallow another bite. She was not at all sure her distress was caused completely by the seasickness.

She was saved from being forced to continue the conversation, however, by forces far greater than those Jason Draper could muster. There was a bolt of lightning bright enough to be startling even through the two small portholes. It was followed by a deafening clap of thunder.

"Damn," Draper hissed. He turned and stared out at the thick torrents of water that suddenly began to fall. Then he pushed himself away from the table. "We're in for it tonight, Liam," he said.

Alyssa realized with a touch of relief that she was effectively forgotten for now, her place in Jason Draper's thoughts usurped by the far more pressing needs of his ship.

Argus, too, began to push himself away from the table. "You'll excuse us, miss?" he said to Alyssa.

But Draper stopped him.

"I can handle things for now," he said. "Finish your dinner with Miss Whitlock and see her to her cabin. I'll see you on deck later."

With that he retrieved a long canvas slicker from a cupboard, donned it, and disappeared without so much as a glance at Alyssa. She found herself wondering whether she was relieved or not at being so completely and easily dismissed by him, and then wondering why she even cared.

Argus returned his attention to Alyssa and his dinner. "You'll like Banaba, miss," he said between bites. "It's certainly a pretty enough island, and the Polynesians are kind and good-tempered. And old Merricomb is pleasant enough company."

"You don't seem to share your captain's dislike of missionaries, Mr. Argus," she returned.

He shrugged.

"I suppose he has his own reasons, miss," he replied

thoughtfully. He brought his eyes to meet hers. "Don't think too harshly of him. He's a good man, fair in his dealings, and the best captain I've ever had."

"It's comforting to know he rouses some sort of sympathetic feelings," she murmured, her tone dry. She once again lifted her fork.

She managed two or three more bites and then the *Empress's* already unsettled movement seemed to increase. She put down her fork and clamped her lips firmly together as the barque's lurchings matched the inside of her stomach.

Argus considered his now empty plate, then Alyssa's still filled one.

"Is the food not to your liking, miss?" he asked. "Is there something you'd rather have? I could ask the cook . . ."

She shook her head, then wished she hadn't, as the movement seemed to be reflected through her torso and only exacerbated the discomfort.

"No, no, Mr. Argus," she quickly assured him. "The food is excellent. It's just the movement."

She put her hand to her mouth as an especially strong wave battered at the side of the *Empress,* causing Alyssa's stomach to heave in sympathy with the ship. The contents of the glasses and the decanter on the table in front of her began to slosh unpleasantly. She turned away, unable to look at it.

Argus nodded.

"No wonder you look so pale," he told her.

Alyssa turned pleading eyes to his.

"Do you think a moment or two on deck would offend Captain Draper so very much?" she begged. "I know it would make me feel a great deal better."

It took him a moment to weigh her request, and then he stood.

"You stay here a moment," he told her.

Alyssa watched him disappear and wondered what he intended, whether he meant to ask Jason Draper if she might be allowed the freedom of the deck for a few moments, or whether she was to be confined to her cabin. But he returned after only a moment or two, bearing two canvas slickers like the one Jason had donned before leaving. He held one out to her.

"Just for a little while, miss," he warned her. "The deck can be a dangerous place during a blow."

"I'll be just fine, Mr. Argus," she assured him as she quickly pulled on the slicker. It was huge, reaching nearly to her feet, the arms hanging half a foot below her hands. She looked up at Argus and smiled. "Really," she said.

"As you say, miss," he replied.

Then he pulled on his own slicker and led her up on deck.

The rain against Alyssa's face was cold and sharp and wonderful. As soon as she had inhaled her first few breaths of fresh air, her stomach settled and felt miraculously cured.

She stared out at the darkness of the night. The storm, she realized with a shock of discovery, was incredibly beautiful. Despite the rivers of rain that ran along the deck to soak her feet and the hem of her dress, despite the waves that raised white-tipped tongues upward to shatter at the rail, still the sea seemed completely different from the cold, angry gray water that had marked the storms on the trip around the Horn. This water was a startling, deep blue, iridescent and glowing in each flash of lightning. For the first time since she'd left Plymouth, Alyssa felt something other than discomfort at the thought of being on the open sea.

Even the rigging was beautiful in the glow of the lightning, like a complex and perfect web backlit against the black of the sky. Sailors were climbing through the rigging, finishing the task of lowering the sail. They'd shed their shirts and their shoes as impediments on the wet and slick rigging. Their torsos were sleek and shining with rain in the brilliance of the lightning flashes.

The deck was heaving beneath her feet, and by all rights, Alyssa knew, she ought to be retching miserably. But for some reason she wasn't. She felt well and more alive than she remembered ever feeling in her life.

There was the press of a hand on her arm and she turned to find Argus standing anxiously beside her.

"I think you ought to go below now, miss," he told her.

"Just a minute longer, Mr. Argus," she pleaded.

He hesitated, indecisive. He wanted to please her but knew the deck could prove dangerous under the circumstances. But he had no opportunity to make a ruling.

"What the devil is she doing up here?" Jason bellowed out from the far side of the deck. He crossed to them, bending into the wind. "Get below, Miss Whitlock. That is an order."

"She was feeling a touch ill, sir," Argus said in an attempt to temper what he saw was his captain's growing anger.

"She can puke her brains out for all I care," Jason snapped at him. "Just as long as she does it in her cabin. See to it, then get back here."

"Aye, sir," Argus replied. Putting his hand on Alyssa's arm, he turned her back to the hatchway.

"It's all right, Mr. Argus," Alyssa told him. "I can find my own way. I've gotten you into enough trouble."

"No trouble, miss," he assured her. "Are you sure you'll be all right?" He held open the hatch for her.

She nodded. "I'll be fine."

She climbed nimbly down to the passageway below, a trail of wind and rain following after her until Argus let the hatch fall closed. And then she found herself once again surrounded by the still, warm air, and as quickly as the queasiness had disappeared on deck, it returned.

By the time she'd reached her cabin and shed the slicker, her stomach was heaving and she could hardly stand. The *Empress* was tossing wildly, and with its every movement, Alyssa became more and more certain she was going to die. She stood for a few agonized moments, braced by a hand against the wall, and considered the possibility of that end with something akin to yearning.

And then she knelt and retrieved the slicker from the place on the floor where she'd let it fall. Even in the worst of the weather the clipper had faced rounding the Horn, Captain Howard had allowed her the liberty of a small, out-of-the-way patch of deck where she'd stood for hours at a time until sheer exhaustion finally forced her to her cabin. And if Jason Draper had even a speck of humanity in him, she told herself, he could do no less.

She pulled on the slicker, her determination to be out in the open temporarily outweighing the paralysis the lurching inside her seemed to impose upon her. She didn't care about Jason Draper's orders, didn't care about anything at that moment. She was going to go up on deck.

Alyssa pushed the hatchway open and stared out, hoping that the *Empress*'s captain was busily occupied elsewhere. She could see almost nothing, for the rain continued unabated, thick, dark torrents of it pouring endlessly down from the sky. The lightning and thunder were, for the moment at least, stilled. She darted out, pushing the hatch closed after her. She would make her way forward, she decided, to the place where Liam Argus had lashed the heaps of barrel staves to the deck earlier that afternoon. With any luck, Jason Draper would not see her. Once there, she could make herself reasonably inconspicuous.

She faced the bow and started slowly forward, her progress impeded by the *Empress*'s sudden lurching movements in the waves and the wet deck beneath her feet. She expected at any moment to find Jason Draper standing in front of her, ordering her off his deck. But either the darkness and the rain obscured her presence or the *Empress's* captain had better things to do with his time than watch for her. She moved unnoticed, leaning forward into the wind, pushing herself against the force of the storm.

She had nearly reached the huge pile of staves when there was an incredibly bright flash of lightning that seemed to fall from the heavens and strike the mast only feet from where she stood. The flash was accompanied by a deafening roar of thunder. It reverberated through the ship, the very deck beneath her feet shaking with the noise and the impact. The flash blinded her for a moment, and she began to tremble as she realized the *Empress* was right in the midst of the worst of the storm.

And then the air was filled with another sound, the noise of timber cracking and ripping apart. In the afterglow of the lightning, she looked up and saw the mast actually had been hit. There was a long, thin line of charred wood reaching down half its length.

As she stared up at it in horror, the mast began to fall.

Jason felt the *Empress* shake with the hurt done her. He had lived and worked on this ship for enough years to feel her pain, to know, even without seeing the lightning strike when she had been dealt an excruciating blow.

He turned to where the bow of the ship was rising and then dizzily falling as the *Empress* met ten- and twelve-foot waves. And he felt her hurt as his own when he saw the forward mast shiver and begin to fall.

It was only then that he caught sight of Alyssa, standing as though numbed by the sight of the heavy mass shaking and tearing itself apart. He realized immediately how much danger she was in by standing where she was.

"Get back!" he screamed as he started to race forward to her, even as he knew he could not reach her quickly enough, even as he saw the falling mast crash against the rail and sweep her forward in its tumbling, lurching collapse.

By the time he reached the rail near where she had been standing, she was falling, limp as a rag doll, sliding downward and into the waves.

He was pulling off his slicker and his boots, letting them drop to the sodden deck, as Liam Argus ran up beside him. Argus stared in shock at the tiny form that bobbed in the water, falling further and further behind and then disappearing under a wave.

"We'll bring her about," Argus shouted to Jason above the roar of the wind.

"You won't be able to in this sea," Jason shouted back. He grasped a handful of the rope rigging, then pulled himself to the top of the rail. "Drop a dinghy. You can come back for us when the storm's over."

Without looking back at Argus, keeping his eyes on the place where he'd last seen Alyssa's head appear out of the water before it was lost again to a white-capped wave, he dived.

Chapter Four

At first Alyssa thought the sensation of falling was just a dream. A strange dream, certainly, and one that had come to her while she thought she was still wide awake, but certainly a dream, for she felt an almost impersonal distance from herself, as though she were far away and watching herself.

And then the dream suddenly ended. She felt hurt, an aching wave of pain that began in her shoulder and seemed to snake through her until it slowly grew numbed by the cold and wet that surrounded her. Water pulled and pushed at her, throwing her, making her body move in strange ways that terrified her. It filled her nose and pressed against her eyes, coloring even the darkness of the night and the storm with an eerie, shimmering tint of green.

She wanted to scream; more than anything she wanted to vent the terror she felt at this sudden and violent dousing. Luckily, instinct made her keep her mouth shut and told her hands to push against the stuff, pulling her upward. If it hadn't, she would have drowned without ever having so much as managed to return to the surface. But despite the fear and the hurt in her shoulder and her side, lessons she'd learned in childhood took control of her muscles and she scrambled upward, fighting for the surface.

When she reached it, it came as a surprise to her, the

realization that her head had broken clear, that there was air surrounding her face and not water.

She inhaled, panting, unable to fill her lungs with nearly enough air before the next wave came, tossing her, turning her over and over until she didn't know which way was up. The weight of the water pounded against her, reached into the folds of her clothing, and grasped them, until the weight of it began to pull her under once more.

She flailed uselessly against the water for what seemed an endless moment. And then an odd calm settled into her. It told her that if she gave in to the panic that filled her then she would surely die. She must use her mind, must control herself, or she would never find the surface a second time.

She forced her arms to pull against the weight of the water, to pull her upward, even though the effort sent a long line of pain through her shoulder and down the length of her side. This time when she reached the surface she forced air into her lungs as quickly as she could, realizing the respite would not last, that the next wave would come as had the last and pull her under again. She tried to look around her, to find some sign of the *Empress*, but she was disoriented, and she could barely see above the churning water that surrounded her.

The next wave hit her, driving away all thoughts of the ship, forcing her to think only of her own immediate survival. It sent even the thought of the hurt in her shoulder and side away in the more imminent terror of the wall of water that struck her. As the water crashed down on her and tossed her, she knew she would not have the strength to pull herself upward many more times, not carrying the weight of her water-soaked clothing.

She held onto the breath of air she'd inhaled, refusing to allow the churning water to force her to give it up too easily, too quickly. She let herself fall, aware that fighting the waves was useless until she'd rid herself of the weight of the waterlogged clothing. Her hands pulled away the heavy slicker and she kicked off her shoes. Then she began to grab furiously at her dress, ripping away the buttons and pulling at the bodice.

Finally she freed the buttons and pulled herself from the prison of the sodden fabric. She pushed the dress down over her hips, then watched the dark fabric fall free through the water, the skirt billowing out like some unlikely, ominous flower as it drifted downward and away from her. It seemed to perform a strange, fascinating ballet as the churning water pushed it first this way, then that. Had her lungs not already begun to ache from the pressure inside them, she might have stayed and watched it sink completely from view.

She put her hands forward then, remembering the things her father had taught about the water, remembering to cup her hands as she reached out and pulled. And slowly, far too slowly, she began once more to rise.

She expelled the remaining air in her lungs as slowly as she could, but it was not slowly enough. There was a searing, sharp pain in her chest, and she thought her lungs would burst before she reached the surface. The fear that had threatened to overwhelm her claimed her once more, sending a frenzy of panic through her. She was sure she would not live to draw another breath.

But some part of her refused to give up, even in the face of what seemed a useless fight. She didn't know why. Perhaps it was the three years she'd spent in her Uncle Silas's home, always accommodating, always doing what she was told. All she knew now was that her life was too precious to be simply forfeited, and that she would not accommodate the forces that seemed determined to claim her by giving up to them. She doggedly pushed herself through the dark water, clawing at it, determined to reach the surface. And just when she knew she couldn't last even a second longer without air, her face broke through.

She filled her lungs with air, tasting it on her tongue, sweeter than any breath she had ever drawn. It seemed to buoy her, to hold her to the surface. Without the weight of her clothing pulling her downward, she could even manage to tread water without falling beneath the waves.

And with the realization that she could stay afloat came a new panic. She turned herself around in a circle, looking for the *Empress*. She saw nothing but darkness around her, darkness and the pale-tinged peaks of the waves.

"Help!"

She shrieked with all her might, in her fear emptying her lungs and falling below the surface. She bobbed back up, sputtering, her mouth filled with the salty water, aware only of the fear filling her ears with the heavy thudding of her heart.

The realization struck her and left her reeling with terror. She was alone. The *Empress* had continued on, with no one even noticing her fall. She would drown after all. No amount of fighting the waves could save her.

"Help!" Alyssa sobbed again, this time hopelessly, her voice ringing with despair.

"Alyssa! Alyssa, where are you?"

It was madness, of course, but she was certain it was Jason Draper's voice calling out to her.

"Here," she cried, not yet daring to believe there was anyone there to hear her. She only knew she was willing to accept the fantasy even if it served to do nothing more than ward off the terror for a few moments longer.

The fantasy miraculously answered.

"Keep talking," Jason called out to her. "I'll find you."

Her heart was thumping again, and there were tears of relief mixing with the rain and seawater on her cheeks.

"I'm here," she said. Then, realizing she couldn't be heard over the sound of the wind, she shouted it out again and again.

The wind seemed to be growing stronger and the waves higher. It was only a few minutes until her arms began to grow numb with the effort of keeping herself on the surface, and she knew she could not keep herself afloat much longer in such rough water. The hurt in her shoulder gnawed at her, draining her. She looked all around her in the water, staring up at the peaks of the waves and finding nothing. She knew then that it had been only her imagination that had spoken to her after all, that she had imagined Jason's voice because she had wanted so much to hear it.

"Please, please come," she begged.

She was, she realized, pleading in the darkness for him even as she told herself she knew he wasn't there. She was too weary to go on fighting the waves any longer, and when the next one struck her, she hadn't the strength to keep it from dragging her under.

Give up, she thought, as the wave tumbled over her and pulled her downward. Give up and be done with it.

She let herself go limp. It was useless to go on struggling any longer against the end fate had so obviously chosen for her.

Something hard was grasping at her arm and tugging. Improbable visions of sea monsters appeared in her mind, and her first instinctive reaction was to fight it, to pull away from it, whatever it was. But then it jerked her arm sharply and she turned and looked at it.

There was Jason's face, his eyes staring down at her, the water making his hair float around his face and pushing it forward and away. This, too, she told herself, was simply part of the vision, a product of her imagination, just as the voice had been.

She was too dazed and too tired to help him as he pulled her back up to the surface. She gasped for the first breath and found herself coughing up water she hadn't even realized she'd swallowed.

"Why?" she sputtered, then coughed again.

He held onto her, steadying her in the churning water until she finally caught her breath.

"Why what?"

"Why did you come after me?"

He shook the water from his eyes.

"I've never lost a passenger yet," he replied. "I wasn't about to ruin my reputation over a missionary."

There was a biting tone of disdain in his voice and Alyssa finally knew then that he was real, that she wouldn't envision him this way, coldly distant and sneering at her.

Jason assured himself that she was able to hold herself in the water, then released her and pushed upward, searching the wave-tossed surface. She stared at him, bewildered and silent, not daring to question him.

After a moment, he let himself fall back beside her.

"Can you still swim?" he asked.

She looked up at him as if he'd taken leave of his senses.

"Swim? Where is there to swim to?" she asked.

He pushed her forward in the water, the touch of his hands sharp against her arm. It sent a wash of pain along her bruised shoulder.

"Just swim," he shouted at her, his voice strong and sharp enough to make her do as he ordered.

She lifted her arms and let them fall, the motions mechanical, for she was too sore and too tired now to really put up much of a battle. She'd half admitted defeat enough times in the last half hour to realize that she was at the point of exhaustion, that she'd reached a numbed state where she would simply accept her own drowning without so much as a whimper of protest. Had she not been aware of Jason moving in the water beside her, she'd have given up. She was continuing only out of stubbornness and pride, and the determination to show him that she was not quite so valueless as he seemed to think her.

He quickly saw that she was weak now, and making almost no headway against the waves. He reached out for her, put his arm around her, and began to pull her through the water.

Alyssa fell against him, thankful for the pressure of his arm and the heat of his body close to her in the chilly water, but mostly for the knowledge that she was no longer alone. She was beginning to think for the first time since she'd been swept from the *Empress's* deck that she might survive, that with him beside her she could not die. The thought faded quickly, however, as she realized that although he might be there with her, they were alone in the water. The storm had pushed the *Empress* on without them.

It seemed to her that they swam forever, a useless, exhausting effort that could have no reasonable result unless it was to make them both so tired that they'd slip into the waves without a struggle, thankful for the final release. But Jason seemed determined and tireless, and, unwilling to have him think her defeated when he so obviously was not, she forced herself to continue to raise her arms and draw them back, pulling against the endless mass of the water.

A flash of lightning filled the sky with light and she saw it, the dinghy, bobbing up and down in the waves like a child's toy. Her first reaction was to think this too was something she'd conjured up, a vision that appeared out of nothingness because she wanted so very much for it to be there. But then she told herself Jason had been real, and this must be real, too.

Her determination found a strength hidden inside her she did not even know she had. She began to strike out, pulling herself through the water, convinced now that she could not let herself drown when refuge was nearly in their grasp. And then they were beside the dinghy, and she was clinging to it, gasping for breath and fighting against the exhaustion that seemed to have paralyzed her muscles. Jason pulled himself up, climbing out of the water and into the small boat. Then he reached down for her.

The waves seemed reluctant to release her. As Jason pulled her up and away from them they seemed to grasp and pull her, unwilling to let her go. She felt them cling to her, holding her until she reached up to Jason and put her arms around his neck, and he pulled her free.

* * *

For a long moment they lay together on the rough planks of the dinghy, clinging to one another as the waves leaped up over the sides and showered them with spray. Alyssa drew in huge gulps of air, not quite believing she could get all she wanted, not quite believing the luxury of it. Her heart was pounding and her lungs ached and no amount of air seemed capable of easing either one.

"You're all right," Jason told her softly.

He realized he was holding her in his arms, and that that particular act was no longer really required. Still, he had no thought to release her. Her skin was smooth and soft and wet beneath his hands. At that moment she no longer seemed quite so much the missionary. Suddenly she had become something else entirely. The thought bewildered him, but he was not ready to question it.

Alyssa caught her breath. The sound of the beat of her heart still filled her ears, and she found herself shaking. She tried to hold herself very still, tried to force some control on her body as she waited for her exhausted and oxygen-starved muscles to realize that she no longer fought the waves.

It was only then that she considered the strangely potent reaction of her body to Jason's touch. Before she'd recognized what it was he was doing, before she thought about the fact that he was touching her as she had never been touched before, she found herself considering the contact, found herself finding it warming and pleasingly comforting after the fear and the cold of the water.

It took her a long moment to realize what it was that spread that pleasant warmth through her, to realize that it was Jason's hands that were touching her skin, that he was softly stroking her arms and her back, that it was this that was creating the pleasantly warm surge inside her. And it took a moment more for her to realize that his touch frightened her.

Startled, she pulled away from him.

Jason released her without comment, if not without regret. He stared at her, watched her as she knelt for a long moment, returning his gaze. He could see her eyes even in the darkness, bright and deep, questioning and curious. He kept his eyes on hers and found himself startled by the wave of desire that swept through him then. It was as though the contact of their glances was physical, as though she were touching him and he was powerless to pull away. A flash of lightning filled the sky, illuminating her to him, leaving her image in his mind, clear and sharp and bright.

Even when the darkness returned, he could see her, the wind tearing at her drenched curls, sending thick tendrils of it snaking against her bare arms and shoulders, against the dark discolorations of the bruise the falling mast had left there as it struck her and sent her over the side. The rain fell on her face and ran down her cheeks like an endless stream of tears.

Perhaps it was the sight of the raindrops on her cheeks. He wasn't quite sure, but whatever it was, it was like a rebuke that swept away the want he had felt when he'd held her, when he'd let his glance touch hers. His physical desire was suddenly sublimated by the urge the sharp vision of her tear and rain-streaked face roused in him, the urge to comfort her, to keep her safe from further harm. The sight of her bruised skin seemed to pain him more than the physical hurts he'd known. He wished he could take her pain from her, wished he could bear it instead.

Alyssa turned abruptly away from him, not understanding the strange expression on his face. She wondered what it meant, why he looked at her that way, without the usual anger or the hint of disdainful amusement. Just as his touch had, the look she found frightened her.

She stared into the darkness, searching for some sign of the *Empress*, searching for the safety the ship represented, safety from more than the storm and the waves that slapped angrily against the sides of the dinghy. There was nothing beyond the curtain of falling rain that surrounded them.

"What do we do?" she demanded. "Where is the *Empress?*"

Jason shrugged. He knew the dangers they faced far better than she did, but he would not allow her to think of them. He could, at least, protect her from that hurt.

"Gone," he said, making his tone sound as close to bored as he could, as if nothing else could be expected under the circumstances. "With a broken mast and in this rough a sea, it would have been a foolhardy effort to try to bring her about."

"But what will happen to us?" she insisted, bewildered by his apparent calm. "What will we do?"

She leaned forward, over the side, peering into the darkness, obviously unaware she was shifting the balance of the dinghy precariously.

"First, you will sit back down before you capsize us," he told her sharply. "And hold on. I don't feel like going back in and pulling you out a second time."

She turned back to face him, immediately chastened by the tone of his voice. He'd risked his life to keep her from drowning. She had no right to question him. She slid back down onto the rough wooden planks and stared up at him.

Satisfied that Alyssa was at least temporarily willing to do as she was told, Jason began to cast about in the six inches of water that had accumulated in the dinghy, searching for oars. It didn't take him long to realize there were none. They had to have been lost when Argus had dropped the dinghy into the water. Not that it really mattered, he realized . . . there was no place for him to row to. All they could do was try to keep the dinghy from being overturned by the waves and wait for the storm to end. He eased his way to the stern and put his hand on the tiller, expertly turning the dinghy so that the waves hit it with the least force.

He glanced at her then and saw her shivering in the wet of the seawater in which she sat. She was cold and frightened, he realized, and there was little he could do to remedy either.

"Don't worry," he told her. "When the storm's blown itself out, Argus will bring the *Empress* back for us."

She nodded, as though she were trying to accept his assurances but was having trouble making herself believe it was all as simple as he indicated it would be.

"There's a good deal of water out here," she murmured, her voice hesitant, as though she were afraid the words might anger him.

He stared soberly around at the endless expanse of dark water and nodded agreement.

"But Liam is a very determined man," he told her. "And I think he considers me a captain worth keeping. He'll find us."

He motioned to her to move to the stern, beside him, and having no thought to disobey him or anger him yet again, she complied.

He smiled down at her and put his arm around her, not pulling her close when she stiffened at his touch, but not removing it, either.

"All we have to do is hang on, not fall over board, and try to keep ourselves warm until he comes along after us," he told her.

She considered his words for a moment, and the warmth she felt where his arm enfolded her. She *was* cold, she realized, and tired, so tired.

The contact was comforting and made her feel oddly secure. Whatever sense of unease had made her cringe away from him fled her. She released her tensed muscles and let herself fall against him. Her heart was still thudding inside her—from the effort of the swim, she supposed, and her fear, although she'd thought both had eased in the previous moments. Nonetheless, the sound of it filled her ears. For a while she listened to it, telling herself that she was no longer fighting the waves, that she was safe.

Eventually the thudding inside her eased and she found herself capable of thought. The one thought that filled her mind was not that she ought to pull away from Jason or the fact that he was holding her, but quite simply the realization that she was no longer cold. For a few moments she considered the strange amount of heat that seemed to flow from his body to hers. The warmth that filled her from his touch seemed oddly disproportionate to the extent of the contact.

But that thought, like all others, soon grew dim, and she quickly drifted into an exhausted sleep.

Jason watched her eyes flutter closed and found himself thinking how pleasant it felt to have her lie in his arms. He pulled her closer, trying to shelter her from the wind and the rain and the sea spray with his body. He forced his attention to their situation.

He knew the certainty with which he'd told her of their rescue had been nothing more than bravado and the desire to comfort her. Not only was there, as she had noted, a good deal of water in which they might become lost, the waves seemed to be pushing them through it at considerable speed. Even if Argus was able to bring the *Empress* close to the location where she had been when Alyssa had been thrown overboard, he would have no way of knowing in which direction the storm had pushed the dinghy. There was every possibility that the two of them would die of thirst out on the open sea.

Or perhaps not. There were scores of islands in this part of the Pacific and a fair number of ships that traveled the sea lanes between them. There was always the possibility that a ship would spot them and pick them up. It would be foolish to anticipate unpleasant future possibilities for disaster when the present offered quite enough opportunities for it.

He raised his arm, trying to shield Alyssa from a particularly huge wave that first lifted them, then set them down and left them with a parting shower of brine.

Alyssa opened her eyes to the dull, indistinct gray light of dawn. Somewhere not too distant there was noise, the sound of waves beating against a shore. She shook herself, trying to clear her mind so she could think.

She realized that Jason's hand was on her shoulder, that it was the reason she'd wakened. She stared blearily up at him, and at the sky that framed him. His expression was absent and dark, but that, she told herself, was only to be expected. He could not be very happy with the position she had gotten them into, especially when it had come about as a direct result of her ignoring his orders to remain in her cabin.

The sky seemed to echo his dark mood. The rain had ended, but dark clouds still hung overhead, threatening and ominous. She could feel the waves slap against the hull and realized they were even stronger than they had seemed the night before. That, too, was threatening to them.

She tried a weak smile at Jason. "Good morning," she murmured tentatively, as though so innocent a greeting might prove to be a point of contention just like almost everything else she had said to him since they'd met had seemed.

"I'm not so sure," he grunted in reply.

He moved to the dinghy's stern and sat staring intently ahead, his hand on the tiller. His expression was grim.

She stirred, pushing herself up. The movement sent a long line of pain through her bruised shoulder and side, and she found herself biting her lower lip to hold back the cry that would otherwise have escaped her. She moved slowly, stiffly, to accommodate the hurt, finally turning and sitting up on her knees, facing him.

"What is it?" she asked him. She listened again to the sound of surf against rocks. "Is it land?"

He pointed and she turned slowly and with obvious discomfort. There in the distance, still indistinct in the early light, was a shadow against the horizon.

"It is land," she said.

He nodded. "And it's a lot closer than it looks," he told her. He pointed again. "Do you see that gray place, where the water changes color?"

She squinted, peering intently. Despite his direction, she could see nothing out of the ordinary in the dull gray light which seemed to mute everything. She decided it wisest to refrain from telling him so.

"It looks like there are shoals there," he told her when she didn't reply, "probably rocks close to the shore, from the sound of it. The surf is taking us in that direction, and if it throws us up on sharp, volcanic rock, this dinghy will be nothing more than splinters."

"But can't we steer away?" she asked.

He shook his head.

"The surf is too strong. I'm doing about all I can to keep us from capsizing," he said. "Maybe with oars and two strong men to ply them." He grimaced. It was obvious he did not like the position of being unable to do much to help himself. "All we can do is hold on and pray."

He saw her eyes grow round with fear and he realized he had frightened her a good deal more than he'd meant to. He'd wanted to make sure that she would follow his directions without question, not terrorize her.

"Just do as I tell you and we'll both be fine," he told her, using his best captain-at-the-helm tone, the one that always made Liam Argus smile. "If the rocks are very close to the surface, we'll see them before we hit them. If we're lucky, they'll be far enough below the surface for the boat to pass over them unharmed. But if not, we simply go over before we hit them and then swim. The shore looks fairly close beyond and the surf will push us toward it."

Alyssa nodded to tell him that she understood, but said nothing. She realized she was too frightened to speak, too terrified by the memory of the time she'd spent in the water the night before to think of returning to the churning waves once again.

He considered her expression for a moment, watched the way her knuckles turned white as they grasped the gunwale. She was terrified and he couldn't help but see it. But then, unexpectedly, she smiled.

"Did I say something funny?" he asked. "I think I missed the joke."

She shook her head and looked up at him.

"I was just thinking that for what seems the first time since I left Plymouth, I'm not the least bit seasick," she told him.

He returned her stare for a second, and then he laughed.

"Damn strange way to make a sailor of you," he said.

His last words were muffled by the roar of the surf. A wave caught hold of the dinghy and held it suspended in midair. For a second they hung there, as if a powerful hand was holding them up above the water. Then they fell and the rolling wave was pushing them forward, moving them faster and faster toward the line of rocks.

Jason could see the rocks clearly now, the gray-tinged stone lifting ragged points up to the surface as the waves broke against them. There was no question that they might pass over them safely. The waves broke against them with an enormous shower of spray billowing upward when they struck. It was obvious that the dinghy would be smashed against them in the pounding surf.

As much as he disliked the thought of returning Alyssa to the waves in that pounding surf, he knew they had no other choice. She'd be tossed like flotsam by the force of the waves. He hated the thought that they would have no alternative but to try to jump clear and swim for shore.

He waited as long as he thought safe, not wanting to force Alyssa to a longer swim than necessary. He sighted what appeared to be a break in the line of rocks and tried to steer the dinghy as close to it as possible, hoping to keep them from being thrown against the rocks. Once they were through the barrier the water beyond looked almost calm, a relatively easy, not too long swim.

Alyssa kept her eyes fixed on the line of rocks. They seemed to be drawing close far too quickly. Wind and salt spray whipped at the tangled mass of her hair, pushing thick locks of it across her face and obscuring her vision, but even so she could not dull the prospect of the impact.

"Look," Jason shouted. "Do you see the break in the rocks?"

She scanned the area where he pointed, then saw it, a narrow break in the line of steaming spray.

"Yes."

She realized that the roar of the surf had become much louder, that they were drawing very close.

"Make for it," he told her. "I'll help you if I can."

His last three words frightened her almost as much as the sight of the rocks that seemed to be speeding closer and closer to them. The knowledge that he had jumped over the *Empress's* side the night before to keep her from drowning, even if she was in his mind the worst of all human creatures, a missionary's wife, had told her a great deal about his pride. He would not have given voice to the thought that he might not be able to help her unless he thought there was a good possibility that he might be killed.

But there was no time for further thought, no time to consider what might happen to them. Jason had let go his hold of the tiller and was leaning forward to her. His hand grasped her arm firmly.

"Now!" he shouted and pulled her with him as he dived over the side.

Chapter Five

Alyssa barely had time to fill her lungs with air before she felt herself plunging into the cold of the water. If her experience the night before had been terrifying to her, it was nothing compared to being grasped by the wildly churning surf. She felt herself being battered and thrown, tumbled with no idea which way was up and which down. Each pounding movement seemed to force away the precious bit of air she held locked in her lungs. Each sharp push sent a wave of pain through her bruised shoulder and side.

It seemed useless for her to struggle against the power of the surf. Caught in its grasp, she was nothing, as inconsequential as a dried leaf in the autumn wind or a dust mote in the air.

But fear and the knowledge of what would happen to her if she were thrown against the rocks made her fight. She began to struggle, clawing out wildly. There was nothing around her, nothing for which she could reach out and grasp, nothing but the swirling, moving green of the water and the ominous dark gray shadows that she knew were the rocks. She fought uselessly against the force that was pushing her forward, toward those shadows. They were growing steadily darker and closer. Even here, below the surface, the sound of the waves striking them was deafening, filling her ears, reverberating through her body.

And then she felt Jason's hand grasping her arm, tugging her what she thought was downward. Her first reaction was to fight him, to pull away, but she stifled the desire. She followed his lead, trying to move in the direction in which he was pulling her, telling herself he would not let her drown.

The rocks seemed to lunge out toward her, and she was certain they would be thrown against them. As she came closer to them, she saw the rough, sharp points, like dark daggers waiting to impale her flesh.

And then, somehow, she saw the rock falling away below her and she realized she was slipping over it. For a few precious seconds the water seemed to cease its endless churning. Jason tugged at her arm and she followed his lead, helping him as he pulled her up.

She bobbed to the surface, gasping for air and spitting up the water she'd swallowed in the wild moment beneath the surface. She turned and saw the spumes of angry spray behind her. Jason had pulled her through the narrow break in the wall of rocks. They'd survived, a voice inside her shouted in relief. She breathed in a long, grateful breath.

But the respite was only temporary. Once again the waves began to move, lifting her, pulling her. She froze with horror as she realized she was being pulled backward, back against the deadly wall of rocks.

"Swim!" Jason shouted at her. He grasped her, shook her angrily and began to pull her. "Damn it, fight!"

Galvanized by his words, suddenly more afraid of his anger than she was of the waves or the rocks, she did as he told her, ignoring the hurt in her side and her shoulder, ignoring the pounding roar of the surf, ignoring everything but the effort of reaching out and pulling against the water and the intent, sharp movements of her legs as she kicked.

When finally there was an instant of calm once again and she realized the undertow had not pulled them all the way back to the rocks, she was momentarily stunned. Her mind clouded with the awareness of just how much control she could exert over her own fate if she fought hard enough.

But Jason allowed her no time to gloat. He pushed her forward, once against shouting at her, and she swam, surprised at the forward movement generated by her stroke in the temporarily still water, and even more surprised as the next wave lifted them and pushed them forward toward shore.

It seemed to go on forever, the forward movement the waves gave them, the endless seconds fighting against the undertow as it pulled them back toward the deadly rocks. But eventually she found that the undertow did not take them back quite as close to the rocks, and she took heart from the fact that they were moving forward, closer to shore.

Jason was able to stand before she was, and as soon as he found his footing he put his arm around her and drew her through the water. She collapsed against him, thankful for his arm holding her close and steady, completely spent from this second battle with the waves.

Eventually she, too, found her footing. Nothing had ever felt quite so welcome as the solidity of the beach beneath her feet. Still clinging to Jason, Alyssa stumbled forward and finally, gratefully fell to the sand at the water's edge.

Jason lay beside her panting, as she was, but smiling.

"I told you I never give a passenger up to the waves," he told her.

She coughed up some seawater and wiped it wearily away with the back of her arm. Then she let her head fall forward, resting it on her folded forearms.

"Remind me to thank you," she breathed wearily.

She didn't even notice it when once again it began to rain.

* * *

Alyssa was hot. She lay for a moment with her eyes stubbornly shut, not really ready to face whatever new trials lay before her. But she felt hot and gritty, and her lips were filled with the taste of sea salt. There was little possibility that she could shut it out and return to sleep. She finally let her eyes drift open.

It was late afternoon. The last of the storm had fled, leaving the sky clear now, a cloudless, pristine blue. The sun had already begun to lower, sending long, feathery shadows from the palms that edged the beach creeping across the sand nearly to where she lay at the water's edge.

She was alone. It was an unpleasant realization, one that left her bewildered and in nearly as great a panic as her near-drowning had generated within her. She was alone on this strange island with absolutely no idea of what she must do to survive.

She peered along the ribbon of pale beach, first to the right of her, and then to the left. There was no sign of Jason, no indication that she was not completely alone.

She began to push herself to her knees, filled with the panicked feeling that her memories of the previous night had all been a dream, that she had been swept from the *Empress*'s deck and thrown, alone, to this deserted beach, the rest simply the wanderings of her imagination. But as she sat up something fell from her shoulders and she looked down to find Jason's shirt on the sand beside her. He'd obviously placed it over her to keep her from burning in the strong afternoon sun. Wherever he'd gone, he was nearby, somewhere.

She picked up the shirt and stared at it for a moment. It seemed an odd symbol of safety, but it was one, nonetheless. He was here, someplace close, she told herself. He would not let anything happen to her.

She slipped her arms into the sleeves, rolling up the excess of fabric to free her hands. The shirt hung, huge, from her shoulders, but she found it comforting and she would not have traded it for a ballgown at that moment. She stood and started slowly across the sand toward the jungle that edged the beach.

"Jason?"

If she'd expected him to come bounding out of the undergrowth, she was quickly disappointed. There was no response from him, no noise, nothing to tell her he was close by.

"Jason?" she called out again, aware of the note of fear that had crept into her voice despite her intention to conceal it. "Captain Draper?"

Her only answer was the sound of the surf striking against the sand and the faint murmur of the sea breeze stirring the fronds of the palms.

"Captain Draper?" she shouted once more, this time not caring that the note of panic was more than obvious. She was alone in this strange place, and it frightened her.

Still there was no answer, but she saw a rustling in the undergrowth only a few feet away. Her reaction was sharp and immediate. Jason, she told herself, would have answered her, called out to her. She should run, hide from whoever was approaching until she could be certain the greeting they offered was welcoming. After all, she'd heard there were islands where the natives were as hostile as those on Papeete were friendly.

She began to run toward the sheltering obscurity of the undergrowth but had taken only a few uncertain steps when she realized she would not make it before she was seen. Whoever was approaching the beach broke through the undergrowth while she was still several feet from any place she could hide.

She looked at him and her fear turned into anger. Jason dropped to his knees and placed the armload of fruit he was carrying on the sand.

She stared at him. He was naked save for his trousers, and his tanned, well-muscled physique reminded her of the feeling of uncertainty the near-nudity of the natives on Papeete had generated in her. A wave of uncertainty swept through her. She felt uncomfortable near him, especially as he seemed so entirely at ease, as though he were a boy on some holiday adventure.

He looked up at her, took the fruit he had clamped between his teeth, wiped the juice that had dribbled onto his chin with the back of his hand, and grinned at her.

"I didn't frighten you, did I, Miss Whitlock?" he asked.

The tone of superior disdain was not what she had expected. The previous night, in the dinghy, she'd thought he'd forgiven her for whatever sin she'd committed, thought he'd come to consider her if not with warmth, then at least without derision. But now it was obvious that she had been wrong.

It seemed to Alyssa that the possibility that he might have frightened her gave him no great pang of conscience. On the contrary, he appeared mildly pleased by the fear he had seen in her expression. It was quite obvious to her that nothing had changed in his feelings about her, that he still thought of her, if not with outright enmity, then with derision and dislike.

"Why didn't you answer when I called?" she demanded, feeling a bit of enmity of her own.

He shrugged, obviously unconcerned by her tone.

"My mouth was full," he told her, and took another bite of the fruit. "I thought you missionaries were fearless. After all, don't you have your faith to keep you safe from earthly harm?" He shook his head, pretending shock at her lack of faith. "Your fiancé on Banaba will find your devotion lacking, I think, Miss Whitlock. You'd do well to repent of your sins of inadequacy and offer up a few prayers before you present yourself to him."

Alyssa found herself ignoring his words save for the mention of Owen Remsen. She cringed at the off-handed way in which he referred to her intended husband, for it brought back to her only too forcefully the realization that she hadn't given him a thought and had no desire to do so.

"You might do well to tend to your own conscience and leave me to tend to mine," she told him in an acid tone.

He gave no indication that he was the least concerned by the rebuke.

"I was going to ask how you're feeling, but I see such an inquiry is unnecessary," he said. "Your injuries can't be very serious if they haven't mellowed your humor."

"*I* am not the one who has behaved rudely," she snapped.

He shrugged. "As you like."

She stared at the heap of fruit he'd brought with him.

"I don't suppose you would care to tell me where you found those, so I could get some as well?"

He waved his hand magnanimously toward the pile. Then, without waiting for her to take one, he picked a piece of fruit from his haul, inspected it, and having determined it fit for her consumption, held it out to her.

"I don't know what they are, but they taste all right and I haven't been poisoned by them yet."

"Pity," she muttered under her breath as she took it from him.

Why, she wondered as she considered the strange fruit, had he seemed so kind and gentle to her when he'd plucked her out of the water, and why had he now returned to this former and far less pleasant self?

But there were no answers for her in the pale yellow-tinged, red-colored oval, and she pushed her questions aside as she poked its soft, thin skin. She was hungry, she realized as she bit it tentatively. It was sweet-tasting, if a bit pulpy. She took another bite, larger this time, surprised to hear her stomach growl in appreciative anticipation. It seemed to her that she hadn't been really hungry since before she'd left Plymouth.

Whatever scrutiny Alyssa had given him a few moments before was minor compared to the way Jason eyed her as she turned her attention from him to the meal of fruit. His shirt managed to obscure the more obvious charms of her body that he recalled had been quite clearly revealed when she had lain clad only in her shift. For an instant he almost regretted having left her the shirt, then told himself it would have been a pity to allow such fine, pale skin to be burned by the late afternoon sun. Still, he wished the shirt was not quite so large on her, covering her to below her knees. He recalled the pleasant curve of her thighs as she lay in the sand sleeping, and the soft, rounded curve of her breasts.

Still, he decided, even disheveled and dressed in his shirt, she was not without allure. The mass of her blonde curls tumbled around her shoulders and down her back and framed her face, giving it an artless, almost childlike look of innocence. Thick lashes edged wide green eyes and almost managed to trap his glance and keep it from straying to a pair of full lips that were at that moment stained and shining from the juice of the fruit. Lips, he thought, that needed desperately to be kissed.

Under just about any other circumstance, he realized, he would be making an effort to convince her what a pleasant and charming companion he could be, to show her how those juice-stained lips might be employed to give both of them pleasure, how that small but entirely pleasant body might be used to the purpose for which it had been designed. Surely the fact that she was to be a missionary's bride ought not to diminish either her attraction nor the natural inclinations her attraction roused in him. Why, he wondered, did he persist in keeping his distance?

It wasn't that she was full of the usual cant and pious quotes. If anything, she hardly seemed the missionary sort. Now that she was shorn of the dark dress and prim little bonnet she'd worn when she'd boarded the *Empress*, there was little if anything about her that seemed even remotely sanctimonious. It would take little urging for him to forget entirely that she was a missionary. Considering the fact that they might very well be alone on the island for an indeterminate period, he amended his assessment and told himself it would not be out of the question for him to forget even without the urging.

She had finished the fruit and was considering the pit thoughtfully.

"I hadn't thought I'd ever be so hungry," she said, and she eyed the remaining fruit on the sand between them.

He laughed. "Here," he said as he gave her one of the two ripe bananas he'd found. "Eat this while I try to find something to use to open these coconuts."

She accepted the fruit, carefully brushing away the sand that clung to it before she pulled back the peel and then, with a complete change of manner, unceremoniously began to devour it. As she ate, she sat back on her heels and watched him search along the edge of the beach for a piece of stone. She finished the banana, eyed the empty peel with regret, then wiped her sticky fingers in the sand. She looked up to find Jason had walked a fair distance along the stretch of empty beach.

She gathered up the coconuts and the remaining fruit that lay in the sand beside her before she stood and started after him. When he looked up and saw her approaching, he stopped, obviously waiting for her to catch up.

"There," he said as she neared.

He pointed to a small outcrop of rock a bit further along the beach.

"What good will that do?" she asked.

"Watch," he told her.

He collected two of the coconuts from her and then led her toward the outcrop.

"Make yourself comfortable," he said, and pointed to the sand. He grinned. "This may take a bit of work. It's a lot easier if you happen to have a blade. I should have thought of that before I jumped into the waves after you last night, but somehow the thought didn't occur to me."

He grinned again and Alyssa found herself smiling back at him.

"No," she agreed. "I don't suppose it would." She looked up at him. "I'm afraid I must admit that I'm glad you didn't decide to leave me to drown while you went about the task of properly equipping yourself."

He stared at her for a long, silent moment.

"So am I," he agreed.

He pointed once again to the sand. Alyssa settled herself there, then watched him wade through the water to the outcrop. He seemed entirely involved in its inspection for a few moments, and she found herself thinking how boyish he seemed, how entirely at his ease. This *was* an adventure to him, she realized. He would quite happily cope with being stranded on this island, for a while, at least—of that she was convinced. He would think of it as being simply a pleasant adventure.

Jason seemed to find what he had been searching for, for he lifted one of the coconuts and then brought it down forcefully against a thin, narrow edge of rock. He inspected the results, seemed pleased enough by them, and set the coconut carefully on the stone. Then he repeated the process with the second.

"Triumph," he shouted and retrieved the first coconut. He returned to where she sat, splashing back through the shallow water wearing a self-satisfied and pleased expression. He held out one of the coconuts to her. "There," he said, and pointed to a two-inch hole in the hairy shell. "Nectar for my lady."

She took the coconut and stared at the hole for a moment, considering the thin liquid inside the shell.

"Would it seem inopportune to propose a toast, Captain Draper?" she asked him.

"Only fitting under the circumstances, I should think, Miss Whitlock," he replied as he settled himself beside her on the sand. He held his coconut out in front of him, toward the ocean and a sky brilliantly colored by the sinking sun. "To fair skies and calm seas," he said.

She nodded. "And brave sea captains who risk their lives to save their passengers," she added, her voice low with emotion she had not expected to be there.

He turned and glanced at her, apparently surprised by the tribute.

"I told you," he said. "I didn't want my reputation ruined by some missionary foolish enough to jump into the ocean in the middle of a hurricane."

She was a bit put off by his words, but then she saw the humor in his eyes and realized he'd not meant anything cruel. She was sure there was none of the disdainful look she'd come to expect to find in them.

"I didn't exactly jump," she replied with an attempt at a laugh.

The memory of that horrible moment when she'd been swept from the deck was not one she recalled with any pleasure. The bruise on her shoulder and side began to ache in sympathy with the memory.

"Details," he said, moving his hand in a gesture of dismissal. He turned to face her and his eyes found hers. "In any case, you're safe and my reputation remains undefiled." He leaned forward, toward her. "At least so far."

Alyssa watched his face near hers. She could feel his breath warm against her cheek. His eyes held hers, blue and clear. They made her feel as though she were floating, losing herself in them.

She felt suddenly awkward, completely unsure of herself, and the wave of heat in her cheeks told her she was blushing. She knew he wanted to kiss her, even the years she'd spent in her uncle's house had not left her so unaware that she could mistake what she saw in his eyes. But Silas's endless lectures had left their mark, and she could not quite dispel the nagging voice he'd planted inside her, a voice that told her it would be wrong to allow him any such freedom.

It hardly seemed to matter that she found the prospect of his kiss entirely pleasant.

She turned away in confusion, looking down at the coconut in her hands, uncomfortable again, as she had been when he'd emerged from the undergrowth and she'd seen his naked torso. She realized now what it was that made her feel this way, that it was guilt that she found it pleasant to look at his body. Surely, she told herself, this was wrong. Surely her Uncle Silas would damn it as sinful.

"Do you think it will take very long for them to find us?" she asked, eager to think of something else, anything else.

He pulled back, shrugged his shoulders, and forced himself to be content with sipping the coconut liquid in its shell.

"I suppose it depends on how far the storm pushed us," he said.

It was a noncommittal answer, and he had no doubt but that she realized he was trying to avoid a more precise one. Still, it was the best he could give her.

"At least we won't starve," he said, trying to sound cheerful. "I didn't go very far, but there's plenty of fruit, bananas, those reddish things, coconuts enough to feed a small army. Tomorrow, with the daylight, we can explore the island."

She raised her coconut to her lips and sipped the sweet, thin liquid in thoughtful silence. She let her glance drift back to the water and the beautifully color-streaked sky. It was hard to think that only hours before, both sky and sea had been so angry and frightening. Now the water was nothing if not peaceful, blue and idyllic. And the sky was breathtakingly beautiful, filled with color, unlike anything she'd ever seen in Plymouth.

A feeling of peace, of well-being, filled her. It was foolish, she told herself, marooned as they were, but she could not deny to herself that she felt suddenly anything but depressed at their circumstances. She was beginning to understand his apparent lack of concern at being stranded in this place. She thought she might be beginning to feel the same way.

Best not to worry about being found, she told herself philosophically. Best not to think too far into the future. She emptied her mind and thought only of the view and the lovely contentment it left inside her.

"Splendor of ended day, floating and filling me!"

She was as startled by the words as he seemed to be when he turned to face her. She hadn't even realized she'd remembered them until she'd uttered them aloud.

He grinned at her, a surprised, pleased grin.

"You actually have read the Whitman," he told her, obviously amazed at the realization. His eyes narrowed. "And you weren't struck down by that vengeful god you missionaries always speak of?"

She ignored his reference to her as a missionary, determined not to let him goad her into losing the feeling of peace that had settled over her.

"He was a favorite of my father's," she replied.

"Your father the missionary?" he asked.

It was another prod, and it nearly pushed her to anger, but again she forced it aside. And suddenly what he had said seemed terribly funny to her.

She shook her head and laughed.

"The sea captain," she corrected. She looked up at him and grinned. "Like you. Only he captained a whaler."

That piece of information seemed to surprise him. He smiled back at her.

"A hard life, whaling," he said. "Not like roaming around the South Seas, letting the wind blow you where it wants you to go."

Alyssa turned away from him, suddenly wanting to explain herself to him, to make him understand that she was not what he had thought her. She stared out at the waves, closed her eyes briefly, and called up memories of her father.

"He lost a leg when I was twelve," she said slowly, her voice low and tight with emotion that she hadn't realized was lying so close to the surface. "They brought him home, filled with infection and fever. He never quite recovered. He'd seem to get well, and then the infection would return, and he'd be ill for months. He spent the next three years reading poetry and slowly dying, bit by bit."

"I'm sorry," Jason whispered.

She shook her head slowly. "He wasn't. He would say that dying slowly meant he had time to savor life. He told me once that he had never realized how much he loved us, my mother and me, until he knew he would soon leave us."

She choked back the hard ball that suddenly lodged itself in her throat. Jason put a hand gently on hers, but she hardly even noticed it.

"That sounded so strange to me then," she went on. "I'm not sure I understand it even now."

"Perhaps death makes philosophers of us all," he offered.

She shook her head once again and slowly drew her

hand from his.

"I think he was a philosopher all his life," she said, "and only had the time to talk about it when death came to claim him." It was odd, the way the hurt suddenly seemed to ease as she talked about it. "In any event, we read to each other a good deal those last years. Whitman was a favorite of his. He loved the poems that sang about life, about finding joy in oneself. Perhaps it was because his own body had failed him so awfully. I remember listening to him when only his voice was still strong and whole. It was one of the things I missed most when he died, listening to him and remembering what he had been like before."

"And that was when you decided on the life of a missionary?" he asked.

She stifled a scowl, thinking how she'd only wanted to survive, to endure life with her uncle until she managed to find some way to escape.

"My mother died six months after he did. Influenza, the doctor said, but I think it was simply because she didn't want to go on without him. After that, I went to live with my uncle. The decision about a missionary's life, if there was one, was his." She grimaced, then grinned, suddenly finding the situation, now that it was past and no longer to be endured, almost amusing. "Uncle Silas was never really pleased with me. He didn't quite approve of Whitman or a lot of other things, I'm afraid. Not poetry or novels or dancing. I'm afraid I must admit to especially having missed being allowed to dance." She turned to stare at Jason and smiled. "I suppose that bit of information will prompt you to tell me again that I should repent of my sins and pray for guidance?" she asked.

Jason grinned in reply. "Hardly," he said.

He swallowed the last of the coconut milk, then set the nut on the sand beside him and pushed himself to his feet. Alyssa stared up at him, surprised to see him bend deeply from the waist in a formal bow.

"As an alternative to repentance," he said very somberly, "might I suggest a waltz?"

She laughed.

"You aren't serious?"

"I am always serious," he replied, his tone and expression entirely earnest.

"Here?"

He motioned to the smooth stretch of sand the waves had left behind them when the tide ebbed.

"A perfect dance floor," he told her.

"But there's no music," she protested with a laugh.

This, too, did not seem to discourage him. He began to hum tunelessly, listened to himself, then shook his head, apparently deciding his attempts at music less than acceptable.

"You hum and I'll lead," he directed.

Then he held out his hand to her and waited for her to take it.

Alyssa sat, staring at him a moment longer, wondering if he was playing some game with her, if he were trying to make her feel like a fool. But he stared back at her unblinkingly, and she pushed aside her suspicions. She put the coconut down on the sand, then extended her hand to him, letting him help her to her feet.

His right hand slid to her waist. She felt a tremble of uncertainty then, as a ripple of warmth rose where his hand touched her and snaked its way outward, potent shafts of heat that she knew could not come from the balmy sea air around her.

If some part of her told her she ought to pull away from him then, she soon found another part, a stronger part, was pleased to have his arm around her, to feel the warmth of his hand touching her. She began to hum, her voice low and tentative, as she tried desperately to remember a waltz tune she hadn't heard in years.

However unsure her music, he seemed to find it acceptable, because he stepped forward, expertly guiding her with a hand on her waist. Before she knew it, Alyssa found herself improbably giddy. She began to sing, softly at first, then louder, and they danced, making huge, sweeping circles that left swirling prints on the damp sand at the water's edge.

When she finally was forced to admit to herself that she had repeated the refrain of the melody all too many times, she let the last note trail off and found herself suddenly standing with his arms around her and the waves lapping against her feet. She stared up at him, at the red and orange and gold fingers that streaked the sky behind him.

And she watched him slowly lower his face to hers.

Chapter Six

Alyssa trembled as Jason's fingers touched her chin. She stared up into the blue of his eyes and found herself thinking of the ocean, found herself wondering if she might not be swept up to drown in them as she had feared the night before she might drown beneath the waves.

His lips touched hers.

She had never felt anything like this before, never thought it possible that deep within her she could feel herself melting, moving, flowing. Never had she ever imagined that there was a molten river hidden somewhere inside her body waiting to be set free.

She grew light-headed and slightly disoriented, and found herself bewildered by her reaction. What was this sweet magic he released in her veins, she wondered. It intoxicated her, like strong drink to one who had never before taken so much as a sip of alcohol.

How strange, she thought, to become drunk on a kiss.

Jason's arms tightened around her and drew her close. Her body, warm beneath the linen of his shirt, bent to him, pliant to the promptings of his hands just as it had followed him when they'd danced. It struck him suddenly that there was something very right about this, about the way her body seemed to fit against his naturally, as if it had been designed for that purpose and none other.

He lowered his lips to her neck, and Alyssa dropped her head back, letting herself become lost in the sweet mystery the contact released inside her. She could feel her heart racing, and remembered how it had raced the night before when she'd fought against the waves. Some part of her again feared she might drown. But the fear was small compared to the pleasure that had been let loose inside her, and it shrank away as her curiosity pushed it aside. He'd released something strange and wondrous within her, and she could only wonder what other mysteries he might reveal to her.

She raised her hands to his neck, feeling his pulse beneath her palms, strong and sharp like her own. A strange sense of power filled her as she realized that she had done this to him. At that moment she knew that if she was being swept up by the tide, the undertow was not carrying her off alone.

She hardly realized when he lifted her in his arms and then lay her on the soft sand, hardly knew when he pushed the shirt back from her shoulders. All she could think of was the feeling of his lips against her neck, the warmth of his hands gently stroking her breasts and her hips and her thighs.

It was like a small echo in her mind, her Uncle Silas's voice, telling her that what she did was sinful, evil. But somehow she could not bring herself to agree with that faint echo from her past. Somehow she knew that this wondrous thing that was happening inside her was right, was part of what God intended for her when he had fashioned her as he had. If there was sin, she told herself, it was in finding evil in what was as nature had intended it to be.

The voice disappeared, and with it all thought of her uncle and his condemnation. She had room now for only one thought, and that was wonder that the capacity to feel as she now did must have always been within her, and she'd never suspected it.

Jason expertly pulled away her chemise, the movement hardly interrupting the survey he made with his lips and his tongue of her breasts and the gentle ridges of her ribs and her belly. She found herself floating, as much at the mercy of his touch as she had been at the mercy of the waves the night before. The only difference was in the fact that the waves he released inside her roused no terror in her, only wonder and the strange stirrings that she did not yet realize were the rising tide of wakening passion.

He pulled away from her and she stared up at him, at his naked torso framed by the setting sun and a fiery-colored sky behind him. He seemed like an idol to her, the idol of some strange pagan god, and she a worshiping handmaiden. It seemed odd to her that this thought, so alien to everything she had been taught right and proper, did not offend her.

Jason stood, removed his trousers, and again lowered himself to her. He stared at her as he covered her body with his, at the beautiful pale skin and the golden mane of her hair.

He suddenly found himself frozen. She was beautiful, he thought, so beautiful it took his breath away.

He ran his fingers through her hair, spreading it out on the sand around her head so that it framed her face like a burnished gold halo, reflecting the last fading fingers of daylight. It was like silk between his fingers, fine and soft and smooth. He brought his hand to her cheek and then trailed it slowly downward to her breast, and thought how her skin, too, was silken to his touch. At that moment she was a wonder to him, her beauty perfect, flawless. He found it hard to believe that she was there, beside him, his for the taking.

He began to lower his lips to hers, but stopped before

he actually touched them. Her eyes were staring up at his, peering into his. He could not help but see the bewilderment in those questioning green eyes, and the trust.

She had only the smallest idea what was happening between them, he realized. He felt a wave of guilt pass through him as he realized he was taking something from her he had no right to take. If nothing else, he owed her the chance to say no, the opportunity to make the decision for herself.

"Alyssa," he whispered.

She gazed up at him, surprised to see the expression of tenderness and doubt. Those were two things that she could not think natural to him. She could picture him only as strong and brave and determined. Doubt, she thought, would be alien to him, and tenderness he would keep well hidden.

She reached up to him, putting her hands behind his neck and pulling herself close to him. She stared into his eyes for a long moment, then offered him her lips. She had no idea why she did such a thing, no idea just what it was he expected of her. She only knew she wanted to taste his lips once again, wanted to keep that molten river he'd released within her from returning to that secret part of her from which it had sprung.

He accepted her lips, surprised with the offer but of no mind to refuse it. And when he put his tongue to them, she parted them in innocent and curious welcome.

He held her to him, savoring that kiss, tasting her lips and tongue with his own, wondering at the sweetness of it, the hint of honey. Whatever second thoughts he had had a moment before fled, dissolved and lost in the wave of passion that swept through him. He had never before wanted a woman as he wanted her at that moment. There was no longer any thought of turning away.

He held her close, almost as though he feared she might suddenly disappear from the circle of his arms. Then he kissed her, pressing his lips to her neck, savoring the taste of her skin. He was determined now to make her feel as he did, to make her want him as much as he wanted her. He'd always thought himself a reasonably considerate lover in the past, but never had he felt a need like this, never had it been so important to him that he bring pleasure to another.

He brought his lips to her breasts, letting his tongue urge the nipples until they grew taut with want. He could feel her heart beating, could feel the heat that radiated from her and knew it came from the fire he'd ignited within her. He brought his lips once more to hers and felt her breath, warm and ragged, against his cheek.

Alyssa had no thought now but to let him take her wherever he intended her to go. When he nudged her legs, she spread them beneath him, unsure of herself but knowing she could no more turn away from him than she could battle the endless tides. Whatever was to happen between them, she told herself, it was fated. She had as much power over it as she had over the sun rising and setting.

He entered her like a shaft of sweet, flowing fire. She felt herself melting where he touched her, and wondered if she were flowing into him, becoming part of him with the joining. Nothing had prepared her for this, nothing had ever felt as this felt, nothing had ever been as shattering or as beautiful.

She moved as his hands urged her, quickly joining him in the eternal dance. And as she did, the tides he'd set free inside her seemed to rise, growing ever stronger, ever higher, until she was sure they would overpower her and sweep her away. It frightened her to think that she was a willingly compliant voyager caught up in those mysteriously potent tides. All she knew was that she had no desire to break free of their powerful hold.

And they tossed her, higher, ever higher, until she thought she might shatter with their force. And when she finally gave herself up to them, she trembled and clung to Jason, not even hearing the low moan of pleasure she uttered.

Jason had waited for that moment, for the knowledge that she'd found the pleasure of release. The feeling of her body trembling and clinging to his was a spur he could not fight, and he found he could no longer hold the wave of passion that he had until then managed to control. He let it sweep through him, more powerful than any he had ever felt before, and he joined her in the sweet, timeless delirium.

They lay together, spent and breathless in the sand. Jason cradled her in his arms, listening to the sharp beat of her pulse and knowing that it echoed his own. It bewildered him to realize that he'd never before felt as he did at that moment, never been quite so content. He wanted nothing more than for that moment to go on forever, to spend eternity holding her in his arms.

It occurred to him that he might do quite well were the two of them to remain stranded alone on this island. Fate had surprised him, had given him something he'd never known he'd wanted.

Alyssa stared up at him as her breathing and pulse slowly settled. This, then, she thought, was what it meant to sin, to spurn those laws her Uncle Silas had held so stringently close and preached so knowingly.

The thought brought her not the least twinge of guilt. Sin was ugly, she told herself, and what she and Jason had done had been beautiful. There was no question in her mind now that she could compliantly accept all those lessons Silas had put so much effort into teaching her. She was changed, a totally different person now. And she was glad. She had no desire ever to go back.

She stared up at Jason, then reached up to his face, putting her fingers first to his chin and then slowly tracing the outline of his lips. How odd, she thought, that she had never before considered what magic could be evoked by two lips.

"Do you know you're smiling?" she asked him. "I didn't think grim sea captains allowed themselves to ever really smile."

"Or missionaries," he replied. "But you're smiling, too."

She was, she realized. She thought she had never before felt quite so contented or happy.

"I think it must be this island," she told him softly. "I think it must be enchanted."

He stared down at her, holding her eyes with his, mesmerizing her with his gaze. Finally he shook his head.

"It's not this place," he told her. "It's you."

He leaned forward to her, and kissed her lips softly, then fell to the sand beside her and pulled her close.

She lay, staring up as the last of the sunlight was extinguished in the sky above them and as the first of the night stars showed themselves overhead. Tomorrow, she told herself as her eyes drifted closed and she nuzzled comfortably in Jason's arms, would be a beautiful day.

Alyssa woke, gritty with sand and alone on the beach in the bright morning sunshine.

She was naked. Jason had once more laid his shirt over her to protect her from the sun, but beneath it she was naked. With that realization came the memory of the reason why she woke to find herself in the sand as she was, and the memory brought with it a thick wave of shame.

What must he think of her, she wondered, what kind of a woman must he think she was? She had no idea why she had done what she had, why she had let it all happen. And the knowledge that she had found pleasure in the act only made the feeling worsen. A woman who behaved as she had would be thought nothing more than a common whore in Plymouth. Certainly some things could not be changed, even if she had come halfway around the world.

Had she been clad still in her chemise rather than naked, she could have told herself she had dreamed what had occurred between them the night before. As it was, she was indeed naked, and her skin felt itchy with the grit of the sand beneath her.

She pushed herself to her feet and eyed the empty beach. No Jason, nothing but her chemise, a crumpled ball of linen, a few feet from where she stood. It seemed like an accusation to her, a symbol of her easily cast aside morality.

The years of her uncle's barely veiled suggestions that she was bound to find an immoral, sinful end came back to her with a painfully accusing clarity. Perhaps, she thought, Silas had been right about her after all.

She could not escape the knowledge that she had allowed a man she hardly knew to take her, a man who had made little attempt to hide the disdain in which he held her. No matter what she might tell herself by way of excuse, no matter how she might try to explain what had happened, tell herself it had been the effect of the moonlight and the talk about her parents and the aftereffects of the fear of the hours spent in the ocean, still she knew there had been no reason for what had happened except that she had let it happen.

She ran into the water, letting the waves splash roughly against her body, wondering if somehow the force of them might in some way wash away the guilt she felt along with the sand that clung to her skin. But no matter that she rubbed herself so furiously her skin grew red with the friction, still she felt no better. If only Jason had been there when she'd wakened, if only he'd been loving to her, if only, if only . . .

She pulled herself up sharply. It made no sense to think what it might be like if he'd told her he'd loved her, if he'd promised to marry her, she told herself. He hadn't. She had no reason to think he considered her with any more feeling than he thought of the doubtless accommodating Polynesian women he'd come in contact with over the years. She couldn't pretend what had happened between them meant anything more to him than a few moments of pleasure.

She'd be a fool to think that what had happened would in any way change her life, to imagine he would marry her and they would live an endless fairy-tale adventure aboard the *Empress*. Life was not a fairy tale, and there were no happily-ever-afters. Her parents' lives were more than example enough to convince her of that. No matter what else she was, no matter what she'd done, she was not a fool. She'd made a mistake, and now she must decide how she would deal with it.

The sand was washed from her skin, but still she told herself she was hardly clean. Feeling totally miserable, she turned back toward the beach. She found her shift, shook it to rid it of the sand that clung to the fabric and pulled it on.

"Morning, Miss Missionary."

She turned sharply, surprised by the sound of his voice, even though she knew she had no reason to be. She found he'd appeared out of the jungle as he had the previous afternoon, his arms laden once again with fruit. He was standing there, staring at her, and something about his glance made her feel unaccountably uncomfortable.

Miss Missionary.

The words echoed in her mind, along with the faintly

amused and derisive tone he'd used. If there had been any slight doubt in her mind that he might think her more than a conveniently accommodating female, it disappeared. She was still a missionary to him, and he'd made it only too clear to her that he considered that classification on a level with reptiles or perhaps something worse. She wondered if it gave him pleasure to think he'd corrupted a missionary, if it amused him to think he'd made her sin against all those beliefs that he considered her kind had come to Polynesia to preach.

"I have a name," she told him sharply.

She turned away, hurriedly picking up the shirt and pulling it on. Despite its covering, she was, she found, still feeling terribly naked.

Jason was disconcerted by her response. He'd only called her that because when he'd stepped out of the undergrowth and seen her, she'd seemed anything but a missionary to him. He didn't understand why she stood with her back to him, why she'd donned the shirt as though it were a coat of impenetrable armor.

He dropped the armful of fruit and crossed to her, slipping his hand around her waist and pulling her back, close to him. He began to lower his lips to the nape of her neck.

His touch told her nothing of the tenderness he felt for her at that moment. Instead, it only reinforced what she had been telling herself, that he considered her a useful and compliant companion, a diversion that might make his time on the island a bit more pleasant.

Before he had the chance to kiss her, she pushed his hand away and stepped forward, out of his grasp.

"I think we should come to an understanding," she told him as she turned to face him.

He raised a brow. "An understanding?" he asked.

"Last evening. What happened." She found she was strangling on the words.

"Yes. I believe I remember," he said with a wry grin.

The grin faded quickly as soon as he realized it was not being returned.

She turned away again, not wanting to look at him, afraid she might lose her grasp if she did.

"It was wrong," she said firmly. "Not that I blame you," she added quickly. "I shouldn't have danced with you, I shouldn't have let it happen. It was my fault. But it can not happen again."

Jason didn't move. "Wrong?" he asked.

Alyssa wrapped her arms around herself, and moved another step away.

"Of course," she replied and she turned once more to face him. "We're civilized human beings, not barbarians. We've . . ."

He cut her off.

"Barbarians?" he asked. "Don't you mean godless fornicators? Like the Polynesians? Don't you mean we're better than that?"

She saw the anger that had edged its way into his eyes, and didn't understand why it seemed so sharp, so coldly fierce. She told herself that he had no right to bear her any anger, that it was she who had been wronged.

She pulled herself stiffly erect.

"Those are your words, not mine," she told him.

He'd been right about her the first time he'd seen her on the wharf in Papeete, he told himself. She was just another self-righteous, morality-spouting missionary. He'd been stupid to think, even for a moment, otherwise.

"Let me assure you, Miss Whitlock," he said through tight lips, "however barbaric I may be, I am not so great a brute as to force myself upon a woman who does not want me."

The vehemence she heard in his voice surprised

Alyssa. She certainly hadn't expected him to react with such angry intensity.

"I didn't . . ."

He interrupted her with a sharp movement of his hand, cutting off the words before she could even think what to say to him.

"And when we arrive on Banaba," he continued, completely oblivious to her startled and confused expression, "I promise to keep your little lapse from your doubtless most civilized and moral bridegroom. We wouldn't want him to think you less than the perfect little morality-preaching hypocrite you really are."

This was more than she could believe. He had seduced her, and now he was accusing *her* of hypocrisy. She felt her cheeks color with the wave of rage that began to sweep through her.

"How dare you?" she demanded. "How can you stand there and accuse me?"

But he wasn't listening, didn't seem to care what she might have to say. He turned away from her and returned to the pile of fruit he'd dropped in the sand. Alyssa fell silent, aware that whatever she might say would fall on deaf ears.

"There's your breakfast," he told her, pointing to the heap of fruit. "I'm sure you'll enjoy it more in the sanctity of your own sinless company. I wouldn't think to sully it."

He started off without even turning to offer her another glance, striding along the beach with a purposeful gait. He was immediately totally involved, staring into the undergrowth that edged the sand, obviously having dismissed her and pushed aside any consideration of her without so much as a second thought.

Alyssa realized she had been totally dismissed. It didn't take the long, hard stare she leveled at him for her to recognize that he no longer was even aware of her presence. She stood and glared at him, angry that he had misinterpreted everything she'd tried to say to him, angrier still that he seemed perfectly content to dismiss her as easily and as completely as he might a stray animal that had wandered into his path and then been shooed aside.

She tore her eyes away from his rapidly diminishing form, telling herself she was glad he was leaving her alone, that she didn't want his company. She wandered over to the pile of fruit, knelt beside it, and chose one of the reddish fruits she'd eaten the day before. She considered it, giving it a moment of intense attention it hardly deserved, before taking a determined bite.

But the fruit did not hold her interest long. Her attention was immediately distracted by movement in the undergrowth behind her, and she turned to the line of greenery that bordered the beach. She saw nothing, just a seemingly endless wall of still leaves and fronds.

It was just the wind, she told herself, a stray sea breeze that stirred some leaves. She turned her attention back to the piece of fruit, not allowing her glance to look along the beach to where Jason's figure was growing tiny in the distance.

And then there was another stirring in the leaves, louder this time, and closer.

"Who's there?"

She realized she was barely whispering, realized that if there was someone hidden among the undergrowth, secretly watching her, she really didn't want to know who it was.

She shook herself and told herself she was behaving foolishly, that there was no one there and that the wind and her imagination were the only active entities near her. But still, despite her resolve to ignore the stirrings in the leaves nearby, she found herself growing more and more uncomfortable with the prospect of being alone on the stretch of beach.

Jason Draper might be callous and without a shred

of common good manners, but he was still company and protection from whatever or whoever might be lurking in the undergrowth.

She took one last long stare into the dark shadows of the greenery, then pushed herself to her feet and ran along the water's edge after Jason.

Jason was well aware that she was following him. She was still a good distance behind him when he heard the padding of her feet in the damp sand that edged the water. She's come wanting to apologize, he told himself, and he felt a smug thrill of victory, as though he'd won a battle.

Part of him wanted to turn to her, to welcome her and forget the angry words they'd spoken. But there was another part of him that could not forgive her for being a missionary's bride, for proving that she was no better than any of the others of her ilk.

He didn't turn to her and he didn't slow his pace. Let her run, he told himself. Let her come begging.

Alyssa was breathless by the time she'd nearly caught up with him. But her ragged breath did not bother her nearly as much as the realization that she was beginning to feel foolish. He'd been rude to her, and purposefully cruel, and here she was, running after him with no other explanation than that she was in a strange place and it frightened her to be alone. She slowed her pace, then stopped entirely, and stood watching him move away from her, further along the beach.

When Jason realized the sound of her feet against the sand had ceased, he continued on for a moment longer, at first determined not to give her the satisfaction of turning to face her. Finally, though, when he'd asked himself why she had followed so far after him only to stop without having spoken, he gave in to his curiosity. He, too, stopped and turned to face her.

"Was there something you wanted, Miss Whitlock?" he demanded.

She was standing some ten or fifteen feet from him, wide-eyed, staring at him. He was amused by the blush on her cheeks and her look of confusion. He had to force himself to keep from smiling.

She looked down, obviously flustered, letting her glance fall to her hands and noticing that she still held the partially eaten piece of fruit.

"I, I realized you hadn't eaten anything," she said, and held out the fruit, making a poor attempt to hide against her palm the place where she'd taken two fairly large bites.

He eyed the fruit, then walked slowly toward her.

"Your kindness overwhelms me," he told her as he reached for the fruit, grasping it quickly, before she could draw it away. He eyed the pulpy place with the bites. "To think you'd offer up your own meal truly touches me," he said, making no effort to hide the sarcasm in his tone. "Such generosity shows a genuinely Christian spirit. I'm sure your intended would be proud of the sacrifice."

Alyssa rankled inwardly at the mention of Owen Remsen, but she forced herself to swallow the feeling of anger. The more she thought about it, the more she realized she didn't want to remain alone very long on the beach.

"Where are you going?" Alyssa demanded abruptly, anxious to change the subject.

He eyed the wavy ribbon of beach in front of them.

"I thought I'd explore a bit," he said, then turned back to face her. "I don't suppose you'd care to come along, would you? Not afraid I might press some unwanted attentions upon you?"

Alyssa found herself shrinking at his words. If only his attentions had been unwanted, she thought. Then she might not feel as guilty as she did.

"I, I thought I heard some rustling in the leaves back there," she murmured, feeling foolish but unable to do anything but admit why she'd come chasing after him.

He smiled a wry smile.

"And you prefer a monster you know to one you don't, is that it, Miss Whitlock?" he asked.

She felt herself blush and found she had no words with which to reply.

"If it would ease your mind, I can assure it was most probably just the wind moving the leaves that you heard. In all likelihood this island is uninhabited save for the two of us." He turned and continued on with his inspection of the beach.

Alyssa scrambled along after him.

"I know," she said, agreeing with his assessment, but finding that despite his assurance, she did not feel anymore like remaining alone on the beach.

"On the other hand," Jason continued, "there is always the possibility that the island *is* inhabited."

He lifted the piece of fruit he'd taken from her and absently took a large bite from it, then chewed thoughtfully as he walked. His eyes continued to scan the undergrowth that edged the beach.

"But if there were natives here, wouldn't they come out and greet us? Wouldn't they know we were here?"

Alyssa found that she had to hurry along to keep up with him, for in his preoccupation he made no effort to shorten his stride to match her far shorter one. Or perhaps he simply didn't care to make it easy for her to accompany him, she thought. Perhaps he was intentionally trying to make her feel uncomfortable.

Intentional or not, he was succeeding.

"Oh, they'd know we were here, all right," he agreed. "And as to their greeting us, that would depend on whether they were of a friendly frame of mind, now, wouldn't it?"

And that remark, she decided, was intended to make

her even more uncomfortable. She wished he would at least turn away from the line of undergrowth and look at her. At least then she might have an idea what he was thinking.

"What are you looking for?" she demanded.

He continued on without answering. Alyssa padded along at his side in confused and miserable silence. Her legs were beginning to ache from the long walk in the sand, and she wished he would stop for a moment so that she could rest.

She was thinking about how she might broach the subject of a short rest when he suddenly stopped and stood staring into the undergrowth.

"What's this?" he muttered softly.

She stared into the welter of shadows, wondering what he saw that was any different from the nearly endless line of shadows he'd simply passed by without notice. She could see nothing but fronds and leaves and palm trunks.

"What is it?" she asked him in a hushed tone.

He crossed the width of the beach slowly, and Alyssa followed, dragging her feet through the warm sand.

"It would seem that we may not be alone after all, Miss Whitlock," he told her when he'd reached the edge of the growth.

Alyssa moved to his side and then stared at what had so obviously caught his attention.

It was overgrown, apparently unused for a long while, but now that she was close she could not miss it, either. They were standing, staring at a narrow path that led into the jungle.

Chapter Seven

Alyssa stared dully at the path. It wound its way into the shadows, quickly disappearing as it twisted and turned, snaking its way through the undergrowth. Roots had worked their way up through the soil and vines had begun to creep across it, claiming the open, bare space, but there was no question in her mind: it was a distinct path through the jungle.

Alyssa caught her breath. A path like this could mean only one thing—that there had been people on the island.

It could mean that they were there still.

"What do we do?"

Her voice, she realized, was hushed, as though she was afraid they might be overheard. She found herself darting a furtive glance along the deserted beach, looking for the unseen owners of the feet that had worn this path through the undergrowth.

"I suggest we find out where it leads," Jason said.

He seemed entirely calm—too calm, Alyssa thought as she watched him step forward, onto the root-rutted path. She found herself hesitating, not quite certain that she wanted to follow him. Going into the jungle seemed to her like walking into a lion's den, and she felt at that moment absolutely no kinship to the ancient Daniel.

But remaining alone on the beach, out in the open

and exposed, seemed equally unappealing to her. Forced to choose between the two, she had to admit that she'd rather follow after Jason than be left alone.

She stepped onto the path, into the shadows made by the canopy of leaves overhead. There seemed to be much more noise here, rustlings in the leaves and the cries of birds that called out angrily as their domain was invaded.

Much to her surprise, a good deal of her fear vanished as she looked around her. She soon realized that the rustlings that had at first seemed so ominous were caused by the birds as they changed their perches overhead. She stared up at them and stood for a long moment gawking at the brightly colored wings she saw flapping in the green canopy of leaves above her. There had been no birds like these in Plymouth.

Even the sunlight seemed entirely different here, filtered to a pale, grayish green by the leaves. Once she was on the path, what had seemed like a blur of solid green became a multitude of differentiated patches of color, each distinct, each set off from those around it. She'd never realized there could be so many different shades of a single color.

But the undergrowth wasn't confined to the patches of green. Surprisingly, despite the lack of direct sunlight below of the shading canopy above, many of the plants showed tiny flowers and berries, a myriad of strange fruits and flowers. She recognized none of them, but the shapes and colors created a pleasing if confusing tumult. It seemed odd to her that a place that had seemed so ominous moments before suddenly appeared welcoming to her, resplendent with this unexpected bounty.

She realized that Jason was a good deal further along the path, but now that she was no longer plagued by the panic that had struck her on the beach, she felt no need to keep up with him, to stay close to him. It was obvious now to her that the noises that had frightened her so had simply been the wind in the leaves, and possibly the movement of some birds. And it was equally evident that the path on which she stood had not been used in quite some time. If the island had once been populated, she told herself, it had doubtless been abandoned long ago.

Let the smug Mr. Jason Draper go on alone, she told herself firmly. It would do him good to realize she was not so dependent upon him that she could not survive quite well without him.

The sight of a large cluster of dark red berries hanging from a vine near the edge of the path reminded her that she'd eaten only a few bites of fruit Jason had brought for her breakfast. Her stomach rumbled ominously, telling her only too clearly that she was still very hungry. She eyed the dark red berries, thinking how inviting they looked.

Not stopping to think any further, she stepped beneath the vine and reached up for the cluster of berries. Standing on tiptoe, she just managed to reach it and pull it free of the vine. She plucked one of the berries from the cluster and brought it to her mouth.

A hand caught her wrist and held it with a sharply painful grasp.

She uttered a small, strangled cry, then turned to find Jason standing behind her. He jerked her hand away before she could put the berry to her lips.

"Unless you've grown very tired of the tedium of island life, Miss Whitlock, let me suggest to you that you never eat anything you don't recognize or have not been told on extremely trustworthy authority is safe."

Alyssa dropped the berries. That was stupid, she thought. She would never have simply eaten berries she didn't recognize back in the woods on the outskirts of Plymouth. It was just that so much was strange here, and she'd somehow come to accept the fantasy that one need only reach up and take whatever one found. During the trip to Papeete, Emily Carver had gone on endlessly about the cause for the Polynesians' laziness and lack of godly reverence, proposing that it was simply that they did not have to work to eat, that they had only to pluck an endless supply of fruit from the trees. Alyssa had thought she'd ignored Emily's lectures, but it seemed that some of it had somehow had an effect, a nearly deadly effect.

She looked up at Jason. "And are you a trustworthy authority?" she asked him.

"As good as you have at the moment," he told her dryly. "Unless you want to offer up prayer to your missionary deity and hope for supreme guidance."

She scowled at his tone, and at the sharply contemptuous glance he leveled at her, but she realized she had little right to complain. It would seem she was dependent upon him after all, despite her moment of bravado when she'd told herself she could survive without him. It was more than obvious to her now that just the opposite was true.

"Are these berries poisonous, then?" she asked.

He shrugged. "I don't know," he admitted. "But I've never eaten any like them and wouldn't suggest you use yourself as a guinea pig. Unless, that is, you're willing to take the chance."

She looked down at the cluster of bruised berries lying near her feet. A bit of bright red juice had leaked from them and stained the dark soil. The sight of them made her stomach growl. She wished she hadn't been so shortsighted as to leave behind on the beach the heap of fruit Jason had gathered that morning.

"I suppose that unladylike noise means you now sorely regret having relinquished your breakfast," Jason said in response to the growl. "A lapse of your selfless missionary sense of charity?" He grinned. "Or could it be part of you at least is willing to admit you're only human?"

He didn't wait to see her angry scowl, but turned and walked back a bit, retracing his steps, then moving off the path and into the undergrowth. He rustled about in the leaves for a moment, then reappeared.

"If you're starving, eat these," he told her and held out a hand of tiny bananas. "They're not quite ripe, but they won't kill you." He grinned again, this time slightly maliciously. "At least I don't think they will."

Alyssa hesitated, wanting more than anything at that moment to reject his offering, to show him she could provide for herself well enough without his help. But a glance at the welter of leaves and fronds told her distinctly that she couldn't. Even staring directly at the place from which she'd seen him take the bananas, she found she couldn't differentiate the dozen or so different fronds, and had no idea where she ought to look to find more fruit.

"If you don't want them . . ." he said, and moved as though he were about to toss the small hand back into the undergrowth.

"No," she said, putting her hand on his arm, keeping him from heaving the bunch back into the mass of greenery.

The contact sent an odd shiver through her hand, a strange, warm, tingling sensation that startled her. She quickly drew it away.

"Am I to assume that you're willing to accept food from my hand, Miss Whitlock?" he taunted. "Aren't you afraid it might be tainted?"

"I . . ." She found she was tongue-tied and nervous and was not the least surprised to see that her reaction seemed to amuse him. Even though she was no longer touching him, she could still feel the strange heat, the oddly pleasant tingling reaction. "Thank you," she said firmly and took the bananas he once again held out to her.

He stood for a moment, staring at her with an absent sort of smile curling the edges of his lips. She wondered what it was he was thinking, wondered if he knew the sort of effect touching him had had on her, wondered if it brought him any satisfaction to know how easily he could unsettle her. She wanted to run away, to find someplace where she could hide from him and the sight of his half-amused, superior smile.

He turned abruptly back to face the path, leaving her to contemplate the sight of his back and just how much she was beginning to dislike him.

"Well, if we're going to explore, we can't spend the whole day standing here while you fill your stomach," he told her. "You can come or not, as you like."

He set off without offering her another glance.

Alyssa half-walked, half-ran after him, not stopping even as she pulled one of the bananas from the small bunch, peeled it, and munched at it in ruminative silence. Jason obviously was in no mood to talk to her, nor did he give any indication that he was interested in her presence at all. He marched on through the jungle, pausing only to tear aside a vine that had grown across the path and was too high to be stepped over easily.

After she had stubbed her toe painfully against a protruding root, she realized she had to direct at least a modicum of her attention to the uneven path underfoot. The combined acts of eating the bananas, considering the extent of Jason Draper's rudeness, pondering the response she'd had to the fleeting contact with his arm, and keeping an eye on each place she stepped seemed about all she could accomplish.

It was no wonder, then, that when Jason stopped suddenly, she simply kept walking until she bumped into him.

"Oh!" She stepped back from him. "I'm sorry."

But he wasn't listening to her. In fact, he was totally oblivious to her now, and was, instead, silently admiring what he'd found.

And once she'd had her own thoughts jogged loose from the track in which they'd been mired, Alyssa realized that the air was filled with a thick thrumming sound, the sound of water striking rocks. She stood on tiptoe and peered over Jason's shoulder in an attempt to discover what it was that had roused his admiration.

A thick stream of water was spilling from a rocky ledge perhaps forty feet above them, falling to a tumble of dark stone, then collecting in a small pool. Surrounded as it was by lush vegetation, Alyssa had to admit the view of the waterfall and pool was more than enough to incite the admiration with which Jason so obviously viewed it.

She edged by him and moved to the water's edge. The water was crystal clear, so clear she could see the stones at the bottom of the pool. She knelt, set the remaining bananas on a slab of stone at the edge of the pool and put her hand into the water. It felt cool and inviting. Venturing a taste, she found it was delicious.

She looked up at Jason.

"It's not brackish," she told him as she brought a handful of the water to her lips.

"I thought I told you not to put anything in your mouth I haven't told you was safe," he muttered, then shrugged, as though the possibility of her drinking tainted water might not distress him all that much anyway.

He knelt beside her and tasted the water himself.

"Do I have your permission to drink, Captain Draper?" she asked him. She smiled a saccharine-sweet smile.

"All you like," he agreed. "Fresh water like this is not altogether usual in these parts, but I'm not about to complain." He pushed himself forward and took a long drink himself, then dunked his head into the clear, cool water.

Alyssa eyed his method of imbibing his fill. "You can lead a horse to water . . ." she muttered with a primly superior air. Then she moved a few feet away from him and quickly drank water she scooped up with her cupped hands, pretending not to notice the water she dripped liberally over the front of her shirt nor the fact that his method was a good deal more effective than hers.

Jason pushed himself back from the water, sighed with pleasure, then stood.

"I don't suppose you'd care to join me in a short swim?" he asked as he began to unbutton his trousers. "I've about tired of the feeling of dried sea salt on my skin."

He didn't wait for an answer but shed his trousers and dived into the deep, clear pool.

Alyssa felt the warmth of a blush filling her cheeks. At first she told herself she was angry with him, angry that he thought so little of her that he would behave as though she was not even there and take no notice of her modesty. But then she realized with a deep sense of shame that she had been unable to take her eyes off him as he'd stripped, that she'd watched the whole time and, perhaps the worst, that she'd found a strange, stirring kind of pleasure in what she'd seen.

Jason had swum to the far side of the small pool, just to the side of the place where the waterfall came in contact with the rocks, and now he turned to her. He was, she realized, smiling a superiorly knowing smile. He'd seen her, she thought guiltily. He knew she had been watching him.

"Come on in," he called to her. "The water's beautiful."

She shook her head.

"I think not," she replied through tight lips.

His smile disappeared, and as he considered her, his expression drained itself of any hint of the amusement he might have felt a moment or two before.

"You needn't worry, Miss Missionary," he told her, his tone grown low and cold. "I've already told you that whatever I may be, I am no rapist."

His tone, she was sure, was calculated to anger her, but no more than the words *Miss Missionary.* He was letting her know just how little interest he had in her, telling her as plainly as he could that he considered her with nothing more than complete disdain and distaste.

She would not let him embarrass her or intimidate her, she told herself. He had no right to make her feel worse than she already felt.

She pushed herself to her feet.

"I'll wait for you there," she said, pointing in the general direction of the rocky rise that led to the ledge from which the water fell. "Perhaps there's a way up to the top. We could see the whole island from there."

She started along the edge of the pool, not waiting for him to object. She kept her eyes carefully averted, taking great pains not to give him any more fuel to feed what she was sure was an already inflated opinion of himself.

She heard a soft splash as he dived under the surface and swam back across the pool. She busied herself peering into the undergrowth, telling herself she was looking for another path even as she realized she longed to turn around and watch him as he climbed out of the pool.

"I've found something!" she called out after a few moments effort clambering through the undergrowth. "It's another path."

He came jogging up behind her a moment later, finishing up the buttons of his trousers as he ran and brushing back the wet hair that had fallen over his eyes.

He leaned close to her, staring into the dim, filtered light of the undergrowth, peering at the path she'd found.

Alyssa felt the cool damp that emanated from his skin and drew quickly away, before she touched him. She had no desire to feel again that unsettled feeling his touch roused in her. Still, she had been close enough to him to envy the comfortable coolness of his skin. She wished for a second that she had joined him in the pool. She felt uncomfortable with the salt the seawater had left on her skin, and away from the beach, sheltered by the surrounding jungle, there was no breeze to blow away the stickiness that clung to her.

She had only a moment to consider her comfort, or lack of it, for Jason was edging by her onto the path she'd found.

"I don't suppose you see anything different about this path from the other we took from the beach?" he asked her absently as he started once more into the jungle.

She started after him, shaking her head as she looked around.

"What is that supposed to mean?" she asked. "It's a path, like the other."

"Not just like the other," he said and he pointed to the bare, root-rutted earth, well worn and richly dark beneath their feet.

Alyssa stared down at the path. Her own feet, stained dark from the dirt, seemed to blend into the thick, damp soil.

"I don't . . ."

"Think," he told her sharply, interrupting her before she had the chance to admit that she saw nothing at all different about this path. "Do you see any vines edging their way across this path, any of the undergrowth reclaiming the free soil?"

She saw it now, realized that this path, unlike the

other, was well worn and bare underfoot. She nodded slowly.

"And why do you suppose that might be, Miss Missionary?" he asked her as he stared speculatively into the pale green gloom of the undergrowth where the path twisted and disappeared.

Alyssa felt a finger of the panic she'd experienced on the beach return.

"Because it's still used," she said in a choked whisper.

"Precisely," Jason agreed.

They had followed the path for only a short distance when it divided. One branch continued on into the undergrowth, the other began to climb up the rocky hillside.

Jason halted, and Alyssa, behind him, stood dully by waiting for him to decide what they ought to do. It was remarkable, she thought, how easily he could make her feel frightened and vulnerable and lost. A few words and here she was, cringing at his side, running to stay close to him, afraid that if she let herself fall behind she might encounter something she was not prepared to face alone.

It took him only a second to determine to take the left-hand path, the one that led up the rocky incline. Apparently he agreed with her assessment that they would be able to see the whole of the island from the vantage point of the ledge above. He began to climb, and she ran along close behind.

He couldn't be bothered to so much as turn to her to see if she was there, Alyssa thought as she scrambled up the steep path after him, or to see if she needed any help. There were places where the rough volcanic rock was without a covering of soil, and her bare feet quickly grew sore from the tiny nicks the sharp edges inflicted upon them. Worse, as the slope grew steeper, she found herself becoming unsteady and losing her balance all too often. She was finally forced to grab hold of roots and branches at the sides of the path and pull herself forward.

When she looked up and saw Jason easily climbing up the steep path as though he barely noticed it was an effort, she felt an irrational anger. It was bad enough that he knew she was totally unable to fend for herself. Now he was no doubt amusing himself with the thought that she was struggling along behind him, barely able to stand on the steep rise. She silently told herself that he was insufferable and totally unlikable.

It occurred to her that the condemnation, were she to voice it to him, would most likely please him. He would tell her how uncharitable she was being, how unworthy she was to be a missionary, and how disappointed Owen Remsen would be with her. She found herself pulling at the vines with a good deal more vehemence than was required for her to keep from falling back down the slope.

After what seemed an interminable time climbing, but was probably not so very long at all, she darted a glance up to see that Jason was nearing the ledge at the top of the hillside, and then one downward, to the foot of the incline. It seemed impossibly steep from where she knelt, clinging to a thick piece of vine, and impossibly far away. She had no idea they had climbed so far. She realized she was looking down at the tops of the trees under which they'd been walking, and felt suddenly unsettled and slightly dizzy.

"If you keep staring down like that, Miss Missionary, you'll find yourself tumbling head over heels. And I'm not in the mood to go chasing after you."

With that pronouncement, and before she realized what was happening, Jason put his hand on her arm. With a none too gentle grasp, he pulled her the remaining few feet to the top of the ledge. She didn't fight him, didn't try to tell him she could make her own way without his help. She was exhausted from the climb, and her bare feet were sore from the contact with the rough stone. She would, at that moment, have gladly let him carry her, had he been so inclined.

"You can see the whole island from up here," she said when she'd had a moment to regain her breath. She was hot and sticky from the climb, and her chemise and Jason's shirt clung uncomfortably to her skin. A few dozen feet from where she sat, water gushed out of the rock face from an underground spring and fell straight down onto the rocks below. From her new vantage, the pool below seemed tiny.

She stood and carefully edged her way along the ledge to the place where the spring bubbled up, then knelt, wetting herself without a care as she gratefully took a long, cool drink. When she looked up, she saw Jason had followed her, and now he was looking with more than a little amusement at the way the drenched shirt clung to her. She pretended not to notice, moving aside to let him drink as well, and settling herself comfortably on the sun-warmed rock of the ledge. She looked around at the view of the island, surprisingly small, she realized, now that she could see it spread out beneath them in its entirety.

"What's that?" she asked and pointed to a barren flat plateau just behind the ledge where they sat. It seemed almost as if some great creature had come along and chopped off the top of the peak, leaving the ledge where they sat as a raised lip.

Jason turned, gave the plateau a quick glance, and shrugged.

"The volcano's cap, I suppose," he said.

"What?" she demanded, shocked by what he'd said. "What volcano?"

"Look," he told her sharply. "All these islands were formed by volcanoes. After a time, if it becomes inactive, the magma in the crater cools and hardens, like this."

"You're telling me we're sitting on a ledge of the volcano's crater?" she asked and swallowed uncomfortably. "Is it safe?"

He shrugged again. "I suppose so. If the thing chooses to erupt, no place on the island will be any safer." She paled and he grinned at her reaction. "Don't worry. If anything was about to happen, we'd feel heat, movement, and God only knows what else. So forget about it and enjoy the view."

She turned away, trying to do as he suggested, but not quite able to forget what it was that lurked behind them. She was more than a bit sobered.

"Look," she said after a while, "there's the beach where we came ashore."

She sat entranced, watching the waves break against the ring of sharp rock where their dinghy had been destroyed. From the distance, the plumes of spray made by the waves as they struck the rock seemed like handfuls of tiny jewels thrown up by a negligent hand to sparkle in the bright sunshine as they fell.

Jason was standing beside her, apparently ignoring her, as he slowly turned and made a survey of the island. But when he'd made half a circle and stood staring at the far side of the island from the beach where they'd come ashore, he suddenly stiffened, then crouched quickly beside her.

"What is it?" Alyssa asked, sensing a change in his manner. She drew up her feet and turned around to face in the same direction he did. "Is something wrong?"

"I'm not sure yet," he said, pointing to the water on the far side of the island.

Alyssa looked in the direction he indicated. There was a natural cove there, filled with calmly placid water that emptied out to the ocean beyond. It was a natural harbor, without the dangerous ring of rocks they'd been forced to pass on the other side of the island. Surrounded by a pale gold ribbon of beach, it seemed the picture of the idyllic South Seas.

She let her glance move outward, to the water just beyond the cove. And then she saw what it was that had made Jason grow wary enough to stoop down and obscure his presence rather than remaining clearly outlined against the sky: a half dozen canoes filled with dark-skinned men were approaching the cove.

"What is it?" she asked again, this time in a hoarse whisper, although there was no possibility that the occupants of the canoes could have heard her from so great a distance. "Who are they?"

Jason did another quick survey of the outlines of the island, then peered out at the ocean past the approaching group and let his glance linger there for a moment. Alyssa felt herself growing anxious and more and more irked with him for taking so long to answer her questions. Finally he pointed outward, to the horizon.

"There," he said. "Look carefully. What do you see?"

"Must we play games?" she demanded. "Can't you just answer my question?"

"Look," he directed her a second time, this time in a tone that told her he was used to being obeyed and wouldn't countenance any further insubordination from her. "What do you see?"

She scowled, then squinted into the sunshine that was reflected from the water. The shape was clouded with the humidity of the air and the distance, but she could just make out a large, dark form floating on the water.

"Another island," she replied. "It's another island, isn't it?"

Jason closed his eyes and rubbed his chin.

"I was hoping you wouldn't see it," he said softly. "I was hoping I'd imagined it."

She shook her head in exasperation.

"What are you talking about?" she demanded.

He opened his eyes again and looked at her. "Since you ask," he said. He found a piece of vine and used it to scratch on the rock an egg-shaped outline with a small nick on one side. "Look," he said, pointing to his drawing. "This is approximately the shape of the island we're on." He scratched another, much larger, elongated shape. "And, unless I miss my guess, the island we see out there looks pretty much like this."

"And is that supposed to mean something?" Alyssa asked.

"To anyone who has studied the charts of this part of the ocean, it does," he replied. "A small, egg-shaped island due west of a larger island, the small one with a tiny bite out of the side that looks just like that cove down there."

"Then you know where we are?"

He nodded, but there was none of the pleased excitement in his expression that that possibility roused in hers.

"I think so," he told her. "I think that storm blew us more than halfway to Banaba. I think we're on the island of Nukuhiva. If I'm right, then that larger island we can just see out there is called Tapuay."

Alyssa gritted her teeth. "I'm delighted to find you so well versed in the geography of the area, Captain Draper, but just what is all this leading to?"

"The natives of the larger island use this one as a ceremonial place," he went on, "a place sacred to their gods. They perform their rituals here, come to sacrifice to their gods."

Alyssa looked down at the canoes that were slowly advancing toward the cove.

"Then they're coming here," she said. "We can

go down to meet them, ask them to take us back to their island. We can wait for a ship to come to trade with them, and take it to Banaba."

"You don't understand," Jason told her softly. "There aren't any ships that come to trade with the natives of Tapuay. On the contrary, these two islands are well marked on the charts with warnings to keep away."

Alyssa nodded toward the approaching canoes, eyeing the passengers and trying unsuccessfully to discern their character from the images that were blurred with the distance.

"They aren't friendly?" she asked in a worried whisper.

"You might say that," Jason replied. His expression grew grim. "The natives of Tapuay," he told her with a nonchalance she found undeniably chilling, "are cannibals."

Chapter Eight

Alyssa sat stunned, completely numbed by Jason's words.

Cannibals . . . surely that couldn't be possible. Surely those were just stories, tales told by sailors who wanted to make their adventures seem more frightening and exciting than they actually were. Surely there really weren't people who ate the flesh of their own kind.

But when she turned and looked at Jason's expression, she knew he wasn't telling some story to frighten her, knew he wasn't lying.

It was true. Those men in the long canoes approaching the island were cannibals.

"What do we do?" she asked in a strained whisper.

He shook his head. "I don't know."

His admission was a second shock to her. The last thing she expected from him was the concession that there might be something he didn't know or couldn't do. Whatever his imperfections, she'd have thought him incapable of admitting to them.

He seemed to sense her reaction, for he suddenly smiled at her.

"Perhaps we should pray?" he asked in a needling tone. "Perhaps if you remind God you're a missionary, He might provide us with a bit of divine guidancc."

Alyssa bristled. Was everything a joke to him, she wondered. Or was it simply that he so enjoyed making her uncomfortable that even the gruesome prospect of facing a tribe of cannibals paled in comparison?

She told herself she would not give him the satisfaction of reacting to his jibe. She pretended she hadn't heard.

"But what if they come up here? What if they see us?" she demanded.

He considered the possibility.

"That wouldn't be pleasant," he agreed. "But let's not panic until they do." He nodded toward the canoes as the ocean waves pushed them toward the cove. "This is as good a place to keep an eye on them as I can think of," he said. "If they seem to be coming up here, we can leave and find someplace to hide."

"Hide," she muttered crossly. "How can we hide on an island they must know as well as their own?"

"As the sun is behind us and will outline us beautifully against the sky," he replied, "I suggest we make ourselves as invisible as possible before we have to consider that question with rather more interest than I would like to devote to it at the moment."

Alyssa shrank down close to the stone. His words made her feel as though she were terribly exposed, as though the cannibals from Nukuhiva were staring at her at that very moment.

Jason knelt beside her. The two of them huddled close to the rock of the ledge so they wouldn't be seen, and watched as one by one the canoes glided into the cove and near to the shore. The passengers jumped out of their craft, splashing through the water as they beached the canoes, pushing them close to the beach.

Alyssa could see them clearly now, could see the bright tattoos that decorated their arms and encircled their necks like strings of gaudy red, green, and blue beads. The younger men, tall, well muscled, and dark, seemed eager to begin whatever ceremony had brought them to the island. The few older men, wrinkled and dark and even more thoroughly embellished than their younger counterparts, moved with determined but unhurried steps.

One of the younger men began directing the others, pointing and gesturing to them, and at his order they pulled the canoes up onto the sand. He must be their leader, Alyssa thought as she considered him. He was tall, taller than the rest, and powerfully built. The other men followed his instructions without argument. At his orders, they emptied the canoes, fetching out large calabashes and leaf-wrapped packages, carrying them up onto the beach and setting them out on the dry sand.

"What are they doing?" she asked Jason as she considered the slightly disorganized flurry of activity.

"It would appear that they're preparing to cook their dinner," Jason replied. "Look," he said, pointing to an old man who was gingerly handling one of the calabashes, emptying its contents over the pile of gray driftwood, dried leaves, and broken branches some of the others had gathered and heaped on the beach sand. "It looks like he's making a fire."

That was indeed what the old man was doing. He took a long, dried branch and used it to arrange the glowing coals he'd emptied from the calabash, pushing and prodding them among the nest of leaves until a thin, bright flame shot up. He fed the small flame, letting it grow slowly, until there was a large fire burning on the bed of sand. Alyssa could smell the wood smoke and even see the sharp crackle of sparks rising from it.

Most of the men had already settled themselves in small groups around the fire, passing the calabashes back and forth, obviously pleased with whatever it was they were drinking from them. Only two remained busily employed, one the young man Alyssa had decided was their chief, the other an old, wizened man, stooped and thin, who carried with him a fabric-wrapped package which he occasionally lifted and considered with an almost comically quizzical interest.

The old man now caught Alyssa's attention. He acted as though the thing he carried were alive, and although it appeared to Alyssa to be nothing more than a bundle of rags, he gestured to it and seemed to be carrying on conversation with it, nodding as he listened for replies to his inquiries. As she watched, he began to move among the group of natives, treating them with complete indifference as he continued his conversation with his bundle of rags.

The old man's strange behavior continued for several minutes, until he stumbled against the feet of one of the men who lazed on the sand, drinking. His stumbling near fall was almost comical, the bundle in his arms flying up and forward as he attempted but failed to catch it. He ran a few steps to keep his balance, his movement suddenly spry despite the stiffness with which he'd moved until then.

He stood for a moment and looked at his fallen bundle where it lay in the sand. Even from the distance, Alyssa could see his concern as he considered the heap of rags. Suddenly angry, he turned and began to shout angrily at the seated man whose foot had caused the accident.

Alyssa expected the others to ignore the old eccentric and go on with their drinking. She was surprised when three of the men hastily stood to help him, retrieving the fallen bundle and returning it to the old man's arms. Then, apparently to ward off any anger, one of them handed the old man his calabash and stood politely as he first put the heap of rags to the gourd's mouth as though encouraging it to drink, then took a healthy swallow of the contents himself.

"What is he doing?" Alyssa finally demanded of Jason. "Why is that old man talking to a bundle of rags?

Why is he pretending to give it something to drink?"

"I'd say he's tending to his god," Jason told her. His tone was matter-of-fact, as though he saw nothing unusual in the old man's odd behavior.

"His god?" Alyssa returned. "How can a bundle of rags be his god?"

Jason turned to her, and she saw his eyes grow hard and distant.

"What makes you think, Miss Missionary, that the god to whom you address your prayers is any more real than his?" he demanded.

Alyssa shook her head slowly, not understanding his apparent anger with her, and understanding his question even less.

"Because we all know, that's why," she replied with a distant, dismissive shrug.

But even as she mouthed the words, she found herself silently asking herself once again the same question he'd asked her. Her only real answer, she realized, was that it was what she had been taught, what she'd been told to believe. God was that entity to whom her mother had addressed prayers for her father's safety when he had been away on his whaling ship, to whom she'd begged for his recovery when they brought him home without a leg and filled with fever. God was the authority her Uncle Silas quoted when he wanted his pronouncements received with due reverence. It was a simple matter, one that needed no explanation. The existence of God, her parents' and her uncle's God, was the one thing she'd never thought to question.

It occurred to her suddenly that god was whoever and whatever you were taught to believe he was. The thought was unsettling to her, and she pushed it away, not wanting to become any more confused than she already felt at that moment.

"Because you know," Jason told her with a sarcastic sneer. "Or so all you missionaries preach, anyway."

He turned away from her, obviously in no mood to debate theology, and returned his attention to what was happening on the beach below. Alyssa realized she was glad, realized that if he'd pursued the subject, she was not entirely sure she would know how to counter what he had said.

She, too, returned her attention to the events on the beach. The chief was handing a large, leaf wrapped bundle to one of the other men. The second man hefted it onto his shoulder and carried it to the fire. There was a good deal of activity as two others helped him to set it, still wrapped in its covering of greenery, carefully amongst the coals.

That feat accomplished, the whole company settled itself around the fire, occupying itself with talking, laughing, and passing the large calabashes from hand to hand. Occasionally one of the men would stand and wander off into the undergrowth for a while, but he'd soon return and rejoin the party.

The sun was beginning to lower in the sky behind them. Despite the distance from the cove, Alyssa could not ignore the distinct odor of roasting meat that rose to taunt her. She realized she and Jason had been lying on the stone ledge for hours and had had nothing to eat since the fruit early that morning. She was cramped and stiff and once again hungry, a condition that was only intensified by the scents from the fire below that wafted upward on the breeze.

"When will they be done?" Alyssa murmured petulantly. "I'm stiff and hungry."

"It would seem that patience is another of the missionary virtues that you lack, Miss Whitlock," Jason told her.

"Could you please stop preaching to me, Captain Draper?" she asked in a pained tone. "I'm well aware of my deficiencies. My uncle spent a good deal of the last four years pointing them out to me."

"To little avail, it would seem," he said, this time with a grin.

She turned and faced him. "And why should that concern you?" she demanded.

"Does it?" he asked.

He was staring at her with those knowingly smug blue eyes, and Alyssa knew that deep inside he was laughing at her. She couldn't understand a thing about him, she realized. They were marooned on this island, stranded in this spot, in danger of being discovered by a band of cannibals, and still he seemed intent on laughing at her, on making her feel unsettled and unsure of herself. If she were ever to get off this island and to Banaba, she told herself, she would take whatever pains were necessary to insure that she never need see Jason Draper again.

She turned away, not wanting to look at him, not wanting to see the amusement in his blue eyes. Whatever this was, she told herself, it was not the way she had imagined an adventure would be when she'd left Plymouth. In her imagination she had never thought an adventure meant being alone with someone who made no pains to hide the fact that he held you with absolutely no respect, never considered it might involve being hungry and frightened. Nothing, it seemed, was at all what she had expected it to be.

She turned her glance back to the men on the beach. They were laughing now, and motioning expansively to each other as they talked. One stood unsteadily, and staggered off into the undergrowth.

"They look drunk," she muttered in disgust.

"They probably are," Jason agreed. "They're probably drinking arva."

"And just what is that?" she asked. "The cannibal version of whiskey?"

She saw his superior grin and wished she hadn't asked.

"A lot stronger than whiskey," he replied. "It's the juice of the root of a large, rather unpleasant looking plant with narrow, spiked leaves. It's a narcotic, said to bring visions, although I'm afraid I can't personally attest to that fact. A good number of the Polynesian tribes make it, at least on those islands where the missionaries haven't outlawed its use."

She pursed her lips primly as she stared at the staggering, rowdy group on the beach below.

"As well they ought," she said.

"Aren't we superior, Miss Missionary?"

She turned to face him, her fear almost forgotten in the wake of a sudden wave of anger with him.

"Will you stop calling me that?"

"Be quiet," he hissed at her. "Or are you trying to announce to them that we're up here?"

She hadn't even realized she'd raised her voice. His scolding cowed her, especially when she considered the gravity of what she'd done.

"I'm sorry," she murmured.

But he was staring down at what was happening on the beach, and seemed to have lost his interest in goading her.

"I think the party is about to begin," he told her.

Alyssa turned back to the beach. The chief put down the calabash from which he'd been drinking, steadying it in the sand, and the others followed suit. The old man who had been carrying the bundle of rags was now carefully tending to his strange burden, cradling it in his arms. The chief stood, lifted what appeared to be a piece of multicolored cloth from a package he'd earlier deposited on the sand, then approached the old man and helped him to his feet. The others came to a disordered attention, becoming suddenly quiet and sitting up a bit more stiffly.

The old man stood, still preoccupied with his bundle, as the chief wrapped the cloth around the old man's shoulders. It seemed to be illogically thick, for there was no need for a warm cloak in this climate, and yet the old man gave no indication that the weight of it affected him. In the pale light, it appeared to shift and flutter in the light breeze. The tiny patches of colored feathers seemed to change and become iridescent in the firelight.

"What a strange cloak," Alyssa muttered.

Jason nodded. "It's made of feathers," he told her. "That old man must be a very powerful priest. Such cloaks are very precious, very much prized."

The chief and the priest walked to the far end of the cove and faced what from above appeared to be a wall of solid rock. They stood for a moment in silence, and then the priest began to sing in a loud, atonal croak. The song went on for a long while, the old man's unmelodious voice the only sound other than the noise of the waves rolling in toward the beach. Finally he stopped, and the silence seemed unnaturally deep by comparison.

The priest raised his bundle of rags over his head. Then the two men stepped forward and simply disappeared.

"What happened to them?" Alyssa whispered.

Jason peered into the shadow where the two had gone.

"I don't know. Maybe there's a cave down there," he said. Then he faced her and smiled wryly. "Maybe they really *do* have some magic."

Alyssa scowled and turned back to watch what was happening below. The sun had slowly lowered, filling the sky with color and the beach below with shadows. The fire danced brightly, the only source of light, giving the natives' faces a darkly demonic luster.

The group of men sat in absolute silence, not laughing or talking or singing now, and not one so much as reached for one of the calabashes. Something was about to happen, and they were anticipating it with a respectful reverence.

All was still and silent for several minutes. Alyssa found herself unable to take her eyes from the place where she'd last seen the old man and the chief, aware that she was following the lead of the men who sat waiting on the beach below.

Overhead, a bright, round moon began to rise, and the beach was soon bathed in a dull, silvery light. The scene, she thought, was made all the more eerie by the moonlight. The men, so silent and still, seemed like statues set out on the beach to ward off some unnamed evil.

Finally, as quickly as they had disappeared, the chief and the priest reappeared at the far end of the cove. They stepped forward, toward the fire and the circle of men, their movements clearly visible in the moonlight. The old man still carried his burden of rags, but the younger one was now carrying something as well, a huge shell which he held straight out in front of him like a totem.

When they neared the edge of the circle, the old man began to strip away the pieces of cloth that covered his burden. He pulled away one piece at a time ever so slowly until there was a small heap of them lying on the sand by his feet. Finally rid of its wrappings, he held up a small carved figure.

There was a murmur of respect from the circle of men, and they moved back a bit, clearing a space for the old man and his carving. The old man moved forward, brushed an area of sand near the fire until it was smooth, and then set down his burden so that it seemed to be standing, facing the circle of men.

The chief moved forward then and placed the huge shell in front of the statue, settling it carefully in the sand. Its contents glowed softly in the reflected fire and moonlight. It looked to Alyssa as though it were nearly filled with small, round, glowing stones.

She heard Jason whistle softly and she turned to face him.

"What is it?" she whispered.

"That shell," he whispered in reply. "It looks as though it's filled with pearls, black pearls." He turned and stared at her, his eyes glowing in the moonlight. "We're looking at a fortune down there, Miss Missionary. A fortune that belongs to a cannibal's god."

He turned his attention back to the ceremony below, and Alyssa followed suit, watching as the chief opened a small pouch he wore on a string around his neck, and emptied its contents into his hand. He bowed and held out his hand in offering to his god.

Even from the distance she could see that he held another of the round stones, a black pearl, if Jason's judgment was correct. It glowed softly in his hand, reflecting the light of the fire.

The old man gestured and danced in a wandering circle around the statue. Finally, when he'd done, the chief placed the offering onto the heap in the shell. For a moment the circle of men stared in silence, as though waiting for something to happen. Then there was a shout from them, and after the quiet, the sound of their voices seemed sharp, almost violent, in the still night air. They scrambled to their feet and began to dance, some in pairs, some in groups of three or four, all the while shouting and singing in strident, loud voices.

"It would seem the god has accepted their offering," Jason whispered.

"How could it not?" Alyssa demanded in a sharp whisper. "It's just a carved statue."

"You have much to learn about the South Seas, Miss Missionary," Jason replied.

Alyssa turned to look at his profile as he watched the scene below, wondering why he seemed so accepting of the pagan beliefs of the natives, why he was so condescending about hers . . . and his own. Surely he had to have been raised to believe what she'd been raised to believe. Surely, despite his scorn, his past was not so very different from her own.

The shouting subsided, and Alyssa turned back to watch the chief lift the enormous shell and return to the side of the cove with it. Once again he disappeared into the shadows, and she found herself wondering what was down there and how he managed to vanish that way.

But her attention was quickly drawn to the old priest. He had put aside the incredible feather cloak and was now busying himself with the statue, setting a calabash beside it and making an inviting gesture toward it, as though he were telling the figure to help itself. This act completed, he found a branch and moved to the fire, where he poked at the leaf-wrapped package that had been set there to roast.

The others gathered around him, obviously hungry for their feast. The old man pushed and prodded, then nodded to the others, and with a shout of enthusiasm they grabbed up spears and used them to pull the thing clear of the burning embers of the fire.

They gingerly pulled away the wrappings of leaves, and Alyssa could see a small cloud of steam rise from the contents as the covering was removed. Then they skewered their feast on two of the spears and held it up to the light of the fire for the approval of the statue, their god.

Alyssa watched them lift their roast meat with complete disbelief. Even browned as it was from the fire, she could see its shape clearly, and she could not mistake it.

It was a haunch and leg. Clearly a haunch and leg.

And it was just as clearly human.

She screamed. Uncontrollably, completely hysterically, she screamed.

The sound of it shattered the night air and drew the attention of the men on the beach below.

Jason clapped his hand over her mouth, but it was too late. The men on the beach had heard. They snatched up their spears and started running into the undergrowth. There was no doubt but that they were heading to the path that led to the top of the ledge.

"Now you've done it," Jason hissed.

He grabbed her arm and half pulled, half pushed her along the ledge to the opening in the growth that was the path. In the near darkness, illuminated only by the moonlight, it seemed to Alyssa that he was pulling her down into nothingness.

As he pushed and prodded her, she stumbled and ran, seeing nothing through terror-clouded eyes. She was too frightened to cry out when she stubbed her toe or fell roughly against a protruding root, too terrified to protest the rough way Jason handled her or even to ask where they were going. All she knew was that the jungle was filled with noise, the screams of birds overhead whose peace had been disturbed, and the shouts of the men on the beach who had been about to eat human flesh.

She had no doubt in her mind that the shouts were angry shouts, cries filled with heat and the thirst for vengeance for the sacrilege she had committed by spying on them and their god.

However long it had taken her and Jason to climb up to the ledge, it took only moments for them to slide and tumble their way down. Alyssa felt as though she had been beaten, her arms and legs sore and bruised from rough contact with roots and rocks and trees, and there was a warm stickiness on her knees that told her they were skinned and bleeding. But she said nothing to Jason, well enough aware that it was all her own fault, and aware as well that if they were caught, that would be her fault, too.

Once at the bottom of the rock ledge, Jason took her arm roughly and began to run, pulling her, nearly carrying her along the path in the undergrowth. The noise behind them was growing louder and louder, until it sounded as though it was only a few feet away.

Jason pushed her roughly into the undergrowth. Unprepared, she slipped in the moist leaf mold underfoot and fell. Her nostrils filled with the scent of the soil and greenery, and her mouth filled with the taste of it. She felt tiny movements beneath her, the movement of insects whose nocturnal activities had been suddenly interrupted. Had she been less frightened, she would have drawn away in disgust at the contact of the things. As it was, she was too panicked to move.

Jason fell to the ground beside her and put his arm over her, holding her close to the damp soil. She could hear her heart beating, a thick, loud, thudding sound that filled her ears, louder even than the noise of voices and movement on the path a few feet away.

She dared to look up and was rewarded with the sight of a half dozen bare feet and naked legs. She found herself without the courage to look further. Knowing that they were so close, that if they chose, they could lift the spears they held and skewer her and Jason just as they had skewered their grisly feast, was more than enough to make her press herself back down into the moist soil beneath her. She closed her eyes and silently prayed, the first sincere prayer she could remember offering up since the day her mother had died.

The prayer must have had some value, or perhaps it was just that they were deep in the shadows of the undergrowth. In any case, she soon heard the padding sound of running feet and realized their hunters had, for the time being at least, missed sight of their prey.

Alyssa opened her eyes tentatively, afraid she might

have been mistaken, afraid the feet might still be there on the path, near enough to her so she could reach out and touch them. But there was nothing in her plane of vision save a seemingly endless sea of leaves and dark soil.

Jason pushed himself carefully to his knees, taking pains to make no noise as he looked around for some sign that the natives might be returning. When he was satisfied there was none, he silently nudged Alyssa's arm.

She pushed herself up, suddenly aware once again of the feeling of tiny movements close to her skin. It startled her to realize that for a few nearly endless moments she had been totally oblivious to the insects that had been touching and biting her skin. Fear, she realized, had a great many strange effects.

Jason was already on his feet, and she scrambled to hers, irrationally afraid now that he might leave her there, alone in the jungle. He put his fingers to her lips, warning her not to speak, and she nodded that she understood.

They set out through the jungle, running along the path they had taken early that afternoon. The noise in the undergrowth around them seemed to have subsided. Alyssa could hear sounds of movement on the hillside behind them, and she knew that any noise they might make could alert the natives to their presence. Each time she felt a twig snap beneath her foot she was sure it would call down all the men of the tribe on them.

The shouts began to grow fewer now and less violent as the effort of the run through the jungle in the darkness took its toll. But Alyssa had no delusions that the hunters had simply given up the search. There was the sound of leaves and vines being crushed underfoot in the jungle behind them and along the path up to the ledge. She realized she and Jason had made it to the bottom just in time.

She was breathless, panting from the run and the fear that gripped her. She could hear the rough, ragged sound of her own breath as she gasped for air, and it felt as if something were about to burst inside her chest. And as frightened as she was, as terrified of what would happen to her if she was caught, still she realized her legs were growing heavier with each step. She could barely lift them.

When the branch seemed to reach out to strike at her waist, it doubled her over with the force with which she met it. She fell and realized with a wave of wrenching fear that her legs felt numb, that she simply couldn't get up.

There was noise behind them, not far behind, and she realized that not all the natives had climbed up to the ledge. Some were still searching along the paths from the beach. She was certain she was about to die.

Jason turned back, quickly recognized the signs of exhaustion on her face, and wordlessly lifted her. He tossed her over his shoulder with as little care as he would a sack of potatoes. Alyssa realized she had begun to sob silently, tears streaming down her cheeks. She didn't know if it was fear that had released them, or the simple indignity of being treated like so much freight.

She was lost and disoriented now, and had no idea where they were going, or what Jason intended to do. It was only when they broke out of the undergrowth and she saw the round, golden circle of the moon reflected on the dark surface of the pool that she realized where they were.

Jason put her down by the water's edge.

"Can you swim?" he whispered.

She nodded, too frightened to speak, afraid that she would be overheard.

He slipped into the water first, moving carefully so that he made no sound as he broke the surface. Then he reached up for her, cautioning her with a finger to his lips to be silent. She let him pull her into the pool beside him, willing to do whatever he told her she must do, but not understanding how they could hide there. Surely, she thought as she felt the cool water of the pool envelop her, they could easily be seen as long as they were in the pool. The moonlight appeared dangerously bright, and the shadows of the jungle suddenly seemed a sanctuary compared to the open, pale expanse of water.

Jason didn't make any effort to explain. He put his hand to her arm and nudged her forward, guiding her. At his prodding, Alyssa found herself pushing away from the edge, out into the open, moonlit calm of the pool. She pulled herself through the water using only her arms, afraid that if she kicked her feet it would make a noise that could be heard.

In a moment they were beside the rocks at the far end.

"Climb up," Jason told her.

He put his hands to her waist and pushed her up, helping her out of the water and onto the rocks.

Alyssa dragged herself out of the pool and into the narrow torrent of the waterfall. She was nearly blinded by the falling water, and inadvertently banged her already scraped knee against a protruding ledge of stone. The contact sent a shaft of pain through her leg.

Jason quickly climbed up beside her. He reached down, putting his hand under her arm, and nearly lifted her bodily. Then he pushed her back, under the weight of the heaviest flow of the tumbling water.

For an instant Alyssa thought she would be crushed by the downpour. She trembled, nearly falling, as the torrent slapped down on her. But then Jason put his arm around her waist and he drew her back.

She was coughing and gasping for air, and clinging to Jason to keep herself from falling. He pushed her roughly back, and she found herself pressed against cold, rough stone. The contact was sharp, and it brought a spasm of pain to her already bruised shoulders and legs. But she swallowed the cry that came to her lips as she stared over Jason's shoulder.

She could just discern the shapes of three of the Polynesians breaking through the undergrowth to stand at the side of the pool.

One, the man she had taken to be their chief, knelt down and stared at a dark stain on a rock. Alyssa realized that it was her blood he was considering, the blood that had oozed from her scraped knees before she'd slipped into the pool.

He put his finger to the dark stain, touching it gingerly, then lifted his hand. He stared for a second at the dark smudge he'd lifted from the rock, sniffing it, then bringing it to his lips and tasting it. His expression became suddenly thoughtful.

He stood then and looked up, considering the still water and the peaceful orb of golden moonlight that floated on it. And then he turned his attention to the far end of the pool and the waterfall.

He was, she realized, staring directly at her.

Chapter Nine

At first Alyssa was sure that she and Jason had been seen. She could see the cannibal chief's eyes, dark and intent, staring directly at her. Surely he was considering the method he would use to kill them, she thought, before he directed his men to jump into the pool and capture them.

She could feel a small trickle of warmth continue to seep from her knee and knew there was more blood, knew it would fall to the stone and blend into the flow of the water. She wondered if it was enough to show a stain, to leave a line of red in the pool that would point directly to the place where she and Jason hid. She doubted if it even mattered, for what she could see of the chief's expression told her he needed no more evidence than he already had to find them.

But it soon became obvious that she was wrong. Apparently the spray, the downward rush of water from the fall, and the night shadows all combined to obscure her and Jason from his view. He finally turned his glance away, shifting it first to the still depths of the pool, dark now and black with shadows, and then toward the jungle that surrounded them.

The other natives shifted uneasily from foot to foot and edged their way along the side of the pool. They seemed unwilling to go too near the edge, as though they were afraid they might fall in. That seemed strange to Alyssa, for surely these people who lived in and on the water ought not to fear so small and calm an expanse.

The natives waited for their chief's orders. They stood staring dully past the waterfall and into the jungle beyond, fruitlessly searching for any sign of something out of the ordinary and finding none. They seemed to be bored with the hunt, almost anxious to be away from this place and to be able to return to their grisly feast.

One of them began to speak, gesturing toward the still jungle on the far side of the pool and waving his arms in a gesture of dismissal. Alyssa thought he was trying to convince the chief that their prey must have gone onward, through the jungle, or perhaps that they were foolishly hunting a ghost. She silently cheered on his effort, hoping he was being convincing.

The chief wanted to hear none of it. He shouted a single, short word and angrily waved the man to silence. The other complied immediately, cowed by what he heard in the chief's tone.

The chief stared in silence at the waterfall for a while longer, his expression tense and wondering. Then he once again lifted the hand he had touched to the small stain of Alyssa's blood. He considered the dark mark on his fingertips. Alyssa held her breath, waiting for him to order his men to send their spears into the waterfall. She could almost feel the sharp point striking her and her life seeping from her.

Jason, however, wasn't frozen with fear, as she was. Seeing the chief's preoccupation, he turned and motioned to Alyssa to be still. Then he knelt, lifting a fist-sized stone he found in a crack between the larger ones on which they stood before he straightened up. Checking first to make sure the natives were not looking toward the waterfall, he edged his way to the side and heaved the stone high up into the jungle growth.

There was a sudden and immediate reaction. Birds, their night roosts upset by the passage of the stone, took to their wings. They called out angrily, and others soon took up the startled outcry. Their voices created a din that was strong enough to be audible to Alyssa, even through the uproar of the waterfall. Sharp and loud, it seemed like a chorus of old women, screaming in anger or pain.

Jason moved quickly back to stand close to Alyssa, pressing her back against the stone and sheltering her body with his own as he waited for the Polynesians to react. If his movement had been seen, if he'd been spotted as he heaved the stone toward the treetops, he knew the reaction would be fatal to the two of them.

But the natives reacted as Jason had hoped they would. Startled by the sudden loud squawking, they stared up at the commotion in the jungle canopy, obviously searching for the cause of the uproar. They began shouting, and the sound of their voices added to the confusion and to the melee.

When the birds' fury had died away and they had once again settled themselves among the tree limbs above, the chief waved his men to silence. He gazed calmly up at the round orb of the moon and spoke softly to it, his manner much like the old priest's when he had spoken to the figure of his god. Then he turned to the others, waving them back into the jungle, motioning them toward the path that would take them back to the beach and their feast. Bewildered, but apparently willing to comply and give up the search, they started off into the undergrowth.

The chief followed them to the path, but turned and glanced questioningly at the pool one last time before he stepped into the jungle. He raised his bloodstained fingers to his lips, thoughtfully licking away the last of the stain. Then he shrugged his shoulders, turned, and followed the others into the undergrowth.

* * *

Jason and Alyssa didn't move for a long while after the natives were gone. When he finally stepped away from her, she found herself trembling uncontrollably, barely able to hold herself upright.

She had no idea what had happened, and could not understand why the chief had decided to give up the search. All she knew was that she and Jason had somehow managed to escape, and that realization sparked a wave of such intense relief that it left her weak and shaking.

"They're gone?" she whispered to Jason.

He nodded. "Back to their feast, I think. With any luck, all those birds helped me to convince their chief that your scream was nothing more than the cry of some bird."

She shook her head, unconvinced.

"But my blood—I scraped my knee coming down from the ledge. He saw the blood that dripped from it onto the stone."

"I know."

Jason had seen the chief considering that dark stain of her blood on the rock, and for a moment had been sure that its discovery would lead to their deaths. But they had been lucky, it seemed. The natives of Tapuay considered this small island sacred and mysterious. It seemed it had not been hard for the chief to convince himself that the blood was a sign from some spirit, probably a sign that he would be victorious in battle, a favorable omen he was eager to accept.

"Luckily, these people are superstitious," Jason said. "They believe in spirits, powerful spirits."

"Spirits powerful enough to leave real blood on a stone?" she asked. This was all nonsense to her, and she could not believe she owed her life to it.

"I suggest you put aside your prejudices just now," he

replied sharply. "Unless you're in the mood to waltz onto the beach to begin your career as a missionary and try to convert them, I'd suggest you pray that these particular Polynesians hold a very strong belief in the power of their gods and spirits. Just at the moment, I'd say they saved us from becoming part of dinner."

Alyssa tried to swallow the lump that sprang to her throat at his words. The prospect he'd offered was sufficiently frightening to keep her from further discussion of the subject.

Jason stared off toward the path the natives had taken.

"Let us hope they accept what happened tonight as some mystery of their gods," he muttered. "I'd rather not have them start looking for us again."

His words reminded her that the natives might still return. She quickly pushed aside her disdain for the pagan superstitions, and heartily prayed that the chief held a fervent belief in the spirits of Nukuhiva.

Jason stared down at the thin trickle of red that ran from her knee down her leg. He knelt and considered the scrape on her knee.

"Why didn't you tell me you were hurt?" he asked as he began to wash the scraped place with handfuls of cool water from the fall.

The contact of his hand to her knee sent a surprised shiver through Alyssa's leg. His hand brushed only briefly against her flesh, and yet it seemed to send sparks flashing through her. She told herself it was the aftermath of fear, part of the wave of relief that they had not been discovered. She tried to force herself to ignore the flow of electricity that poured through her at the contact. Despite the effort, she could not.

What power does he have, she wondered, that he can do this to me?

"I didn't think you'd care," she said, framing her words carefully, determined not to let her voice tremble, not to let him see the effect his touch had on her. "After all, it was my own fault."

"True," he replied, his tone as cool as the water he splashed against the scraped knee. "But blood leaves a trail." He considered the now washed scrape. "This isn't bad. I doubt you could have left more than a few drops on the path back there. Not enough to notice. But still, you should have told me."

She gritted her teeth in anger, wondering as she did why she reacted this way. Was it simply that he seemed to be showing her yet again how incapable she was of surviving without his protection? Or was it that he seemed to feel nothing of the thudding response she now felt to his touch? She suspected the latter and found no comfort in that.

She found she had to force herself to speak civilly in reply.

"I will make a greater effort next time, Captain Draper."

He looked up at her and the corners of his lips turned up in a wry grin that quickly disappeared.

"If there *is* a next time," he told her in an ominously sober tone.

Her anger disappeared at his words and was immediately replaced by a wave of fear. There might not be a next time. They still might be caught. She shivered, suddenly cold despite the heat of the jungle night.

Jason felt her movement and understood immediately what had caused it. Fear, he knew, would be their greatest enemy. It had been fear and shock that had precipitated the scream that had drawn the natives' attention in the first place. He must force her to fight it if they were to survive the night. If they wanted to live until the natives left them once again alone on Nukuhiva, he could not afford to let her give in again to fear.

He brought a final handful of water to her knee, but this time he let his hand linger against her flesh. Rather than removing it quickly, as he had been doing, he pushed his hand gently upward, letting his palm glide over the smooth flesh of her thigh. He felt her tense her muscles at his touch, and she tried to back away from him, only to be stopped by the wall of stone behind her. At least, he thought, he'd replaced the fear with anger.

But she didn't strike out at him as he expected, or try to push him away. Instead, she leaned back against the solid rock behind her, and closed her eyes. She began to tremble again, only this time she was not trembling with fear.

Alyssa knew there was hard stone behind her, but she felt it only indistinctly, as though she were numb where she touched it. But no where else did she feel in the least bit numbed, certainly not where Jason's hand stroked her thigh, where he pressed his palm against her flesh and moved it in slowly growing circles that mirrored the increasingly widespread circle of heat that emanated from it. It warmed her, sent a rapidly coursing flow through her body that left her dizzy and breathless.

Jason rose and pressed himself close, holding her still between his body and the rock behind her. He felt her excitement, and his own body reacted to it with a speed and determination that both bewildered and pleased him. He'd meant at first only to distract her, to make her angry with him, anything to keep her from thinking about the natives returning and finding them, of thinking about what fate would await them if they were to be captured. But at the first touch of his body to hers, all thought of distraction was swept aside.

He realized he no longer had any thought but that he wanted her.

He slid his hands to her hips, letting his palms feel the gentle slope of them, the hardness of the bone beneath the flesh. Her body was smooth and warm beneath his hands, and wet from the swim and the continuous misting of the spray. He let his palms drift over the small, flat plane of her belly, then rise to the mounds of her breasts. Through the fabric of her chemise he could feel her nipples, already hard to his touch.

He lowered his face to hers.

She raised her hands to his neck, then spread her fingers and snaked them through the dark, thick curls at the back of his head.

"If they find us, if we're to die, perhaps this isn't wrong," she murmured as his lips touched hers.

It was an excuse, and a weak one, she knew, but she didn't care. She could almost hear her Uncle Silas's voice, offering the example of dozens of martyrs who had gone willingly to their deaths without a thought to their worldly suffering, certainly with no thought of physical pleasure. But she was no martyr, she told herself, and she was not yet prepared to die, not for any cause. She wanted to feel alive.

The night before, Jason had made her feel more alive than she had ever felt before. She wanted to feel that way again. More than anything else at that moment, she wanted some affirmation of the life that raged within her.

His lips were hard and certain against hers, and she welcomed the probe of his tongue, feeling the mysterious hot flow it released within her and welcoming it, telling herself that she could not feel this way if fate had intended that she were soon to be found, if she were soon to die. She held herself close to him, wrapping her arms around his shoulders and pressing herself to him, savoring the contact and the delicious sense of stirring it roused within her.

She could feel his hands against her breasts, pushing away the thin linen of her chemise. She helped him, letting the straps slide down from her arms, shedding both his shirt and the undergarment at the same time.

When he lowered his lips to her breasts, she closed her eyes and held him close, letting herself dissolve in a sea of breathless excitement.

He was lifting her, his hands on her haunches, and she instinctively spread herself for him, wrapping her legs around his hips, welcoming the first sweet thrust of him inside her with a hunger that she had not known herself capable of feeling. This was life, she thought, hot and surging within her. Nothing, she thought, could take this away from her, not even the cannibals' spears.

Jason buried himself in her, bewildered by this stranger, this unexpected creature that gave herself so hungrily to him. He was lost in the fires she had ignited within him. He'd never before felt his own need so strongly, never lost himself as completely as he now lost himself in her.

Alyssa gave herself to the feeling of him inside her, the contact of his lips to hers, the taste of his tongue on her own. The roar of the waterfall seemed only a dim echo of the pounding she heard inside her, the roar of her own blood racing through her veins. Nothing else could possibly exist beyond this feeling, not the island nor the Tapuay natives, certainly not Owen Remsen nor her Uncle Silas. And if it did, she told herself, it didn't matter.

It was like a moment that had been set apart from time. Her legs wrapped around him, her bare back pressed against the stone, and all that she knew was the sweet rapture of joining him, the ecstasy of losing herself to him. The shattering moment came in an explosion like the eye of a storm, sharp and sure and of such intensity that it could not live long.

It left her too spent and disoriented for her to think again of the fear of capture or of death. She had tasted life in that moment. Now she knew, with a certainty that seemed absolute, that she would not die on that small island, that there was too much life within her for it to be soon extinguished.

They spent a sleepless night, huddled close in one another's arms, waiting for the sunrise.

The first fingers of dawn spread a dull, grayish light through the undergrowth that skirted the pool, turning the nighttime black shadows to varying shades of dull grayish green that were reflected by the water of the pool.

With this first hint of day, even before the sun had risen high enough to fully lighten the sky, came the visitors they had so dreaded throughout the night.

There were only two of them, the old priest and the chief. The leaves beside the path stirred, then parted, and they walked tentatively forward to the side of the pool.

The chief pointed to the stone on which he'd found Alyssa's blood and whispered quietly to the old priest. The older man nodded and stepped forward to place his seemingly perennial burden, the statue, on the stone, as if to show it what little remained of the stain. The chief stood still and silent beside him, and the old priest began to sing in a high-pitched whine.

Jason held Alyssa in his arms. The two of them knelt behind the spray of the waterfall, trying to make themselves as inconspicuous as possible. Alyssa could hear the old man's prayer, a wail that rose above the noise of the falling water. It meant nothing to her, was just unpleasant noise, but it roused her curiosity and she wondered what it was the priest was doing.

It startled her to realize that she was capable of curiosity at that moment, that it could possibly outweigh her fear of the cannibal chief and his priest. She didn't realize that during the night she had built for herself a certainty of her own immortality, and it had not yet quite worn away.

The priest ended his prayer suddenly, with no apparent cause other than that perhaps he had tired of it. Then he retrieved the statue from the place on the rock where he'd set it, knelt at the pool's edge, and carefully lowered his god into the water.

The bath was not an especially careful one, other than that neither man allowed himself to come too close to the edge of the water. They seemed to have a fear falling into the pool, just as the others had shown a similar fear the night before.

The ablutions consisted of little more than the priest dunking the statue, lifting it out, and then splashing some water at it. The ceremony, if that was what it was, was quickly completed.

The old man lifted the statue up and out of the pool and set it down on the rough grass beside him. Then he carefully dried it and wrapped it in a length of tapa cloth. When he was done, it once again appeared to be nothing more than the pile of rags it had seemed when Alyssa had seen it the day before. Then the chief helped the old man to his feet and they quickly turned and started into the jungle, leaving along the same path as that by which they had come.

Alyssa didn't move other than to turn to face Jason.

"Do you understand what just happened?" she asked in a tense whisper.

He shrugged. "It seems to me that we've managed to find the one place on the island that might be taboo to these people," he told her.

"Taboo?" she asked. It was a word she'd never heard before.

"Sacred. Prohibited to them. I'd say from what we saw, they believe this pool belongs to their god, and they are forbidden to use it other than in the god's ritual bath."

"You mean they won't enter the water, won't come back here?"

He nodded. "From what I've seen, it would seem

they're afraid to." He smiled at her. "I'd also say we are incredibly lucky."

She stared out at the pool, considering his words in silence for a moment before she turned back to face him.

"Does that mean we stay here forever, hiding behind this waterfall?" she asked. She looked about at the undergrowth, and saw as the light began to brighten that small patches of color emerged from the dull gray-green. Fruit, she thought . . . food. It startled her to realize that despite everything that had happened in the preceding twenty-four hours she could still be hungry. Her stomach growled in anticipation and she could almost taste the sweet, pulpy flavor of bananas on her tongue.

"We can starve to death here," she told him with a look that implied she was already well along that path.

Jason allowed himself a low chuckle.

"I'd say the statue's bath might mean the end of the ceremonial feast," he replied. "They'll probably leave and return to their island soon." He, too, darted a glance toward the undergrowth. "You'll be safe here. Stay put, and I'll see if I can't find out what they're doing."

With that, and without waiting for her to protest, he slipped into the downpour of the fall, then into the pool beyond. Alyssa hesitated a moment, then followed him, not at all sure she wanted to leave whatever protection the pool might provide her, but completely positive that she did not relish the idea of waiting there alone for Jason to return.

She slid through the water of the pool with a complacent expertise that surprised her, as though she had suddenly become mistress in this place rather than a hunted interloper. But still she was careful to make as little noise as possible and didn't call out to Jason to wait for her as he climbed from the pool. Instead she hurried herself, clambering quickly out of the pool and silently running after him as he slipped into the undergrowth.

She caught up with him quickly, and he seemed pleased, if surprised, to see her.

"Do you miss me already, Miss Missionary?" he asked her in an amused whisper. "I'm flattered."

She scowled, but didn't let the name disturb her, realizing his tone had held none of the derision she'd heard when he'd used it before. She was actually beginning to get used to it, although it hardly pleased her.

"Don't be," she told him. "I simply didn't want to wait back there all alone."

"Afraid of the spirits?" he asked.

She stared at him a moment, not understanding.

"The spirits back at the pool," he explained.

She scowled, and ignored his suggestion. It occurred to her that he carried on about such things only because it seemed to disturb her.

"Do you really think this is safe?" she asked, pointing in the direction of the beach. "What if they see us?"

"The idea is to try to be sure they don't," he told her. "It's better than cowering back there forever, not even knowing if they've left the island." He put his hand on her arm. "If you're coming with me, you will first promise to stay where I tell you to stay, and you will keep your lips sealed, regardless of the provocation."

"I promise," she agreed.

She swallowed, thinking uncomfortable thoughts about the provocation that had led to her unfortunate cry the evening before.

But her answer seemed to satisfy Jason well enough, and he released his hold of her arm.

"Be careful not to make any noise," he warned.

He started along the path, leading the way toward

the beach where the cannibals had held their grisly feast the previous night.

They huddled in the undergrowth watching as the Tapuay natives climbed into their canoes and pushed them off into the still waters of the lagoon.

Jason gritted his teeth.

"I wish I'd had the presence of mind to count how many of them arrived yesterday," he muttered under his breath.

"Do you really think they'd leave any of their men here?" Alyssa asked in a horrified whisper. She'd just begun to feel secure, to think they would soon be alone on the island, and safe.

"I don't know," Jason admitted.

They watched the canoes move across the length of the lagoon, not yet daring to move away from the protective camouflage of the undergrowth. Once the Tapuay natives had paddled out of the calm of the lagoon, through the passage to the open sea beyond, and had grown tiny with the distance, the beach seemed entirely still and quiet to her.

"Shall we look around?" she ventured.

Jason shook his head. "I'll look around. You will stay here."

It seemed foolish to her to continue kneeling in hiding when the expanse of beach looked so calm and deserted. Still, she had given him her word, and if he really thought there might still be a cannibal lurking somewhere nearby, she had no real desire to meet him face to face.

She huddled down among the undergrowth where Jason pointed. He inspected the place when she was still and settled, apparently satisfying himself that she was well enough hidden, then he parted the last of the greenery that separated them from the beach.

It was obvious to her that Jason assumed any native hidden there would come out to face the stranger who dared encroach on this holy place. She wondered what Jason unarmed, could do to defend them from a spear-throwing cannibal in any case. If he was taking excessive precautions to protect her, it seemed he was being unnecessarily careless with his own safety.

Jason stepped out into the bright sunshine that glistened off the sand and water of the lagoon, half expecting to hear the whine of a thrown spear at any moment, or to see one of the natives jump out from behind a rock. But the beach was apparently deserted, and there was no attack as he made his way down the incline that edged the jungle here, across the sand to the place where the fire had burned and where the remnants of the feast still littered the beach.

Along the sand were the remnants of the cannibals' meal, bones and an empty calabash or two. The sight of the bones, he decided, could only upset Alyssa, and he quickly kicked sand over them, covering them completely. He checked the fire, found the embers were still red and glowing. That pleased him, for it meant if he could catch some fish, they could cook it. It also meant he could make a signal fire if they were lucky enough to spot a passing ship. He carefully banked the embers, and found a discarded calabash in which he might transport them later.

He made a final inspection, and determined there was little other evidence of what had happened there the night before. There seemed to be no evidence that any of the natives had been left behind. In all, the beach seemed safe enough.

He returned to the edge of the jungle and called to Alyssa. Anxious to be away from the insect-laden damp of the undergrowth, she stepped out eagerly and slid down the sandy incline to the place where he stood.

"Safe?" she asked with an I-told-you-so look that he

managed to ignore.

"And empty save for us," he told her. "Shall we find out where the chief and the old priest disappeared to last night?" he asked in the same tone he might have used were he inviting her to come with him to a picnic on a town green.

Alyssa stepped out onto the beach feeling as though they were beginning an adventure. A real adventure, she thought, the kind she had imagined when she'd left Plymouth, not the sort of terrifying experiences that had left her shattered and frightened since she had been thrown from the deck of the *South Seas Empress*. No angry seas to try to drown her, no cannibals to fear. Instead, clear, strong sunshine, water gently lapping at a beautiful beach, and a mysterious cave to explore.

"I couldn't think of anything more intriguing," she replied as she offered him her hand.

They saw the mouth of the cave before they'd crossed even half the distance of the beach. It seemed strange, staring at it in the bright wash of morning sunlight, that the chief's and priest's disappearance had seemed so mysterious the night before. But then, Alyssa reminded herself, the beach had been swathed in the shadows of sunset. Now, in the direct light of the rising sun, she found herself staring into a dark gray hole in the rock at the far end of the lagoon.

"What do you suppose is in there?" she asked, pointing to the opening and starting to run across the warm sand. "Besides the pearls, I mean?"

Jason laughed. "Spirits, perhaps," he suggested.

Alyssa stopped and turned to face him.

"You're not serious, are you?" she asked him, her tone suddenly sober. "You really don't believe in any of that pagan nonsense, do you?"

"How can you call it nonsense?" he asked. "After all, the spirits of Nukuhiva saved you last night. Even the good missionary that we both know you are couldn't ignore that."

He was smiling at her, but his tone had been serious when he replied and she couldn't shake the feeling that he wasn't really joking, that part of him had come to accept the beliefs of the Polynesians, at least a little.

"But we know that some carved statue isn't a god," she insisted.

He shook his head. "And those cannibals know just as surely that it is," he replied. "What right have we to say that we are right and they are wrong?"

"I don't understand you," she told him.

"I know," he replied.

Alyssa fell silent, and they crossed the beach and reached the opening of the cave without saying another word. But before he stepped inside, Jason turned to her and grinned wryly.

"Remember, the spirits may not like our entering their cave," he warned.

Then, laughing at the pained expression she gave him by way of answer, he led the way inside.

Chapter Ten

It was almost chilly inside the cave, the interior stone cool with the damp and the darkness. Alyssa was momentarily blinded by the shift in the light, stepping into the dimness after the brilliance of the sunshine on the beach, and she was struck by the sudden change in temperature and by the strange scent of the place before she could really look around her.

There was, of course, the mustiness of any enclosed, damp place, but there was something else about the air of the cave, something faint, but sharp and acrid and unpleasant that seemed to linger even after the breath she drew was expelled. She was sure that if the cave hadn't received the fresh sea by and an occasional breeze from the beach swept inside, the odor would have been overpowering.

She took a step further inside and felt something sharp beneath her feet.

"Ow!"

"Watch where you're stepping," Jason told her in a tense tone. "Or else go back outside to the beach and wait for me there."

His tone irked her, as though it were an admonition for distracting him, but still she ignored him, choosing to say nothing rather than reply that she had no way of watching where she was stepping while her eyes were still unaccustomed to the darkness. Instead, she stood still and waited until her vision cleared. Within a moment, forms began to take shape around her and she found herself able to walk slowly forward into the cave without further mishap.

The floor, save for a narrow path in the center of the cave leading somewhere back into the dimness, was littered with what at first glance appeared to be sun-bleached sticks. She knelt and lifted one. It was long and pale, and it occurred to her that it was far too smooth and straight to have been a branch. It was at that moment, while she was fingering the strange bit of what she had assumed was wood, that she caught a glimpse of a skull. It was lying against the wall of the cave, its empty eye sockets smiling luridly up at her. And as she stared around, she realized there were others, an uncountable number of pale, gape-eyed skulls, scattered among the litter lying on the sand floor of the cave.

Alyssa was filled with revulsion as she realized her error. She dropped the thing in disgust.

The floor of the cave wasn't littered with sticks, she realized . . . all those pale slender rods were bones. The floor of the cave was littered with hundreds of human bones.

Jason turned to face her. He, too, had become accustomed to the darkness, and saw what she had seen.

"Perhaps you'd better wait outside after all, Miss Missionary," he suggested, but this time his tone was gently understanding.

She shook her head. She was as able to walk into this cave without qualm as he was. Or at least, she could pretend to. After all, she told herself, there were no such things as spirits or ghosts. The experience might be distasteful, but there was nothing here that could hurt her. She refused to allow herself to be frightened.

"I was just startled, that's all," she told him, trying to

excuse the wave of revulsion that had filled her at the realization of what she had been holding. She wondered who she was trying to convince more, Jason, or perhaps herself.

Jason turned back to stare into the blackness just beyond them.

"I don't see much," he admitted slowly. "No sign of that shell with the offerings of pearls."

"It has to be in here," she said, trying to sound eminently practical, trying to show him just how unruffled she was. "After all, we saw the chief bring it here."

"Perhaps we'd better get some light," he said. "I'll go outside and make a torch." He grinned a crooked grin. "You can stay here and wait if you like," he offered, thoroughly aware that she had no intention of doing any such thing.

She turned on her heel and preceded him toward the mouth of the cave.

"If it's all the same with you, I think I'd rather get a breath of fresh air."

"And avoid being alone in here?" he jibed as he walked past her and out onto the beach. "I don't suppose you'd care to avoid any stray spirits that might be lurking?"

She turned away with only a disgusted grunt, refusing to give him the satisfaction of admitting that what he said just might have some truth in it.

Jason spent a few minutes rustling around in the undergrowth, gathering up a thick handful of dead and dried fronds and one thick branch which he proceeded to tie into a makeshift torch. Then he crossed the beach to the place where the cannibals had lit their campfire the night before. He pushed away the sand from the banked embers and lit the dried brush from them.

When he'd returned to the mouth of the cave, he made a theatrical bow and a sweeping gesture of invitation with his arm.

"Shall we, Miss Missionary?" he asked, motioning to her to precede him if she liked.

He seemed to expect her to decline the invitation, or at least allow him to take the lead. Instead she marched forward into the cave, hesitating only long enough for him to raise the torch high and follow her.

If the sight of the bones had revolted her before, in the flickering light cast by the torch, it became even more frightening and lurid. Nothing in her imagination had ever been so grotesque, so shocking, as the realization that all these parched and bleached bones had once been the frames of living human beings. She stood still and closed her eyes, trying to force the image away.

Jason put his hand on her arm.

"You needn't do this, Alyssa," he told her gently. "You can wait outside."

It seemed odd to her, to hear him speak her given name, especially as he did, with what she told herself was warmth and affection. She didn't think he'd ever used it before, and the sound of it was comforting to her, far more than she would have thought possible.

She shook her head. "No. I want to see what's inside." She scanned the heaps of bones quickly. "But perhaps you might go first?"

He slid by her, holding the torch high to cast the greatest light and leading the way through the narrow path between the grisly remnants of past cannibal feasts.

They had only to go about thirty feet into the cave to pass the carnage. Once past the outer wide mouth of the cave, the walls narrowed and the roof lowered substantially until it was just above their heads. When she reached out to touch it, Alyssa found the stone cool and rough to the touch.

"What's that sound?" she asked, as a dull but repetitive thudding sound filled the small space around them. She supposed the noise wasn't really as loud as it seemed to her, that it was magnified by the thick stone walls and the tiny size of this part of the cave.

"The waves, perhaps, striking rocks somewhere outside," he replied. "Or it could be underground water. Caves made by lava flows, like this one, often have underwater passages that are filled by the tides."

They continued on, following the twisting path of the cave. Alyssa was sure they were going downward, for the floor of the cave sloped gently, but other than that she realized she was completely disoriented by the continuous turns. She had no idea if they were proceeding toward the center of the island or away from it.

Eventually they found themselves facing a wall. The torchlight reflected off the dark, brittle surface. They'd reached the end of the cave and had found nothing more than a wall of rock for their efforts. Nowhere had there been any sign of the treasure in pearls they'd seen in the cannibal chief's arms the night before.

"What now?" Alyssa asked.

Jason said nothing, but looked around, lowering the torch so that he might examine the walls. He would refuse to admit it wasn't there, she knew, until he had searched every square inch of the cave.

He began to move slowly back toward the entrance, carefully casting the light of the torch on the cave walls as they slowly retraced their steps. Alyssa followed along behind him, saying nothing, not daring to distract him, wondering what he would do if there was no treasure to be found in the cave after all.

They hadn't gone far, a dozen feet perhaps, when Jason stopped and pointed to a place close to its floor.

"There," he told her.

She looked down to the place where he pointed. No wonder, she thought, that they hadn't seen it when they'd first passed it. It was little more than a small, dark hole, barely waist high, and appeared at first glance to be nothing more than a slightly darker shadow among all the others that filled the cave.

She knelt and stared into the hole.

"Do you really think there's something in there?" she asked, not quite sure she believed that anyone, even a cannibal, would put a fortune in pearls in such an unpromising-looking place.

"It's the only opening I can find," he said as he knelt beside the hole and peered inside.

"What's in there?" she demanded. Shc wasn't sure, and it certainly didn't seem likely, but the more she stared at the hole, the more it seemed to her that there was a very faint light at the far side. Not a light, really, she amended, but a lightening of the gloom.

He knelt, pushed the torch into the hole, and looked inside. The light seemed to be gobbled up by the recess, leaving them in near complete darkness.

Jason shook his head. "I can't see much," he told her. Then he turned and looked at her. "Well, Miss Missionary, are you game?"

Not waiting for an answer, pushing the torch ahead of him as he moved, he crept forward on his hands and knees, quickly disappearing into the hole in the stone.

Alyssa found herself plunged into complete darkness save for the flicker of reflected light that came from the hole.

"Are you coming?" Jason asked from the far side of the wall, his voice muffled by the stone.

She could either stand there in the darkness, she realized, or follow after him. There really was no choice. She settled herself on all fours, then carefully crept forward through the hole.

The wall was thick, more than a foot, and while she was still crawling she felt an irrational sense of weight, as though all the stone over her had fallen onto her and trapped her there. She hurried, scrambling forward, uncomfortable with the thought.

Once through, she was not at all prepared for what

she found. The narrow hole opened onto a small room, perhaps ten feet wide and a bit longer. She could stand easily, for the roof of the cave here was several feet higher than it had been in the dark passage from which she'd just come. And, oddly, the whole of the room seemed to be lit with a pale, shimmering sort of light.

Jason whistled softly. "It would seem we've found the god of Nukuhiva's secret lair," he told her. "And his treasure."

Alyssa, too, was shocked. There in front of them was a long low stone, and on it was placed not one, but three huge shells. All of them were filled with faintly glowing pearls.

She slid past Jason and stood staring at the shells. They were each at least an arm's length across. The one set in the center of the stone contained dark pearls and was doubtless the one they'd seen in the chief's arms the night before. The two others, flanking it, held heaps of pale, lustrous, milky white pearls.

"My God," she whispered, awed by the size of the hoard. "These must be worth a fortune."

"Ten fortunes," Jason told her. "Or twenty. Who knows? They've probably been giving every pearl they've found for generations to that foolish-looking little statue, storing them here." He lifted one of the darker pearls, a huge, slightly oval-shaped one nearly as large as a joint of his thumb. "Would you look at this one?" he murmured. "In London, this alone would fetch enough for a man to live comfortably for a lifetime."

He returned the pearl to the shell.

"What are you going to do?" Alyssa asked him.

He shrugged. "Nothing," he told her. "Until we're sure of a way off this island, I think it would be more than a bit foolhardy to disturb anything, don't you?"

She nodded, agreeing. She had no idea what the cannibals would do were they to discover some of their god's treasure had been pilfered, but she was sure it would not be the least bit pleasant. The prospect of their return, and the thought of spending another night as she and Jason had spent the previous one, was more than terrifying enough without the added possibility of having the natives return to hunt them, searching for the thieves who had taken their offering to their god.

But then she told herself the cannibals were gone and might not return for a long while. Until then, she and Jason were safe on the island. And perhaps if they were lucky, they might find some way off the island before the natives saw fit to hold another of their gory ceremonial feasts.

She began to look around.

"What's that odd light?" she asked, referring to the dim glow that seemed to come from the floor behind the offering stone and reflected off the walls and floors.

Jason edged his way around the stone and she followed.

"Careful," he told her, reaching for her arm and steadying her when she nearly slid on the damp rock underfoot.

The light, she found, was coming from a pool that filled the rest of the small room behind the offering stone. The water was pale blue and seemed to glow with light. It was eerie to see that odd glow in a place where there ought to be complete darkness. No wonder the cannibals had chosen to leave their god's treasure here. They must think the place magic.

"Why does it do that?" she asked.

Jason stared at the deep pool. "Probably reflected daylight," he told her.

"Then we're near the ocean here?"

He shook his head. "Not necessarily. Light can travel a fair distance in water. And with the turns we took coming in, there's no way to tell how far we are from the beach here."

She stared down at the deep pool of clear water, intrigued by the faint glow that traveled through it and seemed to make the stone walls of its sides iridescent. Like the huge heap of pearls, it seemed an improbable wonder, a totally unexpected beauty hidden behind the horror at the entrance to the cave.

The torch was beginning to spark and sputter. Jason inspected it, then pulled Alyssa away from the pool's edge.

"Unless you want to walk through that cave in total darkness, I suggest we leave now," he told her.

The prospect was great enough a spur to send her hurrying through the hole to the outer cave.

Once outside, Jason dug up the embers from the cannibals' fire and fanned them until there was a small fire burning on the beach.

"Our nocturnal visitors have left us a present," he told Alyssa as he fed the flames. "How does the prospect of grilled fish for breakfast sound to you?" he asked.

Even the words made her stomach groan in anticipation. He laughed when he heard the noise.

"I expect that means you consider it would do?"

"Quite nicely, thank you," she replied. "But how do we catch fish?" She held up empty hands. "No rods, no lines and hooks. Are the fish supposed to just jump into our hands?"

The idea seemed to amuse him. "I expect the lagoon is filled with fat, friendly fish just waiting to be caught," he said with a grin, "but I doubt they'll go to that extra effort of offering themselves up. No, we use a net," he told her.

"But we don't have a net," she countered.

"We will soon enough," he told her. "Take off my shirt."

She was more than a bit taken aback by the demand.

After her actions of the night before, she realized she had no right to any false modesty, but this was hardly the way she'd expect him to make advances to her.

"The shirt?"

She looked away and swallowed uncomfortably. She was not at all sure she was willing to comply with his demands, whatever they might be, and not sure what he would do when she told him so. But he was standing there, staring at her expectantly, and she realized she could not escape the demand.

"Last night," she stammered, "I, I was terrified. I didn't know what I was doing . . ." Her words trailed away as she realized she was uttering a lie. She had known precisely what she was doing the night before.

Her confusion seemed to amuse him. He looked up at her and laughed. But when he spoke, there was no amusement in his words nor his voice.

"You are a little hypocrite, aren't you, Miss Missionary?" he asked.

She turned back to face him, startled by the sharpness in his tone. "Please try to understand, Captain Draper . . ."

He cut her off with a wave of his hand.

"It's food I have on my mind, Miss Missionary, not amusement." He took a last look at the fire, seemed to find it satisfactory for his needs, and stood. He took a step toward her. "Not that I couldn't be persuaded, however." He reached out his hand and grasped her arm and pulled her to him.

He stood for a moment, staring down at her. Alyssa wondered what he was going to do, wondered what she would do if he kissed her. Part of her, she found, wanted him to. Part of her already throbbed with anticipation at the thought.

But after a long moment he released his hold and stepped back.

"I think this not the proper moment to try to delve

into the bizarre workings of your mind, Miss Missionary," he told her. "You're so tied up with your notions of morality that I don't think you'll ever really learn to separate cant from real piety."

There was a tone of disgust in his voice, and it stung her even more than the words.

"You don't understand . . ." she murmured.

"I understand all I need to," he interrupted. "Now if you want to eat, give me the shirt."

Her fingers shaking, she unbuttoned it quickly and handed it to him.

He took it and started into the water without giving her another glance.

She wondered, as she stood on the beach watching him, why she felt so exposed, so naked. He hadn't even offered her a glance when she'd shed the shirt, and still she felt as though some part of her that she ought to keep hidden lay open and bared to his view.

It wasn't long before he returned to the beach. She saw he had tied the ends of the sleeves and gathered up the fabric of the shirt into a sort of a makeshift bag which was jiggling erratically with the motions of the fish he'd caught.

"Breakfast," he told her as he dropped the wriggling fish onto the sand and quickly killed it with a rock.

She turned away, wandering a bit down the beach while he gutted and cooked the thing. She spent the time telling herself that he was wrong about her, that he didn't understand her at all. But a voice inside her told her that he saw her more clearly than she saw herself. Perhaps, it suggested, despite her determination to reject her uncle's beliefs, she'd somehow managed to adopt them just the same. Perhaps she was the sanctimonious hypocrite Jason Draper thought her.

She was forced to admit that she simply didn't know. All she did know was that as long as she remained on the island, she had no one to whom she might turn, no place she might escape from Jason Draper's damning opinion of her.

And she had no idea how long she must remain there.

The afternoon was a busy one. Jason thought it would be unsafe to keep the fire where it was, on the beach by the lagoon, especially as there was the possibility that its light might be seen from Tapuay if they were to let it burn into the night. Besides, he told her as he gathered up some embers into the calabash he'd found on the beach, if he intended to set up a signal fire for a passing ship, it would have to be on the far side of the island. No knowledgeable captain took the chance of letting his ship pass too close to Tapuay and its unfriendly natives.

They transferred their fire to the beach where they'd first been swept up on the island, carefully arranging a large heap of sand beside it so that they might quickly extinguish the flames and hide it were the need to arise. Jason climbed to the top of the ridge early in the afternoon to scan the horizon, searching for some evidence of a mast and keeping a watchful eye for the canoes that might at any moment arrive from Tapuay. But the water was clear and sharp and empty on both sides of the island. Both the fear of the return of the cannibals and the hope of rescue proved equally fruitless.

Alyssa had trailed along behind him, following him up to the ridge, not at all sure she was eager for his company but still afraid to be alone on the island. Jason treated her with distance and a slight hostility, acting as if what had passed between them during the previous day had simply never happened. She was pained by his attitude, but she realized she was also thankful for it. She wasn't sure she was ready to argue morality or anything else with him, for that matter. At that moment, a bit of cool distance seemed safest.

Jason went fishing with his improvised net in the lagoon in the late afternoon. Once again he returned with a large fish for their meal.

"Lucky those fish are so fearless," he told her. "You can practically walk up to them and pick them out of the water."

She doubted it had been that easy and told him so as she dropped the armful of fruit she'd gathered. She was beginning to recognize different leaves from the general green of the mass, and had discovered how to find the sort of palm that would harbor bananas beneath its greenery as well as those that bore the round reddish fruits Jason had gathered the morning before.

All the while they ate their meal they maintained a careful and polite distance. When it was finished, the sun had already begun to set.

"Neither of us slept last night," Jason reminded her. "A good night's sleep might improve our humor."

Alyssa stared across the fire at him, wondering just what he intended, now that it was beginning to grow dark. The firelight gleamed off the muscles of his bare chest, and she felt a wave of shame that part of her hoped he might want to repeat the intimacies they'd shared in the darkness the previous night.

But Jason gave no indication that that was on his mind. He stood and turned to stare at the darkening shadows that had already filled the length of the beach.

She swallowed uncomfortably. "Yes," she murmured in weak reply. "Yes, some sleep would do us both good."

He turned and stared at her, his eyes meeting hers, making her feel all the more unsettled. But he shifted his glance finally and returned it to the now darkened stretch of beach.

"Have no fear, Miss Missionary," he told her as he started to move away from the fire. "Neither cannibals nor depraved sailors will disturb your chaste and sinless sleep tonight."

She watched him disappear into the shadows just beyond the firelight, telling herself as she did that she was glad the matter had been so easily settled, that the only way to survive on the island was to maintain this uneasy distance from him. After all, if any two people were entirely unsuited, it was more than apparent that they were. Unless they were taking pains to remain calmly distant with one another, they hardly seemed able to pass an hour in one another's company without falling into one subject or another that led to a disagreement.

She settled herself into the sand, preparing for sleep, but found herself replaying the events of the day in her mind. And the one scene that seemed to recur over and over again in her thoughts was the one on the beach by the lagoon. She found herself seeing his expression as he'd looked at her and told her he was interested in food, not entertainment, found herself seeing his eyes as he reached out to grasp her arm and pull her to him.

Entertainment. She wondered why the word hadn't struck her that afternoon, why it hadn't aroused the anger it rightly ought to have aroused in her. Entertainment—that was what he thought of her—little more than a diversion, a way to amuse himself while he was stranded on this island.

She was glad he'd left her to sleep alone on the beach. And she would be gladder still when they got away from this horrible little island, when she finally reached Banaba. Let him openly scorn her for being a missionary. She'd much sooner be that than merely the source of his entertainment.

Still, despite the anger and the determination it aroused, and despite her own exhaustion, she found sleep did not come as easily as did the night.

The next few days passed in orderly, if not entirely

tension free, fashion for them. On the fourth day, however, when they climbed to their lookout place and scanned the horizon, Jason spotted the jutting white of a sail on the horizon.

He grinned at her, and for a moment Alyssa thought the antipathy between them had suddenly melted away.

"Saved, Miss Missionary," he told her with a delighted grin. "There's a ship out there."

She stared into the glitter of sunlight reflected from the water and just made out a tiny white rectangle where the sea met the sky. She turned to him, threw her arms around his neck, and kissed him impulsively. It was, she thought, too good to be true. The cannibals had not returned to the island, and here they were, about to escape it without any of the horrors she'd imagined happening to them.

"It would seem good tidings melt even missionary ice," he murmured.

He was holding her close to him, and she realized what she had done. Awkward, she felt herself blush as she pulled away from him.

She cleared her throat in an attempt to cover the feeling of confusion that filled her, and wondered why she had done such a thing.

"How long before they get here?" she asked.

"It's not that easy," he told her. "They don't know we're here. We still have to tell them."

"The fire?" she asked.

He nodded. "And hope they recognize the smoke as a cry for help."

They scrambled down the slope and ran back to the beach. Alyssa gathered up an armful of dried fronds to burn and brought them to where Jason was uncovering the banked embers.

"Get some green stuff," he told her. "This won't make enough smoke."

She nodded and went about doing as he'd directed as

he fed the fire. It took her only moments to pull up an armful of greenery and bring it to him, a procedure she repeated three times more.

"Enough?" she asked as she watched the dark puffs of smoke rise into the air.

"Let's hope so," he replied. "Keep feeding the fire," he directed. "I'm going back up to see if they're turning in to the island."

With that he disappeared, and Alyssa was left with the responsibility of tending the smoky fire.

He returned not very long after and his expression was composed, almost indifferent. Alyssa felt her heart falling inside her. The fire hadn't been seen, she thought. The ship had continued on without turning in toward the island.

He began to kick sand onto the fire.

"They didn't see us?" she asked through the tight ball of disappointment that filled her throat.

"Oh, they've seen us all right," he said. "They should be here in a few hours."

"Then what's wrong? Why are you putting out the fire?"

"Because they aren't the only ones who are approaching," he told her. "There are a half dozen canoes heading this way from Tapuay."

"Oh, God, no," Alyssa murmured. The lump in her throat had grown larger, and seemed to be threatening to choke her.

"With any luck we'll be away before they get here," he told her.

He turned away from her and started for the path into the jungle.

"Where are you going?" she called after him when she realized what it was he was doing.

"Back to the cave," he told her.

"You can't be serious."

"I intend to get a few mementos to remind myself of

the pleasant time we've spent here," he told her. "You stay here."

There was nothing for her to do but wait, she told herself as she obliterated the last evidence of the fire, carefully layering it with sand. But once that task had been completed she was not really that sure.

She glanced anxiously back out to sea, hoping to catch a glimpse of the approaching ship, and finding she could see nothing from the vantage of the beach but water. Then she turned and stared at the greenery where Jason had disappeared into the jungle.

She hesitated, but knew she could not simply stand there and wait for him to return. He might not realize it, but he needed her, needed someone to watch out for the approaching canoes from Tapuay.

She ran after him, quickly disappearing into the jungle in his wake.

Chapter Eleven

There was no sign of Jason when Alyssa reached the edge of the beach by the lagoon and she decided he had already disappeared into the cave. She darted a quick glance to the water, assuring herself there was still no one near enough to see her. Satisfied, she slid down the incline, then trotted across the open expanse of sand to the far side of the beach.

Once she'd reached the mouth of the cave, she felt a wave of revulsion at the prospect of entering. She stared into the dim, dark hole.

"Jason?" she called. "Captain Draper?"

There was no answer. He's probably too far inside to hear me, she thought. He'll take his booty, and return in a few minutes. Hopefully, she thought, before the canoes entered the lagoon.

There was no need, she told herself, for her to actually go into the cave after him. All she really need do was stay hidden and keep an eye out for the canoes from Tapuay so that if the need arose she could warn him when they were drawing close.

She turned back to the still, calm sheet of water. It was a simple enough matter, standing by the mouth of the cave, keeping her attention riveted on the lagoon, searching for the first sight of the canoes approaching. Jason would come out any second now, she assured herself, and then they would get away from this place. And she would never have to think about the cannibal natives of Tapuay ever again.

She let her feet drift through the damp sand, idly digging her bare toes into the warmth until she felt something hard and sharp beneath them. At the contact, she drew her foot out quickly, remembering what she'd seen inside the cave, realizing what it must be that her foot had touched beneath the surface of the sand.

The thought was frightening, too frightening. It called home to her the fact that if she or Jason were seen, it could mean their deaths. That a ship and safety were close was incidental; it would in no way affect that fate. It was all too chilling to her to realize that she could very easily end with her bones being cast aside to lie among the others littering the floor of the cave.

What, she wondered, was she doing standing here when she knew this was the place to which the cannibals would first look when they approached the island? Jason must be nothing less than mad to venture into the cave when he'd seen the canoes approaching. And she must be equally as mad to wait there for him.

But she wasn't mad, or at least she didn't think she was. Not in the ordinary way she thought of people being mad. But perhaps being in love was simply a form of madness. Surely falling in love with a man like Jason Draper could be thought nothing else.

Because she *was* in love with him. She realized that now. Not that the fact would do her anything but hurt. She was, at least, not so deranged that she couldn't see that as clearly as she could see the bright sunshine reflecting off the blue water of the lagoon.

This island, she thought, with all its beauty, was a horror. She would be glad to be away from it. These last moments, waiting while the ship they'd seen approached, could not pass quickly enough for her. She amended her earlier thought. When she was gone from this place, when she was safely arrived on Banaba, not only would she forget about the cannibals, she would forget everything that had happened here. Everything, including what had passed between her and Jason Draper. And she would never allow herself to think of any of it again.

She turned to look once more into the dark recess of the cave, hoping to see Jason appear out of the shadows, wishing she had the common good sense to get away from the beach, to go to the far side of the island and wait for the approaching ship, even if she did it without him. She could see nothing, nor could she hear a sound. And she knew she could not go until he left the cave, knew she couldn't leave him there to be trapped.

"Jason?" she called softly. Still there was no response. Nothing but a faint echo of her own voice followed by an unpleasant silence returned to her from the cave. "Captain Draper?"

She wanted to cry out to him, to shout his name into the darkness of the cave. But she was afraid that if she raised her voice it would carry over the water to be heard by someone to whom she'd rather not reveal her presence. Not, she thought, if she valued her life.

There was nothing left for her to do but keep a sharp watch out for the appearance of the canoes into the lagoon, wait for Jason to appear, and pray that his greed for the pearls would not blind him to the approaching danger.

She'd been staring fixedly at the same spot out on the water for what seemed to Alyssa to have been hours but what she knew could not have really been very many minutes. Some irrational part of her had thought that if she kept her eyes fixed on the spot at the far end of the lagoon, what she saw there wouldn't change, that the water would stay smooth and calm and empty.

But it had changed. What had been a simple melding of the blue of the water into the paler blue of the sky was now littered with a half dozen dark shapes, shapes she recognized as the canoes from Tapuay.

It seemed impossible that they could have gotten so close so quickly. If the natives had been that near the lagoon when he'd seen them from the ledge, surely Jason would never have been foolish enough to go on this dangerous treasure hunt of his. Perhaps he'd misjudged the distance. Perhaps the tides had carried the canoes more quickly than he'd anticipated. Perhaps, perhaps . . . whatever the reason, it still meant the same thing, and that was imminent approach of the cannibals, the imminent approach of death.

She froze for a moment, unable to tear her eyes away from the rapidly growing shapes on the water, unable to turn away and enter the cave, even though she realized that each second she wasted lessened their chances of getting away.

"Jason?" she called again.

This time she could not mistake the note of desperation in her voice. She wondered if it had been there before. In any case, it had no effect. There was no response from the interior, no sounds at all.

There was no alternative, she realized. She would have to go into the cave, walk through that hideous outer room with its litter of bones, and somehow manage to find the secret inner room. And she'd have to do it without benefit of any light whatsoever. The thought of groping around in the cave in the absolute darkness was terrifying. Only the prospect of the nearing canoes could have spurred her to enter.

She turned, darting a glance at the line of jungle that edged the beach. It took only a glimpse of movement in the undergrowth to make her heart leap uncomfortably in her chest. There was someone there, she thought, someone lurking in the shadows, someone who might see her.

She looked again, but saw nothing. It was her imagination, she told herself, and she stared intently at the spot. And then it was there again, a movement among the leaves, a movement that could not have been caused by the wind.

She jumped back, into the mouth of the cave, her thoughts confused and terror filled as she wondered how one of the natives could have come ashore without her seeing him. But she had no time to ponder such mysteries. She had to find Jason and warn him. The two of them had to get away somehow.

Instinct made her run, but she was blinded by the lack of light and she'd taken only a few steps before she fell. She suddenly found herself on her hands and knees, and there were sharp pains in her arm and her legs and on her cheek. If she'd had the time, she would have recognized the warm seep of blood from the scratches the rough edges of broken bones had left on her skin, but fear and revulsion crowded out other thoughts. She scrambled shakily back to her feet.

This time she forced herself to control the growing panic, and she slowed her step to one that allowed her to navigate reasonably in the darkness. Her hands extended in front of her, she guided her movement along the cleared path through the center of the outer room of the cave by the feel of the bones that littered its edges. Eventually she found herself at the far end of the first room of the cave and near the narrow passage to its rear.

If only she had some light, she thought as she began to grope her way along the narrow passage. In the darkness she was forced to move slowly, too slowly. And the cave's twisting path only made matters worse, only made her hesitant progress even slower.

But there was no light, and she had no choice but to keep on. She tried to move a bit faster, but when she did she only succeeded in bumping into the rough stone of the cave wall, aggravating the places she'd hurt when she'd fallen. The cuts on her leg and arm began to ache, to throb with a dull, nagging hurt that was not so great she could not tolerate it, but far too much for her to be able to ignore.

After a few moments, she realized she had no idea how far into the cave she'd already gone. What if she'd missed the entry to the treasure room? What if she'd passed right by the hole without even noticing it?

But no, she thought. She couldn't have gone far enough yet. And if she had, she would find the end of the cave soon enough. In any case, she ought to start searching for the entry to the room that held the pearls.

She bent forward, holding her hands against the rock face of the cave wall and feeling for the recess that led to the interior room. The stone was rough, and it scratched painfully at her bruised hands. The uncomfortable position made her progress even slower, but she could think of no other way of ensuring that she would find the entry.

She was right in thinking she was close. In a few moments she felt a lip in the rock. Moving her hands carefully, she discovered it was not merely a narrow recess, but a thick cut in the stone wall. This indeed must be the entry to the treasure room.

She could not understand why there was no glow of light from within. If Jason was in there, he'd have brought a torch with him. She ought to see at least some glimmer of the light from it.

She knelt down and stared into the darkness.

"Jason," she called softly.

There was no answer, nothing but the soft lapping sound she remembered from her previous trip inside the cave.

"Why doesn't he answer?" she fumed as she got down on all fours and began to creep through the opening in the rock wall.

The room was darker than she remembered it. She'd thought the reflected glow from the pool had been much brighter, but once she was inside, she realized it had seemed that way only because it brightened the light the torch had made. Now she realized it was little more than a dim luminescence, and was, in any case, nearly completely blocked off from the entrance by the huge slab of rock on which the shells holding the offerings of pearls had been set. If her eyes had not by now become accustomed to the complete darkness of the cave, she doubted she would have been conscious of the pale glow at all.

She peered around the small room, trying to make out the shapes of objects she knew were there, the large slab of rocks, the three huge shells. In the dim light, she could just find them, shadows dimly floating in a world that had, for her, become nothing but shadows. It all seemed exactly as it had that first time. Or perhaps the contents of the huge shells had diminished a bit . . . she couldn't be certain. The only thing of which she was certain was that the room was quiet and still. Too still.

"Jason?"

She felt the panic begin to rise inside her even before she called out his name.

"Jason?"

There was no answer.

The room, like the cave outside, was empty.

She was completely alone.

Jason cursed softly, but with determined vehemence. A quick glance assured him that the canoes were already inside the calm water of the lagoon. It would be only a matter of minutes before they would reach the beach.

Why had Alyssa come after him when he'd specifically told her to stay on the far side of the island? Worse still, why had she run inside the cave when he'd tried to motion her back into the jungle? Who had she thought could be in the undergrowth but him?

He gritted his teeth. There was nothing for him to do but go after her now. And that would not be an easy thing to do. The canoes were coming closer to the beach, and even if he skirted the open sand, keeping hidden in the undergrowth, there was still a short distance he would have to cross to the mouth of the cave that would leave him completely in the open. He was far from delighted with the situation.

He began to work his way through the jungle, asking himself why he was doing this, yet again chasing after her as though she were his responsibility. A missionary. Surely the islands would be better off with one less of her kind. He should have let her drown when the waves swept her from the *Empress's* deck. If he'd had an ounce of sense he'd have looked the other way. If he'd had an ounce of sense . . .

Perhaps he should have told her just how close the canoes were to the island when he'd left her on the beach. Maybe that would have frightened her into doing as he'd told her. But he'd thought she'd make a fuss about his going into the cave for a handful of the pearls, and he'd thought he'd had no time to deal with that. Now he wished he had.

He quickly worked his way as far as he could under cover of the foliage. He stood for a moment, staring down at the open and exposed stretch of beach he would have to cross. Then he darted a glance at the approaching canoes. They were already nearing the center of the lagoon. It would take only one of the men in those six canoes casting a curious glance in his direction and he'd be as good as dead. They'd both be as good as dead, he corrected. Alyssa wouldn't last long, either.

There was no choice in the matter, he realized. He

muttered a short prayer, to no deity in particular but to the pantheon in general, and then pushed himself down the incline and darted forward onto the beach.

It took him only a few seconds to cross the short expanse of sand, but all the while he braced himself for the angry shout that would mean he had been seen, for the sharp point of a spear's tip entering his back. At least that would be fast, he told himself. Not like what would happen to Alyssa.

That last thought was spur enough to goad him to more speed than he thought he possessed. And when he'd reached the mouth of the cave and slid inside, he realized that there had been no shout, that he'd not been seen.

So far, he cautioned himself.

He'd made it this far, but that was hardly any reason to feel cocky. It certainly didn't mean they were safe. He faced the blackness of the interior of the cave and started forward, hoping he would not be too late.

"Jason!"

Alyssa didn't know why she called his name yet another time. There was no possibility that there would be any answer save the echo of her own voice. It was more than apparent that she was alone in the cave, that Jason wasn't there to answer.

She felt herself shaking. Her legs seemed hardly able to hold her, her stomach was heaving, her hands were trembling, and she was powerless to control any of it. She was alone in this cave, the beach outside was about to be filled with cannibals, and she had no idea what she was to do.

Not that she'd be able to do much even if she did have an idea, she thought, not as she was. She couldn't even keep her hands still. She pushed her leaden legs forward until she was able to lean against the rock that held the offerings of pearls. There, she thought as she pressed her hands to the rock's surface to still their trembling. She looked down at them and saw them as dull, grayish shadows in the dim light. A ghost's hands, she thought. Or at least, soon to be.

Stop it, she ordered herself firmly. She had to think.

She slid down to the dirt floor of the cave, and sat with her back against the slab of the offering stone. Staring at the dark recess that was the hole out to the larger cave, she tried to understand what had happened.

Jason had told her he was coming here, she reminded herself. But she hadn't actually seen him enter the cave. What if he'd decided it was too risky after all, what if he'd gone back to the beach on the far side of the island looking for her, and she wasn't there? That was the only logical reason she could find for his not being here. And it in no way lessened the danger of her situation.

Would he think to come here for her? She shook her head, deciding the possibility was remote. Even if he realized she'd gone to the cave, there was no way he could get past the party of cannibals from Tapuay. They must be almost to the beach by now. It would be impossible for Jason to slip by them and into the cave without being seen.

That left her alone here. And sooner or later the cannibal chief and his priest would enter the cave with their foolish little statue and come to this room to show their god his treasure. And they would find her here. And then . . .

She pushed the thought away. She couldn't think about that. If she did, she'd be lost. She must remain calm. If there was to be any chance at all for her, she must remain calm.

She wondered if she could hide, if she could make her way back to the narrow passage and follow it to its end. Would the cannibals go all the way to the end of the cave before they entered their god's treasure store? There didn't seem to be any reason they might. Perhaps she could manage to keep herself hidden from them. Surely they'd leave in the morning, as they had the last time they'd come. Perhaps she could keep them from finding her and wait them out as she and Jason had waited them out hiding behind the waterfall.

But then she reminded herself that there were only a few feet more of the cave beyond the entrance to the treasure room. The possibility that she could remain silent and hidden just an arm's length from them was too slim to contemplate. She'd give herself away, just as she had given herself and Jason away that night when they had lain hidden on the ledge. Fear, despite whatever determination she might muster to force herself to keep calm, would eventually conquer her and she'd move or cough or cry out and then they would find her cowering in the darkness. No, she told herself, there was no possibility that she might keep herself hidden.

Her eyes drifted to the faint luminescence that emanated from the pool and permeated the rear of the room. That light, Jason had told her, probably came from the outside, reflected along the path the water took to get inside the cave.

She pushed herself to her feet and edged past the offering rock to its rear. She stood there, staring at the pale blue, dimly lit water. It lapped rhythmically against the stone, making a soft, not unpleasant sound.

If the water came from the outside, she told herself, perhaps she could follow its path back to the sea. The sunlight and water came in, so perhaps she could trace its path to get out.

She had absolutely no idea how far she might have to swim underwater, no idea, even, if the passage was large enough to admit her passage. There was a good chance that by diving into that pool she would be purposely plunging to her death.

But there seemed to be no other choice. She could either try to swim out of the cave or wait where she was until the cannibals from Tapuay came in and found her.

She inched her way closer to the pool. The water seemed calm enough, inviting enough. But appearances, she had found since she'd come to this island, were decidedly deceiving.

She closed her eyes, intending to offer up a short prayer before she took the plunge. But when she did, the image of the statue that the Tapuay natives called their god sprang to mind, and it spoke to her, telling her that other gods than her own ruled in this place. She quickly opened her eyes, shunting the thought aside. Whatever her fate, it seemed apparent that it was not in her own hands.

She sat on the stone and lowered her feet into the water. It was surprisingly pleasant, cool, and fresh. She dipped her hand in and tasted it. Fresh sea brine, she thought, clear and clean. So the opening must bring in fresh water, changing it regularly with the tide.

She peered down and saw a fissure in the rock a few feet below the place where her feet dangled just beneath the surface. That must be the way the water entered, she told herself. Hopefully it was also a path by which she might escape.

She took a deep breath and plunged down into the pool.

She pulled herself through the water, quickly reaching the fissure in the rock and grasping it, then pushing herself into the narrow opening in the stone. It was like a worm hole, perhaps three feet in diameter, just large enough for her to pull herself along. Her first reaction was one of exaltation. She could do this, she thought. She was going to escape.

But it wasn't long before the feeling disappeared. She

was pulling herself forward as fast as she could, and still there was no end to the narrow tunnel in sight, no indication that she was anywhere near the outside. Still she was surrounded by the faint glow, but it seemed no brighter, and that, too, told her she was no closer to the outside.

And then the tunnel began to narrow.

Her breath was almost spent and she felt the panic begin to rise within her. Her heart was beating sharply in her chest, too sharply. In a second of mindless desperation she tried to turn, to twist her way around to go back in the other direction.

She bumped her head painfully against the rock wall of the tunnel. The hurt wasn't great, but it was enough to make her realize that the tunnel was too narrow, that she'd never be able to turn around. Her lungs began to ache as she felt the need for air fill her. She had been a fool to attempt this, she thought. She was going to drown in this place.

She began to push herself backward, her hands frantically brushing against the rough stone around her. Her arms ached from the effort and her hands were scratched and bleeding from the rough surface of the stone as she pushed herself along.

She was moving back toward the pool and the cave, she knew, but not fast enough. She would never get back there before the air in her lungs was spent. She would die here in this narrow tunnel and her body would be trapped, food for whatever fish might manage to find their way to it. She wondered why fate had saved her from drowning in the open sea only to let her meet that same fate in the hidden recess of this cave.

But something would not let her give up. Something inside her made her aching arms continue, despite the fear, the feeling of hopelessness, and the sharp hurt in her chest. Some instinctive part of her refused to stop fighting.

And it saved her life. One instant she was pushing herself mindlessly along the tunnel, sure she'd never reach the end. The next she found herself floating free, and then rising to break through the surface of the pool.

She was coughing and panting and gasping for air. She pushed herself to the side of the pool and then lay grasping the rock face, holding herself there, trying to still the throbbing in her chest by filling her depleted lungs.

She was still exhausted, and her breathing was still ragged and erratic when she realized that she'd returned from one death only to find another. The cannibals were still just outside the mouth of the cave; they would find her. She hadn't avoided death. She'd merely postponed it for an hour or two.

She pulled her arms out of the pool and lay them on the floor of the cave. She was, she found, too exhausted to pull herself out . . . not that it really mattered. She had no reason to climb out, in any event. The cannibals might just as well find her as she was, clinging to the side of the pool, as sitting on the floor of their god's treasure room.

Her head fell forward onto her arms. She lay there too tired to move, too tired even to notice the thin seep of red from the scratches on her hands and arms. It seemed to take every bit of energy she had simply to draw in breath.

She had, she realized, reached the end. There was no place left for her to run.

She didn't hear any sound of someone approaching. It was probably masked by the ragged sound of her breath. Even though she expected it, however, she was not altogether resigned. She cried out when she felt the hand on her shoulder.

Then she looked up in confusion.

"Jason?"

It didn't seem possible. How could he have gotten inside the cave? He hadn't been there before, and she couldn't have missed him. What was he doing there now?

"You were hoping for some other visitor, perhaps?"

She shivered at the thought of who another visitor to the cave would be.

"You could look a bit happier," he told her. "It could have been our hungry friends outside."

"But how . . ."

"I followed you in here," he explained. "Why you're here is beyond me. Didn't I tell you to stay put on the other side of the island?"

"I thought I was following you. I intended to warn you. The cannibals . . . they must be to the beach by now."

He shook his head in disbelief. "You came to warn me," he repeated. "A noble thought, perhaps, but typically ill conceived. It would seem you've done it again, Miss Missionary."

She chafed at his tone. Her aching arms and scraped skin momentarily forgotten, she stared angrily up at him.

"I wasn't the one who decided to indulge in a bit of greed and come in here in the first place," she retorted. "I came to warn you to get out."

"A warning that was completely unnecessary," he replied. "Or have you forgotten that I wasn't here when you arrived?"

She sobered. "No," she agreed. "No, you weren't here."

"Do you think I didn't know how close they were?" he went on. "Why do you think I told you remain on the other side of the island?"

She shook her head. "I don't know," she murmured. "I suppose I didn't think."

"That will be a great comfort to me when I'm about to be roasted for the cannibal chief's dinner," he said. "The irreproachable Miss Missionary admitted she didn't think."

His words released a wave of regret and self pity within her. Once again she'd acted thoughtlessly, blunderingly. Once again she'd put them both in danger. Only this time there was no way to escape as there had been the other times. They were trapped, and they were both going to die.

An enormous tear welled up in each eye and slowly slid down her cheeks. She was too tired and sore and miserable even to notice it, to feel anything but the sense of loss and regret that filled her.

But Jason noticed the tears. And his anger with her melted at the sight of them and the look of hopeless regret that stared up at him from her eyes. It seemed impossibly irrational to him, but he could not deny that he felt a wave of tenderness for her wash over him. It irritated him to recognize it, and he told himself he was a fool to feel it, but as much as he might want to, he could not ignore it.

Everything she did, he told himself, and everything she said seemed calculated to anger him. And if that weren't bad enough, she seemed a magnet for trouble. She drew disaster after her just as a lodestone drew iron. But one glance at those wide, green eyes of hers, of those tears slowly slipping down her cheeks, and all he could think of doing was comforting her.

He slipped into the water beside her and wrapped his arms around her.

"I'm afraid I'm going to be forced to remind you of that admission of yours when we're away from here," he said softly. "I'll demand a full apology then."

She pressed her face against his chest.

"We'll never get away from here," she said. "I've gotten us both killed this time. There is no way out. They're going to find us here and kill us."

He put his hand beneath her chin and pulled it up until she was facing him.

"Wrong again, Miss Missionary," he told her with a small grin. "We are, at this very moment, literally floating on the path to escape and freedom."

She pulled herself away from him.

"The hole through the stone down there?"

She pointed to the narrow tunnel where she'd nearly drowned.

He nodded. "Precisely."

Her stomach heaved at the prospect of returning to what seemed now to her nothing more than an underwater grave. She shook her head sharply.

"I was down there. It's not a way out. We'll drown down there."

"I assure you that it *is* a way out," he told her. He held out his hand. "I'll show you."

She pushed his hand away and backed away from him.

"No," she told him. "I can't go back down there. I'll drown down there."

The feeling of tenderness for her vanished as he considered the look of determined obstinacy he saw in her expression.

"And you'll die an exceedingly unpleasant death if you stay here," he told her through tight lips. "Our friends out on the beach will see to that."

She shook her head. "I can't go down there again," she told him firmly. "I can't."

He exhaled sharply, exasperated with her. He pushed himself forward, grasping her hand. She started to struggle with him, to try to pull herself free, afraid he might try to pull her back down into the water.

But he pushed her sharply against the side of the pool, stilling her struggle by pressing his body to hers and holding it still.

"No," she cried, shaking her head, trying to pull herself free.

The cry, too, he stilled with his hand, placing it firmly over her mouth and holding it there.

"Damn it, be quiet," he hissed.

She grew silent. Something about the intensity of his expression told her there was need, that he had heard something she hadn't. She stilled the fear that had filled her at the thought of returning to the underwater passage and listened.

And heard the whine quite plainly, the high, monotonous, unpleasant song she'd heard the old priest sing when he'd entered the cave the last time he was on the island. She heard it quite plainly and realized it was growing slowly louder.

She turned to stare up into Jason's eyes.

"They're here," she whispered. "They're coming."

He nodded. "They're coming," he whispered in agreement. "Now you either come with me or you stay here and greet them alone. I'm not going to sit here and die because you're afraid."

"It's not a way out," she protested.

"It is," he told her. "Either you believe me and come with me, or you stay. It's your choice."

With that he released his hold of her. He stared at her a moment and decided the only way to convince her was by example. He took a deep breath, filling his lungs with air before he sank beneath the surface.

Alyssa watched him turn and enter the narrow underwater tunnel. He disappeared all too quickly, leaving only a soft ripple in the water behind him to mark his passage.

He was gone, leaving her alone, just as he had told her he would. And now she could hear the old priest's whine draw nearer.

The natives were in the tunnel on the far side of the stone wall, just outside the room, she realized. And they were about to come inside.

Chapter Twelve

Alyssa stared down through the pale blue water at the cleft in the stone face where Jason had disappeared.

He'd promised her it was a way to the outside, she reminded herself. He'd told her to trust him. But trust, at that moment, was not something that came easily, especially after the frightening moments she'd spent in that narrow stone tunnel. She could almost feel the weight of the stone all around her again, just as she had felt it when the panic had stricken her and she'd been filled with the certainty that death would find her in that narrow underwater passage. Her stomach tightened and heaved at the memory of it.

Her hands began to shake at the mere thought of returning. Despite Jason's promise, despite her desire to believe that what he had told her was true, there was a part of her deep inside that could not be shaken from its certainty that she would die if she went back down there, a part of her that held no value on trust but only on what she had seen and felt.

She could hear the high-pitched whine of the priest's prayer and the sound of movement in the cave beyond the small room. The noise was growing louder; the priest and the chief were coming closer.

She hadn't much time. She had to decide and decide quickly.

Jason had told her she could either believe him and

go with him, or stay. It was her choice, and he'd left her to make it knowing she had to decide alone, knowing he could not sway her, and that to force her down into the underwater tunnel with him might mean both their deaths. She eyed the pale shimmer of the water where it flowed from the cleft in the rock. As much as she wanted to believe him, she could not dislodge the hard ball of fear that filled her stomach at the prospect of returning there. It seemed to her that what he had offered her was a choice of either dying with him or dying alone, hardly a choice at all.

But she could not escape the reality that to stay meant facing the certainty of a horrible, gruesome end. Better to die with one of her own than to be sacrificed and eaten by cannibals. Better to die in that underwater tunnel than to have her bones scattered on the outer cave's floor.

She took a deep breath and released her hold of the stone at the side of the pool, allowing herself to sink into the water. Better, she told herself over and over again, to die with Jason than alone.

As the water swiftly covered her, she heard the old priest's song grow sharply louder. The cannibal priest and his chief had entered the treasure room. She pushed against the stone, forcing herself into the narrow passage before either of them could get far enough into the room to see her.

It was the same as it had been the first time, the unchanging color of the water as she pushed herself through, the seemingly never-ending monotony of the tunnel. And then she was at the place where the tunnel began to grow narrower, the place where she'd panicked and turned around the last time. Terror shook her again, but she forced some calm on herself. If she went back this time, there would be no postponement of death. It would be immediate and inescapable. She could drown, or she could face the cannibal's spears. Either way, she'd be just as dead.

Somewhere on the dulled edge of her consciousness there was the realization that the tunnel in front of her was empty. If there was no way out, then logic dictated that Jason would still be there. He wasn't.

An unexpected spurt of hope filled her. The tunnel ahead was empty. That could mean only that it must remain large enough to pass through after all, that it must lead to the outside. She pulled herself furiously forward, spurred by the energy generated by the prospect that she might yet survive.

Her lungs were beginning to ache, and she felt the fear of the tunnel closing in on her, but this time she forced herself to continue on, pushing herself forward, grasping onto the rough stone and pulling herself through. And when it appeared that the tunnel was about to become too small for her to swim through, when she was sure it was about to close in on her and trap her, she finally saw the water brighten and realized what had brightened it was a shaft of sunlight shining directly down into it.

She was nearly outside, she told herself. The light couldn't be that sharp and still be nothing more than a reflection. Just a little bit further and she would be outside the tunnel and free.

But when she tried to reach forward to grasp the stone around her, she found her arms nearly unable to move. Her lungs felt as though they were about to burst, and her arms ached so much she could hardly lift them, could barely push against the stone around her. Kicking here was useless, for there was no room to move her legs. When she tried to put her feet against the stone and push, they slipped, and she felt herself sliding backward.

She was close, she told herself, almost on the outside. And even the spur of that knowledge was not enough to give her arms the strength to push herself any further.

Jason had gotten through, she realized. And if she'd not been such a fool, if she'd gone with him, he'd have helped her through as well. But she'd refused to go, refused to believe him until he'd already gone on ahead of her. If only she'd trusted him, she'd be safe now, breathing fresh, clean air.

There was nothing left in her lungs, no air left to ease the throbbing ache in her chest, no strength left in her arms to pull against the press of the water and stone that entombed her.

She felt the ocean brine begin to edge its way past her lips and tasted it on her tongue.

The chief and the old priest crawled into the room and stood for a moment before the stone slab and the three huge shells with their precious burden. The old man's wailing singsong stilled to a soft whine, then ended entirely. The two stared at their god's treasure.

It was the old priest who noticed first. He set the carved figure on the slab and gazed at the shells. Then he turned to the chief.

The younger man seemed unconvinced at first, and he stared at the heaps of pearls in the shells a long moment before determining that the old man was right. Then he sidled past the stone slab and approached the pool.

The pale glow from the pool reflected off a stain of dull red water-thinned blood that lay on the stone at the edge of the pool. In the water, a wispy, watery trail of red led to the tunnel. It was slowly dissipating, thinning out and dispersing with the gentle movement of the water, but it was still clearly visible.

He knelt beside the small puddle of watery red at the side of the pool. And as he had done the night he'd chased Jason and Alyssa to the waterfall, he touched his fingers to the dark stain, then lifted them to his lips. This time, however, there was no fear in his expression as he looked around, no sense of awe. This time he did not think the blood had been left by spirits. Spirits, after all, had no need to steal. This time he knew.

He turned to the old priest and a roar of outrage escaped from his lips. Then he vaulted over the large stone slab and hurled himself toward the entrance to the offering room, quickly kneeling and scrambling through the hole and out into the tunnel beyond.

The old priest gathered the statue up with hands that were shaking with shock and anger. But the shock slowly faded from his features and rage replaced it as he followed after the chief at the more subdued pace his aged limbs allowed him.

Alyssa tasted the salty brine on her tongue and knew she had swallowed water. She told herself she must keep her mouth closed lest water pour into her. But there was no strength left in her, and no way she could push herself any further along the tunnel. She peered through the opening just ahead of her into the pale glow of filtered sunlight. There was the end of the tunnel, just beyond her reach, and she hadn't the strength to pull herself to it.

Just as she was about to accept that fate had ordained her death there, an arm appeared and reached toward her. She simply stared at it for an instant, not quite believing it was real. Then she reached out for it, and the hand caught hers and pulled her forward.

She had no cognizance of slipping out of the tunnel. There was only the feeling of the hand holding hers, pulling her, and the realization that she could move freely, that she was no longer surrounded by stone. And still her lungs felt as though they would burst.

And then Jason was holding her, his hands to her face, pulling it to his, his lips pressing against hers, forcing air into her mouth. She drank it in, greedily, her lips pressed to his, accepting the gift he offered her, the gift of her life.

They rose slowly in the water, Jason's arms around

her, holding her, steadying her still weak and shaking body. It seemed to take forever, that trip to the surface.

When finally they broke free, she gasped for air, letting Jason steady her and keep her from falling beneath the surface yet again, trusting him not to release her. For an instant she wondered why he'd bothered, why he'd gone down there and waited by the mouth of the tunnel for her. And then she simply told herself she was grateful that he had.

"Can you swim?" he asked her. "We can't stay here. We're too close to the beach."

She looked around, suddenly aware of what it was he was telling her. They were bobbing among the waves, just beyond the lagoon, in clear view of the beach where the cannibals had pulled up their boats onto the sand, and where they were already beginning to build their fire. If one of them happened to turn, to look out toward the water, she and Jason would be clearly in view.

They would have to swim close to the rocks that edged the rim of the island here, then make their way around to the far side, to where the ship might by now be close enough to pick them up. If only they could escape notice, if only none of the natives assembled on the beach turned and saw them or chose to take an excursion to the far side of the island, they might still be safe.

She nodded, and tried to push her arms forward to propel herself through the water. But the waves dragged at her, and she hadn't the strength left to fight them. Jason put his arm around her and began to swim, pulling her along with him. She gave herself up to him, letting herself float at his side.

His strong stroke carried them forward, and in a few moments they were close to the shore. She felt her feet touch the rocky bottom, and she stood, letting the waves lap against her, grateful for the foothold.

Jason helped her forward, urging her to move as

quickly as she could. In a few moments more she was sitting on one of the large, jutting stones, panting breathlessly and trying to steady herself. She darted a glance backward and was grateful to see the edge of the island curved, to see they were no longer within view of the beach by the lagoon.

She looked up at Jason and smiled. And she found herself again asking herself why he'd been there, at the end of the tunnel, waiting for her.

"How did you know I'd follow you?" she asked him. "Why did you wait there for me?"

This time his smile held a hint of superiority, of knowledge of her that he quite obviously had determined she did not possess herself.

"Because you're not ready to die yet, Miss Missionary," he pronounced. "There's too much life still within you. I knew you'd come."

It wasn't a real answer, she told herself. He might think he knew her better than she knew herself, but he was wrong.

She looked away from the smug certainty in his expression, turning to scan the coastline.

"We're safe," she said. "We're past them."

He shook his head, his smile vanishing as he considered their position.

"Almost. I don't think any of them saw us. But there isn't much time to waste here. That ship should be putting a longboat ashore soon. If they don't find us waiting on the beach for them, they'll assume the smoke they saw was some mistake, and knowing where they are, they won't stay long enough to investigate. Nukuhiva isn't exactly considered a friendly port hereabouts."

Alyssa nodded, understanding the need to hurry. She stood, tentatively testing her legs and finding them far steadier than she had any right to expect them to be.

They started out, moving through the thigh-deep water, picking their way past the rocks that littered the island's coast. Their movement was slowed by the rough surface beneath their feet and the constant beating of the waves tumbling into the shore, but they kept doggedly on.

As they rounded a jutting outcrop of rock and found themselves near the beach on the far side of the island, Alyssa felt the feeling of exhaustion almost disappear in the wash of exaltation that swept over her at the sight of the ship floating on the waves. A longboat was being lowered over the side.

Jason stopped for an instant and stared at the sharp outline of the ship against the blue horizon.

"I'll be damned, it's the *Empress,*" he breathed with obvious delight, "come to look for her lost children." He turned to her and grinned. "I knew Liam wouldn't give up on us."

Alyssa stared at the ship. He was right, she realized. It was the *Empress*, her forward mast still a broken ruin from the storm that had swept her overboard five days before.

Five days, she mused. Had it only been five days? It seemed like a lifetime.

"We can swim out to the longboat," she offered. "The sooner I'm away from this island, the better."

He laughed softly. "My thoughts precisely," he agreed. "But I hardly think you're in a condition to do much more swimming at the moment." He shifted his glance to the beach. It was in clear view now, and he stared at the place where they had built the signal fire. "Besides, there's a small package I need to collect first," he murmured.

Alyssa followed his gaze and saw the package to which he was referring, a small bundle that appeared to be his shirt, rolled into a heap, sitting on the sand. She felt a sudden wash of modesty, realizing that save for her shift she was naked, and that she would have to return to the *Empress* in that decidedly unladylike condition. Funny, she thought, that the lack of the shirt and the covering protection it offered had not bothered her during the past few days. Surely the fact that Jason had looked at her near naked body all that time ought to distress her. She found herself wondering why it did not.

She turned her attention back to the heap on the beach.

"Surely you don't intend to go back there merely to retrieve a shirt?" she asked.

"That unlikely heap of unlaundered linen holds my fortune, Miss Missionary," he told her with a wide, pleased grin, "a healthy pile of the pearls from that horde back in the cave."

She shook her head, not understanding.

"But you never went into the cave until you followed me there," she said. "You didn't take any of the pearls."

"I never said that," he said.

"But you didn't come out," she objected. "I was there the whole time and I would have seen you if you had."

"I left the same way you did," he explained.

"Through the underwater tunnel?"

He nodded. "Precisely."

That bit of information startled her.

"Then you knew for certain it was large enough, that it was a path out?" she asked. "You knew because you'd just been there."

He shrugged. "Actually, I knew that three days ago. I told you I was going fishing, and explored the place."

She chafed at the smug tone of his voice, at the way he assumed such a superior attitude. And then she realized what might have happened when he'd gone off without telling her.

"You could have been caught in that tunnel," she accused. "You could have died there and I'd have never known."

"I'm flattered, Miss Missionary. I'd not have thought you'd miss me."

She scowled. "You could have been trapped and left me alone on this horrible island."

He shrugged. "I wasn't and I didn't."

She shook her head, sure she'd never understand him.

"But why did you leave that way?" she demanded. "Why didn't you just come out the way you went in? I would have seen you then. I never would have gone inside."

"Lest you forget, you were supposed to have remained on the beach," he reminded her. "I'd seen how close the canoes were, and decided it the most prudent course of action to leave by the rear exit."

"You knew they were that close, and yet you went anyway?" She couldn't believe him, couldn't believe he'd do so dangerous and foolish a thing. "Have you no fear, no feelings whatever?"

She'd been right about him, she told herself. He was mad.

He grinned, amused by the expression he saw on her face.

"I must admit, when I got to the beach and found you missing, I wasn't entirely pleased. And when I realized I'd have to go back into the cave to get you out, I might even have been a bit disturbed."

She thought of her fear of being trapped in the underwater tunnel, thought of how much easier it would have been for her if she'd known he'd already been through it, if she'd known for certain that it was a path out to the sea. He had let her cope with that terror, even when a word from him would have allayed it.

"You might have told me," she said in an accusing tone. "You might at least have told me that the tunnel was a sure way out."

"I did," he replied, his tone even and as hard as hers had been resentful and angry. "You didn't believe me."

His tone surprised her as did the reproach she saw in his eyes when he looked at her. She quieted, her anger suddenly deflated, realizing that what he said was true. But still, she told herself, he had no right to be angry with her. She was the injured party. She was the one who had almost drowned.

Put it behind you, a voice inside her told her, put it in the past. After all, you're safe now. It doesn't matter any more.

She let the anger go, and let calm fill her. She fixed her gaze on the longboat, telling herself they were safe, that soon she would be on Banaba and able to forget the whole episode. She was not sure if the prospect was as appealing as it ought to have been, but she told herself it was for the best. Jason Draper was soon to be just a name, some fragment of her past she could think about from time to time. It was best for her if she began to think of him that way right now.

But the sound of a cry made the calm she'd called up disappear. She turned and stared at the island's coast behind them. There, rounding the rock outcrop, splashing through the water and chasing after them, was the cannibal chief. His men were close behind.

She didn't need to know the meaning of the words they were shouting to realize these men were intent on blood.

Jason darted a single, regret-filled glance at the beach. Then he grabbed Alyssa's arm and pulled her. They started to run, only this time out into the water, away from the shore. There was the sound of rifle fire from the *Empress*'s deck, and the men manning the oars of the longboat, realizing the danger they were in, were putting their backs into their work, pulling the craft through the water as fast as they could.

"You get your swim after all," Jason shouted to Alyssa.

They were in waist-deep water now, and he put his hand to her waist as she dived forward, pushing her, helping her move through the waves. There was a series of frightful, dull thumping noises as spears hit the water around them. The sounds of angry shouts filled the air.

It was a terror-filled moment, but it didn't last long. The longboat drew near, and Jason lifted her, helping her up, over the gunwales. She fell into the bottom of the boat, a sodden, shivering heap. Once she was aboard, Jason pulled himself up and climbed in beside her. He shouted above the sound of the cries from the shore and the noise of the waves against the hull, telling Liam to turn the boat around and return to the *Empress*.

"Well, now," Liam Argus said, smiling broadly despite the danger they were in. "And are ye whole and well?"

Jason laughed, the sound of it mixing with the shouts the natives hurled at them and the beat of the oars in the water.

"Well enough now," he told his mate.

Alyssa stared from Jason to Argus and back at Jason. They seemed almost to be enjoying themselves, as though the whole experience were some sort of harmless escapade, not the flirtation with death she knew it truly to be. She pulled herself up from the boat's plank bottom and peered back at the angry natives who were beginning now to fall behind as the longboat pressed through the waves.

The natives were splashing through the water, swimming with determined, angry strokes, trying to reach them before the longboat drew too far away from shore. It was soon apparent, however, that they had come too late. Once their spears had been thrown, they had no weapons to level against the desecrators of their god's cave. Had they brought their canoes with them, matters might have been different, but as it was they could not hope to overtake the longboat before it reached the *Empress*'s side.

"Are we safe?" she asked in a small voice, afraid

the answer might not be one she wanted to hear.

"I think so, miss," Liam told her.

"Things might have been a bit different had you come to the party a bit late, Liam," Jason said. "Remind me to thank you."

"No thanks required, Captain. I've always prided myself on promptness," Liam said, then turned to the sailors who worked at the oars. "Let's put our backs into it, boys," he told them. "We don't want our hungry friends on shore to get the idea we intend to stay to supper." He turned back to face Jason. "I don't suppose you accepted any invitations, Captain?" he asked with a chuckle.

"As you see, they were tendered, but I thought it politic to decline," Jason told him. "Although I had intended to accept a party favor as a small memento of the occasion." His expression grew wistful at the thought of the fortune in pearls he had left behind on the beach.

The boat drew up swiftly to the *Empress*'s side. When she'd been handed up to the deck, Alyssa turned back for a last glance at the natives. They had returned to the beach, but their anger was obviously not abated despite their inability to take appropriate revenge. They gestured and shouted, and some waved the spears they had retrieved from the water. She shivered, thinking of the fate she and Jason had so narrowly escaped.

Jason climbed up onto the deck and stood at her side. He called out orders that the longboat be drawn up. Then he turned and stared for a long moment at the beach.

His eyes darted to the chief, watching him kneel beside the bundle that had once been Jason's shirt and untie it. The heap of pearls Jason had hidden inside it tumbled out, scattering onto the warm sand.

Jason grimaced.

"I've just lost a fortune, Miss Missionary," he murmured.

Alyssa looked up at him. She could see the regret in his eye, almost hear his thoughts. He traded my life for those pearls, she told herself. And he can't keep from wondering if the price was not more than he ought to have paid.

Jason turned away, as though even the sight of that heap of pearls on the sand was painful to him. She stared at his back, not sure if she was angry with him or if she regretted being the cause of his loss.

"Give the order to come about, Liam," Jason said as he started across the deck. "Let's get away from this cursed island before our friends back there decide they might just as well fetch their outriggers and come after us after all."

"Aye, Captain." Argus called out to the men, "Let's show a little haste with those sails, boys. We don't want those heathen on the shore to think we've changed our minds and want to accept their invitation to supper."

Alyssa heard Argus's voice, but it was indistinct, distant. Her attention was centered instead on Jason's receding back. He seemed already to have forgotten her, she realized, or at least to wish he could. When he'd turned his back on her, he seemed to have dismissed her completely from his life.

A hard, uncomfortable lump formed in her throat. She knew it was caused by Jason's apparent indifference, by the way he'd consigned her once again to the status of cargo now that they were back on board the *Empress*. For that was how she felt at that moment, like a bit of expensive cargo for which he'd paid an inordinate price and an extravagance he now regretted. The realization that he regretted the loss of the pearls was like a wound to her, painful and deep.

Argus watched her face, watched the hurt that slowly filled her eyes as she watched Jason disappear below.

"Can I help you to your cabin, miss?" he asked her softly.

She turned to face him, suddenly remembering she

was standing, nearly naked, on deck. She shook her head.

"No, thank you, Mr. Argus," she told him.

She started across the deck. It was about time, she told herself, that she learned how to depend only on herself. Expecting others' help was not only foolish, it was a sure road to disappointment.

And expecting anything at all from a man like Jason Draper was simply a prelude to heartbreak.

"I apologize for the delay, Miss Missionary. That broken mast leaves the *Empress* little more than a lumbering cow in the water."

Alyssa shook her head. "No need for apology, Captain Draper."

She wouldn't admit it to him, but she, too, regretted the delay. From the moment she'd appeared at dinner the night before, once again dressed in a dark, modest dress, she'd regretted the necessity of spending even an hour more in his company, regretted more than she could express seeing the veil of cold indifference that fell over his face whenever he looked at her.

It was as though the previous five days had never happened, as though they had never been stranded on Nukuhiva. It was as though they'd never touched, never kissed, never made love. Even the pangs of seasickness had returned to her the moment she'd entered her cabin, and she'd not managed to rid herself of them since.

The sooner she got to Banaba, she'd told herself, the sooner she would be able to forget what had happened on Nukuhiva. She only wished she could begin now, wished she could wipe its memory from her mind. But the memory, however painful, refused to be dislodged, and the sight of Jason only worsened the pain it brought her.

Now, though, as she watched the dark green blur that

was Banaba slowly grow larger and clearer, she wondered if the life she would begin there would allow her to forget what had happened on Nukuhiva. From what little she could see, the islands appeared much the same. Banaba was a great deal larger, certainly, but this island, like Nukuhiva, was lush and green, with a mountainous outcrop inland and what even from that distance she could see was a ribbon of pale, golden beach.

There was a man there, she reminded herself, one who expected her to become his wife, who expected her to spend her life helping him in his work of turning the island into a God-fearing, Christian place. She would be expected to grow old with him, become gray-haired, and feel herself superior to the natives who served her—in short, become the image of what Emma Styles had become through her years on Papeete. The prospect was distasteful to her, more so than she would have thought possible.

Perhaps the prospect of becoming what Jason Draper already thought her to be was what repelled her, she told herself. Or perhaps she already was as he saw her, perhaps she was the sanctimonious hypocrite Jason considered her. She wasn't sure any more. She wasn't sure of anything—anything, that is, except for the fact that she was in love with him and not sure she could give herself to another man. Even if that man was supposed to become her husband.

"I expect you must be anxious to see your bridegroom, Miss Missionary," Jason told her. "And he you."

He spoke in the distant, mildly indifferent tone he'd used with her since they'd returned to the *Empress* the day before. She wished she could rouse some anger in him for it, or even for calling her Miss Missionary, but she found she ached too much inside to feel anything save the hurt that had been growing since her realization that their return to civilization meant his desertion of her.

It was not as though he'd ever lied to her, she reminded herself, not as though he'd ever led her to expect anything else. He'd even told her she was only entertainment to him, quite explicitly told her she was nothing more than a diversion. She had no right to feel anything but relief at the prospect of his delivering her to Owen Remsen and then leaving. But right or no right, still she did.

She steadied herself, clinging to the rail, holding it so hard her knuckles turned white. If nothing else, she would go through with this with some vestige of her dignity intact, she told herself. She would not let him see what he was doing to her. She would not allow herself to give him that satisfaction.

"Certainly," she replied. "It's been a long voyage."

"I'd almost forgotten," Jason mused. "You've come halfway around the globe to wed this man, haven't you? I should think that a sign of singular devotion."

He turned and stared at her, and she could see it in his eyes, the accusation that her singular devotion had allowed a small lapse or two while they'd been marooned on Nukuhiva. She wanted to shout at him, to tell him that she had never met Owen Remsen, that she wasn't sure she would accept him even after that long trip of which he'd spoken.

But she didn't.

Before she had the chance he nodded to her and, lowering his voice, added, "You needn't fear I shall in any way intervene in your plans. Your fiancé need never know what happened on that island."

He probably thought he was being kind to her, she realized as she stared at his smugly complacent expression. But his words brought a wave of anger at him that a moment earlier she had thought herself no longer capable of feeling.

"Tell him, if you like," she snapped back through clenched teeth. "Tell him everything, every lurid detail. I don't care."

His expression lost the veneer of distance. She took some satisfaction in that, in the fact that she had finally managed to do or say something that he did not expect.

"You're not serious?" he asked.

"Aren't I?" she asked. "Do you really think I care if you announce to him just how unsuitable I am, to reveal to him all my unspeakable sins?" She stepped back from the rail and away from him. She wasn't sure where these words were coming from, had no idea why she was saying them, but somehow she couldn't keep herself silent. "Well, I assure you, I don't. I don't care what he thinks, nor does it make the least difference to me what you think of me. I've had enough of that. More than enough."

"Alyssa," Jason murmured. He reached out and put his hand on her arm.

She pulled back, irrational, almost afraid that the touch of his hand would burn her, would leave an indelible scar on her arm.

Like the scar he has left on my heart, she thought.

"We have nothing further to say to one another, Captain Draper," she said. "Not now. Not ever."

She glanced one last time at Banaba, then she turned away, from both the view of the island and from Jason's bewildered expression, and ran to her cabin. A few hours of peace, she told herself, just a few hours. Even the unpleasantness of the seasickness that would plague her in her cabin were preferable to so much as another minute in his company.

A few more hours and she'd be on Banaba. And then she would have to face Owen Remsen and tell him she could not marry him.

Chapter Thirteen

Alyssa eyed Jason as he swung down to the dock on a rope while the *Empress* was still moving. It seemed to her that he was only too anxious to get about his business on Banaba. She had absolutely no question in her mind but that the reason for his haste was his desire to be rid of her.

On the deck around her there was a welter of activity as the crew began to make ready to offload the cargo of supplies for the mission as well as her own belongings. She hugged close to the rail, putting some effort into trying to make herself as little an impediment to the crew as she could.

She couldn't push herself to go below, however, even knowing her presence on deck was an inconvenience. Between her curiosity and the unpleasant heaving that settled into her stomach each time she ventured away from the open air, she was not without motivation. She couldn't help staring at Banaba.

As the *Empress* slid alongside the dock, she couldn't keep herself from looking up to the path that led down from the crest of the hill just above the inlet. She could just see the tops of three or four roofs peeking out of the treetops. But what really interested her was the sight of the two men who were at that moment hurrying down the path to greet the *Empress*'s arrival.

They were both tall, and both were dressed in the sort

of somber, formal attire she had long ago come to recognize as the uniform of missionaries, even in so unsuitable a place as the South Seas. But there the similarity ended. One was gray-haired and decidedly portly, and his step, Alyssa could see even from the distance, was labored with the effort of his descent on the steep path. The other was lanky and his long legs made far better progress on the hillside. He reached the edge of the dock even before the *Empress* had been secured.

As soon as she saw him standing there, staring up at her, she realized he must be Owen Remsen.

Jason seemed to be completely unaware of either of the advancing missionaries. Instead, he busied himself with the task of seeing that his ship was properly docked. It appeared to Alyssa that he was purposely ignoring the two missionaries, just as he had ignored her since their last unpleasant conversation. She wondered if he was taking pains to be as rude as possible. She told herself she ought to expect nothing better from him.

"Ahoy, *Empress*," Owen called.

He looked up at her and waved with a great, sweeping motion of his long arm.

She couldn't help but stare at him. Despite everything, despite all that had happened in the previous days and even her determination to put off any wedding indefinitely, still she couldn't deny she had some feelings of curiosity about the man her uncle had sent her so far to marry.

He was red-haired and freckled, with the sort of pale complexion she hadn't seen since she'd left Plymouth. She marveled at that, that in the months he'd spent on Banaba he'd somehow managed to hide himself from the sunshine. A picture filled her mind, a vision of those long, lanky limbs of his that were so obvious, despite their somber covering, only she saw them, clothed not in black, but bare and utterly white, save perhaps for a sprinkling of those bright freckles. It startled her that she could even have such a thought about a man, and she chased it quickly aside, but not so quickly that it did not make an impression on her.

She concentrated on his face, telling herself firmly that she ought to have no thoughts about any other aspect of his anatomy. It was a long face, and a pair of spectacles were sitting a bit crookedly on his nose, slightly obscuring wide blue eyes. The nose itself was a bit too long, she thought, and the lips a bit too thin. Still, it was a handsome face more than not, she decided. Not that a smile wouldn't have improved it considerably.

"Miss Whitlock?" he called up to her.

She nodded. "Yes?"

"Welcome to Banaba."

The older man had completed the descent to the edge of the dock and came to stand beside Owen, and he, too, called out a word of welcome. The two did not venture onto the dock, however, until Jason had overseen the lines being made fast and the gangway being lowered.

Once the *Empress* had been made secure, they started across the dock, the older man moving slowly, all the while peering up expectantly at her.

Alyssa found herself feeling that she owed them some sort of a properly impressive entry into their world, and she was not at all sure she knew what they might expect of her. She swallowed, trying uselessly to rid herself of the uncomfortable lump in her throat, and straightened the properly modest collar of her decidedly plain dark blue frock. Then she started down the gangway to meet the man who considered himself her intended bridegroom.

"Watch your step, Miss Whitlock. The dock's a bit slippery."

The dock was more than a bit slippery, she found. It was practically covered with an unpleasant green mold that was fostered by the damp and the shadows cast by the trees that surrounded the small inlet. She was grateful for the steadying arm Owen held out for her.

His arm felt hard and thin beneath her fingers, like a piece of metal rod under the fabric of his suit. Ungiving and hard—it reminded her of her Uncle Silas's arm. Now why, she wondered, must she think of her Uncle Silas just then when she least wanted any thought of him to cloud her mind?

"We expected you days ago," Owen was saying.

She had to force herself to pay attention to his words, and when she realized that he was demanding an explanation in a roundabout fashion, she hurriedly supplied him with one.

"There was a storm," she replied and turned to motion to the broken mast that jutted out of the *Empress*'s deck.

The four words seemed sufficient to satisfy him. He grimaced.

"Yes," he said, and nodded in a knowing fashion. "Nothing is dependable in this place except the weather. It's either hot or it's wet. Or both."

His voice held a hint of displeasure in it, as though the weather had not been brought to him for his approval, but if it had, he would have arranged matters more to his own liking. The tone reminded Alyssa of her Uncle Silas.

The matter of the *Empress*'s late arrival apparently settled, Owen turned to the older man, who had slowly advanced along the slippery dock to come to stand beside him.

"This is Reverend Merricomb," Owen said. He grinned then, as though it had struck him as exceedingly amusing that he had not as yet introduced himself to her. "And I, by the way, am the Reverend Owen Remsen."

"So I surmised," she murmured.

"Welcome to Banaba, my dear," Merricomb said. His voice, surprisingly deep despite his age, was pleasant and warm. He pressed her hand in his. "I can not tell you how welcome you are here. It's long past time we had the civilizing influence of a woman among us."

Alyssa smiled warmly at him. His manner was open and genuine, and she knew immediately that she would like him. She was not quite so sure about Owen Remsen.

"That has been my opinion precisely," Owen said. He

retrieved her hand from old Merricomb's, his manner proprietary, as though he considered that appendage already his, and placed it once again on his arm.

"It would seem you are properly settled in the warm and loving embrace of your intended, Miss Whitlock."

She turned to find Jason behind her, and there was laughter in his expression as he stared at her. She had no need to question the cause. She could almost hear his thoughts, his condemnation of Owen's greeting as hardly fitting the effort to which she had been put that she might receive it. It seemed to please him that Owen had not greeted her with a kiss or an embrace, as though the lack of physical warmth he showed somehow proved something Jason had known all along.

Had she known what was in Jason's mind at that moment, she would have realized her evaluation was right.

Look at the warm and loving man you're to wed, Miss Missionary, Jason thought as his eyes met hers. I hope you find much happiness in his bleakly unimpassioned arms. You probably deserve one another.

His attention was immediately distracted by Argus and two others of the crew. They were offloading the mission's supplies and setting the crates on the ground just beyond the dock.

"Shall I have your belongings left with the rest, Miss Whitlock?" Jason asked in the distant, not quite amused, only too proper tone he had taken to using with her.

"I suppose so," she murmured, refusing to admit to herself that the tone hurt her, that his words and his expression made her feel unwanted and unnecessary, but mostly that they made her realize only too clearly how little he cared about her.

She turned her attention to the trunk that Argus was settling on the ground beside the crates of medical supplies for the mission. She stared at it, finding herself suddenly confused and more than a little ill at ease. Her whole world, it seemed, had been packed into that trunk back in Plymouth. She had come to Banaba with the expectation that she would be able to unpack it and make some sort of a home for herself. But now that she was there, she realized she had absolutely no idea what sort of arrangements had been made for her, no idea how Owen Remsen would act when she told him she could not marry him. What if he refused to allow her to stay on there in Banaba? And if he did, where would she go? What would she do?

Owen, however, was without any feeling of uncertainty.

"Certainly Miss Whitlock's belongings are to be left with the rest," he told Jason in a tone that implied he had become accustomed to dictating to others. "One of the natives will sort things out."

His instructions made clear, he dismissed Jason and the *Empress*'s crew from his attention. He clasped his hand firmly on Alyssa's and started to lead her toward the path.

"I'm sure you're eager to see your new home," he told her in a tone that indicated she was, even if she wasn't really as sure about it as he was.

"Then I'll bid you farewell now, Miss Whitlock," Jason called after her as she started the long climb up the hill at Owen's side. "My best wishes for your happiness," he said, an afterthought he added in a tone sharp with sarcasm he made no effort to hide.

She turned and stared at him, wishing she could feel anger with him for his indifference, instead feeling a growing numbness inside her. When Owen nudged her, she turned back to face the uphill path. Cowed into silence, she started to climb.

Jason stood where he was and watched her for a moment. Then his expression hardened, and he turned away.

"But won't you even be staying to dinner?"

The Reverend Merricomb had come up behind him, and was now staring at him with a hopeful expression.

"I'm afraid not," Jason told him.

She didn't even say good-bye, he thought. It wouldn't have cost her much to say good-bye.

Merricomb seemed crestfallen at the loss of company for the evening meal.

"We don't have many guests," he said, "and word of the outside world is always welcome, you know." He smiled. "More than welcome."

Jason shook his head.

"You will have to make due with Miss Whitlock's news," he said, taking no great pains to hide the impatience in his voice. "As you see, the *Empress* is in need of repair. I want to make port at Beau Rivage before nightfall. Hopefully Noyer will be able to provide me with timber and a carpenter to help with a new mast."

He turned away from the old man to stare at his injured ship. It seemed to pain him that the *Empress* had been so mutilated by the storm. At least, he thought as he gazed at the ruined mast, I can fix what's wrong with my ship.

"Oh, I'm sure Monsieur Noyer can be of assistance," Merricomb assured him. "He was kind enough to send two of his men to help build a room for me on the side of the schoolhouse." He grinned meaningfully. "After all, newlyweds hardly need an old man cluttering up their little cottage."

"Yes," Jason murmured. He looked up at the path where Alyssa was climbing the hill to the mission buildings, Owen a dark stick figure at her side. "Newlyweds," he muttered with distaste.

Merricomb brightened. "But the repairs to your ship will doubtless take a few days. Perhaps you can convince Monsieur Noyer to bring you around to this side of the island. There will, after all, be some small wedding celebration."

The old man's words affected Jason strangely. At the mention of the wedding he realized he felt a stab of angry jealousy. But it quickly dissipated at the prospect of attending the celebration. He might, after all, manage to make his presence felt one way or another. That, at least, might provide some measure of satisfaction.

He smiled at Merricomb. "I think Noyer can most definitely be persuaded," he said. All the impatience had disappeared from his tone, and he even managed a smile for the old man. "After all, a marriage of missionaries. Such merriment has not been seen in Banaba for God knows how long."

Merricomb pursed his lips, not quite understanding Jason's sarcasm, yet not sure he should accept his words at face value.

"Yes, a wedding is always a welcome and joyous rite," he muttered in confusion.

Jason took pity on him. "I can assure you Noyer and I will be delighted to attend," he said in a far warmer tone than he was accustomed to using when he was speaking to a missionary. Once again he stared up at the retreating figures of Alyssa and Owen. "I shall have to find an appropriate wedding gift," he said thoughtfully.

"Oh, that's not really necessary," Merricomb interjected. "I'm sure the gesture of your presence will be gift enough."

Jason turned his glance back to him. "But it will be my pleasure," he said with a knowing grin.

"And this is the schoolhouse," Owen said.

Alyssa stared with disbelief at what seemed to be an effort to recreate a small New England town green incongruously set on the hilltop of this tropical island. A small plot of faltering grass, ill suited to the continuous warm temperatures, struggled to survive in its center. Around it were set several buildings, and at the end a steepled affair which was obviously the mission church.

She turned to the structure at which Owen pointed, a plain, unpainted building at the near side of the compound. There was, she noted, an addition of a small room to its far side, the fresh timber a paler shade than the weathered siding of the rest of the structure.

"I've brought twenty first-form readers with me," she told him. "Uncle Silas sent them as a gift to the mission. He thought you would be able to make good use of them with the children."

Owen nodded. "We can use whatever we can get," he said. "There's never enough of anything, I'm afraid. Except bananas and coconuts. They seem to be the only coin that's ever placed in the offering plates."

Alyssa cocked her head and stared at him, surprised at the attitude he conveyed, that there ought by rights to be more.

"What else would these people have to give?" she asked.

Owen scowled, but pretended he hadn't heard her. He pointed to the mission church. Of the structures that were clustered around the not quite convincing replica of a New England town green, it alone had had the honor of having received a coat of white paint.

"Our church," he needlessly told her. "And there," he adjusted his arm, moving it so that he pointed to what might have been a small cottage on the outskirts of Plymouth, complete with a gingerbread trimmed front porch, "is the manse. Where we live."

Alyssa stopped and drew her hand away from Owen's arm.

"No," she said.

He turned to stare at her, his expression bewildered, as though he'd never heard the word before.

"Excuse me?" he asked in a sharp tone.

"I said no," she told him. "We can't live together in that house. It wouldn't be proper."

He smiled at what he took to be simple modesty on her part.

"Of course, we're not yet married," he agreed. "For a day or two, I can sleep in the addition to the schoolhouse, with old Merricomb. Not that the ceremony need be put off very long. After all, there aren't many arrangements that need to be made here. It's not like Plymouth. No need to post bans. It would be beneficial to invite the natives to the service, of course, as a lesson, to instruct them as to what a real marriage is. We've performed a few marriages since I arrived, but mostly these people don't understand the sanctity of the sacrament. They are, I'm afraid, highly immoral in their behavior. You'll see. It is a hard path we tread to teach them God's way, to show them how to distinguish right from wrong."

Alyssa had put her hand up in the middle of this speech, but it had had absolutely no effect on turning the course of his words. It wasn't until he'd done that he even noticed it.

"You don't understand," she said when he finally gave her the opportunity. "I can not marry you either tomorrow or the next day. Or, for that matter, at any time in the foreseeable future."

His brow furrowed. "Your uncle wrote to me that you understood, Miss Whitlock. He advised me that a wife would bring to the mission the sort of civilizing influence that it is beyond the capability of a lone man to exert. His letter to me said you completely understood that you were coming here to serve that function."

A knot of distaste formed in Alyssa's stomach at the way he spoke of her, as a commodity sent to serve a function. She gritted her teeth, forcing down the anger she was starting to feel.

"I have come here to help in the mission, yes," she said firmly. "To teach in the school, to help, if I can, in the dispensary. But for the time being, those are the only functions I intend to serve." She set her jaw. "I certainly can not marry a man I do not know. And I do not know you."

His expression showed disbelief, and not a little displeasure. But Alyssa refused to be cowed by it. She kept her glance firmly on his, willing to wait him out if need be.

"You don't mean to tell me you intend to live here, alone with two men?" he asked.

There was no question but that he considered even the suggestion preposterously inappropriate.

She pretended ingenuousness.

"But I would be living alone with two men even if we were married," she replied. "From all appearances, you found nothing wrong with that arrangement."

"You know that would be entirely different," he snapped. "It would be completely inappropriate for an unmarried woman to live here with us."

"Inappropriate?" she asked. "Surely you don't mean to imply that either you or the Reverend Merricomb are not to be considered entirely trustworthy?"

"There is the appearance if not the fact of impropriety in such an arrangement," he returned sharply.

"Appearances? Who is there on the island to take exception to appearances?"

She was, she found, almost beginning to enjoy the discussion, realizing just how predictable his responses proved to be.

"We are not alone here," he reminded her.

"Surely the natives would have no reason to disapprove. You yourself just told me that the natives' morals are deplorable. I seriously doubt they'll be upset by my living here, married to you or not."

"We are here to reform them, Miss Whitlock," he told her, his tone growing coldly sharp and lecturing, "not to symbolically condone their immoral actions by example."

"But we would do nothing wrong," she insisted.

"It does not matter what we would or would not do," he said. "It is how our actions are perceived that is of concern."

"Then I could take on one of the native women to act as duenna," she returned. Her chin jutted out and her lips took on an obstinate set. "If that seems inappropriate to you as well, then I fear I shall have no other choice but to ask Captain Draper to return me to Papeete."

For an instant he seemed to consider the possibility as

he stared at her. Finally, however, he shook his head. He reached out to her, touching his hand to hers, as though he needed to convince himself that she was real.

"No," he said finally. "That won't be necessary."

Alyssa grinned, feeling as though she had won something for the first time in her life.

"I'm sure it will be for the best," she told him.

His expression told her he was not so convinced as was she. But as he stared at her, a slight reddish cast washed over his cheeks and the hand that held her hand trembled just the least bit before he released it.

"I cannot say," he said finally, "that your decision pleases me. There are certain pressing reasons why it is wisest for a man living in this environment to have a wife. Especially a young man." He looked away, into the distance, apparently searching for a word that would explain and yet not shock her. "There are temptations, circumstances . . ."

His voice faded away in embarrassment.

Alyssa had to fight the grin that threatened to turn up the corners of her mouth. So the proper and sincere Reverend Owen Remsen must grapple with temptations, she thought, and those the unspeakable temptations of the flesh. Certainly her Uncle Silas would never have openly admitted such a thing. Perhaps Owen was a bit more human than her first impression of him suggested he might be. Perhaps, after a reasonable amount of time, she might even grow to like him well enough to consider marrying him after all.

"All of which you have managed to deal with admirably for the months you have been here," she told him firmly, "and will, I'm sure, continue to do so with proper Christian strength and perseverance." She finally relented and smiled at him. "Certainly it would be wiser, for both of us, if we became friends before we considered becoming anything else," she added gently.

She thought the matter had been concluded at that, and she expected him to do the same. And at first, he gave the impression that he would do just as she expected. He cleared his throat noisily, and the remnants of the blush that lingered in his cheeks darkened a bit more.

Apparently, however, he was not content to end the conversation at so inconclusive a point. When she started forward, returning her attention to the tour of the mission buildings, he reached out his hand and caught her arm. She turned back to face him. She was surprised to see the blush was gone, replaced by a sharp, smoldering look in his eyes that even the presence of the spectacles could not obscure.

"I prefer not to think of the wedding as postponed indefinitely, Miss Whitlock," he told her flatly. "Let us decide to discuss the matter again in, shall we say, one month's time? I expect by then you will realize that it would be for the best if we both accepted the normal conventions of these situations."

The pity she'd begun to feel for him vanished.

"I don't think a time limit would serve any purpose . . ." she began.

He waved her to silence, and started on toward the cottage.

"Perhaps it would be most convenient were you to occupy the room in the schoolhouse in the interim," he said, once again using a tone that said he was in charge, and not to be questioned. "I'll have the boys bring your belongings there. In the meantime, would you care for a cup of tea?"

Merricomb sat on a wicker chair on the front porch of the cottage and pretended absolute concentration on the cup of tea he held in his hand. He nibbled a bit of a rather tired dried biscuit, then looked at Alyssa across the small tea table that was between them and offered her a wan smile.

She sipped her tea very carefully, savoring it, as she openly watched Owen direct three native men to return to the cottage those few belongings Merricomb had brought to the schoolhouse room before fetching her things there.

Merricomb, she realized, gave every appearance of being completely bewildered by the change in his circumstances. She'd explained as simply as she could the decision she and Owen had reached concerning the indefinite postponement of their marriage, but she could see the older man was not entirely happy with what he obviously considered an unorthodox arrangement.

Merricomb studied his belongings as they were borne past him to be returned to the room he had willingly offered up in deference to what he expected to be Owen's changed status from bachelor to married man. His consideration of a slightly sobered Owen Remsen directing the exchange made him wonder if he'd somehow gotten some major matter of etiquette terribly confused.

He nibbled at his biscuit, sending a small spray of pale crumbs across the front of his vest.

"Of course, under the circumstances, I understand your reticence, my dear. But certainly you must agree that this arrangement you and Owen have decided upon is not exactly the most conducive to the purpose of the mission."

Alyssa pursed her lips thoughtfully. "Not at all," she replied. "I shall endeavor to be of help to you both, teaching in the school, helping with the sick, all those things that would be expected of me were Mr. Remsen and I to be married. I intend to work very hard."

"Oh, I'm sure you do, my dear. It is only that there is one thing you can not do without benefit of marriage, and that is to provide an example of proper marital stability, the raising of children, and the like."

She turned and gazed at him steadily. "Then that particular function shall of necessity need be left unfulfilled for the time being," she told him.

He leaned forward to her and lowered his voice confidentially.

"I know young Owen makes a strong first impression," he said. "And that can be a bit off-putting. But he works very hard, and once his edges soften a bit, I think he'll make a good missionary."

She smiled at that, at the reference to Owen's superior manner as his "edges" and at the realization that Merricomb was aware of the younger man's rather obvious lack of warmth.

"I trust your evaluation," she murmured in reply.

Merricomb set his cup on the table and carefully placed the remainder of his biscuit on the saucer. Then he reached out for her hand, and she let him take it and pat it gently.

"What I mean to say," he went on, staring now, not at her eyes, but at her hand, where it sat between his two rather hamlike ones, "is that it is not unusual for a young man to be impatient to change the world. It takes time for a man to grow to the realization that even a small change requires time, and that no good work, no matter how small, is unimportant. But because Owen's perspective is still a bit colored by youthful ambition, it does not mean he isn't a good man at heart."

Alyssa nodded. "I'm sure he is," she replied. "It's just that I'm not so sure, at least not yet, that I can be a good wife to him."

Merricomb sighed, and then retrieved his tea. He finished the remainder of his biscuit ruminatively, accepting what she told him, but obviously not altogether liking it. When he'd drained the remaining tea from his cup and swept the powdering of biscuit crumbs from his vest, he offered her a smile, apparently willing to live with the situation, especially as she seemed determined not to be convinced to change her mind.

"In any case, I daresay the children will be delighted to have a teacher who is prettier to look at than am I," he told her with a smile. He looked up when the native men who had returned his belongings to his room in the cottage filed out the door and past the place where he sat with

Alyssa. "So you've done, eh?" he asked them in a jovial tone.

The three nodded, smiled at him, then turned uncertain glances at Alyssa as they filed past her. It was obvious they didn't know what to make of her nor of the unsettled flow of belongings from cottage to schoolhouse and back to cottage again.

Merricomb put his hands on his knees, a not totally uncomplicated business considering the expanse of belly they had to bypass, and pushed himself to his feet.

"Well," he said. "Can I help you do your unpacking?"

Alyssa shook her head as she placed her teacup on the table beside the now emptied pot.

"Thank you, but no. I can more than manage my few belongings. Most of what I brought are books and such, for the school."

"Would you like me to show you the way?"

"Owen has already shown me the schoolhouse. In any case, I doubt I should have any trouble following the caravan of trunks and boxes," she said. She nodded to where Owen was directing the delivery of her baggage from the dockside below to the school. "I'll tend to the tea things, and then go over."

Merricomb waved his hand. "Oh, no, leave that. One of the servants will clear it away. You've much more important things to do."

Alyssa scowled. She was not used to having servants to clean up after her, and was not at all sure she would become easily accustomed to it. Nor was she sure she wanted to.

"Well, then, I'll be about my unpacking, then," she told him.

She stood, crossed the porch and descended the front steps. She glanced quickly at the schoolhouse and the bustle of activity there. Then she stared across the green.

She wondered what sort of view the hillside above the dock offered and quickly crossed the green to find out. It was, she found, even more beautiful than she had expected it might be, the pale water of the small cove opening onto a great expanse of incredibly blue ocean beyond.

Her appreciation of the beauty of view, however, dimmed as she recognized the *South Seas Empress*, her sails straining against the wind, sailing out of the cove.

A weight seemed to settle over her heart. She told herself firmly it was for the best that Jason Draper was gone from her life. She'd managed to arrange matters just as she had determined she would when she'd left Plymouth, postponing the possibility of a wedding until such a time as it suited her, providing herself with what she could not question would be meaningful and useful work. Still she could not shake the feeling of desolation that settled over her as she watched the *Empress* grow smaller in the distance, the feeling that Jason Draper's departure left with her.

If she was to start a new life on Banaba, she realized, she would have to do it while she silently nursed a broken heart.

Chapter Fourteen

Alyssa sat in the shade of a large banyan tree. Sitting cross-legged around her on the ground, their faces beaming up at her, were more than a dozen enthusiastic young Polynesians. Each child held in his or her lap one of the primers Alyssa had brought with her from Plymouth, and the books were generating a good deal of excitement among her young charges.

Between her own enthusiasm to teach and that of the children, she had expected this first reading class of hers to be a simple matter. But things were not progressing precisely as she had expected them to.

What she had begun as a reading lesson had turned somehow into a class in zoology. Not that she was to blame for the change. Nor, for that matter, were her young students. It certainly was not their fault that they had neither seen nor heard of the animals that were illustrated on the very first page of the primer. It was simply that she had not been prepared for the sorts of questions she was being asked, and she was finding the task of explaining the existence of a cow and a sheep a good deal more difficult than she would ever have expected it to be.

"What are these things?" one curious youngster asked. He held up his primer and pointed to the drawing of a quizzical looking cow, his finger firmly rooted beside the animal's udder.

"Cows give us milk," Alyssa replied. "That is the cow's udder, the place where we take the milk."

"Milk?" her bewildered inquisitors asked.

"Yes," she told them brightly. "We drink milk."

This response seemed to bewilder the children. They all began talking at once, correcting her obvious misconception.

"We drink water from the spring," one told her firmly. "Or from a coconut."

One little girl made an unpleasant face. "Why would we drink from an animal?" she asked. "Dirty."

"Sometimes the old ones drink *arva,*" a small boy whispered, and then giggled as his older brother dug a warning elbow into his side and quieted him with a warning hiss. The younger boy looked suddenly stricken, as if he'd given away a strictly kept secret.

The gesture made Alyssa realize that she wasn't only teacher here, she was also considered by her students as one of those who had begun to set rules of right or wrong. Apparently, on Banaba as on many other islands, the missionaries had decreed the consumption of the alcoholic *arva* as decidedly wrong. She pretended she hadn't heard, much to the youngster's relief she noted, turning her glance away from him and to the group at large, quieting the children with a calming motion of her hands.

"Milk is what a baby drinks from its mother," she told them, hoping she had hit upon an explanation with which they would be more familiar.

They nodded, understanding this far more natural function. Their questions with regard to the bovine species apparently exhausted, they turned their attention to the next illustration in their texts.

"And what is this animal?" another asked, pointing to the drawing of a sheep.

Alyssa sighed. This was not going to be any easier than explaining a cow to them.

"That is a sheep," she said carefully. "The male animal

is a ram, the female a ewe, and their babies are called lambs, but they are all sheep. The grown animals are about so high," she gestured with her hand.

One little girl giggled. "It is very fat." The rest laughed, too.

"Actually, the animal is not nearly so round," Alyssa told them when they'd quieted. "It is covered with a thick coat of very soft fur that we call wool. We cut off the wool, and use it to make clothing to keep ourselves warm."

This explanation, too, was met with quizzical looks.

"But we don't need to keep warm," one small boy told her firmly. "The sunshine keeps us warm." He stretched out his arms and legs, sunning himself in pantomime.

Alyssa considered her young charges. They were all dressed similarly, boys and girls alike, a single sheet of tapa cloth wrapped around their waists. Apart from this minimal concession to modesty (which Merricomb had assured her had taken him many months to enforce) they wore only flowers, tucked in their hair or strung together in colorful ropes and worn as necklaces around their necks. They were charming decorations, she had decided when she'd first seen them, and she had told the children so. Her admiration had quickly won her the gift of one of her own, which she had smilingly accepted and placed around her neck. One small girl had very seriously told her she would be glad to teach her how to make the ropes herself.

"But it is not so warm everywhere," she now told her charges, even as she thought how much prettier the necklaces of flowers were than the plain white collar of her plain dark dress. "Many places are very cold, and the people need more covering than these beautiful flowers. In those places, they take the wool from the sheep and use it to make clothes to keep themselves warm."

"How cruel," a little girl shouted. "They steal the wool and the poor sheep must be cold."

"The wool grows back," Alyssa explained.

"But the sheep is cold until it does," the child protested.

"Not if they take the wool at the beginning of the warm season," Alyssa replied.

The children shook their heads. "Warm season?" they asked.

Alyssa was beginning to feel as though all this was beyond her. How could she explain winter and summer to children whose whole lives were spent in an unending summertime? More than that, how was she to teach them to read from a book that assumed a completely different environment from the one in which they lived? The primers she'd so proudly distributed to them seemed to be creating more problems than they were solving.

She closed her book and told the children to do the same. Their faces shadowed with disappointment, but they obediently did as she directed, filing forward to stack the books neatly in a pile by her feet. Then they resettled themselves on the ground and stared up at her expectantly.

Alyssa pointed to a brilliantly plumed bird sitting on a branch just above the place where they sat.

"Let's talk about animals you know," she said. "Like that bird." She wrote the word on the slate in her lap. "B-I-R-D."

The children stared at the slate when she held it up, and nodded, their expressions solemn, as though this were terribly important.

"Now you write it," she directed.

They took up their slates and began to copy the letters, their faces grave with concentration, some with tongues tentatively on upper lips, others tight jawed with the effort required to perform the task she had set them.

"Excellent," Alyssa told them when she had inspected their work. "What other animals do you know?" she asked them.

One young boy shouted immediately, "Fish. We catch fish."

"Very good," Alyssa said, smiling as she wrote on the slate. "F-I-S-H."

Again there was the momentary quiet, the concentrated looks as the children wrote on their slates, and the smiles of relief when she commended their efforts.

"Beetle," shouted another who was eager to take part, even before she asked. He pointed to a beetle almost as large as a fist that was slowly working its way along the ground not far from Alyssa's feet.

Alyssa swallowed, and drew back her feet, hoping she didn't show to the children the feeling of queasiness the sight of the enormous insect aroused in her. She forced herself to smile.

"Excellent," she said as she wrote once more on the slate, "B-E-E-T-L-E."

The game went on for a while longer, the children joining in enthusiastically, giggling and squealing when their offerings met with approval, then working with that innocent, all-consuming concentration of which only the young seem capable. Alyssa found herself beginning to have almost as good a time as they seemed to be having.

"What may I ask is going on here?"

The voice was unmistakable and the tone sent a shiver down Alyssa's back as it instantly quieted the children.

Alyssa dropped her slate to her lap and looked up at Owen. She attempted a weak smile, despite the fact that his expression told her without question she had in some way sinned. She felt at that moment, she realized, much as she had all too often felt in her uncle's house.

"We're having a reading lesson, Reverend Remsen," she told him, trying not to let the uncertainty she felt become apparent in her tone.

"Wouldn't class be better held in the schoolroom, Miss Whitlock?" he asked.

"It was very warm inside," she explained. "I thought the children would be more comfortable out in the fresh air this afternoon."

"It is the purpose of school to teach the children, not to make them feel comfortable," he told her.

Alyssa considered to the upturned faces of her small

class. They all appeared to be so terribly anxious to learn, to please. For an instant she wondered what it was they were learning at that moment, what facts they were compiling about missionaries from the scene Owen seemed determined to make in their presence.

"That will be all for today, children," she told them. "I'll see you again tomorrow."

"Tomorrow is Sunday," Owen said sharply.

Alyssa smiled. "Of course it is," she agreed. She turned back to the children. "I'll see you all tomorrow in church."

They smiled at her and nodded, and scrambled to their feet. Carefully avoiding looking at Owen, they piled their slates in a stack beside the primers, then filed off into the jungle in total silence. As soon as they had disappeared from view, however, delighted shouts filtered back through the jungle from the direction in which they had gone.

"Was that really necessary?" Alyssa asked as she gathered up the stack of books and slates.

"You don't seem to understand the need to maintain discipline with these people, Alyssa," he replied.

"I wish you wouldn't refer to them as 'these people,' Owen. Children, it seems to me, are children," she told him firmly.

"There you are decidedly wrong," Owen said, his tone sharply lecturing. "These people are savages, and you must instill in them respect for the white man. Bringing them outside and playing games is not a way to instill respect."

"I thought I was teaching them to read," she countered. "And as for respect, I have no doubt it will be tendered to me if I earn it."

Owen sighed. He seemed too close to the end of his patience with her, and very close to anger. Alyssa realized she didn't care in the least.

"These particular children are of a race of people who are, by nature, lazy and cunning," he said. "It is best to keep them aware of their place."

Alyssa darted a sharp, cold look at him. "We are all the same in God's eyes," she said firmly. She smiled sweetly. "Surely that is not something of which I need remind a man of the cloth such as yourself."

Owen's cheeks grew sharply red.

"Be that as it may," he said, "in future, all classes are to be held in the classroom. And a proper atmosphere of discipline is to be maintained at all times. I think it would be wise if you limited yourself to the lessons that are found in the primers, and nothing more."

Alyssa felt her jaw grow hard as she bit back the words that she found herself aching to say to him, to tell him exactly what she thought about his attitudes concerning the Polynesians. But she held her tongue, realizing that antagonizing him would in no way change his attitudes, and would only jeopardize her own tenuous position on Banaba.

But she could not hide from the fact that Owen Remsen was a petty tyrant. She was beginning to come to the conclusion that his "edges," as Reverend Merricomb had called them, were permanent and unalterable. It seemed more than apparent to her that they would never be smoothed away as Merricomb seemed to think they would. Owen Remsen was a bigot, and there was nothing more to it.

"As you wish," she said, and turned away from him, not wanting to look at him any longer, aware she could offer no argument that would change his attitude.

He stopped her with a hand to her arm. She turned back to face him.

"And I'm afraid you are further encouraging the wrong attitude with these children by accepting such gifts as this," he told her as he pulled away the necklace of flowers.

She stared at the crushed blooms he dropped to the ground.

"It's just a handful of flowers, Owen," she said softly. "There is nothing evil about flowers."

He shook his head, as though he regretted the need to explain to her.

"It is unnecessary adornment," he told her. "It is our task to teach these children that it is inner goodness that has value, not outward displays of vanity. That handful of flowers is as much the devil's handiwork as a necklace of gold and diamonds."

Alyssa glanced briefly down at the plain cut of her dress. She'd worn clothes very much like this since the day she'd entered her uncle's house, and had often wished for something else, something prettier. The necklace of flowers had cheered her, had made her feel, for the first time in an endlessly long time, the way a woman feels when she wears something pretty. That, she supposed, probably damned her as vain and sinful in Owen Remsen's eyes. Somehow, she couldn't bring herself to care.

She returned her glance to meet Owen's.

"I will take pains to be more careful in the future, Reverend Remsen," she told him curtly.

Then she pulled her arm free and turned away, hoping she reached the schoolhouse before he found some further sin to inform her she'd committed.

Alyssa rubbed the heel of her hand on the surface of a small silver-framed mirror she had brought with her from Plymouth. Along with the silver-handled brush she was using to smooth an unruly mass of curls, the mirror had been her mother's, and she cherished it. That was the reason she had immediately hidden the small glass when she had unpacked it from her trunk. She simply could not bear the thought that Owen might see it and criticize it as being the devil's instrument, a symbol of sinful vanity.

Not that there was much chance Owen would find it hidden among her undergarments. She had been on Banaba for nearly two full days now, and in that short time she had become absolutely convinced that she had made the correct decision about him. She was certain at that moment that she would never be convinced to marry him. And that fact should at least assure her that he would never have the opportunity to delve into the contents of her dresser drawers and find her mother's mirror.

It did not assure her, however, that her decision would be easily accepted by Owen. At the end of the month he intended to return to the discussion of marriage, and that was one conversation she did not anticipate with any enthusiasm whatsoever. In fact, the thought terrified her. She was beginning to wonder if it was possible that he could bully her into marrying him. She had little doubt but that he would try.

She stared at her reflection in the mirror and told herself she still had nearly a month before she must worry about Owen's intentions. For the time being, her own intentions were to make herself as indispensable to the school as she could. Perhaps that way she could convince Owen to let her tend to teaching while he made his dogged attempts to cultivate the souls of his small flock . . . or whatever it was his carping was intended to do.

From Owen her thoughts slipped somehow to very different ones about Jason Draper. For a moment she told herself she had been a fool, that perhaps there might have been another life for her, a life with him, if she had been somehow different. But she pushed the thought away, telling herself that nothing she could have done would have changed his attitude about her, his condemnation of her as a missionary. She wondered what had happened in his past that made him hate the missionaries so, then told herself that perhaps he only needed the example of people like Owen Remsen to sour him.

In any case, Owen Remsen aside, she could make a life for herself in Banaba, of that she was absolutely certain. All she need do was remain firm about the small matter of avoiding a wedding, and find value in teaching the children.

All of which had very little to do with the cloudy reflection she saw staring back at her from the surface of the small mirror. The heat and the damp, she decided, must have adversely affected the silvering on the glass. Rubbing the heel of her hand along the surface did not improve the quality of the reflection. It pained her to think she might have ruined the mirror. She had little enough by which to remember her parents. The loss of even one of those items would be painful to her.

"You must hurry, miss. The bell will be rung soon."

Alyssa turned. Despite Owen's insisting that her situation was not proper, he had nonetheless made no attempt to find a duenna for her. What he had done, however, was send one of the women who cleaned the cottage to help her.

"Thank you, Lupia," she said. She smiled at the woman and then turned back to taming her curls, pulling the brush through her hair one last time, then setting it down and carefully pinning up the otherwise unruly mass in a stern little knot at the nape of her neck.

"Why do you do that, miss?" Lupia asked.

Alyssa turned back to face her once again.

"Do what?"

"Such pretty hair," Lupia told her. "It is a shame to make it so, so . . ."

The woman stopped, unable to find a word that would not seem too harsh. She shrugged when she could not think of one. But the shrug and her expression were more than enough. Alyssa realized that the word she had originally intended to say was ugly.

She darted another quick look into the glass. It was ugly, she thought, that tight little knot at the nape of her neck. Not like Lupia's beautiful fall of shining, dark hair. She put her hand to the pins, hesitating for a moment, wondering momentarily what Owen would say were she to appear in church with her own hair worn loose as the native women wore theirs. It would, she thought, probably lead to a fit of apoplexy or something worse. She let her hand fall without withdrawing the pins.

She slipped the small mirror back into her drawer, then turned back to face Lupia.

"Shall we go?" she asked. "It wouldn't do to be late on my first Sunday, now, would it?"

Lupia shook her head. Her expression was far more solemn than Alyssa's, perhaps because she had had more experience with Owen Remsen's disapproval. Alyssa stood and took her shawl from the back of the straight chair where she'd left it, and then the two women hurried out of her small room, through the deserted schoolroom, and out onto the green.

They walked quickly, realizing that the flow of worshippers had slowed to a trickle, and they were among the last to enter the church. As they hurriedly crossed the green, Alyssa saw that Owen was standing by the door to the church, stiff and proper in his dark suit and starched white linen shirt. He saw her coming and seemed to be about to turn away and enter. He had been waiting for her, she realized, and was not happy about the fact that he had been put to that bother.

But before he'd gone inside, a small, slender native man appeared at the side of the church. He glanced sheepishly up at Owen and hesitated for an instant, as though he weren't sure what he wanted to do. Then he straightened his shoulders and marched forward to the foot of the church steps.

Much to Alyssa's surprise, Owen barred his way, holding out his arms and preventing the man from entering the church. The two men stared at each other in silence for a moment, and then Owen raised his arm and pointed to the path that led into the jungle. The native man simply stood, his eyes wide and begging, but Owen didn't even glance at him. Finally the man turned away.

Slump-shouldered, he walked away, passing the pen at the far side of the cottage where a half dozen sows lazed in the sunshine with their young. The pigs, indifferent to his obvious misery, grunted and snuffled into the dirt.

Alyssa turned to Lupia. She wasn't at all sure she could believe what she'd seen.

"Whatever is going on?" she demanded.

Lupia shrugged, and shook her head.

"That is Namani, miss. Each Sunday morning it is the same. He comes, and Reverend Owen sends him away."

That made as little sense to Alyssa as what she'd seen.

"But why would Reverend Owen send anyone away from the church?" she demanded.

Lupia grew tight lipped, and shook her head.

"He is *mahu,* miss," was the only response Alyssa could elicit from her.

"What does that mean?" Alyssa demanded.

Lupia only shook her head again, and hurried forward, as though fleeing from the question. She nearly ran across the remainder of the green to the church steps.

Alyssa stood where she was, in the center of the green, watching Lupia dart up the steps, slide by Owen, and enter. Nothing of what she'd seen made any sense to her, and the woman's evasions only made her all the more determined that she was not about to dismiss the incident.

She marched across the patch of scruffy grass to the foot of the stairs. She stood then, and stared up at Owen.

He darted a glance at her, then put his foot to the first step as though to descend the half dozen steps to greet her. Apparently he changed his mind. Instead he turned and called out to someone to ring the bell. There was the sound of feet running, and Alyssa realized there must have been a boy waiting just inside the door for that particular order to be given.

Owen turned back to stare down at her.

"You are late for services, Alyssa," he told her. "Please hurry yourself. I'll escort you to your place and then services will begin."

She didn't budge.

"What just happened here?" she demanded. "Why did you send that man away?"

"He doesn't belong here," Owen told her.

He pursed his lips with displeasure, obviously liking neither the question nor the expression he saw on her face when she'd asked it.

"This is a house of God. Surely anyone who wants to enter belongs here."

"We can discuss the matter at a more convenient time, Alyssa. Will you come into the church now?"

She shook her head. "No, I will not. Not until you tell me what possible reason you could have to send that man away."

He was becoming visibly perturbed with her, but Alyssa stood her ground. Finally, realizing she would not move, he descended the half dozen steps and put his hand firmly on her elbow.

"There are many things you don't understand, Alyssa," he told her through tight lips.

She nodded in agreement. "That is why I've asked you to explain. What does the word *mahu* mean?"

His eyes widened in shock.

"Where did you hear that word?" he demanded.

"Lupia said that the native man was *mahu,* and that was why you would not let him enter the church," she told him. "What does it mean?"

His cheeks colored, and Alyssa stared at the bright red blotches, wondering what sins the native man could possibly have committed. What sins, indeed, could possibly be so heinous that it embarrassed Owen even to consider them?

"There are many things that happen here, things too horrible to be described," he told her.

"What could such a mild-looking man do that could be so terrible?" she demanded, picturing the native man in her mind. "Why, he is so slight, almost like a girl. Surely such a person could not be the monster you would have me believe him to be?"

Owen's expression grew hard as he determined to swallow his repugnance of the subject and tell her what she wanted to know.

"A *mahu* is one who practices onanism, Alyssa," he said tersely.

She shook her head. She'd never heard the word before.

"That means nothing to me."

"I believe I've told you that these people are without morals, that they are promiscuous and without restraint," he went on. "Men like that one, those the Polynesians call *mahu,* are the worst."

"I still don't understand," she murmured, completely confused now.

"That person you described as slight and mild goes with other men," he said finally. "Surely you would not have me admit such defiled filth into our church?"

At that moment the church bell, a rather small bell, actually, with a thin, not quite melodic sound, rang out. Despite the bell's soft tone, the sound of it was more than ample enough to prevent conversation in that moment. It gave Alyssa a chance to think through her confusion.

For she was confused. In the prescribed world in which she'd spent her entire life, such things did not exist, or if they did, were certainly well hidden. They were never even spoken of, certainly not in the presence of young women. And now she found herself filled with a bitter sense of revulsion that she knew she had no right to feel, and yet could not expunge.

When the air fell into silence and the last echo of the bell's chime had faded, she found Owen staring at her still, and she knew from his expression that her shock must be written clearly on her face.

"Do you understand now?" he demanded.

But despite the feeling of revulsion, still she realized she could not condone what Owen had done.

She shook her head slowly.

"No," she said. "Even a murderer has the right to pray, to ask God for forgiveness. Surely you have no right to keep this man from a house of prayer, no matter what it is he has done."

Owen's lips grew tight and thin. After all, he'd taken great pains with her, even overcome his reluctance to discuss the matter in order that she might understand. And still she remained obstinately contrary.

"I've tried to explain to you, Alyssa. I can not help but think this stubbornness of yours malicious and unnecessary. It is something that you would do well to curb once we are married."

Married. The word seemed to Alyssa to hang ominously in the air around her. A lifetime, and all of it spent with Owen Remsen's disapproving stare, with his eyes on her as he watched and waited for her to do something he considered sinful or improper. That, she thought, was as close to hell as she could think life could be on earth. Better for her to have been captured and killed by the cannibals on Nukuhiva. Her hands began to tremble.

Owen realized she was upset, but he misinterpreted the cause. He released his grasp of her elbow and slid his hand down her arm to enfold her hand in his. It was meant to be a gesture of comfort, but Alyssa was not in the least comforted by it.

"I understand how upsetting things must be for you here," he told her, his tone softened a bit now, for he'd apparently taken pity on her. "I would have protected you from this if you'd have allowed it. But perhaps it is best that you realize that there are many ugly things here, that despite the beauty of this island, there is a great deal of evil here, a great deal of God's work to be done." He smiled, the first smile Alyssa had seen from him, and his eyes shone with a sudden fervor. "And together we will do it, Alyssa," he told her. "Together we will make this place truly a paradise."

She pulled her hand from his grasp and turned away.

"I have to think, Owen," she told him.

"Certainly," he agreed. "After the morning services we can have a long talk."

"No," she said. "I have to be alone, to think."

She began to move away from him, walking toward the cleared path that led down to the cove.

"Alyssa!" he shouted, and started after her.

But just then the bell rang a second time and the sound of it halted him. He stood indecisive for an instant. Then he turned back, quickly loping up the stairs, his long legs taking them in twos. He hesitated a moment, straightening his jacket as he darted a last glance at her. Then he turned away and entered his church.

Alyssa didn't even turn back. She walked slowly, trying to understand the shock Owen's explanation had elicited in her. Despite her confused state, she knew that Owen's actions could only be termed bigoted. Surely he had no right to ban that native man from entry into the church.

She was struck suddenly by the realization that Jason Draper would have condemned her, too, for the revulsion she'd felt. He would have told her she was a narrow-minded missionary bigot. Perhaps she was just that, she mused. Perhaps her shock ought to prove that to her, that deep inside she was no better than Owen.

Jason . . . why, she wondered, did her thoughts continually turn to him? She had thought of him more times than she cared to admit during the preceding days, even though she was well aware that dwelling on memories could only sour her life on Banaba, a life that already presaged more than enough problems with which she would have somehow to learn to cope. But try as she might, she found herself continually measuring herself and Owen by Jason's standards. And more often than not, she realized that not only Owen, but she, too, was to be found lacking.

She had by now wandered as far as the top of the rise overlooking the cove. Still lost in her own thoughts, she looked out at the calm blue of the water, sparkling and brilliant in the morning sunshine. It took her a moment to realize that it was not empty.

At first, she told herself she imagined it, that some part of her longed for escape and so she'd simply manufactured the means for that escape and set it on the water, waiting to take her away. She bit her lip and dug her fingernails into her palms, sure that the discomfort would chase away the phantom boat she saw sailing briskly toward the dock.

It didn't.

There really was a boat out there, fore- and aft-rigged, two-masted and sleek, of the sort she remembered was called a ketch. And it was really sliding alongside the dock.

She rubbed her eyes, sure she was seeing things as Jason Draper jumped from the ketch's deck onto the dock and began tying up the lines that were thrown to him.

Chapter Fifteen

Alyssa felt her heart begin to thump wildly in her chest. It was Jason down there, a voice inside told her. He had realized that he loved her, and he had come for her before she could be married to Owen Remsen.

Before she had time to tell herself that the thought was foolish, that the Jason Draper she knew would sooner come to fetch the devil than a missionary, she started down the path toward the dock.

A second man stood on the deck of the ketch, watching Jason make the lines fast. Jason paused a moment and darted an impatient look in his direction.

"Will you hurry up, Jean? I swear, life on this island is too easy. It's made you fat and lazy for lack of any real work."

Jean Noyer, tall and dark haired and anything but fat, slipped his arms into the sleeves of the jacket of his white linen suit and then shrugged to settle it properly on his shoulders. After a cursory inspection of the crease in his trousers, he stepped carefully onto the slippery surface of the deck. It was obvious that he was taking great pains not to have a mishap that might occasion the staining of his pristine clothing.

"For God's sake, *mon vieux,*" he muttered as he ambled with an almost spiteful slowness to where Jason stood impatiently waiting for him, "I told you how these missionary fellows conduct their business. First there will be the Sunday morning services. Nothing is important enough to them to disturb the sanctity of their Sunday morning services. Yes, first they will preach to the poor natives, and tell them how sinful they are, and then and only then will they make time for the wedding ceremony. Now, if it were just old Merricomb, it might be different. But since this Remsen man arrived, there has been no thought of deviation from the schedule. You have heard, *mon vieux,* the bell has only just rung for services, so there is more than ample time to allow us to conduct ourselves like gentlemen, not impassioned schoolboys." He chuckled softly. "But that is just what you are, are you not, Jason? An impassioned schoolboy?"

"I'll thank you to keep your tongue still for once, Frenchman," Jason told him. "You are here to play chauffeur, nothing more. I'm starting to wish I'd left you at Beau Rivage."

"And miss this choice opportunity, Jason? Do you seriously think I would let you take my ketch with the prospect of such entertainment in the offing? You have no idea how dull life can be in a place like this."

"If the *Empress* weren't still under repair, Jean . . ." Jason told him through gritted teeth.

Jean chuckled once more. "As you say, *mon ami,* you would have left me at Beau Rivage. But as it is, you need my ketch, and so you need me. And as for casting me as a chauffeur, I really prefer to think of myself in the role of savior. If this young woman is the goddess you say she is, it would be a sin to let her wed that stick of a man Remsen. Have I told you he had the nerve to call me a godless papist?"

"At least a dozen times, Jean," Jason replied.

"A godless papist," Jean went on, ignoring Jason's disinterested tone. "How can a papist be godless, I ask you? The man's a fool besides being dry as dust and about as interesting. All the world recognizes Jean

Noyer as a pious and devout Christian, a man who dispenses charity as though it were water, a man who . . ."

"Who drinks like a fish and womanizes as though the earth were about to end and he was afraid he would not get his fill," Jason interrupted.

"Ah, but that is only natural, *mon ami.* You must treat each woman as though she were the only one on earth. It is only fair to idolize her, to make her feel like a goddess. It pleases her and then she is willing to please you, *non?* What could be fairer?"

"Will you please shut up and move your fat Gallic ass, Jean?"

They had crossed the dock, and now Noyer took the opportunity to look up at the climb he was about to make.

"Who is this angel come to meet us, Jason?" he asked. "Surely not your Mademoiselle Whitlock?" He shook his head. "*Non, non.* The bride would be wearing her wedding finery on her wedding day, would she not?" He beamed at Jason. "You are a better friend than even I could imagine, Jason. You have brought two beauties with you, one for me as well, and you kept mine a secret so I could be surprised! *Merci, mon ami!*" He clapped Jason firmly on the shoulder.

Jason ignored him. He looked up, spotted Alyssa, and began to run up the steep path, leaving Noyer behind to ponder his wordless departure.

But when he was still some twenty feet from her, he stopped and simply stood staring up at her. Funny, he thought—despite that unbecoming gray dress with the collar nearly up to her chin and the way she's pinned back her hair, she still looks pretty. No, beautiful. Those huge green eyes staring at you, she could have that and nothing else, and still she'd be beautiful. He pondered this thought for a moment and decided it did not bode well for him to be thinking this way, not about a missionary.

Alyssa, too, stopped, feeling suddenly awkward, not knowing what she ought to do, nor how she ought to greet him. She could find no words, nothing that would tell him what the sight of him had made her feel. Instead she stood, smiling at him, waiting, as a thick red blush filled her cheeks.

They were silent for a long moment, until Jason finally cleared his throat. He wanted to wrap his arms around her, hold her, tell her she couldn't marry Owen Remsen, tell her he wouldn't let her. But the sight of her staring down at him so cool and distant and self-assured unsettled him. She could at least tell him that she realized she was about to make a mistake, that she realized that she could never spend her life as a missionary's wife. But she didn't, and the words simply erupted, the baiting words he might have offered her before he'd realized he was in love with her.

"Well, Miss Missionary, am I to understand that your people do not hold with the frivolity of a wedding gown?" he asked. "Or is it just that you decided it would not be quite honest to wear white, knowing that it is a symbol of virginal purity?"

The instant he'd spoken, even before he saw the smile fade from her lips, he knew he'd made a mistake. Too late he wished he could call the words back. He climbed up a step toward her, but she backed away from him.

Alyssa felt as though he'd forced a blade through her heart. What a fool you are, she told herself. He didn't come to take you with him, but to gloat that he'd had what he'd wanted of you and see you married, passed on to another man like a rejected dish of half-eaten sweets. Well, if she was soiled and unfit to wear white at her wedding, that was his fault as much as hers.

"Why have you come here, Captain Draper?" she demanded.

"No greeting?" he asked. "No friendly welcome?"

She glared at him. "Why are you here?"

Noyer had climbed the hillside at a far more leisurely pace and now stood just behind him.

"You must introduce me to this angel, *mon vieux,*" Noyer interrupted, edging his way past Jason, obviously with no intention of waiting for the formality of an introduction. He climbed to where Alyssa stood. He took her hand in his. "As my mannerless friend stands mute, mamselle, I find I must introduce myself." He smiled and stared into her eyes as he raised her hand to his lips. "Jean Noyer, mamselle," he told her before he touched the back of her hand to his lips, "and I bid you welcome to Banaba."

"Mr. Noyer," Alyssa murmured, baffled by this strange interruption, but no more so than by the dapper and decidedly handsome figure of the Frenchman.

"Jean owns a copra plantation on the far side of the island," Jason said finally. He muttered the words reluctantly, almost a touch angrily as he realized the Frenchman had already begun to use his charm on her and not at all certain he approved.

"Ah, I see you've found your tongue, Jason," Noyer said. He smiled again at Alyssa. "He is really not a bad fellow, mamselle," he told her. He touched his forehead with his index finger and darted a conspiratorial look at her. "It is a small problem with his head, I think," he continued, whispering now. "He will not admit it, but I believe his nursemaid dropped him on his head as an infant."

Alyssa laughed. It was such a foolish thing to say, and Noyer's expression was so serious, that she couldn't help it.

"I am most pleased to meet you, Mr. Noyer," she replied. "Alyssa Whitlock."

Noyer pretended shock.

"Not the Mademoiselle Alyssa Whitlock who is to be wed this very day to the worthy Reverend Remsen?" he asked. "Why, we are come here to attend your marriage." (He pronounced it *mahr-ee-aj,* clearly exaggerating his own accent.)

Alyssa darted a look at Jason.

"I fear you have been misled, Mr. Noyer."

"Oh, please, we are neighbors, mamselle. You must call me Jean."

She turned her glance back to Noyer, and smiled. "Jean," she amended. "As I was saying, I fear you have been misled. There is to be no marriage today."

She darted another glance at Jason, and saw his eyes widen at her news. He's afraid I'll try to trap him, she thought. He was so smug and satisfied to think I was marrying Owen, and now he's afraid that I won't.

Noyer pretended concern. "I hope there is nothing wrong with the good Reverend?" he asked. "He was well enough when I last came by to play chess with old Merricomb."

Alyssa shook her head. "No, he is well. We just decided it would be wiser to postpone the wedding for a while," she replied, but she stared at Jason, not the Frenchman, when she spoke.

Jason felt a thick wave of relief sweep through him. At least she's not fool enough to marry that prig of a man, he thought. Let her tire of a missionary's life, he thought. It won't take her long to realize she was not intended for that. After a few months, it would be a simple matter to convince her to leave both Owen Remsen and the sort of life she could look forward to living on Banaba.

He smiled up at her. "It would seem we've come all the way around the island for no reason, then," he said.

Alyssa smiled sweetly. "You might care to attend Sunday morning services, just to make your trip worthwhile, Captain Draper."

Noyer laughed. *"Touché, mon ami,"* he said to Jason. Then he offered his arm to Alyssa. "If I may, mamselle,

I think my presence in that little church of yours is apt to make old Merricomb quite merry indeed. He has been trying to convert me for years, godless papist though I be."

Alyssa laughed. "Surely not godless, Monsieur Noyer?" she asked as she put her hand into the crook of his arm.

"Jean, *ma chérie,* Jean, if you please," Noyer admonished as she turned and they started to climb back to the top of the hillside.

"Certainly, Jean. But surely you can not tell me that the Reverend Merricomb thinks you godless?"

He shook his head. "Now that you mention it, *ma chére,* I do think it was that young man of yours who was of that opinion, your fine Reverend Remsen. But let me be the last to suggest him to be intolerant. That would, after all, be uncharitable and un-Christian, and as I was telling my good friend Jason, I am the most charitable of men."

Jason stood for a moment bewildered, wondering how he'd become so much a third and unnecessary appendage to the conversation. He began to climb the hillside behind them, the sound of Noyer's voice clearly audible to him, and about as interesting to him as the drone of insects on a hot night.

"Have I told you about my plantation, mamselle? It is heaven. You will, of course, come to visit soon. It would be a great pleasure to be the host to so charming and lovely a guest. Beau Rivage, I think, is very close to paradise." He sighed. "Two more years, I hope, and I will be able to leave it."

"But you have just said it is paradise, Jean," Alyssa laughed. "Why would you want to leave?"

"There is paradise and there is paradise, mamselle," Noyer told her. "It is my intention to return to Paris to live as a man of my station deserves. After all, Paris is even better than heaven, is it not?"

He darted a quick glance and a knowing smile back at Jason when Alyssa rewarded him with another laugh.

Alyssa looked from face to face at those gathered around the table that had been set out on the cottage porch. Owen and Merricomb on one side, Jason and his French friend on the other, Alyssa, acting as hostess, at the near end. They were an odd company, after all, Jason and Owen quite decidedly ill at ease with one another. In fact, Owen had seemed more than a bit put out when Merricomb had insisted the two remain for Sunday dinner, and Jason had seemed about ready to decline the invitation when Noyer had loudly and enthusiastically accepted.

Only Merricomb and Noyer seemed oblivious to the tension between the two men. As Lupia and two other servants set out platters of grilled fish and steamed vegetables, they chattered loudly while Owen glowered at Jason and Jason sat in stony, apparently bored silence.

"I can not tell you how delighted I was to see you enter the church this morning, Monsieur Noyer," Merricomb was saying. "I have often wondered at the feeling of triumph I would feel at the moment I saw you walk through those doors, and I must admit it was even greater than I had expected."

"I am delighted to have provided you with such a moment of exaltation, my old friend," Noyer responded, "but I am afraid even the persuasive sounds of the good Reverend Remsen's sonorous tones as he exhorts his little flock to saintliness could not convert me." He darted a glance at Owen. "Excuse me, but I think I am mistaken. We papists are the ones who think of saintliness while you missionaries simply preach sinlessness." He threw up his hands and smiled broadly. "But it is all the same, no?" Then, without waiting for Owen to interrupt, as he seemed about to do, Jean turned back to Merricomb. "But I fear I must disabuse you, *mon vieux*. I came not with the intention of mending my sinful ways, but simply to enjoy the sight of a lovely young woman's face." He turned and smiled at Alyssa.

"Whatever the reason, we are pleased to have you, are we not, Owen?" Merricomb replied. He passed a platter of fish to Noyer. "Try this parrotfish. I think you will like the way Lupia grills it with coconut."

Jean glanced at the platter, but did not reach out to take it.

"What a fool I am," he declared, and struck his forehead with the heel of his hand. Then he reached behind him and found the basket he'd returned to his boat to fetch. "I had meant this to be a small wedding gift to the happy couple," he said as he withdrew a bottle of champagne from the basket, "but I think a toast of welcome to Miss Whitlock deserves nothing less." He smiled broadly at Alyssa as he began to busy himself with the cork.

Merricomb eyed the bottle appreciatively and set the platter of fish back on the table.

Owen grimaced as he watched Alyssa return Noyer's smile. He obviously was not pleased with this burgeoning friendship, nor was he pleased with the strange enforced coldness he felt between her and Jason. It was odd, that coldness, as sharp as a knife and thick with a tension that spoke of things other than the short acquaintance of captain and passenger. He didn't understand what was happening right in front of him, but what he did understand was that he didn't like any of it.

"Perhaps you might save it until the wedding, Mr. Noyer," he suggested. "It has, after all, only been postponed for a short time, a few weeks at most, just time enough for Miss Whitlock to become acclimated to her new home."

"Ah, for such a happy occasion, be assured there will be another, perhaps even two," Noyer told him. "A Frenchman always manages to provide himself with a decent cellar, no matter how difficult the task." He smiled at Alyssa, then grew solemn as he turned back to Owen. "There is, of course, always the possibility that I might persuade this beautiful creature to desert you and your good works and marry me instead, in which case there will be not a mere bottle of champagne drunk, but my whole cellar emptied."

Owen glowered. "I will thank you, sir, to speak of my fiancée with greater respect," he hissed.

Noyer looked shocked and repentant, as though he did not realize he had said anything that could possibly offend Owen.

"No offense was intended, I assure you, *monsieur.*" He turned to Alyssa, and the look of shocked repentance disappeared to be replaced by a grin. "I heartily beg your forgiveness, mamselle. I truly meant no offense."

"And none was taken, certainly," she assured him, returning his smile and ignoring Owen's glowering look.

Jason stirred himself to speak for the first time since the meal had begun.

"I suggest you watch yourself with my friend Noyer, Miss Whitlock," he told her. "Beneath that meek and charming Gallic exterior lies the heart and soul of a born reprobate."

"Mon vieux," Noyer said in a hurt tone, but he grinned and seemed entirely unaffected by the slur.

Instead of turning to Jason, he kept his attention riveted on the task of uncorking the bottle. He pressed his fingers to the cork one last time. It flew off the bottle with a loud pop, and the bubbly wine overflowed.

Noyer quickly filled Alyssa's glass. "Mamselle."

But when he reached across the table to fill Owen's glass, he found a hand firmly covering it.

"I don't drink alcoholic beverages," Owen told him sharply.

Noyer smiled his knowing smile. "Of course you don't," he agreed, and he moved on to fill Merricomb's glass, then Jason's and his own.

"To Miss Whitlock," he said as he raised his glass.

Owen glowered as he watched the Frenchman empty his glass.

Alyssa found herself enjoying the situation. Owen's discomfort, his attempts to appear master of the situation while Noyer so completely upstaged him, was, more than anything else, funny.

She lifted her own glass as the Frenchman refilled his. She'd tasted champagne once before, but that had been a long time before, on a New Year's Eve, while her father was still alive.

"To new friendships," she offered, her eyes drifting to meet Jason's before she brought her glass to her lips.

"Alyssa," Owen hissed and put his hand on her arm before she could taste the wine. "I don't think you ought to be drinking."

She glanced down at the contents of her glass. The bubbles danced and jumped from the surface of the wine, and she felt she was holding a bit of magic in her hand.

She reluctantly let her glance drift to Owen's.

"May I remind you, Miss Whitlock," Jason stirred himself to say while he considered the contents of his own glass, "I warned you about him. Here he is, luring you to sin, and in the company of your own fiancé." He smiled at her, daring her to drink the wine.

Alyssa pretended to ignore him, but she inwardly bristled at his dare, knowing what he was thinking, that she would pretend to be what Owen wanted her to be, that she would be a hypocrite.

"But I recall no interdiction against wine in the Bible, Owen," she said with a sweetly questioning smile.

"Certainly not," Noyer agreed loudly. "Why, did not Jesus share wine with his disciples?"

Merricomb tasted the contents of his glass, sighed with contentment, then nodded.

"I believe Monsieur Noyer is correct, Owen," he said. "And the wine is delicious."

"There, you see?" Noyer gloated. He motioned to Alyssa. "Taste it, mamselle."

He waited expectantly as Alyssa, her eyes defiantly on Jason's, lifted the glass to her lips.

She'd forgotten from that other time long before what the sensation of the bubbles on her tongue and against the roof of her mouth felt like. It sent a shiver of delight through her, the dancing of the bubbles in her mouth, the sweet, heady taste of the wine on her tongue, and the long-ago forgotten sensation of the alcohol as it fell to her stomach and then rapidly through her system. She felt a tingle and a pleasant rush of warmth.

"Well, mamselle?" Noyer demanded.

Alyssa smiled at him. "Lovely," she told him.

"There, you see?" Noyer told Owen. "Will you not change your mind, *monsieur?*"

Owen pursed his lips in disapproval. "Certainly not," he replied. "I've no need for artificial stimulants."

Noyer laughed. "Ah, you missionaries. I admire your staunch refusal to allow yourselves even the smallest pleasures. You come here so determined, so pure minded, you live so sparingly. Ah, yes, I admire you. I don't say I understand you, but I must admit that I admire you."

He refilled his own glass and reflectively considered the contents.

"The reason we live sparingly is that we can find far better uses for what little money comes our way," Owen told him. "That single bottle of wine, the price of that bottle would buy a score of prayer books."

Noyer nodded thoughtfully. "Probably two score, my dear fellow," he said. "But two score of prayer books would not bring me nearly as much pleasure as does a glass of this fine wine drunk to welcome Mamselle Whitlock to Banaba."

"I daresay you'd find less pleasure in the prayer books than in a glass of the wine even were it drunk in a cave in absolute solitude, Jean," Jason suggested with a wry smile.

Noyer laughed. "I think you are right, *mon ami,*" he agreed.

Owen ignored them both.

"And where do you get the money to pay for that wine?" he went on. "From the copra. And the copra comes from the labor of the natives. You steal their labor to make your own fortune." He sat back in his chair, smug and satisfied that he'd finally managed to still Noyer's apparently endless flow of words. "You steal from them and give them nothing in return."

Both Merricomb and Alyssa, surprised with the outburst, turned to face Owen. Noyer, momentarily speechless, simply stared at him.

"Owen," Merricomb began, his tone gently placating.

But Owen swept him aside with a motion of his hand. "It's true," he told Noyer. "That wine is not even rightly Noyer's to offer."

Noyer's dark, tanned cheeks showed the flush of anger. The moment of speechlessness was past, and he leaned forward to Owen, his eyes sharp and hard.

"I pay the men who work for me, *monsieur,*" he replied. "Unlike you, who ask them for a portion of their catch or to work your plots of vegetables for nothing but the honor of having served you. As you Americans say, I think this time it is the pot calling the kettle black."

Now it was Owen's turn for anger. He leaned across the table, his eyes on Noyer's.

"In serving the mission, the natives have the honor of serving the Lord," he said flatly. "And what little we take we return by way of the school, the church, and what little we can do with what medicines we can bring here. What do you give them? The money you pay your natives, what can they spend it on besides what you sell at your store? Even there you steal from them by profiting from what they buy."

Noyer returned his angry stare. "If it is so great an honor you give them, then why is it most of the men come to Beau Rivage and not to you?" he demanded.

"Enough, Jean," Jason told him firmly.

Noyer darted a glance at Jason, then turned back to Owen. He seemed about to continue the argument, but instead suddenly smiled. He was a man of easy temperament by nature, and his anger was quickly dissipated.

"Besides," he said to Alyssa with a self-deprecating grin, "I make only a very small profit on what I sell in the store."

"But you don't deny it has made you rich?" Owen insisted, refusing to let the matter die.

"Please, Owen," Alyssa begged him softly. This whole scene was because of her, she realized, and it made her feel uncomfortably responsible. But more than that, it irked her that Owen persisted in trying to bait Noyer, especially when the Frenchman was making the effort to let the insults pass.

"Why should I deny it?" Noyer asked. "I came here to make my fortune, and that is what I intend to do." He smirked, sensing a hint of weakness in Owen, a hint of jealousy. "But I am no richer than this mission could be. After all, you hold claim to as much land as I have at Beau Rivage. Clear it, plant coconuts or pineapples, and you will have more than enough to buy all the schoolbooks and prayer books and medicine that will ever be needed on this island. Or is the only work you see fit to do the work of preaching, Reverend?"

"I would need to have money to have the land cleared and planted," Owen shot back.

Noyer smiled wryly. "A conundrum, is it not?" he asked. "You hate me because I have money and refuse to give it away, and yet you want it yourself, supposedly so you *can* give it away. I wonder, though, what you would do with it if you really had a fortune. I wonder if you'd be what you say you would be, or if you would become what you say you hate, if you would become me."

Jason was, for the first time since he'd set foot on the missionary land that morning, beginning to enjoy himself. He stared at Alyssa and saw the pained expression on her face. I wonder, he thought, if it's the argument that has upset her, or the possibility that Jean is right about her holier-than-thou reverend.

He drained the last of the champagne in his glass and leaned forward to take the bottle. When he'd refilled his glass, he looked up at Alyssa and smiled.

"I think your conundrum may have a resolution, Jean," he said.

"A resolution, *mon vieux?*" Noyer asked.

Jason sipped his wine. Then he set the glass down on the table, savoring the feel of the four sets of eyes turned to him. He smiled, then nodded.

"Yes," he said. "A resolution. You see, I know how to make our friend Reverend Remsen rich."

The moment he spoke, Alyssa knew what it was he intended to say. She turned her eyes to him and found his waiting for hers, ready to meet them.

"You speak in riddles, Jason," Noyer chided.

Jason shook his head. "No riddles," he replied. "I know how to make the good reverend quite wealthy, and ourselves as well, while we're about it."

Alyssa's mind filled with the memory of the cannibals, the sight of them sitting around the fire on the beach, the smell of their horrid dinner floating upward on the night air. The flush the champagne had given her faded instantly, and she found herself not only totally sober, but wishing that she had never allowed the three men to start their verbal battle. She could have stopped it before it started, she told herself . . . it need never have gone this far.

"Don't do this, Jason," Alyssa begged him softly.

Owen darted an angry glance at her when he heard her use Jason's given name. There *was* something between them, he thought, something more than a few days on a sailing vessel would precipitate.

"What is it he shouldn't do, my dear?" he asked Alyssa through tight, angry lips. He put his hand on her arm and pressed his fingers into her flesh, but she didn't even turn to him. Instead, she pulled her arm away, ignoring his question, keeping her eyes on Jason's.

"It's wrong, and you know it," she told him.

"Wrong?" Jason asked her. "What's wrong is leaving those pearls hidden away in that cave where they can do no one any good."

"Pearls? What pearls?" Owen demanded.

"The pearls the Tapuayans have dedicated as a treasure to their god. Surely you've heard of it?" Jason asked with a slightly goading smile. "The treasure of Nukuhiva?"

Noyer shook his head and again reached for the bottle of champagne. He emptied the last of its contents into his glass.

"That is nothing but a legend, *mon ami,*" he said. "There are hundreds of such stories about the cannibal tribes. The islands are rife with them."

Owen nodded. "And none of them more than words."

Jason smiled meaningfully at Alyssa.

"Why, didn't Miss Whitlock tell you about our little

adventure?" he asked Owen. He turned to Alyssa. "I'm surprised, Miss Whitlock," he said. "I'd have thought you kept no secrets whatsoever from your intended."

Owen slammed his hand down on the table.

"Whatever you're talking about, I suggest you say it out plainly. Now."

"Jason, don't," Alyssa begged one last time. "It will only end in someone being hurt, perhaps killed. Is that what you want?"

"This is none of your business, Alyssa," Owen told her firmly. "You will please allow Captain Draper to answer my question?"

Jason smiled. "Well, since you haven't told him about our little adventure, perhaps I should," he told Alyssa. He turned his glance lazily to Owen, aware that each moment he procrastinated only served to further anger the missionary. "The *Empress* was late arriving here on Banaba because of a storm," he began.

"I know that," Owen interrupted. "Get on with it."

Jason nodded. "It was a very severe storm. Miss Whitlock was thrown from the deck, and, gallant sailor that I am, I took it upon myself to take a longboat and fetch her back from the waves."

"Jason," Alyssa tried one last time.

"Alyssa, be silent," Owen warned her in a tense tone, then turned his attention back to Jason. "And then?" he asked.

"Well, it wasn't quite as simple as I thought it would be. The storm blew the *Empress* out of sight, and eventually took our little boat to an island—a deserted island, we thought, until a group of unfriendly looking fellows showed up from Tapuay. They had an unpleasant looking dinner, sang a few songs to their god, and then showed him his treasure."

"Treasure?" Noyer asked, his interest now piqued. "Why did you not tell me about this treasure?"

Jason shrugged. "I'm telling you now," he replied. "A

shell as big as my arm," he said, holding out that limb in demonstration. "And filled with black pearls. A day or two later, when the *Empress* showed up, I was about to relieve the god of the worry of a few of them. Unfortunately, the cannibals decided to have another picnic on Nukuhiva. We only just made it away with our skins."

Owen glowered at Alyssa. "Why didn't you tell me any of this?" he demanded.

"You never asked," she returned, tired of his tone, thinking only of the harm Jason was about to do. She turned her attention back to Jason. "Besides, Captain Draper is embellishing a good deal. Especially about the pearls. Perhaps he's imagined it, perhaps he isn't remembering quite precisely."

Jason grinned again. "Really?" he asked. "Everything that happened on that island is perfectly clear in my memory. Everything."

Alyssa met his glance and knew what he was thinking, knew it had nothing to do with the pearls. She remembered it, and all too clearly. So clearly, it hurt.

Jason turned his glance from Alyssa's eyes to Owen's. He wasn't sure what he saw in them—greed, perhaps, or jealousy, or a mixture of both. All he knew was that Owen wouldn't have let him stop now, even if that was what he wanted.

He put his hand into his pocket and withdrew a single black pearl nearly the size of his thumb, not quite perfectly round, but with a smooth, darkly glistening surface. He placed it on his palm and held it out for the others to see.

"If I've imagined it, Miss Whitlock, how do I come to have this?" he asked.

Chapter Sixteen

Jean Noyer took the pearl from Jason's palm and carefully examined it. When he returned it, his expression showed nothing less than amazement.

"Have you any idea of the price that single pearl will fetch, *mon vieux?*" he asked Jason softly.

Jason grinned, then nodded. "Probably as good as yours," he replied. "And now I ask you, Jean. Consider that amount multiplied by a hundred, by a thousand. There are more pearls just like it, hundreds more, and they're lying in a dank, dark cave, just waiting for an enterprising fellow or two to come along and find them and provide them with a more acceptable home."

"You wouldn't have anyone special in mind, would you?" Noyer asked.

Jason smiled at him and shrugged.

"If it's so simple a matter, why don't you go back and get these pearls by yourself?" Owen demanded. "Why are you so willing to share this supposed treasure of yours?"

"Actually, I had intended to do just that, Reverend," Jason replied. "But my crew, with the exception of myself and my mate, are all Polynesians. Liam had a hell of a time getting them even to go near the island to look for me and Miss Whitlock. They certainly won't go back there. The gods of Nukuhiva are taboo to them. There isn't a bribe I could offer them that would be big enough to convince them to be a party to entering a sacred cave and removing the god's treasure."

"Perhaps that should tell you something, Captain Draper," Alyssa suggested. "Perhaps you should consider that you oughtn't to go back there, either."

Jason offered her a stiff glance. "Besides," he went on, as though she had never spoken, "the *Empress* is a fairly large vessel, one that can be seen from as far away as Tapuay. It seems to me that if we wanted to sail in under cover of darkness, take the pearls, and get away before we are seen, a smaller craft might be more practical."

"Like my ketch, perhaps?" Noyer demanded.

Jason nodded and grinned. "Precisely, Jean. I've always admired you for your astuteness of mind."

"And me?" Owen persisted. "Why do you offer to share this treasure of yours with the mission?"

"Perhaps being surrounded by all this missionary selflessness, I find myself unable to keep such riches to myself," Jason suggested with a wry grin. But then his expression sobered. He leaned across the table, his eyes on Owen's, and there was no hint of humor in them. "Or maybe I'm just curious and willing to pay handsomely to have my curiosity satisfied. Maybe it's worth a third of those pearls to me to see if you're man enough to do anything besides sit here and talk, Remsen."

"How dare you?" Owen hissed.

Jason leaned back and shrugged. "Prove me wrong, Remsen. Show your fiancée here just how much of a man you actually are. Come with me to Nukuhiva for those pearls."

"Jason, how can you?" Alyssa shouted at him. "You've no right to come here and . . ."

"I've done nothing," Jason interrupted. "The good reverend was telling us what he'd do if he had enough money. I've simply offered him an opportunity to get some. He can come with me or not, as he likes."

Owen pushed himself to his feet, then stood, leaning over the table, his eyes on Jason's. His pale complexion had grown suddenly bright.

"I'll come," he hissed angrily.

Jason smiled blithely up at him. "As you like," he said.

Alyssa stared at Jason's satisfied smile, then at Owen as he straightened and stood glaring at Jason. Of the two, she wasn't sure which frightened her more—Jason, for his complete disregard for the consequences of what he was suggesting they do, or Owen, for his dogged determination to show himself better than either of the two other men.

Owen stepped back from the table and nodded to her and Merricomb.

"If you'll excuse me, I have evening services to prepare," he said, his tone terse, as though he really didn't care whether they excused him or not. "I expect I'll see you at evening services." He turned, walked down the steps and started across the green toward the church.

Alyssa glared at Jason. "This was wrong," she told him. "Cruel and wrong."

He didn't seem the least put off by her accusation. "Such moral indignation, Miss Missionary," he murmured as he reached for his glass. "It would seem you've become the same sort of paragon of moral rectitude as your fiancé."

Alyssa glared at him for an instant, then pushed back her chair, stood, and darted down the stairs after Owen.

"Owen," she said, when she had caught up with him. She put her hand on his arm.

"Really, Alyssa, must I remind you that this is the Sabbath? Surely you can manage to maintain a more solemn demeanor than you have by chasing across the green."

Alyssa gritted her teeth. She was trying to show him

that while he was preaching demeanor, he was foolishly risking his life.

"Owen, it's dangerous."

"Running?" he asked. "Not dangerous, really. Just unduly active for the Sabbath."

"Not running," she snapped. "I'm talking about going to that island, and you know it. Those natives won't just smile and tell you you've done something wrong. If they catch you there, if they even suspect you've stolen from their god, they'll kill you."

"How kind of you to be concerned about me, Alyssa," he replied with a smug smile. "But you really oughtn't to worry about me. I will be with Captain Draper. I sincerely doubt he would put himself in any danger."

"You don't understand," she insisted. "He would. He has not an iota of common sense, not so much as a rational thought to the consequences of what he does."

Owen arched a brow, and his eyes grew sharp as he stared at her.

"You seem to have more than a passing acquaintance with the good captain, Alyssa," he told her. "In fact, you seem to know a good deal about him and his character. I can't help but wonder why that is. Perhaps you might like to reveal why you didn't tell me you were stranded alone with him on Nukuhiva." His eyes bored into her. "Perhaps you might care to explain just what happened between the two of you while you were there."

Alyssa could see the anger in his eyes, and she could feel it in the air between the two of them, something palpable, something nearly alive.

"That's not what matters now," she told him. "What matters is that if you go there you could be hurt, even killed."

"I'm touched by your concern, Alyssa. But after this afternoon I find myself unable to keep from wondering if it is my safety that truly concerns you." He reached for her arm, grasping it hard enough to make it hurt.

"Or is it perhaps the thought that Captain Draper's life might be in danger that distresses you?"

She turned her head away, too angry to speak, too afraid that he would see in her eyes that what he said was true. It *was* of Jason that she was thinking each time she thought of the cannibals, Jason she imagined impaled on one of their bloody spears.

"Well, Alyssa?" Owen demanded. "You haven't answered my question."

She couldn't lie to him. Nor did she expect he'd believe her if she tried. Instead, she decided to take another tack.

"Owen," she said, "you can't just go in there and take those pearls. They belong to the natives of that island, not to us. It would be stealing. It would be a sin."

Owen dropped her arm and glanced back at the three men still sitting around the table on the porch. Then he turned his glance back to her.

"Those natives are cannibals, godless savages," he told her. "And the good those pearls could do for the mission is incalculable."

"Stealing is stealing," Alyssa insisted. "That doesn't change because those from whom you steal have different beliefs than you do."

She could see the anger in his eyes now and realized that questioning his motives only increased what had begun with his realization that she and Jason Draper were not quite the strangers she had led him to believe they were. She turned away again, doing as he had done and glancing at the men seated on the porch.

When her glance drifted to Jason, she found that somehow she could not pull it away. She was in love with him. She didn't like the fact, but she could not deny it. And loving him only made it harder for her to accept that he could do this thing, that he could lure Noyer and Owen into horrible danger for no real reason other than to amuse himself and fill his own pockets.

Owen stared at her profile and realized that it was Jason who held her attention. His hands balled into angry fists.

"Those natives have dedicated the pearls to their god," he told her. "But theirs is a false god. All I will do is channel their offerings to the true Lord."

She turned back to face him. "But Owen . . ."

"I have no intention of discussing the matter any further, Alyssa. And this persistent questioning of the morality of my decisions I find decidedly unacceptable. I will not have a wife who debates me in such matters. Once we are married I will not countenance your questioning my decisions."

"We are not married now, Owen," she told him sharply.

"A matter of which I am only too well aware, Alyssa. I had not intended to mention it, but your behavior with Draper and the Frenchman was not only unbecoming, it was openly flirtatious. I suggest you behave more circumspectly in the future. Remember, you are my intended. Your actions reflect upon me."

Alyssa gritted her teeth in anger. "I am terribly sorry if I have embarrassed you, Owen," she said. But she wasn't. She really didn't care. "You, however, have no right to dictate to me. We are not now married, nor, I think, are we likely to be."

There, she thought. She'd said it, blurted it out, plain and without the possibility that he could mistake what she said. She hadn't wanted to say it that way, but now that it was said, she was glad.

He stared at her in silence for a long moment, as though he were pondering some deep question. Then his expression grew sharp and sly.

"Don't tell me you think that sea captain will offer to marry you?" he asked her. "Or the Frenchman? Perhaps Noyer forgot to mention to you that he takes Polynesian women to live with him, three or four at a time. Do you really think he'd give them up for you? Or Draper? He's as godless as his papist friend. There are stories about him. Did you know he once tried to murder a missionary?"

Murder? Alyssa told herself it wasn't possible, that Owen was lying.

"I don't believe you," Alyssa murmured.

"Believe what you like, but I assure you, I am all you have here. You had best consider that fact before you make any decisions you will come to regret."

"Do you think threats can make me marry you?" she asked.

"I think you should consider your choices more carefully, Alyssa. I offer you a life, a future, a roof over your head and food to eat. Those men offer you nothing."

"You can't buy me, Owen," she told him sharply.

He stared into her eyes for a second, and then he smiled.

"We shall see," he told her.

He turned away and continued on toward the church.

Alyssa walked slowly as she returned to the cottage. It pained her to realize that Owen was not entirely unjustified with his anger with her. She had purposely goaded him, and she most certainly had encouraged Noyer. And she had no reason to justify what she'd done save that of showing Jason Draper she was not the meekly accepting little missionary's wife he'd thought he'd find when he returned to the mission, that she was not the hypocrite he thought her.

And what was she to think of those things Owen had told her about the two men? It seemed more than possible that Noyer kept Polynesian women. In fact, considering even the little she knew about him, she'd have been surprised had matters been otherwise, under the circumstances. After all, he was a man who obviously enjoyed women, who took great pains to be charming. And if she could believe what little she'd been told, the Polynesian women were both agreeable and obliging in such matters.

But what Owen had said about Jason, surely that could not be true. Jason might be arrogant and intolerant and a host of other equally unsavory things, but surely he was no murderer.

Just as she reached the front steps, Merricomb stood.

"I must help with the prayer books," he said as he started toward the stairs. He smiled at Alyssa. "I'll see you at evening prayers, won't I, Alyssa?" he asked her as he climbed down the half dozen steps.

She nodded. "Yes, Reverend Merricomb," she agreed with a wan smile.

"Good," he told her.

He stood beside her, staring at her, then took her hand in his and held it for a moment before releasing his hold and turning to cross the green to the church.

She stood where she was for a while longer, watching the old man walk away from her, watching the way the lowering sun shone off the back of his well-worn black jacket. How easy it would be, she thought, if Owen were a bit more like him, if he were understanding and compassionate. For of them all, Merricomb, she thought, was a truly good and selfless man.

If only Owen were like Merricomb, she mused, she might even be able to love him.

After a while, she turned to face the two men who still sat at the table. They were, she found, both staring down expectantly at her.

She ran up the steps and stood for a moment, glowering at Jason, before she dropped gracelessly into a wicker chair.

"I hope you're satisfied, Captain Draper," she told him angrily.

He grinned at her, obviously delighted with what he'd done.

"It would seem you and your fellow paragon of rectitude are on less than harmonious terms, Miss Missionary. Could it be there is trouble even in this paradise?"

"Mon vieux," Noyer whispered, his tone gently chiding.

"That is none of your business," Alyssa snapped at him. "And if you call me a paragon of anything, let alone rectitude, one more time, I swear I will strike you."

Jason shook his head. "Tsk, tsk, Miss Missionary. Swearing? And violence? From one of your naturally nonviolent temperament and vocation? And on the Sabbath. I am truly shocked!"

"What you are truly is unpleasant and arrogant," she told him. "Don't you realize you're about to go off to a place where you and anyone who is stupid enough to go with you will most likely be killed?"

"Would that really bother you, Miss Missionary?" He seemed almost pleased by the prospect. "Would it really concern you if I were to die?"

"Ah, but no one is going to die," Noyer injected. "I will assure you, *ma'mselle,* I would not allow anything untoward to happen to either of these worthy gentlemen. Or, most certainly, to myself."

Alyssa scowled. "You don't mean to tell me you're seriously considering going with them?" she demanded.

"Most certainly," he told her. "I came to Banaba to get rich. I would sooner plunge a dagger into my heart than give up the opportunity."

"And have you considered that one of those cannibals might just do you the favor of plunging that dagger for you?" she asked. "Have you asked your friend Captain Draper just how he intends to ensure that they won't be there when you arrive, all ready for one of their horrid little feasts and in need of the main course?"

Jason smiled. "I've thought about it. And I believe I can assure both Jean and your friend Remsen that the cannibals won't be there if we leave tomorrow."

"And just how, pray, do you know that, Captain Draper?"

He grinned. "It's quite simple actually, Miss Missionary. The first time the cannibals came to the island was the day after the full moon. The second was the day after the third quarter. It would seem to be apparent that they make their visits in lunar phases. That means we have three full days until the day after the new moon." He held up his hands in a gesture that implied even a fool could have come to the same conclusion. "Simple."

"Simple if you're right," she replied. "And what if you're wrong?"

He shrugged. "Then it would seem I'd have to reconsider the situation."

He seemed entirely undisturbed by the prospect.

"Reconsider the situation?" she repeated numbly. "What good will it do to reconsider the situation once those cannibals are roasting you over their campfire?"

More than anything, the vehemence he heard in her voice seemed to amuse Jason. He pushed himself away from the table and ambled across the porch to where she sat.

Alyssa watched him approach, watched his eyes as he bent and placed his hands on the arms of her chair. He leaned closer, until his face was only inches from hers.

"If I didn't know better, Miss Missionary, I'd think you were worried about me. I might even be flattered."

"Don't be," she shot back. She pushed angrily against him with her hands until he backed away and allowed her to stand. "If I'm worried about anyone, it's about the cannibals. Eating you would probably give them food poisoning."

A loud peal of laughter escaped Noyer's lips.

"I fear Mademoiselle Whitlock may be right, *mon vieux,*" he told Jason. "You are not my idea of a wholesome dinner."

Alyssa turned to the Frenchman.

"And you, you're no better. If you go with him, you're a fool."

She stared at him for a moment, half expecting him to agree. He didn't. She stamped her foot in frustrated anger.

Jason stared pointedly at her foot.

"I'm ashamed of you, Miss Missionary," Jason told her with false seriousness. "I'd have thought in your admirable loquaciousness you could devise a more original way of expressing your disapproval."

Alyssa glanced down at the offending foot, then back at Jason.

"You are arrogant and self centered, and you are risking lives for nothing more than your own stupid greed."

Jason's expression lost the hint of humor. "And the highly respectable Reverend Remsen?" he asked. "Just what do you think your fine fiancé's motives are?"

Alyssa's eyes narrowed in anger. "I hope you get what you deserve," she sputtered angrily at him. "You're a fool, Jason Draper." She glanced briefly at Noyer, then back at Jason. "You're both fools," she shouted.

Neither of them responded to this outburst. She would have to do something, she decided, and it would have to be something more forceful than trying to argue them out of going to Nukuhiva. She wasn't sure just what, but she would have to do something.

She pushed her way past Jason, down the stairs and ran toward the schoolhouse. Jason stood at the edge of the porch and watched her go.

Noyer stood and moved to stand beside him. He put a companionable hand on Jason's shoulder.

"You were right, Jason," he told him. "She's in love with you."

"I'm delighted to know you think so, Jean. I just wish she thought so, too."

"Time, *mon vieux* . . . just give it a bit of time. Il te faut prendre patience." He grinned.

"Time," Jason mused softly. "I wonder just how much time she'll be willing to give me?"

Noyer sobered. He stared out at the empty and peaceful green.

"If she's right about those cannibals, Jason, I warn you, my ghost will haunt you for the rest of eternity."

Alyssa climbed from the dock over the ketch's rail and carefully lowered herself to the craft's deck. The sun was just beginning to rise, and she turned to look to the east, to watch the bright golden fingers of sunlight reach up into the sky. From what she could see, it looked like it would be a beautiful, clear day. A perfect day on the water.

Unfortunately, she thought . . . why couldn't it be stormy? She'd even uttered a sincere prayer the night before that the day would be miserable and the water too rough for even Jason to think of taking the ketch as far as Nukuhiva. But it had been, it seemed, as useless as all her prayers seemed to be of late. Like everything else, she'd probably managed somehow to do it wrong.

Well, it was time she did something right. And that was just what she intended to do: to keep Jason from taking the ketch into the cove at Nukuhiva and going stupidly off, to save him from blundering into that cave and the arms of the cannibals.

She looked around the ketch. It wasn't a small craft, but it didn't afford nearly as many places as she had expected there would be where she might hide. The deck was clear and open, with none of the clutter that had been on board the *Empress* once she'd been fully loaded on Papeete.

She opened the door to the cabin, hoping she'd have better luck there. She was not really happy with the need. The thought of spending any time inside a cabin while the ketch was under sail promised only the misery of seasickness, but she realized she had no other choice.

She nearly tripped down the half dozen stairs. While the sky was beginning to brighten outside, little light made its way through the portholes, and the cabin appeared to be nothing more than a dark hole. She pulled the door behind her closed, felt her way slowly down the stairs, then stood waiting for her eyes to adjust to the meager amount of light that managed to eke its way in through the half dozen portholes.

Her eyes accustomed finally to the lack of light, she began to search the cabin. It wasn't large, but here at least there were cupboards, several of which appeared more than large enough to accommodate a determined stowaway. She opened the first and found it, incredibly, stocked with a complicated rack that was filled with bottles of wine. She uttered a quiet laugh of disbelief. Noyer was, she realized, more dedicated to his wine cellar than even his admitted reverence for the beverage had led her to believe a man could be. As she closed the door, she wondered how many of those bottles contained the same champagne they'd drunk at dinner the day before.

Several of the cupboards, she found, weren't really open cupboards at all, but were fitted out with tiers of drawers. These she ignored. She was searching for a place to hide, not looking through Noyer's personal belongings.

The light, she realized, was beginning to grow brighter, and she felt a twinge of panic. They'd be coming soon, she realized, and if they found her on board the ketch, they'd simply put her ashore. She had to find a place to hide, had to keep herself from being seen until it was the right moment. She scanned the walls of the cabin. Only three more large cupboard doors . . . hopefully one of them covered a reasonably large space where she could secrete herself.

She pulled the next door open and found it did, indeed, cover an open cupboard. But this one contained fishing equipment, rods and nets and two large boxes on the cupboard floor which she assumed contained lines and lures. Noyer, it seemed, took his fishing with nearly the same serious intensity as he took his wine.

She considered removing the contents of the cupboard and trying to hide the rods and nets and boxes in other places in the cabin. There was a good deal that she would have to move and that would take time—too much time. She could hear footsteps on the dock, and they were approaching the ketch.

She pushed the door closed, taking care to make no noise, and opened the next cupboard. And this time she found what she had been looking for all along. The cupboard was a simple closet, with rain gear hanging from pegs on the sides and back. Just as the first footstep fell on the deck above her, she climbed into the closet and pulled the door closed after herself.

Noyer moaned.

"Was it really necessary, *mon vieux,* to leave at such an hour? Hasn't anyone ever told you a gentleman never rises before the sun is fully risen?"

He cast a peevish look in Jason's direction, then climbed into the ketch, apparently resigned, but without any show of enthusiasm.

Jason laughed as he began to untie the lines that secured the ketch to the dock.

"How would you know, Jean? Surely you don't mean to try to convince anyone you're a gentleman?" He tossed the line into the ketch. "Here. Make yourself useful for a change."

Noyer caught the rope and carefully coiled it.

"It seems to me, Jason, I tolerate far too much from you in the name of our friendship," the Frenchman replied. "You may find you have pushed me too far one of these days."

"Think of the pearls, Jean," Jason told him as he unfastened the aft line. "That should keep your spirits from fading too far."

"You haven't explained why we need leave so early, Draper," Owen said. He was standing on the ketch's deck, watching the two other men busy themselves with the tasks of casting off. "It's barely dawn."

"And the perfect time to sail," Jason replied. "The tide is high, and with decent winds, we should make Nukuhiva just after sunset. With any luck, we'll have the pearls and be able to leave before the sun rises in the morning."

He threw the last line onto the deck and leaped aboard after it.

"You have this all thought out, don't you, Draper?" Owen demanded.

"All except what you'll do when you see that cave, Remsen," Jason replied. He smiled, apparently enjoying the prospect, as he edged his way past Owen and began to unfurl the mizzen. "I'm betting that you won't have the grit to go near the place."

Owen turned, following Jason with his eyes. It seemed to annoy him, the way Jason went about his task with such confidence, such certainty that he knew precisely what it was he was about.

"And just what is there about that cave that would require what you so quaintly refer to as 'grit'?"

Jason turned to face him, the mast still half tied, but for the second ignored. He grinned a wide, pleased grin that stretched from ear to ear.

"The dead, Remsen. The whole of the cave is littered with the remains of the dead."

"Skeletons?" Owen asked. "What could be so frightening about a few skeletons?"

"Did you ever think that perhaps the Polynesians have a reason to invoke spirits, Remsen? Did you ever stop to think there might be some things in this world of which you have absolutely no comprehension, things no less real simply because you don't recognize them?"

"This is nonsense, Draper," Owen hissed at him.

Jason shrugged and returned his attention to setting the mast.

"We'll see," he replied. "But I can assure you, whether you care to believe it or not, that cave is filled with the spirits of the dead. And I don't think you're man enough to face them."

"I'm beginning to tire of your suggestions that I am a weak sister, Draper," Owen hissed.

Jason shrugged. "Oh, I'm not suggesting anything, Remsen. I'm telling you straight out that I think the only courage you have is reserved for telling people weaker than yourself what they can or can't do in their lives."

"I preach the Lord's word," Owen told him sharply. "It is what I was called to do."

"Called, were you?" Jason asked. He finished with the mizzen and went forward to the jib as Noyer guided the ketch into the center of the cove. "The Lord's work, is it, that you do?" he called back to Owen. "For the next few days, let me suggest you keep your sanctimonious drivel to yourself. Neither Jean nor I am under any delusion as to why you're coming with us, and it has nothing to do with the Lord's work. It's greed, Remsen, pure and simple, and no different from mine or Jean's. You missionaries come to the islands loudly proclaiming that you intend to do good, and you end doing very well for yourselves."

He looked up at the sails, seemed satisfied that they were set properly for the wind, and started aft, to where Noyer stood at the wheel.

"We come to save pagan souls," Owen insisted, following along behind him. "If a mission prospers, it is the Lord's will, a reward for selfless labor."

"Save it for your flock, Remsen," Jason told him. "They're the only ones who will believe you." He laughed suddenly. "No wonder Alyssa refused to marry you. She's certainly too smart to swallow any of the rubbish you spew out."

Owen grabbed Jason's shoulder and pulled it until Jason turned to face him.

"What has Miss Whitlock to do with any of this?" he demanded.

Jason shook his head. "Nothing," he replied. "And everything. It occurs to me that when we return to Banaba and you're forced to admit to her that you're nothing more than a bag of wind, she may just decide she's had more than enough to do with you already."

Owen's cheeks turned red with rage. "I demand to know what happened between the two of you while you were on that island," he hissed.

Jason shook his head. "If you're looking for answers, Remsen, I regret to inform you that I have none to give you. You'll have to ask Alyssa," he replied.

"Bastard!" Owen hissed, and balled up his hands into fists.

"If you want to fight, however, I'll be happy to oblige you. When we get back to Banaba. In the meantime, let me remind you that I'm captain while we're on board this ship. In case you don't know what that means, I'll tell you: a captain is God while at sea. Remember that. And stow your sanctimonious anger. I'm getting bored with it."

With that Jason turned away and strode to the wheel, where Noyer stood half asleep, trying to steer the ketch out of the cove and into the open water of the ocean.

"You look like hell, Jean," he told Noyer. "You shouldn't have sat up half the night drinking."

"What else was there for me to do, *mon vieux?*" Noyer protested. "The women on this side of the island have all been tainted with that foolish missionary purity. There was nothing for me but to drink and mourn the fact that I will never have the opportunity to make love to that angel, Mademoiselle Whitlock."

Jason scowled. "I suggest you watch what you say about her in front of Remsen, Jean," he said. He grinned then. "I suggest you watch what you say about her in front of me, for that matter."

"Just an expression of my admiration, Jason," Noyer assured him. "Nothing more."

Jason sighed.

"Go on below and get some sleep, Jean," Jason said as he took the wheel.

"Bless you, *mon vieux*," Noyer muttered as he staggered forward to the cabin. "Remind me to name my firstborn son after you."

"You already have a firstborn son, Jean," Jason reminded him. "You already have three."

"Ah, I do, don't I?" The thought seemed to bewilder the Frenchman. "In that case, remind me to name the first one born in wedlock after you."

Jason laughed as Noyer pulled open the door to the cabin.

Chapter Seventeen

Alyssa knew the instant when the ketch left the calm waters of the cove and ventured out into the ocean. With the movement of the craft as it was struck by the waves came the misery of seasickness, a misery that was only intensified by the close air in the tiny cupboard. The space seemed to her to be growing smaller with every passing moment.

She pushed the cupboard door an inch or so ajar and stared out into the cabin. Just as she did, the door above opened and Jean Noyer entered. She froze, unsure as to what she ought to do. If she tried to pull the door to the cupboard closed, she feared the Frenchman might see the movement. But if she left it ajar, he might see her huddling among the slickers.

Her fears were groundless. Noyer stumbled into the cabin, then fell onto the narrow cot on the far wall without so much as bothering to glance toward her hiding place. She carefully pulled the cupboard door closed, until there was just a narrow slit through which she could see out into the cabin. Noyer was asleep in minutes.

In only a few moments he began snoring softly, the sound an even, deep drone that somehow seemed to mesh with the ketch's movement on the waves. The sound only intensified Alyssa's nausea. She was beginning to feel totally miserable.

She wondered if she dared step out of the cupboard. Just for a moment, she told herself, just long enough to open one of the portholes wide and get a breath of fresh air. If she was careful to make no noise, she wouldn't wake Noyer.

But as she pushed the cupboard door open once more, Noyer grunted and turned, frightening her back into her hiding place. Sick but resigned, she slid down the side of the cupboard until she sat huddled on its floor, her arms around her knees.

She closed her eyes, telling herself that she hadn't slept the preceding night, that she ought to be tired enough to sleep even in this cramped little place, even with the misery that slid from side to side in her stomach. If she slept, she wouldn't know how sick she felt.

She wasn't exactly right about how tired she was. For what seemed forever, she sat, hugging her knees and silently wishing she could just die rather than feel as she did. But eventually exhaustion and the sheer boredom of being in the dark, enclosed place had its effect.

She drifted off to an uncomfortable sleep that was filled with unpleasant dreams peopled by leering cannibals dancing around a huge fire over which she, Jason, and Noyer were being slowly roasted. From time to time one of the cannibals would pause, approach the fire, poke one of them with his spear, then returned to his dance. But the strangest part of the dream was when she recognized one of the cannibals as Owen Remsen. Nearly naked like the other natives, his pale limbs and torso shone dully in the light of the flames, differentiating him from the rest. In her dream she followed him with her eyes from her place on the spit, mesmerized by his presence among the cannibals. Finally it was his turn to stop and stab her with his spear. When he came forward, he smiled at her and told her he had warned her about running across the green on the Sabbath. "This is the just payment for sin," he said before he went about his business of poking her with his spear and then returning to the cannibal's dance.

It did not surprise her that she had absolutely no regrets to leave the dream when a clatter on the stairs woke her. She started, but quickly settled herself when she remembered where she was and why she was there. She sat huddled and stiff in the cupboard, listening to what was happening in the cabin.

"Enough, you lazy Gallic drone," Jason called down to Noyer as he bounded noisily down the stairs. "It's well past noon. If you can't make yourself useful as a sailor, you can at least find us some food."

Noyer groaned and stirred.

"Take a bottle," he muttered as he pointed to the cupboard door where Alyssa had found the wine. Then he groaned again and turned his back to Jason, and pulled his pillow over his head in the vain hope of returning to sleep.

"Not wine, you degenerate. I need food," Jason shouted at him, then pulled away the pillow.

He laughed when Noyer sat bolt upright, a pained expression on his face, and put his hands over his ears.

"*Mon Dieu,* Jason. Is there not so much as a shred of humanity in that barnacled nautical hide of yours?" he asked. "Can you not see that I am a man in extreme pain?"

With considerable effort he pushed himself to his feet and began slowly to strip off his soiled shirt.

"I might have been persuaded to feel some sympathy if I didn't know you were the cause of your own destruction, Jean," Jason replied. Apparently, he had no intention of offering any pity. "Get some food out of that larder you keep on this floating private bordello of yours and bring it up on deck."

"You shock me, Jason. Such language! You certainly cannot blame me if the island ladies find me and my little craft irresistible and beg me to take them for moonlight rides."

Jason laughed. "It's only that they take pity on you, Jean. And that they believe a man, any man, should not be forced to sleep alone. The generosity of women, I must admit, never quite ceases to amaze me."

"Your derision pains me, *mon vieux*."

"Not as much as the hangover, I think," Jason replied with a short laugh. Then he started toward the steps, but paused when he noticed the opened cupboard door.

"I thought I'd taught you better, Jean. A good sailor makes his cabin secure, especially at sea," he scolded Noyer and he pushed the door closed.

A small squeal of pained surprise escaped Alyssa's lips as the door struck her elbow.

Jason started.

"What have we here?" he asked Noyer.

He pulled the door open, and then stood staring down at Alyssa.

Noyer came to stand at Jason's side. He peered into the open cupboard, then shook his head.

"I think I'm hallucinating, Jason," he said. "I must have a worse hangover than I thought."

Jason put his hand on Alyssa's arm and pulled her out of the cupboard.

"I don't suppose you'd care to explain just what you're doing in there, would you, Miss Missionary?" he asked.

Alyssa stretched her cramped arms and legs, savoring the feeling after hours spent in the confined space. Then she primly brushed at her wrinkled skirt.

"I came to keep you from getting yourself killed," she said when she'd settled herself and found Jason still staring at her, expectantly awaiting an answer.

Jason turned to Noyer.

"I think I'm the one who's hallucinating," he said.

"Don't be ridiculous," Alyssa told him.

"Would you care to explain, *ma chère,* why you were hiding in so," Noyer glanced into the cupboard, "so unlikely a place?"

"I told you," she replied. "To keep you from getting yourself killed. You should be thanking me."

Noyer put his hand to his head, touching it gingerly as though to reassure himself it was still firmly attached to his neck and that that particular portion of his anatomy was still connected to his torso.

"Merci, chérie," he muttered without much enthusiasm.

He reseated himself on the cot he'd just vacated and sat staring at her and Jason.

"I don't suppose you'd care to explain, Miss Missionary?" Jason persisted.

"Do you have something to drink?" Alyssa asked. She looked around the cabin. "I'm terribly thirsty."

Noyer pointed to the liquor cabinet.

"For God's sake, Jean," Jason said.

He opened the one cupboard Alyssa hadn't explored and revealed what appeared to be a fairly well-provisioned larder. He removed a glass from one of the shelves which he filled from a jug of tepid water.

He handed the glass to Alyssa.

"Thank you, Captain Draper," she said primly as she took the glass. She smiled at him and then slowly emptied the glass, aware that he was growing more and more impatient with her as the moments passed.

"Now, if you're perfectly comfortable, Miss Missionary . . ."

"But I'm not," she replied. "If you must know, I'm feeling decidedly uncomfortable. Could we please go up on deck?"

She started to move toward the stairs.

Jason grabbed her arm. "Not so quickly, Miss Missionary. You owe me an explanation."

She turned to face him and smiled in satisfaction.

"You can't go to Nukuhiva now," she told him.

He shook his head. "I don't think I follow your logic, if you have any, Miss Missionary."

Alyssa shrugged her arm free of his grasp. "You certainly can't condone taking me back to that place. So you'll have to take me back to Banaba. You just told Jean it is already past noon, so that means it has taken half a day to get this far. It follows that it would take you half a day to return to Banaba. And that means you couldn't possibly get to Nukuhiva before the new moon, which, according to your logic, is when the cannibals will be there. So you might just as well give the whole thing up, at least for a while, long enough for your two friends to realize how totally insane this venture is." She offered him a dazzling smile. "It would seem your greed will not be satisfied so easily as you thought it would be, Captain Draper."

"You're wrong on two points, Miss Missionary," Jason told her. "I have only one friend with me." He nodded toward Noyer, who still sat, head in his hands, in obvious misery. "And I don't think I'll let you dictate to me what happens now. I think what I'll do is let your friend and my friend decide whether or not we go back, or if we go on to Nukuhiva. Let's just see how my greed compares to that of your sanctimonious friend Owen."

"You can't be serious," she told him.

"Oh, but I am, Miss Missionary. This is, after all, a completely democratic venture."

"It won't be fair," she told him. "You and Noyer will outvote Owen."

"Let's wait and see, shall we?" he suggested. Then he lifted the shirt Noyer had cast off and threw it at him. "Make yourself presentable, Jean," he said. "After all, it would seem we're traveling with a lady. And hurry yourself up on deck with the food. At Miss Whitlock's behest, we have a small exercise in democracy in the offing."

He motioned Alyssa toward the steps.

"Ladies before gentlemen," he said with a tight smile.

"Pearls before swine," Noyer added with a short laugh.

Disgusted with them both, Alyssa swept by Jason and climbed up the steps to the deck.

Alyssa nibbled at the piece of cheese Noyer had just handed to her, and wondered how she had gone from seasick and miserable to feeling not only perfectly well, but also hungry in the half hour she'd been up on deck. She took a deep breath of the fresh sea air, leaned her back comfortably against the sun-warmed planks of the ketch's side, and stared out at the sunlight on the water. Had circumstances been different, this alfresco lunch on the ketch's deck might have even been pleasant for her.

But circumstances were not different. Owen, she found when she darted a quick glance in his direction, was still silently glowering at her, as he had been since Jason had appeared with her on deck. And Jason, who ate his meal while standing at the wheel, seemed to be taking great pains to pretend she was not there, now that he'd made his little speech about allowing Owen and Noyer to consider their decision over lunch. All things considered, he seemed to be entirely enjoying the situation save for the lack of what he considered acceptable comestibles.

"Couldn't you find anything but cheese and crackers in that larder of yours, Jean?" he mumbled as he gnawed the last of his cheese.

"You should have told me before we left Beau Rivage that you intended us to take a two-day cruise, *mon vieux*," Noyer replied dryly. "I would have had the place stocked with *Pâté Strasbourg* and *Boeuf Normande.*" He darted a smile at Alyssa, offered her a biscuit which she accepted with a nod, then turned back to Jason. "I don't suppose you'd care for a glass of wine to wash down the cheese?"

Jason scowled, but before he had the opportunity to reject the offer, Owen spoke.

"Enough of this . . . we've all had our say. I think it time we decided whether we turn back or not."

"All right," Jason agreed. "Let's get on with our little vote." He smiled at Noyer. "Jean? How do you say?"

Noyer glanced briefly at Jason, and then turned his stare to Alyssa.

"I know this is not going to please you, *mon vieux*, but I fear I must vote in favor of turning back. Miss Whitlock's safety is too important for us to take a chance of endangering it."

Alyssa gasped. She'd been certain from the talk among the three men during their makeshift meal that Noyer would vote to go on despite her presence on board the ketch. She smiled as she filled with the satisfied feeling of having won.

"Think of the money, Jean," Jason muttered angrily. He, too, had been expecting Noyer to vote with him. "The longer we wait, the greater the chance those natives will move the pearls to another hiding place. You could lose it all if we don't go now."

"I understand this, Jason," he replied. "I assure you I have listened to every word you and the good reverend have uttered, despite the pounding in my head. But even if it means losing the pearls, still I think we must return Miss Whitlock to Banaba."

"There," Alyssa said, turning to Jason. "We go back."

"Not quite so quickly as that, Miss Missionary," he told her. "I vote that we go on." He turned to Owen. "Well, Remsen?" he asked. "Do you take the chance that we lose the pearls?"

Owen turned to Alyssa as he spoke, just as Noyer had.

"I vote that we go on," he said without so much as a quiver of indecision in his tone.

Alyssa dropped the piece of cheese she held in her hand. "You're not serious, Owen?" she demanded.

"I most certainly am, Alyssa," he told her sharply. "You are here by your own choosing, as are we all. If Draper's opinion is to be trusted, we have this night to take the pearls without threat from the cannibals, perhaps the last we may ever have. I can not ignore the good captain's point, that the natives might very well move the pearls, which I find entirely logical. Given that you remain on the ketch while we are on the island, I am sure you will be quite safe."

"But you don't need the money that badly," she insisted.

"It would seem you have very little idea of what I do or don't need, Alyssa," he told her. "Those pearls can transform the mission."

"The mission can get along without the money," she argued. "It's done well enough so far."

"Not well enough for me," Owen countered. "I intend to make something of it, to make something of my life. I don't intend to grow old like Merricomb, with nothing to show for a lifetime's effort save a handful of converts and a single suit that's gone shiny from too much wear."

"I should say Reverend Merricomb has a good deal to show for his life, Owen. And if you don't see that, you're blind."

Owen ignored her. He turned to Jason.

"I vote that we go on," he repeated, obviously considering the discussion finished. "And that, it would seem, settles the question."

Jason seemed entirely satisfied with the results of the vote. He grinned at her. "It looks like you don't get the opportunity to save us all from ourselves, Miss Missionary, despite your doubtless fine intentions."

"You're all the same," Alyssa hissed, looking at the three of them in turn. "You're all greedy fools."

She scrambled up off the deck to her feet and turned away from them, walking forward, feeling angry and ridiculous at the same time and wanting to get away from the three men. She'd been so certain when Noyer had voted to turn back.

More than anything else, it pained her to realize that what Jason had said about Owen was true. No matter that she found him personally unlikable, still she had thought him truly dedicated to the mission. But it was now obvious to her that he was dedicated to nothing except his own position, to making himself more powerful and more important than anyone else, even if it meant risking lives as he went about the task of making his own little kingdom for himself. It occurred to her that he might very well have chosen to become a missionary because it provided him with the opportunity to be in charge, something life in Plymouth might never have given him.

She felt shaken and disgusted by what she now saw in Owen, but no less than that, she felt suddenly adrift. Because even if the excursion to Nukuhiva proved to be no more dangerous than Jason assured them all it would be, still she knew she could not go back to work at the mission at Banaba. It would be impossible for her to be party to Owen's delusions. His vote had stolen from her the one thing she had clung to, the certainty that she could always be part of something meaningful, something useful, that by teaching in the mission school her life would serve a purpose. Now, with the realization that the mission was nothing but a way for Owen to find the control another life might have denied him, she knew she could not return there.

"Surely it is not so bad as that, *chérie?*"

She turned and found Noyer had followed her. He still looked haggard, but his pained expression had been replaced by one of concern.

"Isn't it, Jean?" she asked warily.

He shrugged. "Probably it will be as Jason says," he assured her. "He is usually right about a great many things—the tides, the weather."

"Those things do not concern the cannibals, Jean," she replied.

"No, they do not concern people. But still, perhaps he is right."

She nodded. "Perhaps," she agreed reluctantly.

"Then just think," he told her. "We will all be rich."

She shook her head. "I don't want to be rich," she told him. "I have no need of that."

"Ah," he said, nodding. "You missionaries." He grinned. "I forget how selfless you are. Perhaps it is because I myself am so selfish."

"Not so selfish as you would have me believe, I think, Jean," she replied. "You were the only one who voted to go back."

"My great weakness, *chérie,*" he said, and smiled gently. "I am putty when I look into the eyes of a beautiful woman."

She shook her head. "I think you are much better than that, too. I think you are much better than you would have the world think you . . . unlike Owen, who I now see is much worse." She looked down at her hands. "I've been a fool, thinking I could trust him, believe him."

"But not all the missionaries are like Remsen, *ma chère,*" Jean reminded her. "There are those like Merricomb."

"Yes," she murmured. She thought back to the way the Reverend and Emma Styles had treated the natives on Papeete. They'd been kind to her, but to the natives they had been superior and arrogant. She had tried not to see it, but she had not been entirely able to ignore their manner, their way of silently proclaiming themselves and their morals and ethics superior. Now memory of the way they'd acted toward the natives returned to her with painful clarity. She turned back to Noyer. "But most are not like Merricomb, are they, Jean?" she asked.

He could see that the realization was unpleasant for her, but he found he could not lie to her, not even to reassure her.

"I have only my limited experience, *ma chère,* but from what I have seen, I can only say that I fear not," he replied gently.

"That's what Jason tried to tell me at the start," she murmured.

"I think that is what this was all about, *chérie,*" Noyer told her quietly. "I think he began all this just because he wanted to teach you a lesson."

"Well, he should be quite happy. I believe him now," she said. "If all he wanted was to prove he was right, he's won. Why doesn't he give all this up and go back?"

"Because Jason would like to be rich, *ma chère.* Perhaps not so much as I, but still he would like to be rich." He grinned at her. "You will be rich, too, if this goes well."

She shrugged. "I told you, that means nothing to me."

He took her hand in his. "Then what is it you do want, *chérie?*" he asked.

She glanced toward the ketch's stern, to where Jason stood by the wheel. She hadn't meant it to be, but the look was more than answer enough to Noyer's question, and she forced herself to turn away when she realized what she was silently telling him.

"It doesn't really matter, does it?" she muttered as she walked away from him.

* * *

Alyssa stood on the ketch's deck in the near darkness, her eyes straining in the thin glimmer of light cast by the moon to see Noyer and Owen lower the ketch's lifeboat.

"Just stay here, be quiet, and don't light any lamps," Jason told her as he carefully adjusted the shoulder holster he'd donned and settled his pistol into it. "Lights can be seen long distances on the water, especially on dark nights like this."

"You've already made your instructions more than clear, Captain Draper," Alyssa told him.

"If I've made myself completely clear to you, Miss Missionary, then it won't be necessary to remind you not run off and do anything foolish, none of those absurd things I've come to expect from you. Rushing off without a thought to what you are doing is one of your most endearing but exasperating qualities."

She turned to face him, suddenly furious with him, and not quite sure why. Perhaps, she thought, it was simply that she was afraid, afraid he might be hurt, afraid she might never see him again. But the fear was probably completely irrational. The lagoon was as quiet and empty as he had assured them all that it would be. There was absolutely no sign of any native canoes, no sign whatever of the cannibals.

"I'm not the one who's rushing off to that island now, am I, Captain Draper?"

He grinned. "Not if you obey orders," he agreed.

"I don't suppose it would do any good to ask you one last time not to go?" she asked. "We could turn around, leave this place."

He shook his head. No, she thought, nothing would induce him to leave without his precious pearls. That was all that mattered to him, the fortune that lay waiting inside that cave. Nothing else could compete with that. She certainly couldn't.

He started to turn away, to the lifeboat where Noyer and Owen waited with obvious impatience for him to join them, but he changed his mind and turned back to her. He took her hand and held it firmly in his.

"Perhaps when this is over, you and I might come to an understanding, Miss Missionary," he said.

"Understanding?" she asked. "What kind of understanding?"

"It would seem that you're not entirely pleased with the good reverend," he told her.

"Even if that's true, what business is it of yours?" she demanded.

"None, I suppose," he said, put off by her tone. "Unless you want it to be."

She stared at him a moment, wondering if he really meant what he was saying to her or if this was just another game, a way to show her just how foolish she was. She swallowed, trying to rid herself of the uncomfortable lump that suddenly filled her throat, but not succeeding.

"Well, Draper. Are you coming? This was your idea, after all."

It was Owen's voice, sharp and pained. Alyssa wondered if he had been watching her and Jason, wondered if he had been listening to what they'd been saying. Not that it really mattered, she supposed. One way or another, she could not think he expected her to return with him to the mission. That seemed to be the one certainty in her life—no matter what happened on the island, no matter what came to pass between her and Jason, she could not return to Banaba.

Jason gave her a final questioning glance, then followed the others, swinging himself over the ketch's side and into the lifeboat.

"Remember," he hissed up at her as he cast off the line, "no noise, and no lights."

She stood watching then as he and Noyer took up the

oars. They soon disappeared into the darkness, but still she found she couldn't move, couldn't even pretend to find something with which she might occupy herself. It was almost as though she were rooted to that one place on the ketch's deck, her eyes searching in the darkness for Jason's return.

She almost thought her heart would stop beating while he was gone. She silently offered up a prayer for his safe return, and then another, that the first had not been said in vain.

The world seemed to have sunk into a pit of complete darkness. Even the thin moonlight had been obscured by clouds. Never had a night seemed so frighteningly and ominously dark.

Alyssa stared forward, to where she knew the beach lay, but found she could see nothing, no boat, no sign of movement, nothing. She ought to go below, she told herself. It was foolish to stand there and stare out at the blackness when there was nothing for her to see. But still she couldn't tear herself away from the ketch's rail. It was almost as if deserting that place was like deserting Jason when he needed her.

After a few more moments, however, she thought she heard the sound of movement. It was too weak, she thought, hardly enough noise for the boat to be making, even if the men wielding the oars were taking pains to be quiet. She squinted into the darkness around the ketch. There was nothing there for her to see.

"Jason?" she called out softly. "Jean?"

There was no answer.

For the next few moments she just listened, but when she heard nothing save the soft lapping of waves against the ketch's hull, she told herself that she had imagined the sound.

And then she heard it again.

This time she thoughtfully considered what she had heard. The noise wasn't loud, certainly not loud enough to be the sound of an oar pulling through the water. It was more like the noise an animal might make, perhaps one who hunted in the water and took care not to alarm its prey. She peered intently into the shadows by the side of the ketch. She saw nothing, not even the waves as they slapped at the hull. All around her there was nothing but darkness.

She wished she weren't alone. If only Jason had let her go with him and the others, she thought, at least then she wouldn't be standing there, imagining all sorts of insane things. Because there couldn't possibly be anything or anyone swimming through the water around the ketch. There had still been enough light to scan the shoreline before they'd entered the lagoon and there had been no question that it had been completely deserted. There had been no sign of canoes or any life on the beach. So there could be nothing there, certainly nothing that could swim out to the center of the lagoon and near the ketch.

She felt a sudden chill of fear, that they'd been wrong in assuming the island was deserted, that the natives had stayed on Nukuhiva to guard their god's treasure rather than returning to Tapuay. It was possible, she told herself. They could have hidden their canoes in the undergrowth. They could be waiting in hiding in the cave, waiting for the return of the man who had been ready to despoil their god's treasure. And Jason was doing just as they expected, returning to try once more to steal the god's horde of precious pearls.

She hit her hand against the ketch's rail in frustration. There was nothing she could do but try to fight the feeling, the fear that Jason had come blithely sailing into a trap.

She stood gripping the rail, trying to will the lifeboat and its passengers to return to the ketch. Her concentration was so intense that she didn't even hear the soft noise of bare feet as they slid onto the deck, or the thin padding of them as they crossed the ketch's deck to where she stood.

It was only when she sensed movement behind her, felt some slight churning of the air, that she turned. By then it was too late.

She'd seen him before. That thought fleetingly crossed her mind as she turned and saw those dark, searing eyes behind her. He was the cannibal tribe's chief, the one who had entered the cave with the old priest.

But there was no opportunity for her to allow her thoughts to dwell on that fact. All she could think when she saw him standing behind her, a knife gripped between his teeth and his hands extended to reach for her, was that he was going to kill her.

She tried to scream, but his hands were too fast, reaching for her neck and pressing. The scream died in her throat.

There was just time enough for her to stare up at him, to see the hatred in his eyes and uselessly struggle against the pressure of his hands on her throat as she gasped for air.

And then there was nothing but blackness.

Chapter Eighteen

Jason hesitated and he dropped his oars as the lifeboat drew close to the shore. His hand, almost without his being aware of the movement, slid to where his pistol was holstered.

There was no reason for him to be suspicious of anything, he thought. He'd neither seen nor heard anything untoward on the short trip between the ketch and the beach. Still, he felt the hairs on the back of his neck rise, and the reaction bothered him. It was not something that happened often, but on those occasions when it did, it usually presaged danger. He did not think himself prescient, but like most sailors, he chose not to ignore omens. And at that moment the omens were giving him every indication that something was terribly wrong.

"You and Remsen stay here," he whispered to Noyer. "Don't beach the boat."

"Stay here?" Owen demanded, his voice sounding unduly loud and sharp in the night silence that surrounded them. "Why should we stay here?"

"Because I said so," Jason hissed back.

He drew the pistol, then slid into the waist deep water. He held the weapon carefully out of the spray, not wanting to wet the firing pin and disarm himself. He was ready to shoot, but there was nothing at which he might aim in the darkness, not even any noise other than the sound of the surf. He began to wonder if he was making a fool of himself.

He stood still a moment and listened to the silence. It was too sharp, too deep, he thought. There wasn't even the noise of birds calling out or stirring among the branches of the trees bordering the beach. In fact, he could hear nothing but the sound of water slapping against the rocks that edged the cove.

Something was wrong, he told himself. Still, he had nothing but the unpleasant feeling to confirm his suspicions and that feeling at the back of his neck did not tell him in which direction he should aim his pistol.

"What is it, *mon vieux?*" Noyer asked in a tense whisper.

"I don't know," Jason replied. "If it's safe, I'll come back for you. But I have an unpleasant feeling . . ."

He let the words die, and Noyer didn't argue. The Frenchman had come to trust Jason's instincts in matters outside his own experience. This was decidedly one of those times.

Owen, however, was not prepared to be as accommodating. He leaned forward.

"If this is an attempt to cheat us, Draper . . ." he hissed angrily.

"Be quiet," Jason interrupted him. "Take my place and be ready to row," he ordered as he started to push through the water toward shore.

Noyer silenced any further outburst from Owen with a hand to his shoulder.

"Let me assure you, my good Reverend Remsen, that I will not allow either of us to be cheated." He stared after Jason, quickly losing sight of him to the shadows. "No matter what you think of him, I can assure you that the last thing Captain Draper intends is to steal the pearls for himself."

"I have no reason to trust either of you," Owen insisted. But he made no move to go after Jason. Unsettled by the darkness and silence of the night, as well as by the reference Jason had made to the spirits that guarded the pearls, he seemed to accept being left behind without further persuasion. He edged his way to take the place Jason had vacated, fumbling for a moment in the darkness to find the oars.

The two men sat in a tensely antagonistic silence, both staring sightlessly toward the shadow-darkened beach. The seconds passed with painful slowness and the silence became oppressive.

Jason's feeling of impending danger didn't lessen as he approached the beach. From what little he could see, the curved ribbon of sand was still and completely deserted. He was beginning to think his feeling had been a false alarm, that he'd caught some of Alyssa's fears and begun to be afraid himself. The pistol felt unnecessarily heavy in his hand.

He was about to turn and call out to Noyer that it was safe to bring the boat in to shore when the first shout shattered the silence. It was followed by dozens more, blood-chilling in their fierceness. The war cries were accompanied by a frontal attack as dozens of natives burst out of the undergrowth that edged the beach and ran across the sand toward him.

"Jason!"

"Turn the boat around, Jean," he shouted back as he began to race through the water, back to the lifeboat.

His instructions were unnecessary. At the first cry, Owen had begun to turn the craft. Long before Jason was near, he slid the oars into the water and started to row away from the beach.

"What are you doing?" Noyer demanded, trying to grasp the oars from Owen's hands. "We can't leave him."

Owen pushed him back and continued to row, pulling with all his strength against the weight of the water. Behind them, the shouts from the beach grew louder. A spear struck the lifeboat's side.

Jason splashed through the deepening water. He didn't realize the boat was pulling away from him until he realized the water was already well above his waist and still he couldn't see it.

"Jean!" he called out.

There was no response to his call. Noyer was too involved to answer as he struggled with Owen for the oars. The two men, both clumsy in the shaking boat, fumbled in the darkness, striking out at one another, and neither seemed to gain any sort of dominance. But the fight between them at least meant the boat was no longer pulling away from Jason.

"Jean!" Jason shouted again. The water around him was filled with spears, and he had little doubt that if he remained where he was much longer one would find its mark. "For God's sake, where are you?"

Finally, realizing he would be unable to stop Owen any other way, Noyer threw himself forward, striking the missionary squarely on the chin as he fell. The oars clattered from his hands.

"Here," Noyer shouted. "Come toward my voice."

Jason realized the Frenchman's voice came from a good distance away. And the cannibals were coming closer.

He turned back to face toward shore, raised his pistol, and fired quickly, emptying the chamber of all six bullets. He had little hope of hitting anything in the darkness, but he hoped the noise would at least temporarily stun the natives and give him a few moments' respite from the rain of spears, enough time at least to reach the lifeboat.

There was a single shout of pain, and then a momentary silence as the cannibals took stock of the situation.

Jason didn't waste time, well aware that they would soon realize the firing had stopped. He dived into the water, swimming with all his strength to the waiting boat. The situation was all too uncomfortably familiar to him as he remembered fleeing in precisely this way with Alyssa only days before. He wondered if he would be as lucky this time as they had been the last.

He nearly struck the boat before he saw it. Noyer's hand reached down to help him in just as the natives realized their prey was managing to escape. There was the sound of renewed shouts, and once again they began to throw the spears wildly, hoping they would find a mark.

"Take the oars," Noyer shouted at Jason as soon as he tumbled into the boat.

Jason started forward, almost tripping over Owen's slumped body.

"What happened to him?" he demanded.

"Just take the damned oars, will you?" Noyer shouted at him. He had already begun to row.

Jason slid into the stern and took up the oars, plunging them into the water and pulling with all his might. The shouts continued from the direction of the shore, but seemed to be falling slowly behind.

They reached the ketch quickly, Jason and Noyer climbing up and tying the lifeboat's line to the larger craft's side rather than try to get the unconscious Owen over the side with them. Jason gave a few terse orders and the two men hurriedly unfurled the sail. Jason took the wheel, and the ketch started for the mouth of the lagoon.

"We're going to make it," Jason shouted to Noyer.

Noyer released the jib to the wind, made sure the line was secure, then made his way aft, to Jason's side. The ketch's sails filled with the wind and the sleek craft seemed to leap forward. It was soon nearing the mouth of the lagoon.

"As you Americans say, as easy as pie," Noyer laughed, and snapped his fingers. "You know, Jason, compared to the boredom of Banaba, I almost enjoyed this."

He'd no sooner finished speaking when a spear struck the deck only inches from where he stood. Noyer's expression suddenly lost any hint of amusement.

"How the hell . . . ?" Jason muttered.

It seemed impossible that a spear could have been thrown so far from the shore.

It hadn't.

"There!" Noyer shouted and pointed to a canoe not ten feet from the ketch's port side. Six natives were in it, three paddling furiously to keep pace with the ketch, three heaving the deadly spears. There was the noise of another behind it, and a third, this one with a passenger holding a torch, drawing close behind.

"Find Alyssa and get her below," Jason shouted to Noyer.

"Mon Dieu," the Frenchman muttered. "Alyssa."

He darted forward, looking for her, wondering how he could have missed seeing her while he and Jason raced around the deck dealing with the sails.

The ketch slid through the mouth of the lagoon into the open ocean. Here, Jason knew, the canoes could not possibly catch them. A few moments more and they would be safe.

"Where is she?" Jason called out to Noyer.

He couldn't leave the wheel. Much as he wanted to search for her at that moment, he knew they would all be dead if he didn't keep the ketch steadily running with the wind. The thought that she might have been hit by one of the spears haunted him all too painfully. The image of her lying someplace in the dark in a puddle of her own blood sent a chilling finger of fear through him.

Noyer darted down the steps to the cabin and then back up. He stood in the open doorway and faced Jason.

"I can't find her, *mon ami,*" he shouted.

"What do you mean, you can't . . ."

Jason's words were cut off by a sharp moan of pain when a spear, thrown as a final gesture of warning from one of the canoes as they began to fall behind, stuck him. Stunned by the blow, he slumped forward over the wheel.

Noyer darted toward Jason. He looked in glazed shock at the spear that sagged now to the deck, its point embedded in Jason's shoulder blade. Finding his senses, he tried to help Jason as he pushed himself back from the foundering wheel. Above them the sails grew limp and began to luff as the ketch floundered and then turned too close to the wind.

Noyer put his arm around Jason and helped him down to the deck.

"The wheel!" Jason shouted at him.

Noyer nodded and took the wheel, darting a glance back toward the canoes that were once again drawing closer. He took the wheel, furiously turning it, hoping the ketch was not hopelessly caught facing the wind. But the boat's momentum was enough to carry it, and the sails once again filled.

It wasn't long before the ketch had left the canoes too far behind for there to be any further danger of their being overtaken. But Noyer no longer felt any sense of excitement over the adventure. He darted a glance to where Jason lay slumped on the deck. Then he glanced back to get a final look at the last canoc, the one with a native holding a torch like a beacon in the darkness of the night, a warning to stay away or else face death.

There was no mistake, he told himself, a sick feeling beginning to fill his stomach. The torch the native held aloft cast a flickering light that shimmered and reflected off a fall of golden hair lying close by the cannibal's feet.

Noyer had no doubt as to what it was he had seen. Alyssa had been captured. She lay slumped at the cannibal's feet, her body ominously still.

Alyssa stirred. Her throat ached, and it hurt her to breathe. She couldn't move her hands. Her arms, pulled behind her, were sore. For an instant she wondered if this was what it was like to be dead.

She realized all too quickly that she couldn't possibly have been killed. If nothing else, she knew she would not be able to feel anything if she were dead. And she felt things now, all too painfully.

And she could hear. There was the sound of water, the splash of waves striking close to where she lay, the soft whoosh of paddles being wielded. She was on a vessel, she realized. Only this wasn't the ketch. The water sounded too close for that.

She opened her eyes. The bright light of a torch greeted them, and she snapped them shut again quickly, shocked by the intensity of the glare. But she found she could not lie still and sightless. She had to find out where she was, what had happened to her. She opened her eyes again, this time slowly, to let them adjust to the light.

She found herself staring at a pair of bare, muscular legs, a man's legs. A native man's legs, she amended as she recognized the coppery tone of the skin.

And with the realization that she was now a captive came the equally shaking realization that Jason and the others were most likely dead. For the cannibals would not leave an enemy to invade their god's lair, of that she was all too sure.

Her heart filled with a sharp, keening pain of loss. Nothing had ever hurt like this, nothing had ever left her feeling so empty or shaken. If in the preceding days she had resigned herself somehow to the thought of living without Jason, still she knew she had harbored the hope that somehow, someday, it might be otherwise. That hope was crushed now, and she felt herself fill with an endless wave of grief that left her shivering and sobbing with the loss.

A hand reached down to her and pulled her roughly until she was sitting upright. She tried to move her arms and realized her hands were tied behind her. They dug into her back as the man pushed her against the canoe's side. Then he pushed aside the hair that had fallen across her face.

A sharp cry of fear and surprise escaped her lips.

It was him, the one who had come after her on the ketch, the cannibal chief. He was kneeling in the canoe facing her, his dark eyes staring down at her like burning coals floating in the night sky.

Instinct and fear made her draw back, to try to get away from him, away from those sharp, angry eyes. With her hands tied, all she could do was push with her feet. She managed to move only a few inches away from him. It wasn't nearly enough.

Her movement seemed to anger him. He leaned forward, grabbed her arm, and roughly pulled her close to him until her face was inches from his. She knew then that he was going to kill her. There could be no other meaning, she thought, than hatred behind the glowing, intense look she saw in his eyes.

He released her arm slowly, as though he only remotely realized that he was still holding her. He lifted his hand to her cheek, touching it with his fingertips, and seemed surprised by the way it felt. He seemed oblivious to her reaction, to the way she cringed as his fingers touched her skin. Too absorbed by his exploration, he acted as though she were something inanimate, something without feeling or awareness. She shivered as his hand skimmed her face, as it touched her chin and her cheeks and her nose, and then drifted slowly to her hair.

It seemed to hypnotize him, the way the handful of long, blond hair he lifted glimmered in the torchlight.

He let it drift slowly through his fingers, then took another handful and watched as he let that, too, fall.

Alyssa could feel her heart pounding with fear in her chest. Unable to move away from him, she sat by the place where he knelt and watched his eyes follow the golden strands of her hair as he let them fall through his fingers. He seemed transfixed, almost like a child who had made some momentous discovery.

After a moment, though, he suddenly lost his interest in the golden color of her hair, and he released the last strands that rested still in his palm. His eyes moved slowly across her face, then down to her neck and torso, and came to rest at that place where her breasts lay hidden beneath the thick, loose folds of her dress.

At first he seemed bewildered by the loose covering of the dark fabric, but he quickly decided how to deal with it. He reached out and tore open the front of her dress, then smiled when he found his suspicions confirmed.

He put his hand to her now bared breast, cupping it, letting his thumb rub against the nipple. Alyssa whimpered with misery and tried to draw away from him, but he grasped her with his free hand and held her fast.

She hadn't realized she was sobbing, not until the tears fell from her cheeks to wet his hand. The tears seemed to surprise him as well, for he lifted his hand away and stared at the droplet on his hand.

"Please, please don't," Alyssa begged.

She knew he didn't understand, knew he wouldn't care even if he did, but still the words couldn't be stopped, a low, steady stream of words that begged him not to hurt her. He stared at her, apparently bemused by the sound of her voice. Then he lifted the hand that had been wet with her tears to his mouth and thoughtfully licked them away, all the time not taking his eyes from her.

After a moment he put his palm over her mouth,

stilling the sound of her words, and she obeyed him, too frightened to do anything else. When he drew his hand away, she was silent.

Again he put his hand to her cheek, slowly sliding the back of it against her skin. Alyssa stared up at him, her eyes filled with terror. But what she saw staring back at her was not what she had expected to see, not what she had seen in his eyes before. There was something else there now—hunger, perhaps, or longing. All she knew was that whatever his intention, he would not kill her, at least, not yet.

The realization was far from comforting. She had seen this man dine on human flesh. What other horrid, bestial things might such a person do? she asked herself. She stared up into the chief's eyes and shivered. There were no answers to her question there, nothing for her save a knowing look of satisfied expectancy.

She cringed back, uselessly trying to get away from him, away from the feel of his hands on her face, away from the hands that slowly moved downward to her neck and once again to her bared breast.

Whatever it was he intended, she did know it would not be pleasant.

"Hold him," Noyer shouted.

Jason groaned with pain and stirred as Noyer tried to extract the spear's tip. The movement only served to bury the point deeper into the flesh.

Owen stared at the spear that protruded from Jason's shoulder and at the mess of blood that had seeped to the deck around the place where he lay. A look of revulsion crept over his face.

"I said *hold him,*" Noyer hissed angrily. "I can't get that thing out of him without help."

Owen gritted his teeth, then put his hands on Jason's arms, pinning them to the deck as Noyer pulled out the embedded shaft. Jason screamed once as the blade tore his flesh, then slumped into silence.

Noyer looked up at Owen.

"Help me get him below, then come back up here and man the helm."

"You have no right to order me about," Owen replied sharply.

Noyer lifted Jason's pistol from the deck beside him.

"This gives me the right," he said. "Do as I tell you, Monsieur Reverend, or I will use this, I promise you."

"You would kill a man of God?" Owen hissed at him.

Noyer shook his head. "No, not a man of God," he agreed. "But as for you, I would have no compunctions."

Owen colored with anger, but he did as Noyer had directed, kneeling to put his arm around Jason's waist and lifting him.

"Bon," Noyer said, and nodded to the stairs leading down to the cabin.

Between the two of them they managed to get Jason into the cabin and settled on the cot.

"Light the lantern," Noyer told Owen. He busied himself finding a first-aid kit in one of the cupboards.

"Do you know what you're doing?" Owen asked.

Noyer shook his head. "Only enough to bandage the wound," he replied.

Owen struck a match, lit the lantern, and then adjusted the flame. He glanced at Jason and grimaced, but then reached for the first-aid kit.

"I'll do it," he said. "You go back on deck and take the helm."

Noyer shook his head. "I've tied the wheel. We'll be fine for a while."

Owen returned his stare. "If I didn't know better, I'd say you didn't trust me."

"You don't know better," Noyer told him.

The two men stood staring angrily at one another,

then Jason moaned and opened his eyes. He stared up at the two of them.

"What happened?" he murmured.

Noyer turned to him.

"A spear, *mon vieux,"* he said. "We're about to bandage your shoulder. You're bleeding pretty badly, I'm afraid."

Owen took some bandages and a bottle of antiseptic from the kit.

"Turn over," he told Jason as he soaked a piece of bandage. He smiled. "This isn't going to be pleasant."

"I'd say that fact pleases you more than not," Noyer told him. He turned back to Jason. "But he's right. It has to be done."

Jason stared grimly up at Owen's satisfied expression, then turned onto his uninjured side, grunting with pain as he moved.

"Where did you find Alyssa?" he asked Noyer. "Was she hiding in one of the cupboards again?"

"No, Jason, she wasn't down here," the Frenchman replied slowly.

"Then where is she?" Jason demanded, leveling a sharp glance at Noyer.

He didn't have the chance to press his point any further just then. Owen pressed the antiseptic-soaked bandage to the open wound, and the shock was enough to leave him breathless and panting with pain.

Owen had begun to bandage the shoulder before he could spcak again.

"You didn't answer my question," he reminded Noyer. "Where is she?"

Noyer shook his head. "I fear, *mon ami,* that they have taken her."

Jason forgot his pain. He pushed Owen away and sat up.

"What do you mean?" he demanded.

"Just as we were pulling away from the canoes,"

Noyer replied. "I saw her."

Jason shook his head as though the words were foreign, incomprehensible to him.

"You saw her?"

Noyer nodded. "In the canoe," he replied.

Jason pushed himself to his feet and staggered toward the stairs.

"What are you doing, Jason?" Noyer demanded.

"I'm turning this scow around," Jason snarled at him. "We're going back for her."

Owen shook his head. "It won't do any good," he replied. "She's probably dead already."

"She's not," Jason shouted at him, anger seething from him like lava from a volcano. "What kind of a spineless animal are you?" he asked Owen. "She was to marry you."

"Was she?" Owen asked, calm now, and impersonal. "Or maybe it was just a game the two of you were playing. In any event, I don't see that it matters any more."

"Damn you, Remsen," Jason hissed. "We could have left the lifeboat with you lying unconscious in it floating in that cove. If we wouldn't leave you, we're not about to leave her."

He turned and started up the stairs.

Owen ran after him and pulled him back.

"She's dead," he shouted at Jason. "Why should we go back there and risk our lives for nothing?"

"I tell you, she's still alive," Jason hissed.

The two of them stood crouched, ready to fight. Noyer, however, jumped between them.

"He's right, Jason. We can't go back for her, not yet," the Frenchman said.

"Think about what you're saying, Jean," Jason shouted.

"I have thought," Noyer replied. "Don't think it pleases me to agree with this spineless excuse for a man. But the last I saw of those canoes, they were heading back toward Tapuay. The three of us wouldn't stand much of a chance storming the whole of the village, certainly not without any weapons. All we have is that pistol of yours, and that's useless since you went for your little swim. All we can do is go back to Banaba, get some weapons and men at Beau Rivage, and pray we aren't too late."

Jason stared at him for a moment, silent and angry. Then he slumped down to seat himself on the lowest stair. Noyer's words sounded reasonable to him, too reasonable. He wished he could argue against them, but he knew there was nothing he could say.

The Frenchman knelt at his side.

"Let me bandage your shoulder, *mon ami.* You're bleeding."

Jason nodded in reluctant agreement. Noyer collected the bandages, returned to him, and began to bandage the grisly wound.

Owen stared at them for a moment in satisfied silence. When Noyer had almost finished with the bandage, however, he couldn't resist the opportunity to gloat.

"Things didn't go quite as you planned, did they, Draper?" he asked.

Jason looked up at him.

"You think I wanted this?" he asked.

Owen shook his head. "No," he replied. "I think you wanted Alyssa and you wanted the pearls. What happened makes us even. I have neither, but then, neither do you." He stood grinning down at Jason, apparently without regret, now that his own loss was offset by Jason's.

"Get out of my sight, you parasite," Jason hissed at him.

"Or what?" Owen demanded. "You'll shoot me? With a ruined pistol?"

"I won't need a pistol," Jason replied.

Owen grinned. Then he edged by the step where Jason sat and climbed up onto the deck, leaving Jason to stare after him in frustrated rage.

"We'll get there in time, *mon ami,*" Noyer told him as he finished tying the bandage. "They won't kill a woman immediately. We still have a little while."

Jason nodded. Noyer was right, the cannibals wouldn't kill a woman immediately. But he knew what they would do, and he wasn't comforted by the thought.

It was still dark. Except for the half dozen lit torches stuck in the sand of the beach, Alyssa could see nothing but blackness around her. Her captors, however, were either more keenly sighted or simply more accustomed to their surroundings. They began to shout and paddle faster until the front end of each canoe struck sand and suddenly stopped.

Unbalanced, she slumped forward when the canoe suddenly ceased its forward movement. A large hand roughly righted her.

The chief climbed out, then reached in and lifted her bodily out of it, handling her without concern, as though she were a doll or a sack of flour. He threw her to his shoulder and strode the remaining few steps through the water, then up onto the beach.

She offered him no resistance. She wasn't sure why she didn't try to fight him, try to free herself. She told herself it was because it would do no good, that there was no place to which she might run, no chance she might escape. But she knew that deep inside she was simply too afraid.

He dropped her carelessly, and she landed on her back, her hands, still tied behind her, feeling the impact painfully and then transmitting it up her arms. Ignoring her, he started back to the canoes, shouting orders to his men as to where they should be beached and making sure the task was done as he instructed.

Alyssa watched him for a moment, and then her eyes drifted to the thick growth that edged the beach. Perhaps she could get away, she thought. It was, perhaps, an irrational idea, but it was born of desperation. Anything was better than lying there in the sand waiting for whatever fate the cannibal chief had decided for her. She could not simply sit there and wait for him to kill her.

She was stiff from the position she'd been in during the canoe ride, and clumsy with her hands secured behind her, but she managed to push herself first to her knees, and then to her feet. Once she was standing, she didn't hesitate, but simply started to run.

Even before the first hand grasped her, she told herself it had been a useless effort, that she could not have really escaped. But the thought was pushed from her mind as she realized there were other hands reaching for her, touching her, searching for her flesh beneath the torn dress. They were laughing, leering at her, their expression more than enough to tell her what they intended to do to her.

She twisted and turned, trying uselessly to get away from the hands that would not release her. And then she screamed and her ears filled with the sound of her own terror.

Chapter Nineteen

There was a single, angry roar that cut through the men's jeering laughter. The sound of it froze them. They dropped their hands away from Alyssa's body and turned to face their chief.

He pushed his way through the circle they formed around Alyssa. He was no longer shouting at them, just talking with a cold, distant anger that she found far more chilling. She stared at the natives' faces and realized that they, too, considered this controlled anger dangerous. Several actually trembled when he leveled his stare at them. There was no question at all in her mind as to who ruled Nukuhiva.

The natives stood silently accepting his rebukes, staring at him, seemingly dazed by the ferocity they heard in the sharp, controlled tone of his voice. When he reached Alyssa's side, he pointed to a prone figure lying on the beach, and barked out a terse order. Half a dozen men nodded, apparently relieved to be sent away. They ran back to where the man lay on the sand.

At first Alyssa thought it might be Jason lying there. She peered past the group that still surrounded her, trying to catch a glimpse of the injured man. He groaned in pain when he was touched, and then grew still and silent as he was lifted up from the sand. His leg, covered in blood, hung limp.

Alyssa gasped when she saw the blood-covered leg,

but the glimpse she had was more than enough to still whatever hopes she had that it might be Jason. The man's dark skin and the many tattoos on his torso and arms told her it had to be a native. She wasn't sure whether the realization was a relief or not. It would have been easier for her to bear whatever was to happen to her if she thought she was not entirely alone. And the thought that if he had not been captured he must already be dead left a shaft of aching grief within her. Still, she told herself, perhaps a fast death was kinder to him than whatever cannibals would do to him.

Or perhaps he might have escaped; perhaps even now he was coming after her.

The wounded native was borne away into the undergrowth, and as she watched the party of men carry him past her, Alyssa wondered what had happened on the beach while she lay, tied and unconscious, in the cannibal's canoe.

She darted a glance at the chief's face and decided his expression was far too complacent to think his men had recently suffered a defeat in battle. She would be a fool, she told herself, to think that Jason might still be alive, might somehow find her and rescue her. He and the others probably lay in that horrible cave, their bodies left as a warning to any others who might try to enter, perhaps, or else simply stored there until the time of the next feast like the one she and Jason had witnessed that night. Either way, it could hardly matter to them now. What did matter was that she would never see Jason again, that she would never have the chance to tell him she loved him.

When the wounded man was out of sight, the chief once more spoke to those still standing on the beach. Whatever it was he told them, they did not seem entirely pleased. Most of them, however, drew back immediately and began to melt into the darkness of the undergrowth. Only a few held their ground, staring sullenly at him and glancing hungrily at Alyssa. He brandished a spear, challenging them, and then they, too, decided it was wisest to let their chief have his way. They turned, mumbling angrily among themselves, and then they too disappeared into the shadows.

Once they were gone, the chief turned to face Alyssa. His naked torso shimmered in the flickering light of the torches. The many tattoos on his arms and chest seeming to move, almost to crawl across his skin like legions of vividly colored insects. It made him seem all the more frightening to her, and she cringed from him, despite the fact that she realized he had saved her from the rest.

He spoke to her then, the words just sounds to her, thickly sibilant, completely unintelligible. Although she couldn't understand a word, somehow she knew he was scolding her for trying to run away, warning her of what would happen if she did it again. She understood he really had no need to warn her. She was too frozen with fear now, too terrified from the realization of what had almost happened to her to think of fleeing.

He put his hand on her arm, grasping her firmly, and began to pull her after him into the undergrowth.

She stumbled along beside him in the darkness, blind by the lack of torchlight once they'd left the beach behind. She realized they were traveling along a well-worn path, though, for the ground was smooth and even beneath her feet.

Eventually they reached an opening in the wall of jungle growth. She looked up, surprised that she could differentiate the black, moonless sky above her from the general darkness of the shadows cast by the trees. She realized that the sky had faded just a bit and that dawn must be approaching, that without the trees to obscure the view above, she could see that it was beginning to turn from black to a dull gray.

She wondered if the approach of dawn meant she

faced at least a short reprieve, if the cannibals would wait until that night to do whatever it was they intended to do to her. Jason had said they performed their rites according to the phases of the moon. Perhaps they would wait until the moon once more showed its face before they dealt with her.

It wasn't really as comforting a thought as it ought to have been. Jason had been wrong, she reminded herself. The cannibals had been on Nukuhiva when Jason had assured her they would not be there. And even if there was to be a reprieve for her, it would be no more than a few hours, just time enough for her to become completely mired in her fear.

The chief did not linger long in the clearing. Pulling her along beside him, he approached a small structure made of bamboo and woven rush at the clearing's edge. He pulled the door open, nudged her inside, and entered behind her.

Once inside, he pushed her to the far side of the small shack, then stood, pointing at a pile of woven mats. When she did not immediately obey his implied order, he knelt and pulled her roughly down beside him.

She fell forward, unprepared for the way he'd pulled her. Her hands were still tied behind her, and she was unable to move them to ease the fall. She landed heavily, hurting her arm and shoulder, and letting a short cry escape her lips.

He seemed surprised by the cry. He put his hands to her shoulders and turned her until she was facing up at him, his touch this time almost gentle. She looked up at him, and her stomach filled with a thick feeling of dread.

He stared at her in silence for a long moment. Then his hand strayed to his waist, where a knife was sheathed. He pulled it out and held it in front of her face. She stared up at it, watching the way the thin finger of light that drifted into the shack glinted from its smooth stone blade.

Her eyes grew wide with fear. So there was to be no reprieve after all, she thought, not even the hours until darkness. It was just as well. She dreaded the hours of thinking about what was to happen to her almost as much as she dreaded her fate.

Whatever she expected from him at that moment, he surprised her. He grasped her shoulder and turned her to her side, then he carefully slit the hemp rope that bound her hands. Her arms fell aside, so numb she could hardly move them. She slowly pulled her hands together in front of her and tried to rub away the numbness.

He returned the knife to its place in his belt, watching her shaking hands and her look of strained discomfort. Then he took her hands in his and deftly massaged her wrists.

He was smiling at her when he released his hold of her wrists. She stared down at them, realizing that they were no longer completely numb. She moved them tentatively, stretching the cramped muscles and feeling the tingling hurt that told her the circulation was returning to them.

He turned and began to edge his way to the far side of the mat.

Now, she thought, now it was to come. Not death, at least not yet. First he had other uses for her. And the fear that had seemed to paralyze her since he'd taken her from the others on the beach disappeared in a wave of revulsion. She was still terrified, but she knew she could not meekly submit to him.

His back was to her, and her eyes fell from the dark, tanned skin of his back to the knife. She flexed her still clumsy fingers and watched him as he reached for what appeared to be a large piece of tapa cloth at the side of the mat.

Alyssa lunged forward to grab the blade.

He turned as she pulled the knife away from his belt and stared at her as though he could not believe what she had done. His eyes, dark and shining, stared out at her in the dim light, watching her as she scrambled to her feet. She held the knife in front of her, her eyes on his as she backed away from him to the door of the shed.

Before she reached the door, he sprang forward, the motion as smooth and supple as a cat's. He grabbed her arm as he fell against her, the force of his movement carrying her to the ground with him, pinning her beneath him. She flailed uselessly with the knife until he pushed her arm back and stilled it at her side. When she could no longer move, he pried the weapon from her hand.

For a moment he held her still and stared down at her. Alyssa heard the ragged sound of her own breath, the short, gasping sobs, sounds she had not realized she was making. Then he lifted the blade and brought it close to her neck. The touch of it to her skin somehow sobered her. She stilled the sobs and stared up at him.

In that moment she decided it would be better to die then and there than to live any longer, waiting in dread for whatever it was he intended to do to her. She returned his stare, unflinchingly defying him, almost inviting him to plunge the knife into her neck.

The boldness of that challenging look, the courage he knew it took for her to welcome death, seemed to surprise him. A slow smile edged up the corners of his lips. He let the knife fall aside.

He spoke to her again, the flow of his words oddly pleasant despite the roughness of his voice. Then he pushed himself up from her, put his hand on her back, and pushed her back to the mat.

This time he held the knife, making a point of not letting her take hold of it again, when he leaned over her and took the sheet of tapa cloth from the far side of the mat. He shook it out, the action oddly domestic, and spread it over her.

He pushed himself to his feet, then stood for a moment, staring down at her. Even in the dim light she could see that he was still smiling. Alyssa felt a wash of bewilderment as she realized he intended for her to sleep.

She watched him as he turned around and strode through the structure to the entrance. When he went outside, ducking his head to keep from hitting it against the lintel, Alyssa could just see the dimmest light of dawn thinning the shadows in the clearing.

He swung the door shut behind him, and she heard the scrape of a pole being placed to secure it. She scrambled to her feet and ran to the door, waiting a moment, listening to the night noises, wondering if he'd left. There seemed to be nothing but silence, and she tested the door, somehow knowing, even before she found it firmly unmoving, that she would not be able to get out.

She returned slowly to the mat, then sat, pulling the tapa cloth around her, although she wasn't really cold. There was nothing for her to do, she realized, nothing she could do save what he intended for her to do—sleep. She lay back on the mat, for a long moment thinking about his smile, wondering what it meant. It left her feeling shaken, and no less frightened than she had felt when he had knelt over her with the knife to her throat.

And then her thoughts turned back to Jason. Just as when she had awakened in the canoe, she felt herself fill with grief. He was dead—of that she was entirely sure now. She pictured the cannibal's expression and once again decided it had seemed too pleased for her to think Jason and the others might have escaped.

The morrow, she thought, couldn't come fast

enough. Better to face the cannibal's knife than to go on feeling as she did, awash with fear and grief. Death, she thought, would at least be a release from the pain that gnawed at her.

Her thoughts drifted back to the cannibal chief's smile, to the way he'd stood and stared down at her.

Death, she thought as misery crept through her, might be all too long in coming.

Jason stood by the ketch's rail searching the horizon when the first glimmer of dawn revealed the outline of Banaba looming suddenly ahead of them.

"You should go below and try to rest, Jason," Noyer called out to him from where he stood manning the wheel. "That hole in your shoulder isn't just going to disappear."

Jason shrugged in a gesture of dismissal. He seemed to be willing the ketch forward, hurrying it on its way. An hour or two more, he realized, until they reached Beau Rivage . . . and then he could be on his way to Tapuay, to Alyssa. That was, assuming the *Empress*'s mast was repaired, assuming he and Liam could convince enough of his men to come along to the cannibal island as crew, assuming the winds didn't suddenly die and leave them becalmed. There were far too many things he could not control for him to have any sense of command. It irked him that there was nothing he could do to hurry matters along, that he could not feel more certain of what he intended to do, that he could not even know if she was still alive.

Owen appeared on deck, letting the door from the cabin swing open with a loud clatter, then neglecting to close it behind him. He marched to the rail several feet away from where Jason stood and considered the growing outline of the island.

After a moment he turned to Noyer.

"Why are we approaching from the north?" he demanded. "I insist you return me to the mission as soon as possible."

"Insist all you like, Remsen," Jason told him. "After he's brought me to the *Empress,* Noyer can take you round the island. But first I get to my boat."

"I'm going with you, Jason," Noyer interjected. "If the good reverend is so anxious to return to his mission, he can take the ketch himself."

Jason turned to face the Frenchman. "I can't ask you to come along, Jean," he said.

"I don't expect you can, *mon ami,*" Noyer replied. "But then again, you can't ask me not to come."

"I don't know what's going to happen," Jason warned.

"What is going to happen is that you'll be walking into a nest of murderous heathens and most likely get yourselves killed," Owen interposed abruptly. He looked at Jason and smiled unpleasantly. "Don't let me stop you."

"True and noble sentiments from a selfless man of the cloth," Jason muttered at him. Then he turned to Noyer. "The wind must have shifted, Jean," he said. "It's suddenly become unpleasant on deck. Call me when we reach Beau Rivage."

The sound of the bamboo pole being drawn away from the door awakened Alyssa. She opened her eyes and stared up at the woven rush roof of the small shed and spent a long, confused moment trying to remember where she was. When she finally oriented herself, she wished she hadn't made the effort.

She pushed away the tapa cloth that still covered her. The interior of the shed was quite warm, the air thick and still. She realized she was covered with perspiration. As the door was drawn open, she saw it was already full light.

Three old women appeared in the doorway, all large and gray-haired and displaying open curiosity as they gazed in at her. All three were clothed in large sheets of tapa cloth, and that portion of their flesh that was left exposed showed old and faded tattoos, oddly distorted by the swollen folds of their skin.

They chattered among themselves, the sound of their voices high and strangely melodic, the softly sibilant flow of the words sounding to Alyssa more like music than anything else. She sat up, pulling the front of her torn dress closed to cover herself as one of the women entered.

The woman was holding a gourd and a small bowl. The latter, Alyssa realized, was actually half a gourd, and from where she sat, she saw that it was filled with some sort of mushy paste. These she held out in front of her, an offering, it seemed. She knelt beside the mat and motioned to Alyssa to take them.

More bewildered than anything else, Alyssa took the gourd first and peered in at its contents, then sniffed it. Water, she thought, as the stuff seemed to have no odor at all. She took a careful sip, then emptied the gourd completely when she found her suspicion had been right. She had been thirsty, she realized, and hardly even noticed that she let a good portion of it dribble onto her bodice.

She returned the empty gourd to the old woman and took the offered bowl. For a moment she simply sat staring at the pale yellowish mess it contained. Her hesitation prompted the woman to motion to her, holding out a finger and pantomiming dipping it into the bowl and bringing it to her mouth. Alyssa realized she was to eat.

"Ka pai," the woman told her and once again went through her pantomime. *"Poi-poi."*

Alyssa had tasted the native taro paste while on Papeete and had found it tart tasting, but not terribly unpleasant. She put the tip of her finger tentatively into the soft goo, fully intending to eat some of it as her stomach, despite the addition of water, was nonetheless groaning in miserable emptiness.

But as she brought her finger to her mouth, she remembered what it was she had seen the men of this tribe eat during their picnic on the beach. The thought sent a wave of revulsion through her. She looked at the pale, sticky mess on her finger and her stomach began to heave. She pushed the bowl back into the woman's hands.

The woman shook her head and tried to return the bowl to her.

"Ka pai," she repeated.

When she found she could not induce Alyssa to take the gourd from her, she turned to her two companions who stood still, watching, in the doorway. The three of them began an intent discussion, and they seemed oddly disturbed at her refusal to eat.

They were still chattering when the chief appeared. The old woman who had tried to offer the bowl of poi was the first to see him. She quieted immediately and moved back. The others quickly followed, making room for him to pass into the small room.

The filtered daylight that made its way inside the shed in no way lessened the impression of muscled strength he inspired. His naked torso glistened with droplets of moisture, and Alyssa assumed he had bathed before coming to see her . . . readying himself, she thought, for the ceremony of her death.

He took the bowl from the old woman, then knelt in front of Alyssa and spoke to her as he held it out to her, telling her, she supposed, she should eat. But seeing him brought back a flood of memories of the night before, the sight of him suddenly appearing behind her on the ketch's deck, the hard look in his eyes when he'd torn the bodice of her dress, the knowingly hungry way he'd stared at her before he'd locked her in the shed. He frightened her. There was no hunger great enough to induce her to eat from his hand.

She shook her head, rejecting the offered bowl.

He grunted in displeasure, then put his forefinger into the bowl and withdrew it covered with the sticky paste. He extended his hand, bringing the coated finger toward her mouth. She turned her head away before he could touch it to her lips.

He seemed displeased with her refusal to eat, but evidently accepted it, handing the bowl back to the woman and licking the coating from his finger himself. When Alyssa turned back to him, she found he was staring at her, waiting for her to return her attention to him.

He brought his hand to his chest.

"Mehevi," he said, articulating the word carefully. *"Mehevi."*

For an instant Alyssa felt as though she was going to laugh. She was struck with absurdity of the situation. To all appearances he was introducing himself to her. It was like a wolf walking up to a lamb and offering a bit of pleasant camaraderie before he made the weaker creature his dinner.

The laughter, however, died stillborn as she considered his stare. It was deadly serious.

"Mehevi," he repeated, then waited for her to respond.

She returned his gaze. *"Mehevi,"* she murmured.

He smiled and nodded at her, as though she were a child who had managed to accomplish some great feat of logic.

"Mehevi," he repeated, pointing again to himself. Then he put his hand out, bringing it to rest against her chest, touching the valley between her breasts.

She drew back, but he ignored her wariness. He leaned forward to her, again pressing his hand against her chest, obviously demanding she complete the introduction.

She complied, murmuring "Alyssa," relieved that when she did he withdrew his hand.

"Ah-lee-sah," he repeated slowly and nodded. Then he repeated her name and his own, smiling at her as he did.

Alyssa was relieved when he stood, seemingly satisfied with the exchange. He turned to the old women and began to talk to them, apparently giving them orders as to what was to be done with her. She wished the flow of words held some meaning for her, wished she had some idea of what they intended to do to her. Knowing, she thought, could be no worse than the terrifying visions supplied by her own imagination.

He turned suddenly back to face her.

"Arioi," he said, his expression proud and solemn as he stood in front of her. He pointed to himself just as he had when he'd told her his name.

She didn't understand, but she nodded, hoping he'd leave.

"Arioi," she repeated and pointed to him.

This time the formula didn't seem to work. He frowned at her, then turned to the three old women and barked out a few words at them. Immediately they knelt in front of him, lowering their heads to the ground. He turned back to Alyssa.

"Arioi," he repeated firmly and again pointed to himself.

And this time she understood that he was telling her he was royalty on his island, king to his people. Not that the revelation especially surprised her. Whether chief or king, she had realized from the very start that he was the leader of his tribe.

She nodded. *"Arioi,"* she repeated. She wondered if he expected her to bow as the others had.

He stood an instant longer, staring down at her. He put his hand to her head, lifted a handful of her hair as he had the night before, and let it fall through his fingers. He seemed mystified by the golden tresses.

Alyssa was struck by the possibility that these people, with their straight, dark hair, had never before seen anything like her blond curls. Was it possible, she mused, that she owed the fact that she was still alive to something as mundane as her hair?

"Ah-lee-sah," the chief said softly, and he touched her cheek with the back of his hand.

Then he turned and barked a few more instructions to the old women. They scrambled clumsily back to their feet, made noises that Alyssa took to mean they understood whatever directions he had given them, and stood aside as he left the room.

Alyssa sat, still and unmoving, trying to make some sense of what had happened.

The old women did not leave her to consider her status, whatever it might be at that moment. Two of them moved forward, motioning to her to stand and follow them. When she didn't obey immediately, one stepped forward, put her hand on Alyssa's arm, and gave it a rough tug. When this action did not produce a speedy enough reaction to suit her, she slapped the flat of her hand sharply against Alyssa's shoulder to hurry her along.

Alyssa scrambled to her feet and rubbed the smarting place on her shoulder where she'd been slapped. She quickly realized that the chief might have afforded her some special consideration, but these women had no intention of fawning over her. She was being told in no uncertain terms to do as they directed. She had no doubt but that the slap would be repeated were she not to perform to their expectations.

They escorted her outside, into the sunlit clearing, then along a well-worn path through the jungle growth.

They stayed close to her, not allowing her much freedom to move except as they indicated.

She was surprised with the speed with which they moved. Bulky and large, all three showed an animation that belied their age and size. They seemed entirely unaware of the heat and humidity that seemed to grow more and more oppressive to Alyssa with each moment they spent tramping through the jungle.

The march ended at a large pool, not unlike the one that had provided her and Jason with their hiding place that night on Tapuay, with a small waterfall at its far end. But unlike the deserted pool on the smaller island, this pool seemed to be the social center of the tribe.

Three dozen or more women were there, bathing in the clear water, lying or sitting beside it, talking, arranging flowers in one another's hair. They were a mix of young and old, some quite beautiful, Alyssa thought, save for the tattoos that decorated their skin, indiscriminately scattered over necks and arms and haunches. Those who were not naked wore pieces of the same white tapa cloth the old women wore, some wrapping theirs around their waists, leaving their breasts bared, others choosing instead to cover themselves from breast to knees. Alyssa's one thought when she and her warders left the jungle and came upon them and the pool was that this must be some drunken sailor's dream of paradise.

The women stopped their chatter as soon as Alyssa and the three women appeared at the jungle's edge. A strained silence fell on them and they all turned and stared at her. Alyssa saw an evaluating look in more than one woman's eyes. Was it, she wondered, the consideration a butcher showed a calf before its slaughter, or was it something else?

One of her warders pushed Alyssa toward the pool. She moved forward, feeling strange now as she grew aware that she was the center of all these women's attention. They stood and moved forward to her as she approached the pool. When she reached its edge, she found herself completely surrounded.

They all started talking at once, reaching for her. It seemed as if a hundred hands were grasping for her, touching her skin and her hair, exploring her, considering her feel, her texture, as if she were a length of cloth in some tailor's shop. Part of her realized the hands were relatively benign, for none of the women made any gesture to hurt her, but still she could not quiet the panic she felt as all those strange hands touched her, as the fingers waved close to her eyes as they reached forward to her. The rising babble of their voices only intensified her fear. It was a strange nightmare to her, only she knew it was real.

She screamed and tried to get away, but it was impossible. There was no place for her to go, no way for her to get past the wall of bodies that surrounded her. A moment of flailing against the hands, and then she found herself hunkering down, bowing her head and folding her arms in front of her face, trying to protect herself.

It was only then that they seemed to realize they had frightened her. They fell silent and backed away from her, leaving her huddled and kneeling as they stared silently at her.

The three old women who had come to the shed forced their way through the group. One pulled Alyssa to her feet while the others began to tug at her clothes. They seemed to think the dress would fall away from her body with the same ease as did the pieces of cloth they wore wrapped around themselves. When the dress didn't fall away from her as they expected, they began to pull harder, tearing at the already ripped bodice until it was little more than tatters.

"Stop it!" Alyssa screamed at them. "Let me be."

Her cry froze them momentarily, and they drew

back, apparently bewildered by her reaction. But the woman who had slapped her when she hadn't moved quickly enough back in the shed now stood stony faced in front of her and motioned to the pool. Alyssa realized they intended for her to bathe.

It was hardly an unwelcome prospect. The hours she'd spent locked in the small structure dealing with her fear and the long walk through the humid undergrowth had left her sodden with perspiration, the thick fabric of her dress clinging uncomfortably to her skin. She realized she would gladly have shed the dress herself if they'd made their intention clearer from the very beginning.

She began to unfasten the buttons of the dress, then realized how foolish the effort was as the front was already torn. Instead, she pulled her arms from the sleeves, then pushed the dress down and over her hips.

She could almost feel the women's eyes stray to the thatch of hair between her legs. This seemed to intrigue them even more than the blond hair on her head. The babble began again, this time a bit more subdued than it had been before, and the women pointed to the wiry curls.

Alyssa pretended to ignore them. It was foolish to feel modest, she told herself, when she was surrounded by so much naked flesh. She stepped out of the circle of fabric her torn dress and underthings made on the ground and took a step toward the pool.

It doesn't matter, a nagging voice inside her added, the bath was probably nothing more than a preamble to her execution.

Chapter Twenty

"How does the shoulder feel, *mon ami?*"

Noyer, Jason noticed, was staring at him with the sort of ghoulish look a particularly bloodthirsty surgeon might use when contemplating an especially challenging patient, one who required an extensive operation such as the removal, perhaps, of some vital organ. The fact that Noyer knew absolutely nothing about medicine did not make the expression any less ominous. Jason couldn't keep himself from wondering just how ill he appeared to be . . . not that it really mattered. He wouldn't have allowed his friend to keep him from making this trip, regardless of the consequences.

"I told you," Jason replied, "I'm fine."

He was lying. And he knew Noyer knew it. His shoulder ached with an unremitting throb that seemed to travel down his arm to his finger tips. The wound in his shoulder had become infected, and other than bathing it with antiseptic, there was little he could do about it. Despite the hurt, though, he was not about to leave the *Empress*'s helm, certainly not about to admit to Noyer that he wasn't physically able to captain his own ship.

Until that moment, he had actually given the throbbing in his shoulder very little thought. He'd been wounded before, and he knew what to expect. His only real concern was the fear that the fever would come too quickly, that it wouldn't leave him time to do what he knew he had to do.

Whatever that would be. He wished he knew more about Nukuhiva, wished he had some idea of how many natives were there and how to deal with them. But he had only one way to answer his questions, and that was to trespass on the cannibals' island and face them. There was one thing of which he was entirely certain at that moment, and only one: he would not leave Nukuhiva alive unless he had Alyssa with him.

And if anything went wrong, he wouldn't have to worry about the infection in his shoulder killing him. Not that that particular possibility frightened him nearly as much as logic told him it ought. The thought of going on living without her, knowing that he had been the cause of her fate, was far more terrifying to him even than facing death.

"You don't look fine, Jason," Noyer told him firmly, interrupting his thoughts. "Not that I expect you'd let a bit of fever send you to your sickbed. Certainly not under the circumstances." He stared out at the sunlight that glinted off the waves, searching the horizon even though he was well aware it was far too soon for them to have come close enough to catch sight of the island. "How many men did your mate say will come with us?" he asked casually, as if the question were of the same interest to him as a consideration of the weather.

Jason shrugged, then wished he hadn't as the movement sent a sharp stab of hurt through his shoulder.

"Liam only got the crew to come along by promising them they won't have to leave the *Empress*. They'll defend the ship if they have to, but they won't set foot on the island. Nukuhiva is taboo to them, and they won't break their taboos." He scowled. "Peli is the only one who'll come ashore with us."

"Peli?" Noyer asked. "That big Samoan?"

Jason nodded. "That's the one."

Noyer ventured a grin. "Perhaps he'll be enough. The thought of coming upon him on a dark night would give any normal man nightmares."

"I'll tell him you said so," Jason replied. "I'm sure he'll consider it a compliment."

Noyer laughed, but when the laughter died, his grin quickly disappeared. When he spoke again, his voice was low.

"Then it is just the four of us—you, me, Argus, and your Samoan?"

Jason nodded. "Just the four of us," he said.

Noyer scowled, but recovered quickly. "Not so bad as it seems, I think, *mon ami*. Four well-armed men. And we'll have the darkness and surprise with us. It will be enough. But I could have wished for another man or two."

"I'd go alone, if I had to," Jason said in a tone that spoke more of determination than anything else.

"There will be no need of that," Noyer assured him. He was silent a moment, thinking. When he asked it, the question was heavy with indecision, as though he had thought it best not to ask, but then allowed it to escape despite his reticence. "What do you think our chances are? Of our getting there before they . . ."

"We'll get there before they kill her," Jason interrupted. "I'm not thinking about anything else yet. I can't."

Noyer nodded. He understood Jason's reluctance to give words to his thoughts. After all, he himself felt that talking about what the cannibals might do to Alyssa, actually giving vent to the words and hearing them spoken aloud, might somehow make it worse. And however painful he found the prospect, he knew that for Jason the hurt was ten times greater, a hundred times greater. Jason was in love with her.

He quickly changed the subject.

"Do you believe that stick of a man Remsen, turning

the ketch around and sailing to the mission as though he didn't have a concern in the world?" he muttered. "I fear I shall never learn to understand mankind."

"I think classifying that hypocrite as a member of the human race is being excessively liberal, Jean," Jason murmured in absent reply.

He looked up at the sails and then forward to where Argus directed the crew in trimming the sails. He realized he didn't want to waste so much as a minute on Owen Remsen. Just the memory of the way Remsen had left without so much as a thought about Alyssa sent him into a murderous rage, and he had neither the time nor the energy just then to waste on anything so valueless as nursing anger. Getting the *Empress* to Nukuhiva, that was what he need consider.

From all appearances, Argus and the carpenters at Beau Rivage had done an excellent job with the new mast, but Jason could have wished for a stronger wind to test its strength. The raw wood was still bare and unvarnished, for that particular task had of necessity been postponed by their need to get under way. The mast looked like a pale white, sickly limb sticking out of the *Empress*'s deck. He wished there was enough wind to give it a real test, enough wind to hurry them on their way to Nukuhiva. He'd never before found anything but pleasure in the time he'd spent at the *Empress*'s helm. Now he begrudged every second.

Noyer watched him as he stared up at the wind filling the *Empress*'s sails. His eyes gleamed with fever the Frenchman realized, but with something more than fever as well. He wondered what Jason would do if they did not find Alyssa in time. Even if they did, he doubted she would be the same once the native men had had their chance with her.

The Frenchman wondered if she would ever recover from that. And he wondered if Jason would ever recover from the guilt, knowing that he had been the one who had initiated the trip to Tapuay in the first place, knowing that he was partly responsible for what happened to her. In many ways the fever that burned in his friend's shoulder must be mild compared to the fever that must now fill his mind.

"We should reach Tapuay just before sunset," he ventured.

Jason turned to him and nodded.

"We hold to the south side until dark, then cross over to Nukuhiva. It won't be easy approaching the island without light, but I don't see that we have much choice."

"I've checked the charts," Noyer said. "They don't show any reefs or shallows."

Jason nodded. He, too, had given the charts more than a bit of his passing attention.

"We shouldn't run into any surprises," he agreed, "assuming the charts are correct."

He turned back to his consideration of the wind-filled sails. Charts of the seas near Nukuhiva were, of necessity, incomplete. He knew it and so did Noyer. After all, few captains bothered with measuring the water's depth when they were being chased by canoes filled with cannibals. There could be any manner of hidden danger lying just beneath the surface of the water surrounding the island, and as they intended to approach in the darkness, they would not know it until they were fully upon it.

The cautious captain in him warned him that the venture was folly. He ignored his own advice, his concern for his craft and his crew vastly outweighed by his concern for Alyssa.

Whatever the dangers, he could not get there fast enough.

Noyer patted the pistol with which he had armed himself before they had left Beau Rivage.

"Let's hope," he said, "we can provide a few surprises of our own."

* * *

Alyssa tried to ignore the eyes watching her as she slid into the water of the pool. It was cool and clear and felt wonderful against her skin. It seemed strange to her that she could actually feel capable of enjoying anything under the circumstances, but she could not deny the fact that she was thoroughly enjoying the swim.

Six or eight of the younger women dived in after her, following along as she swam, giggling and splashing water at her. At first Alyssa could not understand what they were doing, but after a few moments she realized they were trying to play with her. She turned away from them and began to swim out into the center of the pool, letting the others follow her or not, as they saw fit. She was as bewildered by their treatment of her as she had been by Mehevi's.

She stopped in the center of the pool treading water and eyeing the clearing and the distance from the pool's edge to the jungle. She returned to her swim wondering what chance she had of reaching the undergrowth if she tried to get away from the women. After a moment's consideration, she gave up the thought, telling herself that there was no place she could hide for very long, that escape from the island was impossible.

And she had to admit that the natives seemed perfectly willing to make whatever time they intended to allow her to live among them reasonably pleasant. Assuming, that was, she behaved as they wanted her to behave. Perhaps, she thought, it was better to simply accept whatever fate the tribe had decided for her and do as they wanted.

But the more she considered the situation, the more she found herself picturing in her mind the pigs that happily mired themselves in the mud of the mission's pen back on Banaba. They lazed and grew fat with no thought to the fact that they were all too soon to be set on Owen Remsen's dinner table. Unlike their fellows who rooted wild on the island, they happily gave up their freedom for indolence, not realizing their days of ease presaged an early, certain death.

Was that all she was, she wondered, an indolent beast, accepting of her fate in exchange for her food and comfort until her keepers decided it was time for her death? Didn't her own humanity require that she fight against them, that however futile the effort, she face death not with meek acceptance, but rather boldly striving for her life?

Once again she turned her attention to the area surrounding the pool, this time taking greater pains to be more observant. She could see several paths opening into the jungle, not only the one by which the old women had brought her, but several others radiating outward like spokes of a wheel. She and Jason had managed to hide from the cannibals on Tapuay, she reminded herself. Surely on this much larger island she could find someplace to secrete herself, someplace she might escape their notice.

If not, at least it would be better to die quickly while trying to escape then to wait for her slaughter like some dumb, penned-up animal.

The three old women, she noted, sat, sharp-eyed and attentive, at the side of the pool. The others, save for the half dozen or so in the water around her, seemed to pay court to the three matriarchs. She had only to lose the honor guard of swimmers that surrounded her, she told herself, and perhaps she could climb out of the pool and reach the jungle before they realized she had bolted. Then she would find someplace to hide.

But what then, she asked herself.

She told herself to think of one problem at a time. First, get away from the women. Then she would have time to consider.

Before anything else, she would have to rid herself of

the half dozen women swimming in the pool with her. If she were to have the opportunity to get out of the water and run into the jungle before they caught her, she must distract them.

With that in mind, when they gathered around her, she smiled and splashed water at them, hoping that they would return to the mood of playfulness they had first shown her when she'd entered the water. They seemed surprised at first by her gesture, but readily joined in, giggling and calling out as they splashed her and one another.

When she pointed and then darted forward to the edge of the pool opposite the side where the old women sat, it took them a moment to realize she was challenging them to a race. After a confused moment, they started after her, their strong strokes carrying them across the pool close at her heels. But with her head start, Alyssa won handily, and as one by one they reached the side after her, she clung to the rocks at the edge of the pool and crowed over her victory.

She didn't give them much time to consider that she had cheated them, that they were decidedly better swimmers than she and in a fair race would have certainly outstripped her. Instead, she again pointed to the far side of the pool, this time toward the old women, and began to swim.

This time the others took off after her immediately, quickly passing her by in their efforts to win. And Alyssa let them go, barely swimming a few strokes before she halted, treading water and watching the curtain of splashed water they left in their wake.

She took a deep breath, oriented herself in the water, then turned around and began to swim. She returned to the far edge of the pool, grasped the rocks at its side, took a deep breath, and scrambled out.

She barely darted a glance at the others, only long enough to let her see that the swimmers had reached the center of the pool and the old women had not yet noticed her defection. She turned her back on them and began to run.

There was the sound of an angry cry behind her as one of the women at the far edge of the pool realized what it was she was doing. Alyssa ignored it, concentrating instead on reaching the path in the undergrowth. A little way into the jungle, she told herself, and she would be able to find someplace to hide. Surely she could reach it before any of the women could get back across the pool to follow after her.

Despite herself, she found she was surprised when she reached the edge of the jungle and still there was little more than confusion behind her. She darted onto one of the paths that snaked into the undergrowth, feeling the shade of the trees that formed the canopy above as welcoming as anything she had ever known. She realized she had not really believed she could get away. For the first time she began to think she might actually find some way to escape.

The path she had chosen, she discovered after she had run only a few dozen yards, led upward, into the lava mountain that was the mother of the island. The path began to rise sharply in front of her, and she looked up at it in dismay. It was rough and rutted, hardly ideal for a fast escape.

But there was little alternative for her, she realized. She certainly couldn't go back and choose another path. At least the undergrowth at either side was thick, she told herself. If need be, she could always slip into it and hide.

She began to climb, her bare, wet feet slipping on exposed roots, forcing her to scramble along, catching at low branches to keep her balance. Behind her the shouts seemed to have grown in intensity, but there did not seem to be any sign that the women were catching up to her, no movement that she could see on the path or in the jungle just behind her. She wished she could understand what it was they were screaming so sharply. She began to run faster, even though she could feel her heart beginning to pound in her chest. She told herself that the cries didn't mean anything.

But she was to soon discover that they did mean something. She had slipped on a loose stone and fallen, bruising her knee as she landed. When she pushed herself back to her feet and looked up again to the steeply rising path in front of her, wondering how far she'd come from the pool and how much further she must go before she might feel safe enough to find someplace to hide, she saw the leaves rustling and heard movement.

For an instant her heart felt as though it had stopped beating, but she recovered quickly, forcing herself off the path and into the undergrowth. She felt the sharp edge of fronds scratching her skin as she slid past a stand of low palms. She moved quickly, hoping she hadn't been seen, moving behind a thick-trunked coconut with a welter of huge-leaved colocasia plants at its feet.

The greenery was easily dense enough to hide her, she decided. She crouched down and tried to slow the pounding she felt in her chest, certain that it was loud enough to be heard.

But rather than slowing, the sharp thud grew stronger as she saw a file of native men on the path she'd just left. They were moving down the slope, approaching the place where she had stepped off the path.

They carried spears and huge nets and looked as if they had been part of a hunting party, probably searching through the jungle for the wild boar that was the Polynesian islander's sole source of meat (save for *these* islanders, she reminded herself, who supplemented their diet in unspeakable ways). All she knew was that the women's cries had alerted them, and now they were most certainly a hunting party.

And what they were hunting now, she knew, was her.

A glance at them was more than enough to convince her. She ducked lower into the foliage, falling onto her knees and hoping they had not seen her, praying she was well enough hidden and had been fast enough to evade them. She didn't dare move, not even to glance back at the trail, until long after the faint noise they made as they moved along the path had died. Then she ventured only to part enough of the leaves in front of her to give her access to a view of a narrow piece of the path.

It was empty. She continued to stare at it, assuring herself that nothing there stirred, that no one still remained. It was only then that she rose slowly from her knees to her feet and, still crouching, took a more thorough look around.

The path was still and empty. She peered first uphill, the direction from which the hunters had come, and then back toward the pool. In both directions the path was deserted.

She stood then, absently wiping away the mud that stuck to her hands and knees as she cautiously began to move back toward the path. But she'd taken only a few steps when she heard a stirring in the leaves behind her, not far from the place she had hidden herself.

She turned, stricken, expecting to see one of the cannibals standing there facing her, his spear held extended and ready as he took aim at her. Instead she saw nothing but a movement of leaves close to the ground.

She was bewildered at first, but not so curious that she had any intention of trying to find out what it was rooting through the undergrowth. Not that she needed sight of the thing to tell her it was a wild boar.

The scent of pig swept over her in a wave as the animal came closer. As if to confirm her suspicions, the boar made a short, thick snorting sound, as though warning her away. It was more than enough incentive.

Alyssa began to step backward, her eyes glued to the movement of the foliage as she stumbled toward the path. The men had definitely been hunting, she realized. They had, most probably, frightened this creature down from its lair further up the mountain. And that would mean the boar was both angry and unpredictable in its fear.

A picture of wild boar formed in her mind. These animals, she knew, were entirely unlike their domestic cousins, the docile creatures with which she had been familiar back in Plymouth. They were not only large, they were violent, with thick, spiny hair and long, dangerous tusks. A charging boar was a challenge even to a strong, well-armed man, a man well versed in hunting. And she was none of those things. She was a woman alone, naked, and empty handed.

She felt the worn, packed earth of the path beneath her feet before she realized she had gotten that far. She took a deep breath and told herself that perhaps the creature hadn't seen her. Perhaps she could still get away from it.

She turned and started to run.

But the sudden noise of crushing leaves and of hooves rapidly striking the ground told her only too clearly that the boar had indeed seen her and that it was following. She had no real need to turn around to see it charging after her, but, dazed by fear, that is just what she did.

Its shiny, dark little eyes shone angrily as it ran toward her. Driven from its den by the cannibals, unable to fight the whole hunting party, it had been forced to flee for its life. But the boar was angry, and it was ready for a fight. Now it found a single adversary and determined that the time had come for its revenge for the indignity it had suffered.

The boar lowered its head, ready for combat that

Alyssa knew all too surely would not be combat at all, but slaughter. Her slaughter.

The fear of alerting the natives to her presence had vanished.

She screamed as she stood frozen with fear, and watched as the boar lowered its head to charge.

Jason gave the order to reef the *Empress*'s topsails, then stood at the rail and narrowed his eyes, staring at the distant beach and the rocky reef that sheltered it. It was the beach on Tapuay at which he stared with such concentration, the beach where he and Alyssa had first made their way to shore after the terrifying battle with the surf and the rocks. The water was calm now, and the memory seemed distant, like something that had happened years, not merely a few weeks, before.

It might have been a lifetime before, he told himself.

A short lifetime, he amended, but still long enough to have left his life completely changed. It had been a different Jason Draper who had dragged himself onto that beach. Part of him almost wished he could go back and become that man again, if only to lift the burden of guilt he carried at that moment.

Noyer joined him by the rail.

"They're probably still there," he said.

"What?" Jason asked, lost in his own thoughts and having no idea to what his friend referred.

"The pearls," Noyer replied, his expression thoughtful as he considered the long shadows that had begun to creep across the beach. "They're probably still there, lying in that cave."

Jason nodded absently.

"I suppose they are," he agreed. He hadn't given the pearls so much as a thought since the moment he'd learned Alyssa had been taken. Without her, they no longer interested him.

Noyer grinned.

"After we get her off Nukuhiva, we could try to find them," he suggested.

Jason scowled.

"You look for them if you like, Jean," he said. "I've told you all I know. If they're still in the cave, you won't need my company to find them."

"I would sooner we were both rich men, *mon ami,*" Noyer insisted.

Jason shook his head. "I don't begrudge you them," he said. "All I'm interested in finding is Alyssa."

Noyer nodded, understanding.

"There are all kinds of fortunes, *mon ami,*" he agreed softly.

"And I was a fool to leave her at the mission," he went on, talking more to himself than to the Frenchman. "I should have made her go with me to Beau Rivage. I should have kept her with me on the *Empress.*"

"You went back for her, Jason," Noyer reminded him. "You went back to keep her from marrying Remsen."

"And behaved like an idiotic schoolboy," Jason replied. "I should have just told her I love her, convinced her to come with me. But no . . . I had to show her what a fool Remsen was, what a fool she was to agree to marry him. And look where it all has led."

"It's easy to be wise with hindsight, *mon vieux.* But there is no value to torturing yourself with thoughts of what might have been. We'll get her back."

"I wish I were sure of that, Jean."

"I have confidence enough in you for the two of us, *mon vieux,*" Noyer told him. He was about to slap Jason on the shoulder but paused, his hand in midair, when he remembered the wound there. "Before you know it, the three of us will be back at Beau Rivage, emptying my cellar of champagne in celebration."

"From your lips to God's ears," Jason muttered.

"A prayer? I think, Jason, she's already reformed you." Noyer laughed, but the sound of it was empty and faded quickly.

Jason turned his gaze back to the beach. The *Empress* had made the trip more quickly than he'd anticipated. Despite the growing shadows, he knew it would still be at least two hours before it would be dark enough so that they could skirt the island and cross to Nukuhiva without being seen. In the meantime there was nothing for him to do but sit and wait and think.

And none of his thoughts provided him with anything approaching comfort.

Alyssa closed her eyes and waited for the pain of the boar's tusks striking her. She prayed her death would be a quick one.

But then she heard a battle shout behind her and turned to see Mehevi bound down the path and pass her. He held his spear ready to strike and charged down at the advancing boar.

There was a moment of confusion, the air suddenly filled with the animal's anguished squeals as it blindly ran into Mehevi's spear. The point caught the boar just behind its head, and the wound immediately spouted a thick stream of red. The scent of fresh blood and dirt filled the air.

The huge muscles of the cannibal chief's arms and chest strained with the effort of holding the spear and driving it further into the animal's flesh. The wounded boar struggled blindly, its charge useless against its enemy's spear. The frenzied movements served only to drive the shaft deeper, and it cried out its pain in sharp, fitful squeals and grunts.

Alyssa stood for a long, dazed moment, watching the struggle. But she quickly gathered her wits. She turned and began to run, hoping to lose herself in the confusion while the cannibal chief battled the beast.

And in her own confusion she ran into the remainder of the hunting party, those men who had been with Mehevi and were now running down the path to join him. They held their spears extended in front of them as he had, ready for the attack. And Alyssa nearly impaled herself upon them just as the charging boar had raced into the instrument of its own death.

She halted and stood facing the dozen natives. Several pushed their spears aside and swept by her, continuing past her, intent upon helping their chief give the boar the coup de grace. The remainder turned their spears' shafts sideways to bar her way, then slowly began to force her back down the path.

It took her a moment to realize they would not use the spears on her too, that she was not to be treated to the same fate as the boar. And when she did, she pictured again the penned-up creatures on Banaba. Better to die as the boar had, she told herself. Better to struggle and die quickly than go meekly to the knife.

She put her hands out in front of her, grasping the shafts of the spears and pushing against them. The surprised natives only stared at her, dazed and without understanding.

"Why don't you kill me?" she shouted at them when they made no move to raise their weapons to her. She put her hand to the closest man's chest and pushed him. "Kill me!" she shouted at him in heated, frenzied anger.

Amazingly, the natives began to fall back, murmuring "Taboo" at her and making an effort to keep away from her flailing hands. And while one of them stared openly at her naked body, the rest looked away as though they feared even the sight of her might somehow contaminate them.

It took her a moment, but Alyssa soon realized they were forbidden for some reason to touch her. And she determined to use that reluctance, whatever its cause, to her advantage.

She reached out to them, pushing her hands forward, reaching for their arms and their chests. And at her touch, they drew back.

She lost all fear of them and their weapons. She found herself feeling an odd sense of power over them. She waved her hands at them and nearly laughed as they tried to avoid her touch.

But she had not lost sight of her original intention to try to get away. She had managed to edge her way to the side of the path and turn. Now she darted forward, expecting them to give way rather than touch her. Instead, they pushed the shafts of their spears forward at her, apparently recovering from her bewildering charge, and blocked her passage.

"No!" she shouted at them, trying to reach forward, to use again whatever power her touch might have over them.

But they held their ground, and a moment later she felt a hand close firmly on her arm.

She turned. Whatever taboo had prevented the others from touching her, apparently their chief was exempt from it. Mehevi's hands, stained and wet with the pig's blood, grasped her arms, leaving a dark red smear where he touched her. She tried to pull herself away from him, but he held her firmly, his strong hands as ungiving as steel bands.

His eyes, she saw, were pained with disappointment. She wondered if he had actually expected her to remain passive, to wait for his ritual for her death. He spoke a half dozen words, but gave up the effort when her expression remained blankly uncomprehending.

"Mehevi," he said firmly. *"Arioi."*

She remembered the word, realized that he was trying to impress upon her, as he had earlier, his stature, his position, to remind her he was king. She could only shrug in reply.

He turned her around, and ushered her down the path.

She'd tried, she told herself. At least she'd tried.

But then he led her past the place where the boar lay on its side in the blood-soaked dirt, the spear was still embedded in its flesh. It snorted and squealed, and its legs twitched in a last, weak struggle against inevitable death. With each movement a thick surge of red spurted from the wound, leaving the sharp, thick hairs matted with a sticky red coating. As she watched, the boar gave one final spastic shudder and then sank into silence and death.

Was this to be the way she'd die too, she wondered, impaled on Mehevi's spear? At that moment she felt so alone, so pained with the grief of having lost Jason, that she found herself wondering why she even cared.

Chapter Twenty-one

Mehevi brought her back to the old women and handed her over to them with a few stern words. Alyssa had absolutely no question in her mind that he was scolding them for allowing her to escape. Then, turning his back on them and without so much as a glance at Alyssa, he dived into the pool. The women glared at her, obviously blaming her for being the cause of his anger with them.

Alyssa watched him glide beneath the water, his large, muscular body surprisingly fluid, even graceful, as he swam. He covered more than half the distance of the pool before he returned to surface. Completely self absorbed, ignoring the openly admiring glances his performance elicited from his tribeswomen, he devoted his attention to washing away the blood and dirt the pig hunt had left on his skin.

This time the three old women made a point of allowing her no freedom to bathe herself. They gave orders to several of the others to fetch water in calabashes, and carefully stood guard until it was brought. This they emptied on Alyssa's soiled limbs, roughly washing away the smears of dirt and pig's blood from her arms and legs, treating her as they would a willful child. Their voices were sharp with her, and they made no attempt to hide their displeasure at her attempted defection.

When she was washed well enough to suit them, a sheet of clean white tapa cloth was given to her. Alyssa stared at it numbly for a moment before she realized it was meant to substitute for the clothing she had shed before her swim in the pool. She dully took it and wrapped it around herself so that she was covered from breasts to knees.

It was odd, she mused as she tucked the end of the cloth snugly under her arm, that she no longer felt any bodily modesty at all. She'd not only swum naked among the women, she'd also raced through the jungle in the same condition and been seen by more than a dozen men. There had been so many more pressing thoughts in her mind that the fear of being seen undressed, it seemed, paled in comparison. Or perhaps, she thought, she no longer cared about such matters. Perhaps being among people to whom nakedness was natural had dulled the more 'civilized' attitudes she'd been raised to accept.

Quite suddenly she felt the undeniable urge to laugh. Her Uncle Silas, she knew, would be scandalized. She pictured the look of shocked disgust she'd seen him wear so many times when admonishing her for her sins. Public nakedness, she thought, must be by far the worst.

She sobered abruptly before she had the chance to give vent to her laughter, however. Certainly she need not fear Silas's anger ever again. Silas and Plymouth were behind her. So, too, were all but the few days, or perhaps even hours, that remained of her life. Whatever he intended to do with her, surely Mehevi would not wait much longer to do it.

The old women considered her appearance. Then, apparently satisfied, they led her to the far side of the pool and pushed her down to sit on a large, flat stone. She did as they directed, at that moment without any strength or volition to do anything else. The stone, heated by the sun, felt smooth and warm beneath her.

There was the sound of a male voice and Alyssa assumed the chief had finished with his toilette and come to see if she was being properly guarded. But when the circle of women parted, it was not Mehevi who stood before her, but an old man, small and dark and wrinkled, his skin toasted to a dark nut brown by the sun. But it was not the brown of his skin that impressed itself upon Alyssa, but the green and red and blue.

Alyssa had grown almost accustomed to the sight of natives' tattoos, but this man's body wasn't merely embellished with them, it was nearly covered with decoration. From his ankles to his neck, practically every inch of exposed skin had long before been enhanced with tangles of vines and flowers, ropes of shells and simple geometric shapes, an endless series of designs of greens and reds and blues. Some of the shades had faded through the years to become muted with the contrast to the darkening bits of skin that edged the areas of color. The whole was oddly distorted, and the designs seemed to fold in upon themselves as the skin itself grew slack and wrinkled through the passage of time.

Alyssa considered the picture of this strange creature, and he seemed to be equally interested in her. He came to a halt a few feet from her, then knelt and stared at her for a long moment. His dark eyes moved rapidly, as though he was afraid to let his glance linger long on any one feature. Instead, it darted from her face to her legs to her arms and back again to her face, his head nodding as his glance shifted. When his odd inspection was completed, he raised a hand, then suddenly reached out and grasped her arm.

She pulled away from him, but not before he'd let his hand slide along her arm, touching her in a way that made her feel he was considering the texture of her skin, the quality of it. This feat accomplished, he scrambled to his feet and disappeared through the crowd of women, pushing his way negligently past them in his eagerness to be about his business.

Alyssa had little time to consider this bizarre creature before he had once again returned, this time with a large leather sack in his hand. He hunkered down in front of her as he had before, but this time he concentrated all his attention on the contents of his bag. He untied the leather strap that held it closed and carefully removed several small gourds from it. These he set out on the stone near where Alyssa sat. When they were arranged to his liking, he returned to the sack and removed an assortment of thin bone needles.

It was the sight of the needles that sent a shiver of disgust through Alyssa. She had no idea what purpose they served, but she was certain that it could be nothing pleasant. She tried to draw back, away from the old man, but found herself completely hemmed in by the circle of women. She darted hopeful glances at half a dozen of them only to find a complete absence of recognition in the looks they returned her. She had, she realized, alienated them all by outwitting them and trying to get away. They had obviously lost any desire to befriend her.

She returned her attention to the old man. He had pulled small round pegs from the tops of the gourds and was now busily dipping his needles into the liquids inside them. He hummed tonelessly to himself as he prepared for his work, obviously delighted with the pale, clean canvas he had been given upon which to work. Alyssa shuddered. When he withdrew one of the needles and leaned forward toward her, she screamed.

Twenty hands reached out to hold her still yet she screamed and writhed. The old man drew back, muttering angrily to himself, obviously displeased that he was unable to begin his task as long as she continued to struggle.

And then two more hands were holding her, and although the rest were quickly withdrawn, Mehevi's grasp was strong enough to still Alyssa's frantic struggle. He considered the fear be saw in her expression, then barked an order to one of the women. She disappeared, darting away from the group and into the jungle.

Alyssa sat, suddenly painfully aware that she was surrounded by silently staring women, even more sharply aware of Mehevi's grasp on her arms and the greedy look in the old man's eyes. No one spoke. The silence seemed to grow heavier, almost oppressive. Alyssa could hear the noise of birds fluttering in the treetops above, even the dull drone of the insects that inhabited the undergrowth.

In a few moments the woman Mehevi had sent away returned, now bearing a calabash and a gourd. There was liquid in the calabash, Alyssa realized. She could hear a sloshing noise from inside it as the woman came closer.

Mehevi took the small gourd, and the woman tipped the calabash, filling the gourd with a pale, milky liquid. He nodded, waved her back, then turned to face Alyssa.

He offered the gourd to her, holding it close to her lips, but Alyssa turned away, afraid to drink. The stuff in the gourd had a sharp, slightly acid smell to it.

Mehevi took the gourd and sipped the stuff, and spoke a few words which she assumed were assurances that the liquid was harmless. When he returned the gourd to her, she reluctantly took a small sip.

It took only a few seconds before she felt the effects. At first it was just a slight warmth and tingling sensation in her cheeks and fingers, but it spread, a feeling as though she were withdrawing, as though nothing around her could actually touch her. When Mehevi offered her the gourd again, she took a larger swallow.

He was talking to her, pointing to a place on his left

shoulder, to an asymmetric arrangement of a half dozen small triangles that had been tattooed there, the whole no larger than a copper penny, a sprinkling of tiny red and blue darts. Then he pointed to first one of the women, then another, to the same places on their shoulders. Through the growing haze that filled her mind, Alyssa saw that each woman had the same small tattoo on her left shoulder.

And somehow, when he put his arm around her and held her, she had no mind to object. The old man moved forward to her, his needle in hand, and when she tried to shrink back, Mehevi put his hand to her cheek and turned her head so that she didn't see. He pressed the gourd to her lips and she swallowed, feeling only remotely the prick of the needle.

When Mehevi released his hold of her, Alyssa turned dull eyes to the place on her shoulder where she, too, now wore the same small tattoo as the other members of the tribe. She pondered that fact for a moment, wondered why they had done this to her.

Mehevi was speaking to her, nodding, carefully touching the dark mark on her shoulder. She ignored him, instead keeping her eyes on the old man. There was something about the way he was looking at her, as though he was not yet satisfied with his handiwork.

He moved toward her once more, his outstretched hand reaching for her cheek. She was not so drunk with the liquor Mehevi had given her, she realized, that she could not see that he wanted to decorate the pale, unblemished skin there. She struck out at him, and when she did, Mehevi stopped him, speaking a few sharp words.

The old man seemed about to argue, but instead he shrugged and shook his head, as though he could not quite understand the logic that stayed him but would honor it nonetheless. He turned away, concerning himself with his inks and needles, carefully returning them to his sack.

The procedure completed, Mehevi stood. He stared down at her for an instant, then turned and walked away, leaving Alyssa to the care of the old women as he disappeared into the jungle.

It seemed to grow dark too quickly, as though it were full daylight one instant and night the next, with no intervening period of dusk to ease the transition. Alyssa wondered if the effect of the drink Mehevi had given her was wearing off, if that was why the darkness seemed so sharp and thick now, when everything that had preceded it was little more than a fuzzy memory.

She looked down at herself, considering the white of the tapa cloth against her skin, the sharply vivid colors of the ropes of flowers that now encircled her arms and ankles and neck, and had been woven into her hair. She had no memory at all of being adorned in this way, only the hazy memory of sitting beside the pool surrounded by perhaps a dozen of the women. The others all had disappeared, and these few, including the old women, were left to guard her. Their task had been easy. The narcotic drink had left her groggy and lethargic, too lost in a hazy dream world to consider fleeing yet a second time.

But now, as her head began to clear, she realized that the flowers and the wrap of tapa, even the strange mark that was now on her shoulder, were all to prepare her for some ceremony. When the old woman offered her the gourd filled with the milky white liquid, she took it and stared at the stuff a moment, aware of a nearly physical need to return to the peace it had brought her before. She drank, telling herself it would be easier to face her death with the help of whatever narcotic it contained than to look at it clearly. She'd tried to escape and failed. There was nothing more she could do.

Once she'd emptied the gourd, the women led her through the jungle, and she went quietly, hardly even aware of their presence except as guides. Once again the thin veil of the narcotic enveloped her. She found herself considering her situation with an illogical objectivity, as though it was not her, but some stranger being led to whatever ceremony preceded death.

They brought her to a wide clearing. Alyssa was startled, coming on the place as suddenly as they did, by the light of dozens of torches. She squinted her eyes, which stung from the rapid change from darkness to so much light, letting them readjust. They were not far from the beach, she realized. Despite the fact that the clearing was surrounded by undergrowth, still she could hear the sound of the waves quite clearly.

The place was crowded, she realized. Although there had been little sound from them when she'd appeared, dozens of voices now rose as though cued by her entrance. She wondered if she inspired them to discussion of the attributes of their intended dinner.

Her eyes had adjusted to the light, and she could see faces now turned to stare at her. The clearing was nearly filled with people reclining on mats on the ground. Many of the women, she realized, wore the same ropes of flowers as she did. There seemed to be an air of expectancy about their stares.

One of the old women offered her the gourd once again, and in her fear Alyssa accepted it, draining the contents, wanting now only to make herself insensible to whatever was to happen. She closed her eyes for a moment, hoping that she'd simply drift away completely. Unfortunately, when she opened them, nothing had changed.

From the far side of the clearing, Mehevi rose from the high, woven chair where he had been sitting among a group of men. Alyssa immediately knew it was him, recognized the way he stood, the sharp stare of his dark eyes fastened upon her. He started forward to where she stood with the women, and as he did, a slow, deep throb of a drumbeat began. He walked toward her, never taking his eyes from her, crossing the clearing.

He took her hand and nodded his head by way of greeting, his expression now totally sober. Then he turned, motioned to her, and took a step back into the clearing, expecting her to go with him.

She didn't move. Despite the narcotic haze through which she saw him, she could not still the voice inside her that told her that to go with him would be to go to her death. The drug had made her arms become numb, her legs rooted, unable to move, but unfortunately it had not dulled her mind enough to let her escape the knowledge of what was happening or to still her thoughts entirely.

Mehevi finally put his arm around her waist and held her, practically lifting and carrying her with him to the center of the clearing.

He set her down on a thick mat that had been laid out, then settled himself close beside her, sitting cross-legged and apparently devoting his interest completely to the steady, dull sound of the drums. But despite his appearance, he was very conscious of what she did. When she tried to edge away from him, he put his arm around her waist and pulled her back, then left it there, holding her still.

The sound of the drums grew slowly louder, and the crowd that surrounded them settled itself into a respectful silence. And then the drums suddenly stopped.

An old man had appeared at the side of the clearing. He was dressed wildly, in a short grass skirt, in anklets of leather with large, white objects, rounded and strangely indented, hanging from them. It was only after staring at them that Alyssa puzzled out the fact that the pale objects were skulls. The drums began their throbbing beat once again, this time louder and faster than before, and as they did, he began to walk forward, toward the place where she and Mehevi sat. Alyssa trembled, but the cannibal chief held her, not letting her move even if her deadened muscles would have responded to the command.

As the old man approached, Alyssa realized that she had seen him before, that he was the old priest she'd seen on Tapuay. In his arms, just as he had during the ceremony on Tapuay, he carried the strange carved figure, the thing Jason had told her was his god.

When he reached the edge of the mat upon which she sat with Mehevi, the priest began a graceless, spastic dance, made all the more eerie by the motion of the skulls strapped to his ankles, by the way the torchlight cast moving shadows around him. As he moved, he sang in the same toneless singsong she'd heard him use on Tapuay. An odd prayer, if that was what it was, she thought, her dulled mind trying to remember if this was the song he'd sung to his god before that other gruesome feast had begun.

She had no idea how long the dance went on, but suddenly it ended, the drums stopping with him, and the night silence hung thick and foreboding around them. The priest hunkered down and held out the wooden carving he had held in his arms all through his dance.

Alyssa stared at it, oddly mesmerized by the ugly thing with its skeletal head, grinning mouth, bulging eyes, and strangely swollen, disproportionately large, erect member. The doll's eyes seemed to be staring back at her with something akin to loathsome pleasure that probably had more to do with the narcotic she'd been given than to any metamorphosis of the wood from which it had been carved. She shivered and drew back, but only as far as Mehevi's arm allowed her.

The priest began to sing again, the dull drone of his

voice growing louder with each word he intoned. As he sang, he leaned forward, bringing the horrible little doll closer to Alyssa, putting it near her face. She shivered with revulsion and tried to turn away, but even that small movement now seemed beyond the power of her drug-atrophied muscles.

The tempo of the old priest's song soon changed, growing faster, the sound sharper. He pressed the doll forward, touching its swollen member first to Mehevi's lips, then to Alyssa's belly. Alyssa felt a sickly queasiness stir within her when he pressed the thing to her, as though she had been invaded, as though the carved creature's spirit had forced its way inside her. The touch of it left her feeling shaken and somehow dirty.

The priest pushed himself to his feet and danced a bit more, twirling, skipping about, suddenly almost graceful in his movement. The skulls that had been bound to his legs struck one another, the sharp clicking sounds they made sending chills down Alyssa's spine. The dance ended quickly, possibly because the old priest lacked the strength and agility to continue, or perhaps by design. In any case, he soon stood, breathing heavily, beads of perspiration trickling down his cheeks and across his naked chest. The drums continued to beat sharply, throbbingly.

A large, open gourd was brought to the priest, and he lowered the doll to its contents. When he withdrew it, the carving's swollen tumescence was wet and shiny from the liquid that coated it.

The priest gave the gourd to Mehevi, and the chief drank from it. Then he lifted it to Alyssa's lips. Mehevi held her head firm, not letting her turn away, and she realized they intended her to drink more of the narcotic milky liquor they'd given her earlier. At first she refused, able only to keep her lips clamped shut, refusing for no greater reason than out of stubbornness, a determination not to give in so easily. But the pressure of Mehevi's hand at the back of her neck grew sharp. She gasped with the hurt and swallowed some of the drink despite her best efforts to avoid it.

The priest took the gourd away and lifted the carved doll high, holding it above his head. As soon as he lifted it, there was a great shout from half a hundred mouths. With the sound of it, Mehevi turned to Alyssa and smiled a proprietary smile.

Whatever the ceremony had been meant to prepare her for, Alyssa realized it was now completed. A thick narcotic haze filled her mind, and her reasoning, she knew, had grown dull. But despite that, still she knew that the night had only just begun. Whatever it was she was to face, it would come soon.

"What in the name of . . . ?"

Noyer put a hand on Jason's arm.

"Softly, *mon ami,*" he whispered. "It would not do to have our hosts know we are here, at least, not just yet."

Jason nodded, but did not take his eyes from the center of the clearing where Alyssa sat beside the cannibal chief. A thin fringe of undergrowth hid them from the clearing. It was only that and the darkness that kept them from the notice of the natives and, doubtless, from death.

"This isn't what I expected," he said softly.

Noyer nodded. They had all expected to find Alyssa locked in some small shed near the ceremonial place in the clearing. Not that they knew much about the island, but Peli had told them that they could expect a place of ceremony where the priest would probably prepare the sacrifice, and they had no reason to doubt the big Samoan. From what little information Peli had been able to offer them, they'd formulated a plan of sorts as they'd rowed ashore in the darkness. They had hoped opportunity would allow them to create some sort of diversion while the tribe was assembled, enabling them to spirit Alyssa away in the confusion.

But though the clearing was pretty much as Peli had told them it would be, nothing else fit their expectations. It had been a shock to them to see Alyssa being brought into the clearing, an unpleasant shock when the chief had escorted her to the place at its center where she now sat surrounded and beyond their reach.

"I think it's a wedding," Noyer ventured after a few more moments' consideration. "They aren't getting ready to kill her at all. The chief is taking her as his wife."

Jason considered the way Alyssa was now dressed, the white tapa cloth, the flower chains around her neck and head and limbs. He had never heard of any rite where a victim to be sacrificed was adorned in this way. On the other hand, a bride could most certainly be arrayed in such island finery. He felt a fire begin in his stomach at the thought, a fire, he knew, that was nothing more than base jealousy.

For a moment he considered the picture she made, pale and withdrawn, probably with fright, but unutterably beautiful in his eyes. It was no wonder, he thought, that the chief had determined to keep her rather than turn her over to the priest as a sacrifice.

If he'd been less of a fool, he brooded, he would have done what this cannibal chief was doing, he would have married her rather than leave her alone with Remsen at the mission. If he had, none of what had happened would ever have come to pass. The burning hurt in his stomach grew stronger, the jealousy laced now with anger and regret.

Argus stared, like the others, considering the strange ceremony. As the cup was pressed to Alyssa's lips, however, he understood what it was they were giving her to drink.

"And they're making sure she'll cooperate. She looks

drugged already, and unless I miss my guess, that's *arva* they're giving her."

Jason clenched his teeth. "How the hell do we get her out now?" he hissed beneath his breath, talking more to himself than to the others. It had been dangerous enough coming ashore, skirting the clearing with all the natives moving about. But there was no way they could simply run through the assembled mass of them and snatch Alyssa away.

Peli nodded. "We wait." He spoke rarely, but when he did, it was with the strength of conviction and certain knowledge. "There will be the chance soon enough," he assured Jason.

Jason turned to him. "When?" he asked.

"He will take her to a wedding hut," Peli told him. "It will be away from the rest, where the chief can enjoy his first night with his bride undisturbed by the presence of his other wives and children."

The thought sickened Jason, the sure knowledge of what the cannibal chief would do to her.

"Where will it be?" he demanded.

Peli shook his head. "I don't know. Somewhere away from the rest, I think. We will have to wait, and follow them once they are alone."

"Assuming we manage to avoid being seen until then," Argus said.

"Assuming we manage to avoid being killed," Noyer added ominously.

It was all some strange dream, Alyssa thought. She wanted to close her eyes, to sleep and then wake to find it all had disappeared. The noise, the throb of drums, the constant movement around her, it all seemed to her *arva*-numbed mind part of a grotesque, unending nightmare.

But through it all was the tense sense of waiting, of

expecting Mehevi at any moment to lead her forward to the priest who would welcome her with a knife in one hand and the horrid little carved creature in the other. She almost wished the moment would finally come. It could be no worse than the anticipation.

The feast was growing wilder and noisier. Calabashes of the milky *arva* were being passed, and as they drank it the natives grew louder and more enthusiastic in their celebration. Huge gourds filled with food had appeared, heaps of fruits, huge grilled fishes, and enormous slabs of roast meat. Part of her wanted to believe the meat was from the boar she'd seen Mehevi kill that afternoon, but each time she glanced at it she found herself picturing not the dying boar as she'd last seen it, but the human haunch she'd watched being drawn from the fire that night on Tapuay. When Mehevi offered her a piece, she gagged and pushed his hand away.

And through it all was the continual sound of the drums. It seemed to seep into her, become part of her, almost like the beat of her own heart. Like some sort of fever, it coursed through her veins until her body began to sway with the beat.

She was not alone. All around her the half drunken natives were springing to their feet, leaping into spontaneous movement, shouting out in drunken glee. Their bodies moved, hips shaking seductively to the drums' throbbing cadence, arms and legs moving now gracefully, now with jerking, bizarre movements that seemed beyond the natives' control. When they grew finally too exhausted to continue, they dropped back to their places to revive themselves with food and more of the seemingly endless stream of *arva*.

But all this seemed almost remote to Alyssa, for Mehevi was too close for her to think long of anything or anyone else. He didn't move from her side, nor did he long release the hold he had on her. As he ate, he tore bits of his food and put it to her lips, allowing her to reject it as she seemed intent on avoiding the meat, but not content unless she sipped the *arva* each time he offered it. He kept his eyes on her, watching her as she slowly relinquished the last of her control to the effects of the *arva.* The more drunk she became, the more satisfied he seemed.

When he stood and lifted Alyssa to her feet, she was almost oblivious to what was happening to her. She'd fallen into hell, she thought, her eyes lingering on the flames of the torches that danced in the breeze and the sea of bodies that seemed to her to writhe in agony as they twisted and contorted in time to the drumbeats. The thought of her uncle filled her mind, telling her he'd always known she'd be damned. It seemed to her that he had been right. If this was not hell, she could not think what it might be.

Mehevi began to lead her through the sea of celebrants, pushing roughly against those who inadvertently did not make way for him quickly enough, pulling Alyssa in his wake. She stumbled along behind him, her numbed feet dragging more often than stepping forward, her nostrils filled with the mixed odors of *arva,* the roasted meat, and the heated, thick scent of strange bodies wet with perspiration.

It had finally come, she thought. He was taking her to the priest and his knife. Her head throbbed and she felt ill with the smells and the smoke and her own dread.

They reached the edge of the clearing and Mehevi paused there for a moment, turning to look back at the celebration that continued on despite his departure. And Alyssa, too, stared numbly at the strange moving creature that filled the space. For the bodies no longer seemed individual to her, but one huge, writhing monster with countless heads and arms, all moving, pulsing to the single dull throb that filled the air.

She looked away, more terrified by what she saw than reason told her she ought to be, turning her eyes instead to the undergrowth, searching for something less alien to her, less frightening. And when she did, she saw something that froze her, that left her shaking and bewildered.

There, on the edge of the clearing, just behind a torn fringe of banana leaves and palm fronds, were Jason's eyes staring back at her.

Her heart seemed to stand still and she gasped in disbelief. Suddenly she felt completely sober, totally in control of her drugged body. But the feeling was fleeting. Mehevi began to pull her away, onto some path into the jungle, and she stumbled and nearly fell.

He steadied her and watched her as her eyes drifted back to the place at the edge of the clearing where she'd seen Jason. He followed her glance and found the same emptiness she now found, just the mass of wind-tattered leaves and fronds and nothing more.

It had been an illusion, she told herself, a wraith the drink and her own wishful thoughts had manufactured because Jason had come to her those other times when she'd needed him. But there was no possibility that he could come to save her now, she realized. He was dead, lying in the cave back on Tapuay, most probably, and there was nothing his ghost could do to keep her from whatever the cannibals had decided to do with her. He was dead, and he'd taken part of her with him, leaving her empty inside and more alone than she had ever been before. It didn't matter what the cannibals intended to do with her, she told herself. Jason was dead, and nothing else would ever mean anything to her again.

Mehevi pulled her after him into the shadows of the jungle, and she followed along numbly, grateful when the drug's haze seemed to settle over her once again.

She had no idea how long they walked, minutes perhaps, or a good deal more. She felt numb inside, even more numb than the deadened feeling the *arva* had left in her clumsy limbs. The glimpse she'd had of Jason's ghost, or whatever it had been, seemed to have scraped out any vestige of fear or feeling she had left within her. She would, she told herself, welcome the old priest's knife.

Finally Mehevi halted and turned to face her. Behind him she saw the light of a single torch that had been set into the ground to light the entrance to a small hut. Set on the ground before its entrance were heaps of flowers and fruits laid out on beds of large leaves, and a calabash like the ones from which the natives had drunk the narcotic *arva*. Her eyes searched the circle of light cast by the torch, looking for the old priest, for some sign that her sacrifice was to be made in this place.

There was none.

Mehevi smiled down at her, and his breath grew short. The want for her he'd begun to feel the night before, honed by the day's wait, the throb of the drums, and the drink, now grew sharp within him, too sharp for him even to wait until he had brought her into the hut that had been prepared for them. He pushed her against the trunk of a tall palm that edged the path, pressing his body to hers, and began to pull up the drape of cloth that covered her.

Alyssa felt his hand, hard and hot, groping against the flesh of her thigh.

She gasped with sudden awareness and began to push, uselessly, against the weight of him.

She had been right in part about what was to happen to her that night. But she had been completely wrong about its manner.

There was to be a sacrifice, but it was not her life that the cannibal chief wanted from her. It was something else entirely.

Chapter Twenty-two

Mehevi leaned forward to Alyssa, pressing his lips against the soft flesh of her neck.

She screamed, her reaction stemming more from anger than from fright. The haze and dizziness that had clouded her mind seemed to have been swept away with a single stroke by the press of his lips against her neck. She knew clearly now what was to happen to her, and the prospect made the old priest's blade seem an almost inviting alternative. If she'd been resigned to accept death without a struggle a few moments before, her resignation vanished along with the drug-induced haze. She would not submit meekly, she swore to herself, not to this. She would not allow herself to become the cannibal chief's docile victim.

She quickly realized that she could not free herself from him. He was far too big, and she had nowhere near enough strength to push him away. She started to flail at him, her hands balled into fists, striking out wildly. The response was one of panic, not thought. Had she considered the possibility, she would have immediately realized that the impact of her fists would seem like little more than gnat bites to so strong and powerful a man.

The first few blows, however, seemed to startle him. He pulled back, his expression filled with surprise. He seemed completely unprepared for the possibility that she might not be entirely willing to cooperate. It occurred to her that none of his own women had ever before refused him, that the prospect was alien to him.

But his surprise was not so great that he was willing to allow her to escape. When she tried to twist herself free from his grasp, he caught her arms, pulling her back. Then he reached down and caught her hands in his before she could strike him again, and held them pinned to her sides as he pushed himself close once more.

She could feel his breath, hot and moist, against her neck, could smell on his breath the *arva* he had drunk, as well as the anxious perspiration that dampened his skin. In the distance there still came the sound of drums, the beat faint now, but as inescapable as the press of Mehevi's body and the heated groping of his hands against her skin.

She closed her eyes and thought of Jason. His death, her abandonment to the cannibal chief's hands, suddenly became unbearably real to her. Just as Jason had been unable to escape from Nukuhiva, she realized she would never escape from Mehevi. All that was left to her was a yearning for a return to the narcotic haze, a wish for her mind to escape his attack even if her body could not.

But there was no reprieve for her. She felt his hands lift away the tapa cloth, felt the press of his flesh, hot and hard with anticipation, against hers.

She struggled, but they both knew it was useless. She could not free herself from him without his leave, and he had no intention of releasing her until he had had what he wanted from her.

"Go back and tell the others to take care of the canoes," Jason hissed.

He started to rise from the place in the undergrowth

where they knelt hidden from view, but Peli pulled him back.

"You need me," the big Samoan told him.

Jason shook his head.

"No," he insisted. "I can deal with him alone. But we'll be pressed to outrun them in the darkness, so you'd better see they won't be able to come after us. And you'd better find some diversion, maybe a fire." He glanced distractedly at the place in front of the small hut where Alyssa struggled with the cannibal chief, and again he felt the burning rage in his belly. He jerked his arm away from Peli. "Hurry."

"No noise," Peli reminded him. "If you make any noise, you'll bring the whole of the tribe down on you."

Jason nodded. "I know," he said, distracted, wanting only to end what he saw happening by the hut. "Go!" he repeated.

Jason started out from the place where they hid, reaching the path in a step. He did not even wait to watch Peli melt into the night darkness of the jungle.

Jason needed only a glance to tell him that Mehevi was not going to wait to take Alyssa to the hut, to see that the cannibal intended to finish what he had begun there, by the tree at the far side of the path. Already Mehevi had stripped away the cloth that had been wrapped around her body, and his hands reached hungrily for her breasts.

Jason started to run.

"Jason?"

Alyssa couldn't believe her eyes. He was standing not half a dozen feet from her, staring down at Mehevi's prone body on the ground at his feet, and still she could not quite believe what she saw. She'd felt the pain of his death so keenly that for an instant she almost believed this was his ghost come to save her. A thick, thudding beat filled her chest. He was alive, a joyous voice inside her proclaimed. He was alive!

Jason hardly realized what he'd done until he stood over the cannibal chief, staring down at him as Mehevi returned the stare groggily from where he lay on the ground. It was the anger that spurred him, Jason assumed, the sight of Alyssa struggling against the huge native's forced advance, kindling something like animal rage in him, something he did not remember ever having felt before.

He had no memory of the wild charge nor of the staggering impact that had felled Mehevi. He had only the sharp, throbbing ache in his injured shoulder to assure him that he had been responsible for the cannibal chief's sudden and obviously unanticipated tumble.

What was real to him was the sound of Alyssa's voice, the touch of her hands as she reached for him. He kept his eyes on the sprawled figure on the ground at his feet and gently pushed her back, out of the way, aware that the fight was not yet finished.

Mehevi turned slowly until he sat staring up at his unexpected assailant. His expression was at first puzzled, but as soon as he saw Jason's face, it contorted with fury.

He kept his glance on Jason's as he pushed himself slowly to his knees. The men eyed one another in wary silence, each evaluating, weighing what he saw in the other. The cannibal's movements were still not sure or measured, no doubt as much a result of the *arva* he'd drunk at the ceremony as of the blow, but his rage was great enough to push hard at the fog that threatened to cloud his mind and rob him of his ability to fight. Jason quickly realized he was facing an opponent that was his measure.

Or more than his measure. For the first time since he'd left the *Empress* behind in the darkness, he was conscious of the painful infection the wound in his shoulder had caused and which now raged within him. It had been sheer stupidity, he realized, for him to send Peli back to help Argus and Noyer and leave him alone to face the cannibal chief.

His hand fell to his holstered pistol, but he quickly let it fall away. The sound of a shot would call down the whole of the tribe. This would have to be a fight on the native's ground, using only those weapons nature had provided them both.

For an instant Jason wondered why the cannibal did not simply cry out to his men, and then he realized that to do so would be to belittle himself in their eyes. This was to him a fight over a woman, a fight for honor. He would not admit he was so weak that he could not vanquish this enemy alone and unaided.

Mehevi stayed a moment on his knees, watching as Jason backed a step away from him, letting his breath steady and marshaling his forces. Then he sprang forward, his intent to strike Jason low and throw him off balance.

But if Mehevi was bigger, Jason was faster. He sidestepped the attack, raising his leg as Mehevi's body fell past him and feeling a sharp satisfaction as it connected with the other man's abdomen, hearing the cannibal's moan and sharply exhaled breath as he fell yet a second time.

Mehevi hit the ground heavily, but he rolled away from Jason and pushed himself immediately back to his feet. This second blow had driven away the last of the euphoria the feast and the *arva* had given him. His eyes narrowed in determined anger. He spread his feet, steadying himself, and then started forward.

Jason avoided the first two blows and landed one of his own before Mehevi's fists managed to find their mark. That single blow, however, was more than enough to show the cannibal chief that his adversary was not without weakness. He saw Jason's wince of pain as his fist came in contact with the wounded shoulder, and he made use of what he saw, directing his fists to the same spot, finally felling Jason with the third blow.

He intended to offer Jason no chance to catch his breath or remarshal his forces. He smiled, sure he was about to end the fight and take his revenge on the man who had dared to violate his tribe's sacred cave. He dived forward, aiming to bring his knees down on Jason's chest as he fell.

But Jason managed to roll to the side just as Mehevi dropped to the ground. The cannibal was left reeling forward, temporarily stunned by the impact of the earth to his knees, as Jason scrambled to his feet.

Mehevi, too, quickly recovered, and was once again on his feet, facing Jason, evaluating the effect of the fight on him. His smile had vanished, and he was flushed with rage now, incensed that this interloper had so far managed to better him. He seemed to be tired with the game, eager for its conclusion. He edged backward, moving closer to the hut until he could feel the heat of the torch that had been set in the ground near its entrance. As Jason advanced on him, he pulled up the torch and swung the burning end forward.

Jason managed to jump out of its path just in time as the flaming brand swept past his chest, singeing his shirt and leaving his face wet with sweat. He backed away, his eyes on the cannibal's. Mehevi advanced on him, holding out the burning torch threateningly.

Jason realized he could not win. Other than his pistol, he had no weapon, and to use the pistol would mean bringing the whole tribe running. More than that, he felt himself growing weaker. The blows to his shoulder had started the wound bleeding. He could feel the warm trickle of blood on his back. There was no possibility he could fight off the cannibal chief for much longer, and Mehevi was pressing him, thrusting the burning torch closer, forcing him backward. The cannibal was waiting only for him to stumble or fall before he made use of his advantage.

But perhaps, Jason thought, using the pistol and calling all the tribesmen down on him could save Alyssa. It would create the diversion that would leave her and the others time to escape. It was not quite the way they'd planned matters, but close enough. The only difference would be that he would not be among those who would leave the island.

It was not so bad a trade, he told himself, his life for hers.

"Alyssa," he called out to her. "Go to the beach. Find Noyer and Argus. Tell them to get out of here."

He began to reach for the pistol.

For a moment Alyssa stood frozen by what she'd seen, but not so numbed that she did not realize that he meant to sacrifice himself to give her the chance to get away. If her muscles still seemed clumsy and alien to her, her mind was now clear and sharply perceptive.

"No," she cried. "I won't leave you here."

"Don't be a fool!" he shouted at her. Still, he dropped his hand away from the pistol. He couldn't use it as long as she was there, couldn't chance that she would be found with him and the dead chief's body.

She realized she was still clumsy, her limbs still numbed from the *arva,* but somehow she forced them to move. She ran forward, skirting Mehevi and darting toward the entrance to the hut where the food and drink had been set out for the chief's wedding night.

She snatched up the calabash and threw it.

She'd meant only to distract Mehevi, hopefully to knock the burning torch from his hand. But her aim was poor, and the force with which she threw the heavy calabash was not nearly enough to make it strike the cannibal's hand. As it flew forward, the huge gourd sprayed an arc of the alcoholic liquid into the air. Then, when it fell, it burst open and wet the ground a few feet in front of the place where Mehevi stood.

The cannibal chief's eyes did not so much as stray from Jason. He ignored the calabash and the puddle of *arva* as he moved forward, pushing his advantage, advancing on Jason and swinging the torch.

"Get back," Jason shouted to Alyssa as he saw the torch come close to the wet line the spray of *arva* left on the ground.

She did as he told her, darting back, forcing her numbed muscles to move away from the milky white trail even as the torch ignited it. The flame shot forward to the place in front of the hut where she'd been standing and back to the puddle left by the broken calabash where Mehevi now stood in mystified shock.

There was a thick whoosh as the puddle of *arva* went up in flames, and then Mehevi's agonized scream.

Alyssa felt Jason's hand tugging at her arm. She was rooted by the horror of what she saw, sure she would never be able to move from that spot. But Jason pulled her away, into the undergrowth, just as the first sparks struck the thatched roof of the hut. She turned back to glimpse the hut as the fire quickly consumed the dry thatch and, far more frightening, to gape at Mehevi's fallen body encased in flames.

"Hurry," Jason shouted to her, pulling her arm, forcing her to turn away from the thing that Mehevi had become, a horror that lay on the ground writhing in its last death throes.

Alyssa tried to sweep away the image of Mehevi from her mind, concentrating her attention on the need to avoid roots and low branches as she ran. But she knew what she had seen would stay with her for the rest of her life, just as would the sound of the cannibal's dying scream. She had no idea where Jason was leading her, had no thoughts at all save for the tearing knowledge that she had been the cause of a gruesome, horrible death. She was too numbed by the memory of that to think.

But after a few moments of running, she realized the sound of drums had grown much louder. For an instant she thought it might be the beating of her own heart, but then she saw a flicker of torchlight snaking through the darkness of the undergrowth. They were, she realized, close to the large clearing where the tribe was still celebrating Mehevi's marriage.

Jason pulled her from the path. She stood panting for a moment, trying to catch her breath as she stared at the dancers in the center of the clearing. But Jason did not leave her time either to gape or to think.

"This way," he whispered, pulling her through the thick foliage that edged the clearing. "Try not to make any noise."

Not that a little noise would really matter, he knew . . . the feast would not go on much longer, in any case. It would not take long before the flames from the burning hut would be seen. And when they were, all hell would break loose.

He was right. They were still skirting the clearing when the first bright tongues of flames became visible. The fire had spread, and the tribe turned to stare up at the treetops, first in an *arva*-dazed awe at the brilliance of the light, and then with panic as they realized what it must be that had caused it.

Jason hoped the others had destroyed the cannibal's canoes and gone back to the beach. It wouldn't be long, he realized, before the natives found Mehevi's body. When they did, they would search for the intruder who had been the cause of his death and for the pale-skinned woman their chief had taken for his bride.

"Come on," Jason said as he pulled Alyssa through the undergrowth, distracting her attention from the shouting panic that was now spreading through the members of the tribe. "We have to get out of here."

Another endless period of running through the undergrowth, but this time there was no sound of drums to echo the pounding of Alyssa's heart. This time the air was filled with shouts, with cries of anger.

She no longer noticed the branches that slapped against her face and arms and legs. She'd grown numb with fear, she thought, as the realization fixed itself in her mind of what would happen to her and Jason were the cannibals to find them. They would take great pleasure in revenging their chief's grisly death, she had no doubt of that. This time capture would mean a slow and horrible end.

She was panting, and so it did not seem strange to her that Jason's breath, too, was unusually labored. And she was too lost in her own thoughts to realize immediately that he was moving more and more slowly, that it was becoming a greater and greater effort for him to keep moving.

And then finally they were by the shore, peering through the fringe of greenery across a wide swath of sand to where three shadows disappeared into the darker shadows further along the beach.

Jason grasped Alyssa's hand. "Come on," he whispered as he parted the curtain of the undergrowth.

She pulled back. "There's someone out there," she whispered. "I saw movement."

"Let's hope so," Jason replied. "We'll never be able to find the others if they haven't gotten themselves back to the boat."

And there wasn't much time, he realized. He could hear movement and shouts not far behind. The cannibals had doubtless already discovered the fire had claimed more than just the hut, that it also had taken Mehevi's body. In any case, it wouldn't be long before they were on the beach, hungry for the blood of whoever had done this thing to their chief.

The two of them started out, onto the sand and to the water's edge, running along the shore. But they hadn't gone very far when Jason began to lag, and then he stumbled.

Alyssa turned back to him. "What is it?" she asked. She realized finally that he was breathing heavily, far too heavily. Each step he took seemed to take more and more effort.

He shook his head. "Go on. The boat's hidden in that outcropping just ahead. Noyer should be there."

"What's wrong?" she demanded. "Are you hurt?"

"Just winded," he told her. "Go on."

But she refused. "You came after me," she told him. "I can't leave you here."

His eyes narrowed. "It was my fault they took you," he told her. "It's my responsibility to get you back."

"Then the only reason you risked your life to come here was to do your duty as a conscientious captain?" she demanded.

"I've my reputation to keep." He managed a weak grin.

"Liar," she told him. "Let me help you."

She put her arm around his waist before he could object, and found her fingers touching something warm and sticky. It took her several seconds to realize it was his blood. She drew her hand back and stared at the dark, sticky stain it left on her fingers.

"You're hurt," she gasped. It was impossible, she thought. She would have seen it if he'd been wounded. But she couldn't argue with the warm, thick liquid on her hand.

"A scratch," he told her.

"What happened?" she demanded.

He only shook his head and refused to say more.

She put her hand back around him, trying to steady him and help him forward. But her mind was racing, telling her that if she had not seen him being wounded, then the wound had most likely, come from the foray into the cave on Nukuhiva. She realized that he had come after her. Even wounded, still he'd come after her.

They stumbled on for a few moments, aware now of the flash of light from the flames burning in the jungle behind them. There had been no need for Noyer to provide Jason with the diversion he'd requested to distract the natives while they escaped. With Mehevi's unwitting help, they'd made their own diversion, and it was proving to be as much a hindrance as a help to them, for the flames were growing brighter as they leaped into the air, bathing the beach in a frightening, red-streaked light.

There were shouts coming from behind them, in the jungle, and the sound of movement. The noise seemed to be growing louder, closer, and Alyssa realized the cannibals were once again hunting as they had hunted that afternoon, but this time their prey was human, not boar. This time she and Jason were the prey.

Jason pointed further along the beach to where three men were pushing a small craft from the bank at its edge into the deeper water beyond.

"There they are," he told Alyssa.

He put his hand to hers, forcing it from his waist, and then pushed her away.

"What are you doing?" she demanded.

"Go on," he told her. His tone was rough, almost angry, as he tried to convince her to go on without him. "Send Peli back for me."

"I'm not leaving you," she told him, and tried to put her arm around him once again.

"Damn it, Miss Missionary, do as you're told for once," he hissed at her. "Go."

The sound of shouts and movement from the jungle's edge behind them was growing louder. It wouldn't be long, they both realized, before the natives were on the beach, before they would see the two of them fleeing.

"Go," Jason shouted again, and gave her a sharp push forward. "You can't carry me, and I can't go much further. Go, and send back Peli. Or else you'll get the both of us killed."

One of the man-shaped shadows splashed back through the knee-deep water to where Alyssa stood with the waves lapping at her knees. She didn't even notice he was there until he spoke.

"Get into the boat," Noyer told her.

She turned and looked at him, then shook her head.

"No, not without Jason," she objected.

She darted an anxious look to the length of beach to watch Peli racing back to where Jason staggered at the water's edge. There were more shadows, a lot more, appearing now beside the fringe of green that bordered the beach. They were still in disarray, calling to one another, crying out as though they could not quite believe what had happened. But Alyssa knew they would organize themselves quickly enough. And when they did, it would be only a matter of moments before they began a systematic search of the beach.

If Peli didn't reach him soon, Jason would certainly be seen in the growing light cast by the flames. When he was, the cannibals would be after him, hot with the taste for revenge. He would not last long alone on the beach once the pursuit began.

"You can do him no good here, *ma chère,*" Noyer insisted. He put his hand on Alyssa's arm and tugged, pulling her backward, forcing her into the deeper water.

She turned angrily to the Frenchman. "I'm not leaving without him."

"No one's leaving without him," Noyer told her sharply. "But you are of no help to him here. Now get into the boat."

It was the first time she'd heard Noyer use any tone but one of good-humored lechery with her, and it momentarily stunned her. She let him pull her forward, further into the water, then finally hand her up to Argus's waiting arms. Then she watched him turn and start back for Jason.

Peli had reached Jason. He'd pulled his captain's arm around his neck, steadying and supporting him. They were running, or at least the big Samoan was running. Jason could do little more than stagger, making an effort to help himself, but having little success. And then suddenly he slumped forward and Peli was forced to carry him.

They were perhaps fifty feet from the boat when Noyer reached them, and between them the two men half carried, half dragged Jason the remaining distance. It was none too soon. As they pushed Jason over the side and into the longboat, there was a sudden burst of directed, angry shouting. Noyer and Peli clambered into the boat as Argus took up the oars.

"Stay still," Argus shouted at her as Alyssa tried to scramble forward, to where Jason's body lay in a still heap. "And get down."

There was no deference in the first mate's tone, none of the respectful admiration she remembered him showing her. He'd given her an order, and from the way he'd spoken, he expected it to be followed. She nodded, mute and cowed, and resettled herself at his feet.

By the time Noyer and Peli had settled themselves with their oars, the first of the natives had begun racing toward the water in chase. There was a rain of thrown spears, and the sound of splashing as a score of angry natives dived into the water, knives gripped between their teeth, swimming in frenzied pursuit. And despite the three men manning the oars, the boat was not moving quickly enough to escape them. Strong swimmers, the cannibals were drawing closer.

But as the boat neared the *Empress*'s side, the night air was suddenly filled with the sharp, cracking sound of rifle fire. It was enough to make the natives reassess their hunger for revenge, making them weigh the possibility of their own deaths against the death of their chief's murderer. In the end, fear seemed to win out. Alyssa turned back to see them turn away and swim back toward the beach, intending, perhaps, to better arm themselves and attempt a more organized attack in their canoes, one that might give them a greater chance of winning.

She felt herself being roughly handed up onto the *Empress*'s deck, and then watched as Jason's limp body was handed up after her. She knelt on the deck by his side when he was set down there, taking his hand in hers, bewildered and stunned to see him so still. She put her hand to his neck, searching for his pulse, needing to feel it to assure herself that he was still alive.

Around them, the *Empress*'s deck and rigging sprang to life with motion as her crew unreefed the sails and turned her toward the open sea. But Alyssa was aware of none of that, just as she had no cognizance of the frenzied shouts from shore as the natives found their canoes with fresh holes hacked into the hulls and realized they had lost their chance for revenge.

No longer threatened, the *Empress* sailed away from Tapuay with a nearly leisurely nonchalance, an odd anticlimax to the frenzied hour that had preceded her flight.

Noyer put his hand to Alyssa's shoulder, finally rousing her from the dull reverie that claimed her as she knelt beside Jason's unconscious body.

"I think, *ma chère,* it might be best if we got him below."

She nodded, scrambled to her feet and helped the Frenchman lift him.

"He's wounded," she told Noyer. "His shoulder."

"Oui, *chérie,*" Noyer told her. He grinned at her, returning now to his accustomed mien. "But do not look so stricken. We'll tend to his little scratch, and you will see, he'll soon be as evil-tempered as ever."

Alyssa ignored his levity. She was not at all sure that the wound was the little scratch Noyer seemed to think it was. If it was minor, she asked herself, then why was Jason so still, so pale?

Between the two of them, they managed to get Jason to his cabin and onto his bunk. Noyer set him down, intending to rebandage the now reopened and profusely bleeding wound in his shoulder.

Alyssa gasped. Embedded in Jason's back, surrounded by the blood that now drenched his shirt, was a small, feather-tipped dart.

"What's that?" she demanded.

Noyer, too, stared, then reached forward and pulled the dart from where it had stuck in Jason's back. The shaft, a finely honed, sharp sliver of bone, glistened with Jason's blood. The Frenchman shook his head, as bewildered as Alyssa by the small barb.

But Peli, who had followed them to Jason's cabin and now stood by the door, staring in at them, was far less confused. He entered the cabin, quickly moving to Noyer's side and taking the dart from the Frenchman's hand. He sniffed the dart's tip, and then the side of its shaft.

And as he stared at the dart, Alyssa replayed in her mind Jason's flight from the beach, seeing again the way he had staggered along with his arm around Peli's neck, remembering the way he'd suddenly slumped forward, unconscious. One of those dark, moving shadows that had emerged from the undergrowth behind them had shot that dart into him, she realized. And this sudden stillness was the result.

The big Samoan shook his head.

"What is it?" she demanded.

Peli stared at her with wide, dark eyes, considering his response.

"*Urali,* I think, miss," he said slowly.

Alyssa gaped, uncomprehending, at him, then turned to Noyer. The Frenchman's concerned expression in no way lessened the thick feeling of dread that began to fill her stomach.

"What is it?" she asked again, this time barely able to force the words from her lips.

Noyer put his hand on hers.

"Poison, *ma chère,*" he told her softly.

She snatched her hand away.

"No," she shouted. "It can't be. It's not fair."

"Perhaps it isn't *urali,*" Noyer replied, "perhaps it's just the wound."

He glanced up at Peli, and his look was more than enough for Alyssa to realize that he was simply trying to calm her.

"What do we do?" she asked in a hoarse whisper.

"What little we can, *chérie,*" Noyer replied gently. "And we pray."

Chapter Twenty-three

Jason's breathing was shallow and labored, he was burning with fever, and his face was sickly pale. Alyssa stared at him and felt the knot of fear in her stomach grow tighter.

"He's no better?"

She turned, looked up at Noyer, and shook her head.

"He's worse," she murmured.

She stared into the Frenchman's eyes, wondering why Noyer didn't accuse her, why he didn't blame her for being the cause of what was happening to his friend. Because even if the Frenchman didn't blame her, she blamed herself, she knew. Each time she heard Jason draw a painfully rasping breath, she told herself that this never would have happened if he hadn't come after her.

She managed to get Jason to swallow a few drops of water, then rinsed out a cloth and put it on his forehead. It wasn't much, but there was little else she could do. Together she and Noyer had cleaned and rebandaged the wound in his shoulder, but there was nothing either of them could do for the poison the dart had left in his blood, and even Peli could offer them little advice.

"We'll be back in Banaba soon," Noyer told her. "There's medicine at the mission."

He offered her a weak smile, and Alyssa knew he was trying to keep her from giving in to the growing despair that filled her. But there was, she realized, nothing he could say or do that would loosen the thick knot in her stomach or make her feel alive again. Back on Tapuay, she'd believed Jason was dead and she'd felt as though a part of herself had died with him. Seeing him again, learning he was still alive, had been as great a release for her as being saved from the cannibal chief. She knew she could not bear coming to grips with his death all over again.

"How much longer?" she asked Noyer.

"A few hours at the most," Noyer replied. He edged his way to the cabin's side and stared out the porthole. "It's nearly full light."

"It's been the longest night of my life," she murmured.

It was true. Nothing that had happened to her since she'd left Plymouth had been as hard for her as quietly sitting beside Jason during those long hours and watching his life slowly slipping away from him. Not even the thought of her own death had been as hard for her to bear as this.

"Why does he hate missionaries?" she asked.

There had been a protracted silence, and the sound of her own words startled her. She had no idea why she had asked that particular question, but now that she had, she was determined to know.

Noyer stood silent for a moment, then seated himself facing her.

"It was because of me, actually," he replied slowly, then looked down at his clasped hands and sank into silence.

Alyssa waited, not knowing what to say and assuming he would tell her when he found his own way. She was right. After a moment's silence, Noyer began to talk.

"It was a long time ago," he said, "more than ten years, before old Merricomb came to Banaba. There was another missionary then, a man named Rickens, as dried up and hard as a crust. And there were others, two others in particular, the local chief and his wife, his beautiful wife. Her name was Pelari."

He closed his eyes and smiled as he spoke her name,

and it was more than apparent that merely unlocking her image in his memory was more than enough to bring him pleasure. Then he paused and swallowed, as though he really didn't want to say any more, but realized he'd gone this far and might as well go on. Alyssa stared at him, completing the story in her mind, wondering if Jason had loved this Polynesian woman whose very name made Noyer smile.

He returned his glance to her and smiled. "Until I saw you, I'd never seen a more lovely woman," he told her. "And I wasn't long on the island before it became clear to me that she was not happy in her marriage. Her husband beat her, abused her." He turned his eyes away, looking up to the cabin's ceiling, again searching his mind for the memory of this woman Pelari. "And I became infatuated with her, filled with a young man's hungers and a young man's ego, both of which were only fed by the knowledge that she did not find my company without a certain amount of charm. I pursued her, thinking only of what I felt for her. Finally I seduced her."

"But what had that to do with Jason?" Alyssa asked softly.

"I think he may have been a bit in love with her himself," Noyer told her. He shrugged. "No matter. The whole incident would have been nothing had she not become a Christian, for the Polynesians have a very forgiving attitude about matters of this sort. But Rickens had converted her and her husband, you see, and they were both firmly entrenched in the dogma he preached to them each Sunday. As soon as she and I became lovers, she began to feel guilt, and it wasn't long before it overwhelmed her. I begged her to leave her husband, but she couldn't, you see, because Rickens had preached to her that marriage was forever. She went to Rickens, told him what she'd done, begged him to help her. And rather than help, he told her to go to her husband and confess her sins and beg his forgiveness, or she would be damned."

"And?"

"Her husband beat her, then threw her out of her home, and told her she could never see her children again. It was more than she could bear. She was so accepting, so childlike in her beliefs. She was cut off from her children, and she believed, as Rickens had told her, that she was damned. She walked into the ocean and drowned herself."

"And her husband?" Alyssa asked after a short silence.

Noyer's expression grew fixed. "He died a few days later," he said. "A hunting accident."

Alyssa's throat grew tight. "Was it Jason?" she asked in a hoarse whisper.

"No, *ma chère*. Jason had been gone from the island for more than a month when all this occurred. Responsibility for her husband's death lies elsewhere." He looked away, telling her perhaps more than he meant to say. "When Jason returned and learned what had happened, he went to Rickens, demanded why he had done what he had, knowing what sort of man her husband had been. And Rickens told him only that she'd earned her fate, and that she'd damned herself. There was no sign of regret in him, no mourning for the pain he'd caused. I think that was all Jason was looking for, some recognition of what he'd done, some sign of regret. There was none, nothing but that superior, unbending lecture about sin and its rewards. Jason lost his temper, there was a fight of sorts."

"And Jason nearly killed him?" Alyssa asked, remembering what she'd been told.

Noyer shook his head. "Not nearly so bad as that, *ma chère*. Rickens wasn't worth killing. Jason gave him a bloody nose and left him. But Rickens left the island soon after, out of fear, I think, that with me there, and Jason visiting often, something more dire might befall him. Merricomb came, and life returned to the way it had been, more or less. But Jason never forgot, never forgave Rickens, and only spread his blame as he found there were a great number of missionaries who all believed as Rickens did, who had as little compassion or human understanding and spread their self-righteous cant among the Polynesians without regard for the harm it did."

"I don't blame him," she murmured.

Noyer stood. "It is odd, but I got over it all far more quickly than he did. Maybe he really did love her, perhaps even more than I."

He fell silent for a long while, and Alyssa turned back to Jason, thinking about the woman who had been called Pelari, wondering what she had been like, wondering what she had done to make Jason love her. She forgot about Noyer, assuming he'd left and gone back on the *Empress*'s deck. When he spoke again, the sound of his voice startled her.

"He loves you, you know."

She turned wide, hollow eyes back toward him.

"Loves me?" she murmured.

Noyer nodded. "That was why he persuaded me to go to the mission with him in the first place," he said, "to convince you not to marry Remsen. But when there was no wedding for him to interrupt, when you didn't seem to need to be rescued from your missionary fiancé, he seemed to lose sight of his intentions. He's a man who enjoys making noble gestures, and you cheated him of the chance."

Alyssa swallowed the lump that had crept into her throat. "He certainly made one last night," she said.

"He had no choice. It was all that was left to him. He was not about to lose you. Even when Remsen had me nearly convinced you were already dead, he would not let go."

Owen . . . Alyssa realized suddenly that she hadn't even questioned the fact that he had not come after her as well. She hadn't so much as thought of him, and she didn't want to think about him, she realized, not then, not ever. If he thought her dead, so much the better. As far as he was concerned, she was.

Noyer suddenly grinned. "And that is why, *ma chère,* you must believe he will not die. Jason has, for the first time in his life, something for which he very much wants to live. I assure you, he's too stubborn to let you slip away from him."

She turned back to Jason, putting her hand against his fevered cheek. She'd never had the chance to tell him she loved him. She'd not wanted to admit it to herself, but she supposed she'd known it all along, from the first moment when he'd held her and they'd danced, alone, on the beach at Nukuhiva.

She loved him and now she knew he loved her, too. And now there might never be the chance for her to say the words, for her to tell him what she felt.

Please, Lord, she prayed silently, please give me the chance to tell him I love him.

"I'll pray you are right, Jean," she said.

"And I will pray, too, *ma chèere.*"

Merricomb shook his head slowly, his expression filled with regret.

"I have no skill to deal with this, my dear," he told Alyssa. "Other than what I've given him to bring down the fever, there is nothing I can do."

"Surely there must be something," Alyssa protested. "Perhaps one of the natives . . ."

"We do not deal with witchcraft and native magic," Owen snapped. "Here we serve the one true God. There's nothing else to be done."

Alyssa turned around to face him. She'd ignored Owen's presence until that moment, too busy with helping Noyer settle Jason into the small bed and too concerned as she'd watched Merricomb treat him. But now Owen stood stolidly in front of her, demanding her attention by his presence and making no attempt to hide his anger that she had not offered it to him prior to that moment.

She grimaced at his words and his tone and started to turn away from him, hoping to avoid the unpleasantness she knew would end any conversation she had with him then. She was not yet ready to deal with him when Jason's condition was so very much more important to her. But Owen put his hand on her shoulder, forcing her to turn back to face him.

"Let it be, Owen," she told him through tight lips. "I've no interest in your opinion of the Polynesians, or anything else, for that matter."

"Perhaps you'd better find some interest, Alyssa," he told her. "There is nothing more we can do for your captain friend. He is going to die. Perhaps in view of that fact you should decide it is time you channeled your interests where they ought to have been from the start."

Alyssa felt her cheeks grow bright with anger. He had no right to speak to her that way. She had no intention of allowing him to treat her as though she were his servant, as though he owned her.

"Is there really nothing more you can do, Owen?" she demanded in an acid tone. "Or is it only that you don't want to do anything more?"

"My dear," Merricomb began, putting a comforting hand on her arm, trying to calm her, to fend off the storm he saw brewing.

But Owen didn't let him go on. His eyes narrowed and his jaw set, he seemed unaware that the older man was even present.

"How dare you question my motives?" he hissed. "Look at you, half naked, wrapped in a piece of cloth like some heathen, hovering over that godless sailor. You should kiss my foot for even offering to take you, despite the things you've done."

Alyssa felt numb, as though he'd struck her. She clenched her hands, trying to control her anger.

"That is, I think, more than enough, monsieur," Noyer said in a carefully controlled tone that did little to dispel the impact of his anger.

Owen darted him a threatening glance, as though he were daring the Frenchman to interfere further.

"From the moment you abandoned me to the less than gentle care of that cannibal, you relinquished any claim you might have held on me, Owen," Alyssa told him. "*Thank* you for offering to take me back? I wouldn't have you if you were the last man on earth."

"He's your lover, isn't he?" Owen hissed at her. "You lay with him before you even came here."

"What I have or haven't done is none of your business," she shot back.

"Whore!" he shouted at her. "Your uncle will be pleased to know what you've become."

She was shaking now, barely able to control herself enough to speak.

Noyer darted forward. "I told you that was enough," he shouted, and struck Owen in the jaw.

Owen fell back against the wall, a bright line of red spouting from his lip. He stayed where he was, leaning against the wall, staring at Noyer, his eyes filled with hatred.

"Get out of here," Noyer told him.

"I'll leave," Owen replied, touching his fingers gingerly to his split lip and pushing himself away from the wall. He turned to Alyssa. "Fine friends you've found," he hissed, then turned toward the door. But when he reached it, he turned back to her. "And you can keep your lover. He'll do you little good." He smiled an unpleasant smile. "He'll be dead by morning."

Alyssa didn't watch him leave but turned away, dismissing him in her mind, too shaken by his viciousness to contain the rage she felt within herself.

Merricomb put his hand on her arm. "Don't think of it, my dear," he told her, "and don't think he means what he said. He's been distraught, and worried about you."

But she shook her head, dismissing Merricomb as well.

"He meant it," she told him. "And I don't even care."

She looked up at Noyer. "What do we do now?" she asked, her eyes begging him to think of something, some way to help Jason.

He could only shake his head.

"We pray," Merricomb said firmly.

He urged Alyssa forward, to kneel with him beside the bed. Then he clasped his hands and lowered his head.

Alyssa didn't hear the prayers Merricomb murmured, nor did she even notice him push himself back to his feet when he'd done. She stayed where she was, kneeling beside the bed, staring at Jason's pale, still face.

"Did you mean it, miss?"

Alyssa stirred herself, part of her not wanting to let anything outside herself and Jason in. But part of her, realizing there was little time left and hoping to find some help, forced her to turn to face Lupia. The native woman was standing just outside the door, staring in at her. Alyssa had no idea how long she had been there, no idea what she had seen or heard.

"Mean what, Lupia?" she asked.

"What you asked the Reverend Merricomb about having one of us help him." Lupia nodded toward the bed, toward Jason's still form.

Alyssa thought for a moment, remembering that Owen had called what Lupia seemed to be offering her witchcraft and native magic.

"Yes," she replied. "I meant it. Is there someone who can help him?"

Lupia shrugged. "I am not sure. Namani has ways." She darted a questioning glance at Merricomb, but apparently she had determined not to be scared away, now that she'd ventured this far. "Reverend Remsen," she said softly, "he preaches against Namani because he is *mahu,* and against his medicine, too. But still there are some that go to him to ask for his help."

"Alyssa, my dear, these people use incantations, strange herbs . . ." Merricomb began.

Alyssa waved away his objection, not even turning her glance away from Lupia. "Please," she begged the native woman, "if he can help, please bring him."

Once again Lupia looked at Merricomb, her expression questioning. "Reverend Remsen, he has banned Namani from the mission," she said.

Alyssa thought of the way Owen had chased away the effeminately dressed native, remembered how he had denied him entrance to the church. She, too, turned to Merricomb.

"If you don't let him come," she said, "we'll have to take Captain Draper to him. It might make the captain worse, moving him."

Merricomb considered her set expression for a moment. "Are you sure you want this, Alyssa?" he asked. "There is no knowing what this Namani might do to him."

"He can do no greater harm than has already been done," she replied. "Please let Lupia bring him. Surely his presence cannot harm the mission."

Merricomb bit his lower lip. He was obviously less certain than she, and of much the same mind as Owen with regard to Namani. But he found he could not deny her request. He turned to face Lupia.

"Bring this person, Lupia. Let him help Captain Draper if he can."

Namani stood beside the bed, sniffing the shaft of the dart Alyssa had handed him, and then considering Jason's pale complexion and labored breathing.

"Urali," he said finally, confirming Peli's diagnosis.

He set the dart down on the bedside table, placing it fussily, tidying the arrangement of the bowl of water and pitcher that had been set there and clearing a space at one side. And as Merricomb had predicted, Namani began to chant.

Alyssa stood back and watched him, wondering if perhaps she hadn't made a foolish mistake after all, thinking that this toneless song could do Jason no good, all the while telling herself there was nothing else she could have done.

When he had arranged the table to his satisfaction, Namani set down the small cloth bundle he had brought with him and carefully untied it to display a jumble of dried roots, leaves, and berries. It looked to Alyssa like the rubble the fall frost left behind in her uncle's garden in Plymouth, like the heap that had to be cleared away and burned.

But Namani obviously considered his small treasure with far greater reverence. He put his finger into the center of the heap, flicking through the dried mess with an exceptionally long nail until he found what he was apparently seeking. He stopped his chant as he removed a piece of shriveled, gray-brown root. His eyes glowed and he smiled at Alyssa as he held it up to the light to examine it.

Apparently satisfied with his prize, he turned to Lupia, directing her to bring some hot water, and she immediately disappeared to fetch it. Once again he took up his chant, this time in a toneless, almost indifferent manner as he chose a half dozen leaves and a few berries and began to press the lot along with the bit of root between two flat stones he had removed from the bottom of his bundle. As soon as he had crushed the first bit of root, a pungent, sour smell rose up to fill the room. He worked diligently until he had ground the mess into a handful of dirty-looking powder.

By the time he had finished preparing his powder, Lupia had returned with a teapot filled with hot water. Namani took it from her, dropped the powdered root and leaves into the pot, and stirred it. The unpleasant scent grew much stronger as the steam from the herb tea rose and filled the room.

Once again he ceased the drone of his chant.

"You look so frightened, lady," he said to Alyssa, darting a look at her, then turning his attention back to the malodorous tea he was brewing.

She nodded. "I'm frightened for him," she replied, nodding toward Jason.

Namani shook his head and smiled at her. The look was more than a little disconcerting, his darkened eyes and abnormally red lips unsettling her as she realized he had adorned himself in this way.

But his tone was calm and sure when he spoke.

"The new sicknesses, for those I have no cures," he told her. "But this, this I know. Your captain will not die." He turned back to Jason, and once again he began to chant.

'New sicknesses,' Alyssa realized, were those plagues explorers and whalers and other Westerners had brought with them to the islands over the preceding fifty years, measles and syphilis and any number of other diseases the Polynesians were defenseless to fight. She found herself numbly wondering why these people so openly welcomed the missionaries and those other settlers, like Noyer, who continued to come to the islands. The missionaries took away from them their natural joy in life, condemning them as godless heathens, and the others left them with disease that often brought them death. For a moment she wondered if Namani, with the noxious tea he was brewing, was planning to take his own small measure of revenge.

But she held back, making no attempt to keep Namani from putting the cup of evil-smelling tea to Jason's lips. She had no choice, she realized, but to accept what Namani offered at face value. If she interfered, she had no doubt but that Jason would die.

Somehow Namani got Jason to drink some of the foul tea. Despite the fact that he choked and coughed, the Polynesian persisted and eventually Jason swallowed some of it.

Over the next several hours the process was repeated, Namani holding the cup of hot herb tea to Jason's lips and forcing him to swallow until the whole pot was gone. Between the doses of tea, Namani sat at Jason's side and chanted, occasionally jumping to his feet and performing some complicated series of hand and foot motions before reseating himself and continuing on with his seemingly endless drone of song. Alyssa stood at the side of the room, unable to be of help or even to understand what Namani was doing, and yet unwilling to leave Jason.

As the moments grew to become hours, she found herself thinking that it had all been a stupid, useless error, that Namani's chants and his dried roots and leaves were little more than the heathen witchcraft Owen had called them. But by the time the sun had begun to set, Alyssa realized that Jason's breathing had eased considerably, and that his fever seemed to have subsided somewhat as well.

The treatment continued all through the night. Each time Namani brewed more of his evil-smelling drink, Alyssa was certain that he chose different roots, leaves, and berries. She dared not question him. In fact, she dared do little more than watch him force Jason to swallow some every so often, and continue on tirelessly with his chants and his peculiar dances.

If nothing else, Alyssa marveled at his stamina. Lanky and slight, still he showed no signs of fatigue as the hours wore on.

She herself was exhausted, and her body ached for sleep although she could not leave Jason's side. She told herself she couldn't risk sleeping lest Owen, or even old Merricomb, come and try to send Namani away, but she knew it was as much because she needed to see Jason, to reassure herself that he was still alive. Each moment he survived, she told herself, meant that he and Namani's vile potions were defeating the poison with which the dart had tainted his blood.

When the sun rose the next morning, Alyssa realized that Owen's prediction had not come true, that Jason was not only not dead, he was definitely recovering. A shaft of early sunlight filtered into the room through the window and lit his face, and she saw that his skin had regained a bit of its normal, healthy color. She put her hand to his cheek and found his skin far less fevered. A wave of relief swept over her and she turned and smiled up at Namani.

He stopped his chanting, and for a moment Alyssa felt strange, as though the silence was abnormal, missing the necessary adornment of the dull, droning sound of his voice. He leaned over Jason, touching his cheek, letting his thin fingers with their long, carefully tended nails linger against Jason's skin. It was like the touch a mother offers her child, a slow, tender caress. A day before, Alyssa realized, she would have been repelled by the sight of that caress. At that moment, however, she could offer Namani nothing but her thanks.

And as Namani drew his hand away, Jason opened his eyes. For a moment he stared at her in silence, and the ball that sprang up suddenly in her throat prevented her from doing anything more than returning his stare. Then he smiled.

"Am I dead?" he asked in a hoarse voice. "Aren't you an angel?"

Alyssa choked back tears of joy.

"No," she murmured, and shook her head. "No angels here."

Jason slowly lifted his hand to her cheek. She put her hand to his and hugged it. Nothing, she was sure, had ever felt so good to her as that touch, nothing had ever meant more to her.

"Are you sure?" he asked. "You look like an angel."

She shook her head again.

"Positive. No halos. No wings."

Jason's eyes drifted to Namani, then back to Alyssa. "Who?"

She smiled. "Your doctor."

Her response seemed to confuse him, but he didn't argue as he watched Namani back away, then turn to busy himself with his teapot and herbs. Instead, he turned his attention back to Alyssa and considered the liquid-glazed eyes with which she stared down at him.

"What's this, Miss Missionary?" he asked her softly. "Tears? They couldn't mean you're happy to see me, could they?"

"Just relief, Captain Draper," she replied. "Despite everything, I'd hate to have been the cause of your death."

But she was smiling, and they both knew she was lying.

Namani returned to the bedside with another cup of his unpleasant-smelling brew. Jason wrinkled his nose in distaste as Namani pushed the cup close to his lips.

"Am I expected to drink that?" Jason demanded, incredulous.

Alyssa nodded. "You most certainly are. You have to have faith in your doctor's skills."

Jason glanced up at Namani. "It smells like poison," he objected.

"It's saved your life," Alyssa told him firmly.

Jason took a reluctant swallow, large enough to satisfy Namani and to make him growl with distaste.

"It will make you sleep now," Namani told him. "When you wake, the *urali* will be gone from your body."

Namani stepped back and set the cup down beside the pot on the table. Then he began to resettle his small heap of dried leaves and roots, arranging it neatly along with his stones on the piece of cloth and making a tidy bundle of it.

Meanwhile, Jason lay back and stared up at Alyssa. There were things he wanted to say to her, things, he realized, he needed to say to her. But his thoughts were beginning to swim, and he was sure he wouldn't be able to organize them properly, was sure it would all come out wrong if he tried to say them now. His eyes were already beginning to close and he had to fight to keep them open.

"You'll be here?" he asked.

She nodded. "Right here," she promised.

He smiled up at her, and his eyes drifted closed. In a few moments she could hear the regular, even sound of his breathing and knew he was asleep.

She looked up at Namani. "I don't know how to thank you," she told him.

He shook his head. "No need," he told her. "It is what I do." He darted a glance at Jason, then gathered up his cloth-wrapped bundle. "He will be well. I will leave now."

"Please," Alyssa insisted. "There must be something I can give you, something I can do."

For a moment Namani's shoulders slumped, and Alyssa saw him again as she had first seen him, a tall, lanky creature dressed like a woman, begging Owen Remsen for admittance to the church that had been denied to him. There were circles beneath his eyes, and Alyssa realized how much the previous day had drained him.

And then Namani straightened his shoulders. His eyes narrowed as he stared at hers.

"You can tell Reverend Merricomb that I am as human as he," he said.

He turned quickly, crossed to the door, and then he was gone.

There was a soft knock at the door. Alyssa turned and saw Noyer had pulled it open and now stood staring in at her and Jason. She put her finger to her lips to warn him that Jason was asleep, then stood and crossed the room to him. When they were outside, she silently pulled the door closed behind her.

"You wear a smile, *chérie,*" Noyer told her. "He is better?"

She nodded. "The fever is nearly gone. Namani gave him some evil-smelling tea to drink, and it's put him to sleep," she replied.

Noyer's eyes narrowed. "Perhaps you should have a sip yourself," he said. "You look exhausted, *ma petite.*"

"No," she said. "I promised him I would be here when he wakens. I can't leave him."

"I could stay for you," the Frenchman offered.

She smiled again. "There are things I must say to him that you cannot say for me, Jean," she said. Then she blushed.

Noyer laughed softly. "I think I envy my old friend Jason," he said. He returned her smile. "Could not these things you must tell him wait for an hour or two?"

She shook her head. "They've waited too long already," she replied.

"As you like, *chérie.* As for me, I think it only fitting I go to the ketch and find a bottle of wine with which to toast Jason's recovery. Do you suppose old Merricomb would be averse to sharing it?"

"You are an irremediable reprobate, Jean," she accused him, then laughed.

He nodded in mock solemnity. "It is part of my charm, *chérie.* I'll come back later to see you both. Perhaps I'll bring a bottle and we can all toast Jason's recovery." He offered her a sly grin. "Perhaps we can find some other reason to celebrate as well?"

"I'm certain I don't know what you could possibly mean, Jean," she replied in her primmest tone.

"Nor do I, *chérie.* My mind wanders." He leaned forward and pressed a brotherly kiss to her forehead. "*Á bientôt.*"

Alyssa watched him as he started across the green, then turned and went back inside, taking care to close the door softly so that she wouldn't wake Jason.

Owen Remsen stood on the porch of the cottage he shared with Merricomb and listened to the thin murmur of talk from inside. That godless Frenchman was still there, he told himself, still polluting the old man's mind with his talk and his wine. Owen wouldn't go in there, not until Noyer had gone. He would not infect himself by so much as breathing the same air as that papist Frenchman breathed.

He'd been standing in the very same place when his attention had been drawn by a movement from the far side of the compound. As he had watched, Namani had appeared, walked across the open green of the mission compound, turned onto a path at the compound's edge, and then disappeared into the greenery. Owen's jaws clenched and his hands balled into fists at the memory, and he felt the anger once again as he'd felt it earlier, hot and thick and pounding in his veins.

He'd come to stand in this same place several times during the previous night, looking at the lamplight that escaped from the window of her room, aware that she was there, that he was there with her, as well as that unnatural, godless creature she'd asked to help her lover. And now that Namani had gone, she was alone with him, he realized. The two were alone together, and the indecency of it seared him and left him shaking with shame and anger.

It wasn't enough that she had spurned him, he thought. Now she flaunted her rejection of his authority, openly belittling him in front of the natives by inviting that unnatural creature and his heathen rites onto the very grounds of the mission, openly remaining in indecent intimacy with that godless sea captain. He seethed with an anger that threatened to boil over and choke him.

It wasn't fair. Since she'd come to the mission, everything he'd done had ended in disaster. First she'd postponed the wedding that ought to have taken place on her arrival, that had been the start. If she'd behaved decently, if she'd married him, then none of the rest would have followed. There would have been no abortive attempt to take the pearls Draper insisted were lying in that cave on Tapuay. But she hadn't, and everything had soured for him since. She hadn't even had the good sense to die at the hands of the cannibals, instead returning to the mission to flaunt her relationship with that sea captain when by rights she ought to have given herself to him in sanctified, holy wedlock. It was all her fault, and it made no sense to him that God had chosen him to suffer for what she had done to him.

She should be made to suffer for her sins, he thought. Retribution, holy and pure—that was the only way to wash away the stain she had left on the mission and on him. He closed his eyes and raised his face to the sky, murmuring a prayer for guidance, seeking divine help to wash him and his mission clean from the mark of her godless, sinful transgressions.

He stood as he was for a long while, unmoving, lost to his prayers, searching within himself for the sign that would show him what it was God wanted him to do. He didn't move until he smelled the smoke from the fire Lupia had made over which to prepare his and Merricomb's dinner. The first scent of that smoke sent a chill through him. He shivered with the intensity of the knowledge that settled into him along with the smell of the smoke.

He knew what he was meant to do, he told himself, knew what God wanted him to do. The sinful had to be cast out, the evil had to be shriven and an equitable penance exacted. And it was his duty to be the instrument of the penance, for it was him and his mission that had borne the stain of her sins.

He started forward, crossing the open green, relishing as it slowly settled over him the first feeling of certainty and peace he'd known since Alyssa had come to Banaba. Everything had suddenly become clear to him, what he was to do, why he needed to do it. But mostly he took comfort from the realization that she had been sent to test him, to try the mettle of his beliefs and his dedication to his calling. For he knew now that if he were to let her escape without punishment, every precept by which he lived, every standard of morality in which he believed, would crumble and become as meaningless as dust.

He darted a glance around the compound before he put his hand to the door, assuring himself that there was no one there to see him. Then he carefully pulled the door back, taking care to make no noise as he entered her room.

For a moment Owen simply stood and stared at Alyssa, watching her sleep with her head lying in her folded arms on the bed beside Jason. Her hair was unbound and wild, and she was still wrapped only in the sheet of white tapa cloth. Like a native woman, he thought, like the heathen she'd let herself become.

He crept up silently behind her and clamped his hand over her mouth, enjoying the look of shock in her eyes as she woke and stared up at him before he struck her solidly at the base of her neck. She immediately slumped forward, still and senseless.

Owen darted a glance at Jason, assuring himself he hadn't wakened him, then put his hands around Alyssa's still body, lifted her, and silently bore her away.

Chapter Twenty-four

Alyssa opened her eyes and stared dully around her. There was only the narrow shaft of sunlight that entered from the porthole by which to see, and it took her a long while to realize she was lying on the bunk in the cabin of Jean Noyer's ketch.

The back of her head ached, and she found the warm, moist air of the enclosed cabin oppressive. The rhythmic lurch beneath her told her that the ketch was under sail, a fact that was not altogether comforting as she had no idea of either how she had gotten where she was nor of where she was being taken. More immediate, however, was the unpleasant sensation that began in her stomach at her first recognition of the ketch's movement.

Her stomach began to heave, and she knew that she was saved from forcefully emptying it only by the fact that she'd put nothing into it in the previous twenty-four hours. She needed nothing more than the seasickness to confirm that the ketch was indeed under sail.

But that was all she knew. Everything else was a complete muddle. Try as she did, she could conjure no memories of the preceding hours. She had been with Jason, in her room at the mission school, and then there was nothing but confusion, no matter how hard she tried to remember.

She sat up slowly and put her hand gingerly to the back of her head. Even the light touch of her fingers released a stab of pain, and she drew her hand away quickly, leaving a dull, thick throbbing in its wake.

The pain had one positive effect, however, for it reminded her that she'd felt the same hurt before and served to order her confused thoughts. She remembered now that she had fallen asleep with her head on her arms at Jason's bedside, and she remembered waking to look up at Owen before the first wave of that pain struck her. That was all there was—the pain, and then darkness.

At first it seemed impossible that Owen had struck her, that he would actually do her physical harm. But the more she thought and remembered, the more she told herself the look she'd seen in his eyes in that instant when she'd glanced up at him had been the look of a man capable of anything. Something had happened to him, she told herself, something had called up whatever devils he'd hidden away inside himself. And she, apparently, was the target he had chosen to use to excise them.

She put her hand to her temple, forcing herself to breathe deeply, telling herself that she must be imagining things, that surely Owen had not suddenly become some monster. But she still had no idea why she was on the ketch, no memory of how she'd gotten there, and she thought it safe to presume that she had none because she had not been conscious when she'd been brought there. That, at least, would explain the pounding hurt in the back of her head.

What little she did remember was slowly being pushed aside by the image of Owen's face just before that first wave of pain. The memory of the look in Owen's eyes when she'd wakened was enough to send a shiver down her spine.

She pushed herself off the bunk and crossed the

cabin, quickly climbing the few stairs that led to the deck. The door was closed, and she put her hand to the latch, but found she couldn't budge it. The door had been barred, she realized, from the other side.

"Jean?" she cried out, trying to ignore the note of desperation that had crept into her voice. "Jason?"

She knew there would be no answer from either Jason or the Frenchman, even before she cried out their names. Her mind was filled with the image of Owen's eyes, and it told her more plainly than anything else could that there would be no answer from either Noyer or Jason, that neither of them had brought her to the ketch.

"Owen?" she shouted. "Owen, let me out of here!"

She pounded on the door with her fists, but stopped when she heard the sound of his laughter returned to her. The sound of it frightened her more than the silence that had preceded it.

The laughter ceased abruptly, and she could hear his footsteps on the deck. They came close to the other side of the door before they stopped.

"Awake, whore!" she heard him shout at her. "Awake and find the just retribution your sins have earned you."

The sound of his voice was changed, she realized. It was Owen's certainly, but different. Its timbre was lower, stronger than she remembered it, and there was something about it that was unquestionably menacing.

She backed away from the door, afraid now that he would open it and she would be forced to face him.

His voice followed her. "Awake and repent before it is too late to save your immortal soul, whore!" he shouted.

And then he laughed again.

This time Alyssa had no doubt but that she heard madness in his laughter.

* * *

Noyer stood by the door and smiled as he watched Jason pull on his trousers.

"I would have thought, *mon ami,* a man of your intellect would have learned to take advantage of the benefits to be gained by temporary infirmity."

Jason looked up at him, realized the Frenchman was smiling in a slightly alcoholic haze.

"Benefits?" he asked before returning to the task of his trousers, a task that had grown immeasurably with the ache in his shoulder and the feeling of weak dizziness he'd felt since he'd wakened. He supposed he ought to be thankful for those relatively minor discomforts. He realized he might just as easily never have wakened at all.

"Are you not aware that a woman's heart melts at the sight of a man who needs her?" Noyer arched his brow and grinned suggestively. "Under the circumstances, I should think you are certainly entitled to a bit of specialized nursing care."

Jason laughed. "I should think so too," he agreed. "Why don't you rouse Alyssa and tell her I'm in need of it?"

Noyer's smile disappeared.

"Is she not here with you?"

"Do you see her?" Jason asked, and motioned to the small, empty space.

Noyer wandered into the room and looked around. He shook his head as though he were trying to dislodge the cobwebs that had settled there.

"But she must be here," he insisted. "She told me she was staying here, with you. And she did not come to the cottage. I've been there for hours, with old Merricomb."

"She must be around someplace," Jason replied. "The schoolroom?"

Noyer shook his head. "Empty," he said and gestured behind him.

Jason stood. The abrupt movement made the dizziness worse for a moment, and Noyer stepped forward to help him steady himself. He was not yet quite over the effects of the poison, he realized. But he was well enough. He finished pulling up his trousers and quickly buttoned them. He winced slightly as he reached for his boots, but he ignored the pain in his wounded shoulder. He was beginning to get an unpleasant feeling that something was very wrong.

"When did you last see her?" he demanded.

"Not since I came to check on you, early this morning."

"You're sure?"

Noyer's muddled expression vanished completely. The slight alcoholic haze disappeared as he realized Jason thought him too drunk to be a reliable witness.

"Of course I'm sure," he replied. "I'm not so great a sot as that, Jason. The witch doctor had gone, that Namani. Alyssa told me you were much better, that he gave you some foul thing to drink and you were sleeping."

Jason nodded, remembering the smell and, more distinctly, the unpleasant taste of the infusion Namani had given him to drink. And then he remembered Alyssa promising to be with him when he woke.

And she hadn't been.

Something *was* wrong, he realized, something was very wrong.

He started for the door, but had to stop and steady himself by grasping a chair and leaning against it.

"Damn it, will you help me, Jean?"

"Certainly, *mon vieux,*" Noyer replied, and quickly offered him an arm.

When they were outside, Jason stood and stared at the deserted green, at the mission buildings, still and hazy in the afternoon sun. There was a feeling of emptiness that he'd never noticed about the place before, a sense that something was missing.

"Where's Merricomb?" he demanded.

"I'm afraid I left him in need of an afternoon nap," Noyer admitted. "We had a toast or two celebrating your recovery."

"Remsen?"

Noyer shrugged. "Now that you mention it, he wasn't at lunch. I'd almost managed to forget about him."

"Damn," Jason muttered as he started across the green.

"Where are you going?" Noyer demanded. "You are supposed to be sick."

Jason pointed to the far side of the green, to the place where they could look down at the cove and the pier where the *Empress* was docked.

"There," he said.

Jason was breathing heavily with the effort of the walk by the time they'd crossed the green. But his discomfort was quickly forgotten as he stood on the rise and looked down at the *Empress* and the pier.

Noyer saw his alarmed look. "What is it, Jason?" he asked.

"Was your ketch here when we arrived?" Jason asked.

"Certainly, *mon ami,*" Noyer replied. "The good Reverend Remsen brought it back here when we left him at Beau Rivage, do you not remember?" He looked down at the pier, realizing only now that Jason had mentioned it that the ketch was missing. "It is gone," he murmured.

"Remsen?" Jason demanded. "When was the last time you saw Remsen?"

Noyer thought. "Not since early this morning," he said finally. "Shortly after I saw you and Alyssa." His eyes narrowed. "What is it you are thinking, *mon vieux?*" he asked.

Jason swallowed as he stared out to the open sea beyond the cove.

"He has her," he said finally. "And there's only one place I can think of that he would take her."

Noyer shook his head. "But why? Where?"

Jason ignored his questions, and started down the slope toward the dock.

"We need to find the crew if you intend to take the *Empress,*" Noyer shouted after him.

Jason stopped, checked by his words, and turned to face him.

"Where are they?" he demanded.

"They've gone off, with the islanders, all save Argus," the Frenchman replied. "We all thought you'd need a few days to recover."

Jason hesitated only a moment longer, then turned back and started down the hillside.

"There's no time," he shouted back at Noyer. "If the men have found some ladies to entertain them, it will take hours to get them back on board. The three of us can handle the *Empress.*" He stopped again and turned back to look at Noyer, who still stood, hesitant, at the top of the slope. "Hurry, Jean," he shouted back. "There's no time to waste."

Alyssa retreated and sat huddled on the narrow bunk wondering which was worse, being shut up in the close cabin or having to face Owen up on deck. It didn't take her many moments' consideration of what she had heard in his voice to make up her mind. She would decidedly prefer even the heaving in her stomach to the prospect of facing Owen Remsen.

She had no idea what he intended to do to her, but a nagging voice inside warned her that it would not be pleasant. There had been madness in his tone when he'd shouted at her, madness in his laughter, of that she was sure.

She had to force herself to move, for she realized she

couldn't simply sit there, huddled on the bunk, waiting for him. She had been through too much in the previous days to let him render it all futile. She had nearly lost Jason, and she'd still not had the chance to tell him she loved him. She'd thought of what Noyer had told her and decided it was true, that Jason did love her. If it was not true, he would not have gone to Tapuay after her. That realization was more than enough to give her the resolve not to give up, not now, not when she seemed so close to having what she wanted, what she needed.

She pushed herself off the bunk and stood staring at the wall of cupboards. Surely, she told herself, there must be something in one of them that she could use as a weapon. She started to open the cupboard doors as she had done only days before, when she'd hidden herself away the day Jason, Owen, and Noyer had taken the ketch and gone after the pearls at Nukuhiva. Only this time she wasn't looking for a place to hide. This time she knew she needed more than that.

She found the cupboard that contained Noyer's fishing gear, and as soon as she saw it, she breathed a sigh of relief. There would be knives there, she told herself. Fishermen needed sharp knives.

She pulled out the boxes from the cupboard floor, opening the first and finding it contained only reels of line and an assortment of hooks. She swore under her breath as she caught her finger on the sharp edge of one of the hooks and brought it to her mouth to ease the hurt. Then she shut the box, pushed it aside, and opened the second.

And this one, as she had hoped, contained a knife, a large-handled, thick-bladed knife like the ones she'd seen the fishermen use back in Plymouth. She lifted it from the box carefully, knowing it was not a toy. She'd heard that drunken sailors who got into fights had been known to use blades like this to kill one another. Even

Owen Remsen could not fail to be intimidated by such a knife.

She set the knife aside, then returned the boxes to the cupboard. She satisfied herself that the cabin looked as it had before she'd begun her search, that there was nothing to arouse Owen's suspicion. Then she resettled herself on the rumpled bunk, looking around for a place to hide the knife. She wished now that she'd thought to change into her own clothes. A pocket or the folds of fabric of a skirt would provide the perfect place to secret a blade and yet keep it close. In the end she was forced to push the knife beneath the pillow within her grasp.

For a long while she sat huddled into the corner of the bunk, her eyes glued to the cabin door. But as the afternoon stretched on and she saw the long shadows that presaged dusk begin to fill the cabin, she began to doubt that even the knife would do her very much good. The uneasiness in her stomach had grown steadily worse as the ketch was buffeted by the ocean waves, their effect, no doubt, worsened by Owen's inexpert handling of the craft. She found herself miserably heaving, despite the fact that her stomach was empty. She knew that if it continued much longer, she would not be able to do very much at all to defend herself.

She lay down with her head on the pillow, letting her hand slip beneath it, hoping to find some small comfort in the solid feel of the knife she'd hidden there. Whatever relief it afforded was scant. She drew her knees up to her chest and lay curled and miserable, praying that when the time came she would have enough strength to defend herself against Owen.

The wave of relief that swept over her surprised her. It took her a moment to realize that the ketch was no longer being tossed by the waves, that with the less violent movement, her stomach was no longer protesting with anywhere near the intensity that it had been and the heaving had ceased entirely. She lay as she was for a moment, telling herself that they'd reached sheltered water, letting herself simply breathe comfortably for the first time in hours.

Despite the fact that she would have liked to close her eyes and let herself fall asleep, she pushed herself out of the bunk as soon as she felt she would be able to stand. She peered out the small porthole, seeing by the last of the fading afternoon light that the ketch had indeed found sheltered water. They were in a cove, she realized, and the water that lapped against the ketch's hull was smooth and calm.

She stared out at the shadows of land that loomed up before her, the trees that edged the beach glittering dark in the last of the day's light. For a moment she was simply lulled by the beauty of the place, until she realized that the view was familiar to her, painfully familiar.

"Oh, no," she moaned softly as she stared out at a beach whose sand was tinted a deep, burnished gold by the fading sunlight. She knew this place. There was no question in her mind where Owen had brought her.

She turned her glance to the dark shadows she knew were the entrance to the cave when she heard the splash of the ketch's anchor being thrown overboard. Owen had brought her back to Nukuhiva, she realized. She could only imagine what he planned to do now that they were there.

The sound of his footsteps approaching the cabin door sent her scurrying back to the bunk, back to the protection the knife she'd hidden beneath the pillow afforded her. She was sitting on the edge of the bunk, her hand slipped beneath the pillow, her fingers just touching the blade, when he pulled the door open and started down the stairs.

"Get up, whore," Owen hissed at her. "Come here."

Alyssa didn't move. I'm not afraid of him, she told herself, even though she knew she *was* afraid, that there was something vicious and alien in his eyes as he looked at her, something coldly removed about the tone he used when he spoke to her.

"Why have you brought me here, Owen?" she asked him, trying to keep her tone calm, to keep him from hearing the fear in her words. "This place is dangerous. The cannibals might come at any moment. We should leave before they see us, before they kill us both."

He smiled down at her, his expression superior, knowing.

"I heard what your heathen friends did on Tapuay," he said. "They destroyed the canoes. There won't be any cannibals here, at least, not for a while. By the time they do come, I'll be back at the mission." He smiled again. "They will have to satisfy themselves with you, whore."

Alyssa shook her head. "You can't be serious," she said in a voice suddenly hoarse with fear.

"Oh, but I am," he replied as he descended the last of the steps and started across the cabin toward her. "A fitting punishment for your sins."

She cringed back, away from him. When he reached forward for her, she quickly pulled the knife from beneath the pillow and held it up threateningly at him. The flash of the metal blade caught his glance and he stopped, unsettled by the sight of it in her hand.

"Stay away from me, Owen," she warned him as she slowly edged along the bunk to its foot, trying to put a little distance between them. Then she stood and started to back away from him, toward the stairs.

He kept his eyes on hers as he shook his head.

"You're not going to use that," he told her. "I am your one chance for salvation. God sent me to save you from your own evil. He will not let you keep me from what I must do."

One glance at him told her he really believed what he was saying, that however insane it was, he considered himself her redeemer. She wondered if she was to blame for his madness, if something like jealousy for the love she bore Jason had pushed him over the edge. Whatever the cause, she knew he would not be persuaded by reason to let her go.

If she could get up the stairs, she told herself, she could lock him in the cabin. She could sail the ketch back to Banaba, to Jason. If only she could get up the stairs and away from him . . .

"I will, Owen," she said as she backed further away from him, knowing she could not be far from the stairs, praying she could reach them before he started toward her.

Because she knew he was right. She hadn't the physical strength to struggle with him, nor did she think she had the emotional strength to use the knife on him, to lunge forward at him and force the blade into him, to see the blood and know that she had shed it. Her hands began to shake.

Owen saw the way her hands trembled, saw the knife begin to shake, and he smiled.

"You won't, or you will be damned, whore," he said, and started to move forward, stepping slowly toward her, keeping his eyes on hers. "The Lord has bidden me be the instrument of the salvation of your soul. Your only hope is with me."

He held his hand out toward her, and began to move forward.

She took a few more backward steps, then, realizing he was drawing closer, she turned and bolted for the stairs.

She scrambled up the steps and managed to keep out of his reach, to put her hand to the door latch and push it open. But he was right behind her, and when she darted out and tried to slam the door closed behind her, it struck his shoulder. He uttered a groan of pain, then lunged against the door, sending her reeling backward. The knife flew from her hand as she fell, skittering along the deck.

After that it all happened too quickly, the weight of his body as he fell on her, pushing her, then turning her face down as he jerked her hands behind her and tied them. He rolled away, first reaching for the fallen knife and then standing and retrieving a lantern he'd left near the wheel.

Alyssa pushed herself to her knees and breathed the cool night air for a moment. When she raised her head and looked at the island, she saw something she did not quite understand.

There was a glow coming from the peak of the mountain in the middle of the island, just above the ledge, she realized, where she and Jason had watched Mehevi and his tribesmen have their feast of human meat. What the glow meant was a mystery to her. But she was sure it was important.

Owen returned to her, holding a lit lantern in one hand, the knife in the other. He stood staring down at her as he set the lantern on the deck.

"Get up, whore," he shouted. Then he grabbed her arm, pulling her to her feet and threatening her with the knife, placing the edge of the blade close to her neck.

Once she was standing, she tried to pull away from him, but he pressed the side of the blade to her skin. She acknowledged the threat immediately and ceased her struggle. To continue, she realized, would only tempt him to use it.

He began to push her, forcing her toward the rail, then lifting her and dropping her roughly into the waiting dinghy. She cried out when she landed in a painful heap, unable to break the fall with her hands. He was smiling when he settled himself in the center and took up the oars. She thought it was the sound of her cry that had amused him.

"We can't go there, Owen," she told him as he began to row toward the beach. "Look, up there, on the mountain."

He looked up reluctantly, but when his eyes found the light, he seemed transfixed by it. His eyes glowed with a fire of their own, and, lit as they were by the lantern's flickering flame, they looked wild to her, demonic. She did not see the knife now, but she told herself he must still have it. She would have to be careful in what she said to him.

"It's the Lord's fire," he told her, "purifying and holy. You will be shriven by it, your sins will be expiated."

She shook her head. "No, Owen, it's something else." Her mind worked desperately, searching for the one thing that might send him away. "It's what the cannibals worship, Owen, it's their god. You wouldn't dirty yourself by bowing to the heathen god, would you?"

He dropped one of the oars, leaned forward to her, and slapped her, hard, across the face. She fell back, stunned by the blow.

"Be silent, whore!" he shouted. "It is a sign from the Lord, and I will not allow you to blaspheme by calling it anything else."

He leaned over her, his eyes blazing and his hand raised again and threatening. He is mad, Alyssa told herself, there is no doubt but that he's mad. She darted a glance at his eyes, then shrank back, unable to think of anything else to say to him and afraid to anger him any more than she already had.

She sat still and huddled as he rowed the rest of the way to shore. She was too numbed by what she'd seen in his eyes to offer much resistance when he pulled her out of the dinghy and dragged her through the shallow water to the beach. He lifted the lantern high, searching in the darkness for the cave that he'd been told was there.

It took him only a moment to locate the shadows that were the mouth of the cave.

"So your lover didn't lie," he hissed as he jerked her arm and pulled her through the moist sand. "At least, not about the cave."

"You intend to steal the pearls, don't you?" she asked. An irrational anger flared up within her, that he could think himself so sanctimonious that he could damn her for her sins when he had really brought her to this place so that he might steal. "This has nothing to do with piety," she accused him, "or what you think I may have done. This is simply about greed."

"Steal?" he bellowed. His grasp on her arm tightened enough to make her gasp with the hurt. "I do the Lord's work!" he shouted, shaking her. "If I take from the heathens, it is to save their souls, to do what God has sent me to do." He shook her again. "Do you hear me, whore?"

He began to race toward the mouth of the cave, pulling her with him, eager now to finish what he'd begun. When they reached the opening, he held the lantern up high and stared in at the floor, at the heaps of bone scattered across the sand.

His hand shook slightly, and the light from the lantern skittered off the stone walls of the cave, making the shadows at the far end and the bones seem to move as though they were living things.

"The Lord is my shepherd . . ."

Alyssa barely heard the drone of Owen's voice as he pulled her through the first ghastly room of the cave. Her mind was too full of the sick realization that he meant to leave her in this horrible place for her to dwell on anything else.

Owen remembered every word Jason had said about

the cave and the location of the pearls. He pulled Alyssa through the dark passage beyond the first outer room, searching for the entrance to the hidden treasure room beyond with as much ease as he might had he been there before.

All the while he kept murmuring psalms, over and over, his voice a monotonous drone that reminded Alyssa of the old cannibal priest's prayer. It seemed ironic to her that this place seemed to make Owen so like the natives he disdained.

"It's here!"

There was surprise in Owen's tone, as though he had not really expected the opening to be there, as though he'd expected it all to have been a lie Jason told after all. He'd stopped his chant and now knelt staring through the hole in the thick stone wall, apparently amazed by the fact that it was all as he'd been told it would be.

He pulled Alyssa down to her knees and began to push her forward, through the opening. But before she could inch her way into the treasure room, she was deafened by a deep, dull roar that seemed to well up from the mountain itself. She was thrown to the floor as the stone seemed to shake beneath her.

She cried out and rolled herself into a ball, trying vainly to pull her hands free of their bonds to bring them to her head. Behind her, Owen was thrown against the far wall of the passage. She heard his grunt of pain as he struck the stone.

It was over quickly, the noise and movement subsiding and leaving the cave in unnatural stillness. Alyssa backed away from the opening and turned to face him.

"We have to get out of here," she told him. "Something's happening."

But he wasn't listening. His eyes were looking upward, to the stone above them, and he was smiling, his expression filled with satisfied expectancy.

"He knows we're here," he said.

He wasn't talking to her, Alyssa realized, but to himself.

"This place is dangerous," she told him.

He seemed not to hear her. "He's telling us he knows we're here." He turned his glance to Alyssa, and his smile disappeared. He pushed himself away from the wall and reached for the lantern that had fallen at his side. "Forward, whore," he hissed at her. "It's time to face the payment you've earned for your sins."

He leaned forward to her, pushing her once more toward the opening. Alyssa had no choice but to kneel and crawl through. He was right behind her. She saw the light from the lantern in his hand edging past her and moving into the treasure room beyond.

It was all just as she remembered it, save for the fact that the glimmer from the pool was so pale it was hardly noticeable in the lamplight and that the room was a good deal warmer than she remembered it being. The great slab of stone with its burden of the huge shells filled with pearls seemed untouched, exactly as she remembered it from the first time.

There was a soft gasp from Owen as he entered, straightened up, and saw the heaps of pearls, and then a moment of silence as he considered the wealth displayed in front of him. He pushed his way past her, too busy admiring the heaps of pearls to be bothered with her.

But when she tried to edge her way back toward the opening, she found he was not completely oblivious to her. He turned on his heel, reached down, and dragged her back to the stone slab.

He shook his head. "It will not be so easy for you, whore," he hissed.

Then he plunged his hands into the piles of pearls as though he needed to feel them between his fingers to believe they were real. His eyes grew bright with the visions of what they would bring to him, to his mission.

It seemed almost to pain him to turn away from them and look down at her.

"On your knees, whore," he hissed at her. "Pray. Pray for your soul's salvation."

She stared up at him. "You can take all the pearls you want, Owen," she told him. "All that you need for the mission. And we can go."

He smiled at her words, and his hand stole to his pocket. She began to tremble, remembering the knife. But when he withdrew it, he was holding a length of rope.

"I intend to do just that," he told her. "But you, I'm afraid, will not be coming with me. I am offering the cannibals payment for what I take," he said. "I'm sure they will be pleased to have you returned to them. And in the meantime, while you wait for them, you will have ample time to beg God for forgiveness for your sins. Who knows? Perhaps when the time comes he will welcome your soul."

He pushed her down, quieting her by pushing her face down to the stone as he tied her ankles. Then he lifted her and threw her down on the stone slab beside the pearl-filled shells.

"Pray, whore," he told her as he began to fill his pockets with the jewels.

But she was silent, listening to the deep grinding sounds she now heard in the stone around her. The air seemed warmer, closer. Something was happening in the volcano that had made the ground vibrate, she realized. And whatever it was, it was growing stronger.

If Owen left her in the cave, a voice inside told her, she would not live long enough for the cannibals to find her there.

Owen stood back and considered Alyssa's eyes, watched the way they roamed to the walls of the room, as they turned to the pool behind the slab of stone on which he'd left her along with the remaining pearls.

Her eyes disturbed him, the way they shifted and searched. He reminded himself that he'd thought the cannibals would kill her the last time they took her, yet she had survived. He wondered if it would be possible that she might escape her just punishment this time as well.

He knelt and began to pray, asking for guidance, for the strength to do what must be done. But the prayer didn't last long, and when he looked up at her, he told himself that she was unrepentant for what she'd done, that if he left her there, she would escape as she had escaped before. His had been chosen to be the hand of retribution. It would be wrong of him to leave her without completing what he had been selected to do.

He straightened up, then leaned forward, over her, and put his hands to her throat.

"Owen, don't," she begged.

"I am but the messenger," he told her. "Pray for forgiveness for your sins, whore."

She screamed, and then his fingers began to tighten on her throat.

Alyssa felt the pressure of his fingers, felt her breath slowly being pressed away. She jerked and struggled, but it was useless. She was going to die and she knew it.

Chapter Twenty-five

"The ketch, it's here."

The moon had finally risen, a thin sliver of a moon that cast a weak shimmer that was reflected by the water. It wasn't much light, but it was enough to reveal the indistinct outline of a vessel floating in the center of the cove.

Noyer seemed surprised by that, as though finding the ketch sitting there silent and dark was some sort of miracle. Jason, however, was not in the least surprised.

"I'm not likin' the way that looks, Jason," Argus told him. He pointed to the glow from the top of the volcano in the center of the island. "I've seen that sort of thing before, and it bodes no good."

Jason nodded. "I think we're none too soon. You take the wheel, Liam. You'll have to tend to the *Empress* alone. I'm taking Noyer to the ketch, and then I'm going ashore."

He handed off the wheel to Argus, and then he and Noyer lowered the longboat. By the time Argus had turned the *Empress* into the wind and the sails had fallen and begun to luff, Jason and Noyer had swung themselves down to the boat and were rowing steadily toward the ketch.

"You do not suppose they are still there, *mon vieux?*" Noyer asked.

Jason shook his head. "No. There's no light, no

noise. Besides, I can't believe he brought her here to sit in the cabin. He's after those pearls, Jean, I'm sure of it. We can be thankful for the fact that he's an incompetent sailor or he'd have done what he intended and left by now."

"And Alyssa?" Noyer asked.

Jason's jaw tightened. More than anything else, he was convinced that Owen had brought Alyssa here for a purpose, and he doubted very much that it was to help him steal the cannibals' treasure.

"He wouldn't take her back with him, or he wouldn't have brought her at all," he replied.

"Then you think he has her in the cave?"

Jason nodded. "Yes."

"The man must be insane," Noyer muttered. He nodded up toward the increasingly glowing mouth of the volcano. "It will erupt soon. I've seen such things before."

"You may be right," Jason agreed, "on both counts."

"Where do we put ashore?"

"You don't," Jason told him. "Bring me a little closer to the beach, and I'll go after him alone. You get back to the ketch and take it out to deeper water and tie her in the *Empress*'s tow."

"You might need me, Jason," Noyer told him.

Jason shook his head. "I'm all right now. The shoulder doesn't even bother me."

"If the volcano begins to erupt . . ."

"Then it's best that you get yourself away before it does."

"I'll keep watch for you," Noyer told him. "I can be back for you in minutes."

Jason dropped his oars and pulled off his boots, then put his hand on the gunwale. "This is as far as you come, Jean. Go back to the ketch." He put a leg over and slid into the water.

Noyer stayed as he was for a moment, staring after

him, and then looked up to the glow in the sky above the volcano's mouth. It was growing brighter, he realized, even in the short time since the *Empress* had approached the island. There wouldn't be much time.

"Que le Bon Dieu te protège, mon ami," he murmured before he once again took up the oars and turned back to the ketch.

Jason swam the last of the distance to the beach, and then, as soon as he was close enough to shore, began to run. It took him only a few moments to cross the narrow beach and approach the mouth of the cave. He paused briefly, orienting himself, remembering the path through the outer room of the cave to the tunnel beyond. It was dark, and he would have to rely on his memory and his senses in the absence of any light.

He felt the sharp edges of the bones beneath his feet and nearly walked into the stone wall at the far side of the room before he found the entrance to the tunnel, but he had missed the passage by only a few feet and quickly found the opening by feeling along the stone wall.

Once in the tunnel, he moved steadily, dreading what he might find when he reached the treasure room, praying that he was in time. He thought he'd covered about half the distance to the opening when he heard Alyssa's scream.

Jason began to run. He had no idea how he managed to avoid slamming himself against the stone wall of the passage, but some sixth sense seemed to be guiding him. Then he saw the glow of light coming from an opening in the wall and he realized he'd found them.

There was no sound from inside the room now, and he felt a constriction in his throat and a tightening ball of fear in his stomach that he might have come too late. He knelt and scrambled through the opening, scraping his wounded shoulder against the stone, not even feeling the throb of hurt it caused in his anxiety for Alyssa.

And then he was inside the treasure room, looking up to see Owen leaning over the stone slab, his hands on Alyssa's throat.

Jason lunged forward, grabbing Owen, pulling him back and away from her. The scuffle that followed was a hort one, for Owen, surprised by the attack, put up little resistance. Before he knew what had happened, ason found himself standing over Owen and staring down at his dazed expression and the blood that dripped from his nose down to his shirt.

But Owen was not Jason's primary interest at that moment. He stepped over him, turning his attention to Alyssa, feeling the tight ball of fear in his stomach begin to ease as he saw her move and heard her gaspingly ndrawn breath. She was alive, he told himself. That was all that mattered.

He gathered her up into his arms, holding her close to him as she coughed and finally began to breathe nor-nally.

"Jason?"

She seemed momentarily dazed, as though she couldn't believe he was there, couldn't understand how he had found her or why she was not dead.

"It's all right," he told her. "He's not going to hurt you."

The sound of his voice was more comforting than anything she had ever heard before, she thought. He was there, and nothing could happen as long as she was near him. Her vision cleared, and she looked up at him, drinking in the sight of him, the scent of him.

There was a movement behind him, the flash of metal in the lamplight.

"Jason, look out!" she screamed.

Jason spun on his heel, his arms extended, bracing himself to ward off the blow. He hadn't expected to see a knife in Owen's hand, but he reacted by instinct, hit-ing Owen's forearm with the tensed side of his hand, focusing all his might into the blow. The knife fell, and Jason followed through without giving Owen the chance to recover, hitting him once, hard, in the abdomen and then standing back and watching the missionary double over with pain.

"You've chosen the wrong adversary, Remsen," Jason told him as he bent and retrieved the fallen knife. "Missionary school gives no lessons in the sort of things a man learns in ten years at sea."

Owen looked up at him, and his eyes filled with hatred. "You lift your hand against me, heathen?" he shouted. "You dare defy God's word?"

"Not God's," Jason replied dryly. "Only yours."

With that he returned to Alyssa, using the knife to cut away the ropes on her wrists and ankles.

"Jason," Alyssa told him as he pulled the ropes from her ankles, "something's happening in the volcano. We have to get out of here."

He nodded. "That's why we're leaving," he told her. "Come on."

He dropped the knife to the offering stone and lifted her down. Then, hesitating only an instant, he started to move his hand toward one of the shells filled with pearls.

He didn't have the opportunity to take any of the glowing pearls. There was a deafening rumble, and the stone beneath their feet began to shake. He turned to Alyssa, grabbed her hand, and started toward the opening.

Luckily, they didn't have the chance to leave the room. The stone floor of the cave shifted violently, throwing them both back, against the offering stone. The noise continued, and bits of rock began to fall from the ceiling of the cave. Jason threw himself over Alyssa, covering her body with his own. The noise and movement seemed endless, as though the mountain were trying to tear itself apart from the inside.

Finally the noise and the movement abated.

"Are you hurt?" Jason asked her as he pushed himself up and away from Alyssa.

She nodded. "I'm all right," she said. She reached up to his cheek, wiping away a thick drop of blood that sprouted from a long scratch a falling bit of stone had left there.

Jason took her hand and helped her to her feet.

"Look!"

Jason turned, looking to where she pointed.

The opening in the cave wall, the way to the passage that led out of the cave, was completely filled with stone.

"Oh, my Lord, why hast thou forsaken me?"

Owen's agonized cry filled the small room, but both Jason and Alyssa ignored him. The air had grown noticeably warmer and moister, and the rumble had begun once again, low now, but clearly growing louder. The activity in the volcano was forcing the mountain to shift and settle around them. Jason had little doubt but that the next shift would collapse the cave entirely.

"You know what we have to do?" he asked Alyssa.

He pointed to the far side of the offering stone, to the pool they both knew led to the underwater passage.

She nodded. "Yes, I know."

"Can you do it again?" he asked.

"If you're with me," she replied.

He took her hand and together they skirted the stone slab.

"What are you doing?" Owen screamed at them as Alyssa slid into the water. He scrambled to his feet.

Jason turned to him. "It's the only way out, Remsen. You can come or stay here and die. It makes little difference to me."

Owen started to edge his way past the stone slab, but as he passed them his eyes drifted to the pearls. The fear in his expression dissolved and was supplanted by something else, something feral and grasping. He hesitated a moment, the last vestige of his fear battling with his greed and losing. He reached to the shells, taking handfuls of the pearls and stuffing them into his pockets, for the moment thoughts of Alyssa and Jason and the path out of the cave forgotten.

Jason turned away in disgust.

"Fool," he shouted at Owen.

Then he dived into the pool.

Alyssa filled her lungs with air, then, following Jason's lead, she dived into the darkly murky water of the pool.

Jason pulled her into the underwater passage after him, and for a moment she felt the same fear she'd felt the first time she'd entered it, the fear of being trapped, of dying surrounded by the mountain of stone. But the sound of rumbling from the cave behind her told her there was no returning, that if she gave in to it, the fear would certainly kill her this time. She could do this, she told herself. Jason was with her and she could do it.

Unlike the previous time, there was no sunlight filtering through the water, nothing to guide her but the sides of the cave and the encouragement of Jason's hands reaching back for her. It was enough, she told herself. She did not plan to die, not here, not yet. She still had not told Jason that she loved him.

There was one moment of terror as the passage grew narrow and the wrap of tapa cloth she wore caught on the stone. She fumbled wildly for a second, pulling herself free of the cloth, feeling the constriction in her chest as she expended the last of her breath in her panic.

She told herself that the narrowing of the passage meant they were close to the place where it opened into the ocean, remembering from the last time that the tunnel grew narrow just before it ended. She forced herself to push away the feeling of panic. She noticed a thin, reddish glow in the water, caused, she realized, by the reddish light from the mouth of the volcano. She was right, she told herself. They were close.

Then they were no longer surrounded by rock but by the strangely reddened water instead. Jason held her and they swam upward, finally breaking through to the surface just at the moment when she thought her chest would burst from the need for air. She gasped for breath, coughing and spitting out water as Jason held her steady and kept her from being swept under again by the waves. Finally the thick ache in her chest began to ease.

"We're alive, Miss Missionary," Jason told her.

Then he laughed, a low rumble from deep in his chest that spoke more clearly than words might of the sheer joy he felt in that fact, the fact that they had escaped from the last of the cannibal god's wrath. The joy was contagious, for she felt it deep within herself, too, like a surge of life beginning anew. She found herself laughing with him as she clung to him.

Jason pulled her close and kissed her, first with simple happiness, and then, as their bodies warmed to one another, with something more. They fell beneath the surface again, and, startled, pulled themselves back up to the air.

"This will have to keep, Miss Missionary," Jason told her.

He nodded toward the island, toward the mouth of the volcano. Fingers of red flame were shooting upward, then falling back to coat the side and slip down the mountain.

"Jason! Jason?"

It was Noyer's voice, and they responded to it, calling out, splashing and waving until they saw the boat appear out of the darkness.

It was like the ferry across the River Styx, Alyssa

thought, the boat floating on water that had turned red from the reflected flames. It was a chilling thought, the image of the boat that carried the dead across the flames to hell, and she quickly chased it away as Noyer rowed close. Jason lifted her up first, then pulled himself up after her.

She stared at the surface of the water, searching the sea of red as Noyer took up the oars again and began to row back out to the *Empress*'s side.

"Do you see Owen?" she asked as the boat pulled slowly away from the island.

Noyer shook his head. "No," he replied.

"He must have trapped himself," Jason told her. "When I dived into the water, he was filling his pockets with the pearls."

"Then he died for his treasure," Alyssa murmured.

Jason put his arm around her. "I brought the greatest treasure in that cave out with me," he told her softly.

"He was going to leave me there," she told him. "In exchange for the pearls, he said. A gift to the cannibals. He intended that cave to be my tomb."

"Instead he found his own," Jason told her.

"Ahem!"

Noyer cleared his throat noisily. He had been staring at her naked body, wet with droplets that glowed with reflected light. When they turned to face him, he put down his oars, looked away and began to pull off his shirt.

"I think my good friend Jason will not be such a good friend if I continue to enjoy that particular view, *chérie,*" he told her with a hint of regret in his voice as he held out the shirt.

Jason took it from him and wrapped it around her. Noyer took up the oars once again.

"At last you've gotten something right, Jean," Jason told the Frenchman. Then he turned and smiled at Alyssa. "I don't intend to share my wife with any man," he said. "Not when I've gone to so much trouble to win her."

She had been fastening the buttons, but at the sound of his words her fingers grew suddenly clumsy. She abandoned the effort and stared up at him.

"Your wife?" she whispered.

He nodded and smiled at her. "If you'll have a weak sinner, Miss Missionary," he told her.

She let a smile slowly turn up the corners of her mouth.

"It would be an opportunity to effect a reformation," she said thoughtfully.

"And you'd have a good deal of time," he told her with a smile. "A lifetime, to be precise."

"I think this may be an opportunity of the sort that ought not to be dismissed," she countered.

Jason considered the mock seriousness of her expression.

"I might end in corrupting you instead, Miss Missionary," he warned.

"I shall have to consider that possibility, but I think I'll come to the conclusion that it's a chance I'm willing to take, Captain Draper."

"Don't frighten her off, Jason," Noyer told him with a laugh. "I've been looking forward to a celebration, and I will not have you ruin it for me. I like nothing better than to toast another man's marriage."

They'd reached the side of the *Empress,* and Jason handed Alyssa up to Argus, who stood waiting by the rail.

"You're none too soon, Captain," Argus told Jason as he and Noyer climbed up after her. He pointed to the deep red glow in the night sky that was the volcano.

They turned and stared at the thick river of red, molten rock that was now flowing downward, toward the beach and the cove beyond. As the first of the molten rock touched the water, a thick hiss of steam rose into the air.

"Are we far enough away, Liam?" Jason asked.

Argus nodded. "I think so, Captain," he replied. "Still, we might take her a bit further out, just to be sure."

"Then see to it," Jason told him. "We'll spend the night here and leave for Banaba at first light."

He put his hands on Alyssa's shoulders and turned her to face him, forcing her attention away from the stream of lava and the leaping fires at the mouth of the volcano.

"We decided I'm a weak sinner just a little while ago, Miss Missionary," he told her.

Surprised at the serious tone he used, she nodded.

"I think I may be weaker than we both supposed." He put his hand to the torn and dripping bandage wrapped around his shoulder. "I don't suppose you might be willing to perform a bit of nursing, would you?"

"Oh, I'm sorry, Jason," she murmured. "I didn't think. Are you in a great deal of pain?"

He grimaced. "Not too much," he told her. He glanced at Noyer, decided to ignore the Frenchman's knowing smile, then looked back at her. "Could you help me to my cabin?"

But she'd seen the look Noyer had given him and realized that perhaps he was not in as much pain at that moment as he would have had her believe.

"Certainly, Jason," she agreed, willing to play his game if that was what he wanted to do. She helped him put his arm around her neck and then put her hand on his waist. "Perhaps you should lean on me," she suggested as they started across the deck. She smiled coyly up at him. "You've been through a great deal. Perhaps once we're back on Banaba we should ask Namani if he has any other native cures that might help."

Jason scowled at the recollection of the unpleasant tea the native medicine man had forced on him. "I don't think we need go to any extremes, Alyssa," he told her. He looked down at her, saw the laughter in her eyes, and smiled. "In fact, with any luck at all, I expect to be fairly well recovered with only your tender ministrations."

"I'll do what little I can, Jason," she promised and smiled back up at him.

Noyer was grinning from ear to ear as he watched them disappear.

"Now, what do you suppose that was all about?" Argus asked. "The man's as strong as a bull."

"Special nursing care, Liam," Noyer replied as he turned back to watch the spectacle of lights the volcano was providing for them.

"Shame they're missin' the fireworks," Argus noted as he turned away.

"Oh, I think they will make a few fireworks of their own," Noyer said. He laughed. "After we pull the *Empress* out to sea a bit, Liam, what say you to a bottle of champagne?"

"Champagne?"

Noyer nodded. "I'd say there's a wedding soon to be celebrated. And I don't mind starting the celebration a bit early, do you?"

"There," Alyssa said as she tied off the end of the fresh bandage she'd wrapped around Jason's shoulder.

He was sitting on the edge of his bed, uncomplainingly allowing her to treat the wound in his shoulder despite the fact that his thoughts were on other matters entirely.

He inspected her handiwork.

"You do that quite well, Miss Missionary," he told her.

"I had a bit of practice, Captain Draper," she told him. "Not that you were in any condition to be aware of the fact at the time."

He took the remainder of the roll of bandage from

her and dropped it on the table. Then he took her hands in his and pulled her to him.

"I believe I have you to thank for my life, Alyssa," he said. "Jean told me you forced old Merricomb to allow a native medicine man to treat me."

"I couldn't think of anything else to do," she replied. She put her hands on the back of his neck, splaying her fingers through the thick, dark curls.

"Still, it seems to me that I've already begun to corrupt your fine missionary standards," he said.

She lowered her face to his. "Perhaps I'm not so terribly opposed to a touch of corruption just now, Captain," she said before she pressed her lips to his.

It was a long, slow kiss, her lips parting to the expectant probe of his tongue, his arms encircling her and pulling her willingly down to him as the thick tide of passion rose in them both.

She was panting when finally she pulled back from him.

"I thought you were in a weakened condition, Jason," she said and smiled down at him.

"I am," he said as he began to unfasten the buttons of the shirt she wore. "We've been alone here for more than a quarter of an hour, and I've behaved like a perfect gentleman. I must be ill."

"Or perhaps I've already begun to reform you," she suggested.

He'd freed the buttons and now pulled the shirt from her and dropped it negligently to the floor.

"I doubt that very much, Miss Missionary," he told her as he pushed her down and positioned himself over her.

"I love you, Jason Draper," she whispered.

"And you have from the start," he told her.

"Excuse me?" she demanded. "Such presumption!"

He was smiling at her, and he knew she wasn't really angry.

"Admit it, Alyssa," he said as he pressed his lips to her neck. "You've been in love with me from the first moment you walked onto the *Empress*. That was why you refused to marry Remsen. Because you were in love with me."

The touch of his lips and tongue to her neck sent a sweet shiver of fire through her veins. He was right, and she knew it, but despite that, she was not about to let him gloat. She pushed him away.

"You are arrogant and conceited and have a decidedly overblown opinion of your attractions, Captain Draper."

He smiled. "Guilty," he admitted. "But I'm also right. Admit it, Alyssa. You've been in love with me from the very first."

She shook her head. "Not from the very first," she protested.

"No?"

"No."

"Strange," he told her. His voice grew deep and husky. "Because I'm sure I fell in love with you the first moment I saw you."

He put his fingers on the mark the cannibals had left on her shoulder, the small scattering of colors bright against the pale skin. It was painful to Jason to realize that in his own way Mehevi had treated her with greater respect than he had, marrying her according to his people's rites, sharing with her his power and his position.

She brought her hand to his fingers, and then covered the tattoo with her hand.

But he pushed her hand aside and brought his lips to the marks on her skin.

"I find it most becoming, Miss Missionary," he told her, then kissed the place again before he lifted his lips to hers.

She put her hands on his shoulders and held him

close, welcoming his kiss, no longer of a mind to push him away. This was what she wanted, more than anything, to be close to him like this, to know that he loved her. Nothing, she realized, could ever be more precious than this moment.

"I love you," he murmured before he brought his lips, warm and hard, to hers.

She again welcomed the probe of his tongue just as she welcomed the liquid fire it ignited within her. This was the forbidden fruit, the great sin, the apple that had caused the downfall of Eden that her Uncle Silas had preached against with such vehemence. Only she knew there was no sin here, not between her and Jason, and there never could be. The fruits of their love would always be sweet.

His lips roamed to her earlobe and neck, and then to her breasts, leaving her flesh flushed and warm in their wake. The passion rose in her, a thick, hot stream like the lava that flowed from the volcano. She felt as though her body were melting, and she wondered how his touch could have this strange, powerful effect on her. She reached up to hold him, intent on the feel of his body beneath her hands, the hard ripple of muscle beneath his flesh. His body was a wild, alien landscape to her, so different from her own, a beautiful mystery that she knew would forever remain a wonder.

He lowered himself to kiss her breasts and her belly, and she pulled him to her, her fingers in his dark curls, accepting the knowing survey his lips and tongue made of her body as it filled her with wave after wave of liquid fire.

Finally he brought his lips to the downy soft forest between her legs, and this, too, he kissed, stroking her with his fingers and his tongue until she thought there was nothing left to her but the molten surgings of her own desire.

He lifted himself from her then and pulled away his

trousers, then returned naked to her, lowering himself to her, leaning forward to kiss her as he slid into her. He felt her enclose him, surround him, an indescribable joining that completely filled his senses. Never before, he realized, had it been like this for him. There could be a lifetime of this, and never would the wonder of it leave him. It was like a narcotic that made everything else fade, that left him with only one need, and that need was her.

Alyssa reached up to him, pulling him closer, wanting nothing more than to feel herself a part of him and him a part of her. They were meant for one another, fated from the first moment they'd seen one another, just as he had told her. She could not have escaped him had she chosen to do so. And she knew the last thing she would ever choose to do would be to flee from the protecting circle of his arms.

For she knew she had no desire to run from the touch of his hands and his lips, no desire to flee the sweet, heady press of him inside her. She wanted nothing more than the fate of a lifetime spent making love to him.

She clung to him, joining him, pressing her hips to his, letting herself melt with the feel of him. She had been made for this, she realized, made for her body to be one with his. That knowledge, like the liquid heat in her veins and the hard press of him inside her, was precious and intoxicating.

She welcomed the waves that rose within her, accepting them, and finally welcoming the shattering, tumbling moment of ecstasy. And with her trembling release, he let himself join her, let the sweet, hot flow explode from him. They let themselves drift off on a sweep of passion, letting it carry them, both marveling that they'd managed to hold onto one another when the fates had seemed so determined to tear them apart.

Alyssa lay in the circle of his arms, listening to the

thick thud of the beat of his heart, realizing that i
sounded much like the throb she felt in her own chest
When he pushed away a thick rope of hair from he
cheek, she looked up at him, saw him smiling down a
her. She lifted her lips to his and found him more thar
willing to oblige.

Then he lay back, pulling her close to lie with he
head against his chest.

"I think you've found the cure," she said after a lon
moment of silence.

She looked up at him to find he was staring at he
with a look of amused bewilderment.

"Cure?" he asked. "I've done my damndest to corrup
you, Miss Missionary, and you tell me I've found
cure?"

She nodded and smiled. "Here I am, below deck ir
this closed cabin, and the *Empress* is even moving with
the waves."

He nodded. "And?"

"And I'm not even remotely seasick," she said.

He laughed. "If I'd known, I'd have offered you the
cure when you first set foot on the *Empress*'s deck the
night of that storm. It would have saved us both a gooc
deal of bother."

She grew silent, remembering that night, remembering being swept from the *Empress*'s deck.

"It all came from that night, didn't it?" she asked. "I
you hadn't come after me when I fell from the
deck . . ."

"I'd have ruined my reputation as a responsible captain," he interrupted. He put his hands on her waist anc
lifted her until she lay on top of him. Then he put his
hand on her cheek, stroking it gently as he stared up
into her eyes. "And even worse," he said softly, "I'd have
lost this opportunity to make my small contribution tc
medical knowledge."

She laughed, a deeply throaty, knowing laugh that

urprised him until he realized she was as aware as he vas of just what it was he intended at that moment.

"I suppose this means you plan some further investi-gation into the matter?" she asked.

He pulled her gently down to him.

"Just one of the small sacrifices one must make in the name of research," he replied before he pulled her close and kissed her.

Owen climbed over the rail and then slid down until he was sitting in the shadows on the *Empress*'s deck. The sky was filled with a sickly red glow, and a voice inside him kept telling him he had been wrongly sent to hell.

He lifted his arm and wiped away the drips of red from the dozens of scratches that lined his face and neck. He'd barely escaped from the cave before it col-lapsed on him, and his memories were a bit confused as to how he'd managed to pull himself through the under-water passage. It was a nightmare, one he'd sooner for-get, for like the red glow in the sky, the reflected red of the water reminded him of hell. And the voice inside him was telling him he had only one way to escape, and that was by finishing what he'd been sent to do.

The whore had escaped him, escaped her rightful punishment. He'd let her slip through his fingers, and God was showing his anger with Owen's incompetence, showing him the fires of hell. Until he'd seen her re-ceive what she'd earned, Owen knew he would never find peace.

He was tired, more tired than he had ever been in his life. It had been a long swim out to the whore's lover's ship, and he knew only one thing had kept him from giving up, the sure knowledge that God had sent him to see that she received what her sins had earned her.

There was noise at the bow, and he shrank further into the shadows, knowing he could not allow himself to

be seen. It was the papist Frenchman, he told himsel
and the ship's mate. The sound of their laughter drifte
back to him, and he told himself they were drunk
Drunken sinners, he thought, no better than heathen.

He pushed himself wearily to his feet. Taking pain
to make no noise that would alert them, he crept to th
hatch and slipped down the stairs to the passage below
He felt a wave of calm strength wash over him as h
stood outside the closed door. He was on God's errand
he told himself, and God would protect him.

Then he put his hand on the latch and drew it back
Slowly, taking care to be silent, he pushed the doo
open.

He stood in the doorway for a long moment, starin
at the two of them entwined on the narrow bed, thei
naked bodies tinged with red from the finger of ligh
that passed through the porthole. Red, he thought—
the color of sin.

A thick rage surged through him as he looked a
Alyssa's naked body. She'd spurned him, then give
herself wantonly to this godless sailor. There was n
punishment great enough for her crime.

He raised the hand that held the knife, holding i
ready to strike as he crossed the room to the bed an
stood over them.

"Whore!" he screamed as he brought the knife down

Chapter Twenty-six

Alyssa's eyes popped open at the sound of Owen's ry. The first thing to greet them was the sight of the nife as it plunged toward her. She screamed.

Jason reacted more from instinct than from thought, rapping his arms around her and rolling back, pulling er away from the falling blade. It struck the mattress nly inches from her, and he knew that had he not ulled her away, it would have found her heart.

For an instant Owen stood and stared at the knife, azed by the fact that it had missed its target. It was all ıpposed to be so simple, he thought. The whore was) die for her sins. It took him a moment to realize that ıe hadn't, that she was still alive. His eyes found hers, ıen slid down the length of her naked body. At the ght of it his face contorted with rage and he reached ır the knife to strike again.

Those few seconds of shock and indecision were time nough for Alyssa to realize that he would not stop ntil both she and Jason were dead. Before he had the hance to pull the knife back for another attack, she rabbed for the weapon. He already had his hands on it nd had begun to pull it back. Her fingers, reaching for ıe hilt, instead found the blade.

She screamed in pain but didn't release her hold on ıe knife. Jason was pushing himself forward, reaching ır the knife now, and she knew the only chance he had

to get it was if she did not let Owen gain control of i
first.

And then Jason had his hands on Owen's wrist an
she let go of the blade. Jason pushed himself forwar
from the bed, grappling for the weapon. Owen backe
away, frightened, trying vainly to free himself from Ja
son, suddenly realizing that this was not to be an unop
posed act of violence against a sleeping victim, but
fight, man to man.

Alyssa pulled back her bloodied hand, huddling int
the corner of the now blood-spattered bed. But it wa
not her cut fingers that held her terrified attention; i
was instead the horrifying image of the two men locke
together in the struggle for the knife, one naked, th
other dressed in somber missionary black, both bathe
by the hellish red glow that filled the night sky, cast b
the erupting volcano.

Despite the fact that Owen had the initial element c
surprise on his side and that he'd attacked a wounde
man, it was in the end ordained that the missionar
would lose. Jason was the stronger of the two, and i
Owen raged with the force of his insane visions, Jaso
was strengthened by the knowledge that he was fightin
for the life of the woman he loved. He and Alyssa ha
gone through far too much in the preceding weeks fo
him to so much as consider the possibility of losing he
now to Owen's crazed attack.

He dug his fingers into Owen's wrist, tightenin
their hold and then twisting. Eventually Owen had n
choice but to give way to the pressure. His hold on th
knife faltered and, Jason wrestled the weapon from hi
grasp.

No longer armed, Owen cowered back toward th
cabin wall, his rage turned to terror.

Jason stood over him for an instant, and felt a wav
of revulsion as he watched the cowering missionary sin

slowly to his knees. Then he turned away in disgust.

Jason strode back to the bed where Alyssa sat cradling her cut hand. He darted a glance at the spray of red from her palm and fingers, Owen temporarily forgotten, all thought of him, now that he was disarmed, replaced by the more pressing concern of Alyssa's wound. He knelt beside her and reached for her lacerated hand.

But Owen was not to be cowed for long. He pushed himself back to his feet and stood for an instant staring at the two naked figures huddled close on the bed. The rage once again began to fill him, the disgust for what he considered the insult their actions had done both to him and to his god. His eyes fixed on Alyssa, on her bared breasts and thighs, and he could not ignore the reaction that sight initiated in his own body. He fixed the blame for his own rising lust not with himself but with her. It filled him with rage and resurrected his conviction that his must be the hand of retribution that would expiate her sin.

"Whore!" he hissed at her, moving slowly forward once again. "You cannot escape."

Jason turned back to face him. He held the knife out, letting Owen see the red-stained blade and consider what that meant, assuming it would be enough to rekindle Owen's fear.

"Get out," he shouted. "Get out or I swear, Remsen, I'll use this knife of yours to split you end to end."

But Owen didn't move. His fear had vanished, washed aside in a wave of religious fanaticism, in his singular fixation on his belief that he must make Alyssa pay for her sins. His eyes were not on the knife but on her. His scratched and bruised face, tinted red by the glow of light from the volcano, was a horror, a devil mask. His eyes flashed with insane hatred.

"You can't escape, whore!" he shouted at Alyssa.

She shrank back, close to Jason.

"He's mad," she murmured in dazed bewilderment.

Still ignoring the knife, Owen turned his gaze to Jason. "Fornicator!" he shouted. "Godless sinner!" He smiled at Jason. "Don't you know you can't hurt me?" he hissed, and waved his hand at the knife. "I am God's messenger. And nothing can stop me."

He knew himself to be invulnerable, knew with the certainty of the insane that he had been chosen and sent by God. So great was his certainty of mission that he ignored the knife in Jason's hand.

He held his hands out, reaching for Alyssa's throat, and lunged forward.

There was a shriek of pain as he fell on the blade. He pulled back, the madness gone from his eyes now, replaced only by surprise as he stared down at the hilt of the knife embedded in his chest. And then he simply crumpled and fell to the floor.

Alyssa cried out with shocked disbelief. Then she fell into Jason's arms, sobbing and shaking as she realized what had happened to Owen and what had almost happened to her and Jason.

"Is something wrong, Captain? I thought I heard . . ."

Argus stopped in mid-sentence as he and Noyer found themselves confronted by the sight of Owen's body lying on the floor. They froze, their expressions evidence to their shock and surprise.

Jason looked up at them.

"Get him out of here," he ordered.

Then he turned back to Alyssa and held her close.

The first light of dawn was beginning to fill the sky. Alyssa, dressed in a too-large shirt and trousers borrowed from Jason and gingerly holding her bandaged hand so that it would not jar against the rail, stared out at what had once been the beach and cove. It was now a heap of dark red, glowing, molten stone that grew steadily larger as the lava continued to flow downward from the mouth of the volcano.

"It's gone," she murmured. "The entrance to the cave, the beach, all of it—gone."

Jason nodded. "The cave's probably collapsed," he said. "If not, it's certainly sealed by the lava."

She was still shaken, still bewildered by everything that had happened, by Owen's actions.

"I don't think I'll ever understand why he did what he did," she said.

Jason, who was standing behind her, put his arms around her waist.

"Jealousy and greed are not such great mysteries, Miss Missionary," he told her. "I'm sure it wouldn't have pleased him to realize that he was driven by man's basest emotions, but in the end it was simply greed that brought Remsen back here, and jealousy that pushed him to the edge."

She shook her head. "No," she objected. "He had no reason to be jealous of me. He may have wanted a wife, a good missionary wife who would be his unquestioning servant, but I told him from the start that I was not what he wanted, what he expected. And he certainly didn't love me. I don't think he knew how to love."

Jason pressed a kiss to the top of her head, inhaling the perfume of her hair and feeling the silken softness against his cheek.

"But I do," he whispered. "All I want is a chance to show you."

She turned around and faced him. "A lifetime, Captain Draper," she said softly. She reached up and put her hands to his neck. And then she smiled, remembering what he had offered her the night before. "Or was I imagining that you proposed to me?"

He grinned. "Missionaries have no imagination," he told her emphatically. "That particular capacity is banned, along with the ability to dance."

She closed her eyes and remembered the way they'd danced on the sand that evening that seemed so long ago, remembered where that solitary dance had led them.

"Will you dance with me at our wedding, Jason?" she asked.

"And every night after that," he agreed. "After all, I've decided to corrupt you, and that seems a fair place to start." He smiled down at her and pressed a gentle kiss to her lips, then released her. "It's time to leave," he told her.

She nodded, and watched him as he and Argus went about the task of setting the *Empress*'s sails. Soon the wind was pushing against the canvas and there was the creaking sound of straining cordage. The *Empress* slowly began to move away from Nukuhiva.

Alyssa's glance reluctantly drifted to the canvas-wrapped object near the *Empress*'s prow. At first it was hard for her to think that it was a body, Owen's body, but when she reminded herself that that was exactly what it was, she grew uneasy. Jason had wanted to bury it at sea, but she'd begged him instead to return it to Banaba, to the mission. She could not help but feel she was partly responsible for what Owen had done and, she felt she owed him at least that small courtesy.

She returned her attention to the unfamiliar new outline of the island that was fading now with the growing distance as the *Empress* left it behind. She tried to dismiss thoughts of Owen from her mind, telling herself that Owen and all that had happened was the past and she need now think instead of the future, her future and Jason's.

She was still standing by the rail, watching the island

shrink into the blue of the ocean, when Jason rejoined her. He put his arm around her.

"Still thinking about Remsen, Miss Missionary?" he asked her softly.

She shook her head. "About the cannibals and their treasure," she replied. "It's safe now. Their god has claimed it."

"Not all of it," he told her.

She turned and stared up at him.

"What do you mean?"

"Perhaps you'd better come see for yourself."

He took her hand and led her to the stern, to where Noyer was leaning over an overturned barrel.

"I think you'd better show Alyssa what you found, Jean," Jason told the Frenchman.

Noyer straightened up, stared at her, and smiled, hen backed away from the barrel. He motioned to her o look for herself.

The makeshift table top was covered with black pearls, dozens of them, more than she could count.

She swallowed, and then looked up at Noyer.

"But how?" she asked.

Noyer darted a glance at Jason before answering.

"Owen, *chérie,*" he told her softly. "It seems he could not leave such fortune behind. His pockets were filled with them."

It took a moment for his words to sink into her, for her to puzzle out their meaning. She looked down at he pearls again, and finally reached out and took one n her hand.

"Is this a great fortune, Jean?" she asked.

The Frenchman nodded. "More than all of us could spend in a lifetime, *chérie,*" he said. "Even were we all as extravagant as I am."

She looked down at the smooth, darkly glowing pearl, still bewildered by the import of it.

"Then you are rich?" she asked in a whisper.

Jason grinned. "We're all rich, Miss Missionary," h
told her. "Liam and Noyer and you and I."

"But—but how can we keep this?" she murmured.

Noyer stared at her, not quite believing what she wa
saying.

"We certainly can't return it to the cave, *chérie,*" he re
minded her.

Alyssa's eyes turned to meet Jason's. It seeme
wrong to her to keep this fortune, to make herself rich
Westerners had come to the South Seas and exploite
the natives, taking their fortunes away with them, leav
ing disease and death for the Polynesians when the
left. Then the missionaries had come to take even th
natives' joy by imposing a foreign religion on them an
offering them little in return. After all she had seen, sh
knew it would be wrong for them to simply take thi
fortune and return nothing. She found herself silentl
praying that Jason would understand how she felt, tha
he would feel it, too.

Jason returned her stare for a long, silent moment
then he turned to Noyer.

"I think Miss Missionary would like us to donate
share to old Merricomb and the mission, Jean. Perhap
build a real hospital and staff it with real doctors," h
said. He turned back to her and smiled. "And I mus
admit I find myself agreeing with her."

Alyssa grinned and nodded. "Yes," she said. "Coul
we?"

Noyer eyed the heap of pearls and sighed. He wa
obviously not quite so convinced as Jason, but he fi
nally seemed willing to accept their decision.

"Perhaps you are right, *chérie,*" he replied after a pro
longed moment of concentrated thought. "Perhaps a bi
of charity would pave my way into heaven. After all,
can not claim to have led a sinless life." He nodded to

vard the heap of pearls. "Besides, there's more than
nough there. I agree." He turned to Jason, his expres-
ion a bit perplexed by this unexpected turn of events.
I think your missionary has managed to reform both of
is, *mon vieux*. I fear this will lead to a bad end. I might
ven find myself marrying the mother of one of my
hildren."

He turned and walked away, shaking his head as he
imbled to the rail. Neither Jason nor Alyssa could stifle
heir laughter at his apparent dejection.

"I fear Jean is on the verge of taking monastic orders,
Miss Missionary," Jason said. "The thought of marriage
errifies him."

She sobered quickly. "And you, Captain Draper?"
he asked. "Does it terrify you as well?"

He nodded. "That it does," he murmured, his voice
uddenly deep and husky. "But not nearly so much as
osing you."

He held his arms open for her and she went to
im, standing close as he wrapped his arms around
ier.

"Perhaps," he whispered as his lips found hers, "we
night assuage that fear with a bit of scientific research."

He pressed his lips to hers, and Alyssa felt the liquid
ieat blaze and surge inside her at the contact. His kiss
ind the feel of his hands on her back, pulling her close,
vere enough to make her forget Owen and everything
hat had happened in the preceding days, enough to fill
ier mind with only one thought, to fill her body with
nly one need.

"Research?" she asked, confused and a bit breathless
vhen he reluctantly lifted his lips from hers.

He grinned wryly.

"Purely medicinal, Miss Missionary," he told her.
And then he swept her up into his arms.

She wrapped her arm around his neck and laughed

with the sheer joy of the knowledge that they were bot
alive and together.

"And to precisely what sort of medicinal research ar
you referring, Captain Draper?" she asked archly, al
though she already knew what he intended and was a
willing and eager as he.

"There was that matter of finding a cure for your sea
sickness, Miss Missionary," he told her.

Her laughter mixed with his as he carried her acros
the deck, making the way to his cabin and to his bunk